50
CREEPY
AND
BLOOD-CURDLING
TALES

50 CREEPY AND BLOOD-CURDLING TALES

Published by
Rupa Publications India Pvt. Ltd 2023
7/16, Ansari Road, Daryaganj
New Delhi 110002

Sales centres:
Bengaluru Chennai
Hyderabad Jaipur Kathmandu
Kolkata Mumbai Prayagraj

Edition copyright © Rupa Publications India Pvt. Ltd 2023

All rights reserved.
No part of this publication may be reproduced, transmitted,
or stored in a retrieval system, in any form or by any means,
electronic, mechanical, photocopying, recording or otherwise,
without the prior permission of the publisher.

P-ISBN: 978-93-5702-291-0
E-ISBN: 978-93-5702-276-7

Second impression 2024

10 9 8 7 6 5 4 3 2

Printed in India

This book is sold subject to the condition that it shall not, by way of
trade or otherwise, be lent, resold, hired out, or otherwise circulated,
without the publisher's prior consent, in any form of binding or
cover other than that in which it is published.

CONTENTS

Introduction ix

1. THE OCCUPANT OF THE ROOM 1
   Algernon Blackwood
2. THE BOARDED WINDOW 12
   Ambrose Bierce
3. THE OVAL PORTRAIT 18
   Edgar Allen Poe
4. THE INCUBUS 22
   Hamilton Craigie
5. JUNGLE DEATH 34
   Artemus Calloway
6. THE HIDEOUS FACE 44
   Victor Johns
7. A CASE OF EAVESDROPPING 54
   Algernon Blackwood
8. THE MEZZOTINT 71
   M.R. James
9. THE BLACK CAT 85
   Edgar Allen Poe
10. PRESENT AT A HANGING 96
    Ambrose Bierce
11. DAGON 99
    H.P. Lovecraft
12. THE VOICE IN THE NIGHT 106
    William Hope Hodgson
13. COUNT MAGNUS 121
    M.R. James

14.	THE WERE-WOLF *H.B. Marryatt*	137
15.	WHAT WAS IT? *Fitz-James O'Brien*	156
16.	THE MASQUE OF THE RED DEATH *Edgar Allen Poe*	171
17.	THE HALL OF THE DEAD *Francis D. Grierson*	178
18.	THE GRAVE *Orville R. Emerson*	190
19.	THE GHOUL AND THE CORPSE *G.A. Wells*	201
20.	THE UNKNOWN BEAST *Howard Ellis Davis*	216
21.	TWO MILITARY EXECUTIONS *Ambrose Bierce*	227
22.	THE SPECTRE BRIDE *William Harrison Ainsworth*	231
23.	HOW HE LEFT THE HOTEL *Louisa Baldwin*	242
24.	"AND NO BIRD SINGS" *E.F. Benson*	248
25.	THE OUTSIDER *H.P. Lovecraft*	264
26.	THE COLD EMBRACE *Mary Elizabeth Braddon*	272
27.	THE FACE *E.F. Benson*	283
28.	THE MARK OF THE BEAST *Rudyard Kipling*	299

29.	DICKON THE DEVIL *J.S. Le Fanu*	314
30.	CELEPHAÏS *H.P. Lovecraft*	326
31.	THE DEVIL IN A NUNNERY *Francis Oscar Mann*	334
32.	THE FLAYED HAND *Guy De Maupassant*	345
33.	THE CONJURER *Richard Middleton*	352
34.	THE VAMPIRE *Jan Neruda*	357
35.	THE MASS FOR THE DEAD *Edith Nesbit*	362
36.	WHEN I WAS DEAD *Vincent O'Sullivan*	373
37.	A DREAM OF RED HANDS *Bram Stoker*	378
38.	THE CASK OF AMONTILLADO *Edgar Allen Poe*	390
39.	THE RED ROOM *H.G. Wells*	398
40.	THE SQUAW *Bram Stoker*	410
41.	A GHOST STORY *Mark Twain*	424
42.	THE SHADOWS ON THE WALL *Mary Eleanor Wilkins Freeman*	431
43.	THE TERROR BY NIGHT *E.F. Benson*	449

44. THE NIGHT-DOINGS AT "DEADMAN'S" *Ambrose Bierce*	458
45. THE PHANTOM COACH *Amelia B. Edwards*	468
46. THE SECRET OF THE TWO PLASTER CASTS *J.S. Le Fanu*	484
47. MADEMOISELLE COCOTTE *Guy de Maupassant*	491
48. BRICKETT BOTTOM *Amyas Northcote*	496
49. THE TELL-TALE HEART *Edgar Allen Poe*	509
50. A PHANTOM TOE *W. Bob Holland*	515

INTRODUCTION

Horror is a genre that has been around for centuries, but it is still as popular as ever. The reason for this is simple: we are all drawn to the unknown and the macabre. Horror stories tap into our primal fears and remind us that we are mortal beings, vulnerable to the dangers that lurk in the world around us.

In this anthology of 50 ghastly and gruesome stories, you will find tales that explore the full range of the horror genre. There are tales of supernatural entities, ghosts, and monsters, as well as stories that focus on the darker side of human nature. Some of these stories are set in ancient times, while others take place in the early twentieth century heyday of the horror genre. But regardless of the setting, each story will leave you with a sense of unease and a desire to turn on the lights.

The authors featured in this anthology are masters of the horror genre, and some of the very best at rousing fear. From the all-time greats such as Edgar Allen Poe, Ambrose Bierce, and Bram Stoker, to the slightly lesser known but just as effective American pulp writers, the stories in this collection cater to all the sub-genres of horror and the eerie. Their stories are not for the faint of heart, but for those brave enough to venture into the dark corners of the human psyche, they are a must-read.

So, if you're ready to experience the thrill of horror and the fear of the unknown, join us on this journey into the depths of depravity a human soul can venture into. But be warned, once you enter this world, you may never be the same again.

1

THE OCCUPANT OF THE ROOM

Algernon Blackwood

He arrived late at night by the yellow diligence, stiff and cramped after the toilsome ascent of three slow hours. The village, a single mass of shadow, was already asleep. Only in front of the little hotel was there noise and light and bustle—for a moment. The horses, with tired, slouching gait, crossed the road and disappeared into the stable of their own accord, their harness trailing in the dust; and the lumbering diligence stood for the night where they had dragged it—the body of a great yellow-sided beetle with broken legs.

In spite of his physical weariness the schoolmaster, revelling in the first hours of his ten-guinea holiday, felt exhilarated. For the high Alpine valley was marvellously still; stars twinkled over the torn ridges of the *Dent du Midi* where spectral snows gleamed against rocks that looked like solid ink; and the keen air smelt of pine forests, dew-soaked pastures, and freshly sawn wood. He took it all in with a kind of bewildered delight for a few minutes, while the other three passengers gave directions about their luggage and went to their rooms. Then he turned and walked over the coarse matting into the glare of the hall, only just able to resist stopping to examine the big mountain map that hung upon the wall by the door.

And, with a sudden disagreeable shock, he came down from the ideal to the actual. For at the inn—the only inn—there was no vacant room. Even the available sofas were occupied.

How stupid he had been not to write! Yet it had been

impossible, he remembered, for he had come to the decision suddenly that morning in Geneva, enticed by the brilliance of the weather after a week of rain.

They talked endlessly, this gold-braided porter and the hard-faced old woman—her face was hard, he noticed—gesticulating all the time, and pointing all about the village with suggestions that he ill understood, for his French was limited and their patois was fearful.

"*There!*"—he might find a room, "or *there*! But we are, *hélas* full—more full than we care about. To-morrow, perhaps—if So-and-So give up their rooms—!" And then, with much shrugging of shoulders, the hard-faced old woman stared at the gold-braided porter, and the porter stared sleepily at the schoolmaster.

At length, however, by some process of hope he did not himself understand, and following directions given by the old woman that were utterly unintelligible, he went out into the street and walked towards a dark group of houses she had pointed out to him. He only knew that he meant to thunder at a door and ask for a room. He was too weary to think out details. The porter half made to go with him, but turned back at the last moment to speak with the old woman. The houses sketched themselves dimly in the general blackness. The air was cold. The whole valley was filled with the rush and thunder of falling water. He was thinking vaguely that the dawn could not be very far away, and that he might even spend the night wandering in the woods, when there was a sharp noise behind him and he turned to see a figure hurrying after him. It was the porter—running.

And in the little hall of the inn there began again a confused three-cornered conversation, with frequent muttered colloquy and whispered asides in patois between the woman and the porter—the net result of which was that, "If Monsieur did not object—there was a room, after all, on the first floor—only it was in a sense 'engaged.' That is to say—"

But the schoolmaster took the room without inquiring too closely into the puzzle that had somehow provided it so suddenly. The ethics of hotel-keeping had nothing to do with him. If the woman offered him quarters it was not for him to argue with her whether the said quarters were legitimately hers to offer.

But the porter, evidently a little thrilled, accompanied the guest up to the room and supplied in a mixture of French and English details omitted by the landlady—and Minturn, the schoolmaster, soon shared the thrill with him, and found himself in the atmosphere of a possible tragedy.

All who know the peculiar excitement that belongs to high mountain valleys where dangerous climbing is a chief feature of the attractions, will understand a certain faint element of high alarm that goes with the picture. One looks up at the desolate, soaring ridges and thinks involuntarily of the men who find their pleasure for days and nights together scaling perilous summits among the clouds, and conquering inch by inch the icy peaks that for ever shake their dark terror in the sky. The atmosphere of adventure, spiced with the possible horror of a very grim order of tragedy, is inseparable from any imaginative contemplation of the scene; and the idea Minturn gleaned from the half-frightened porter lost nothing by his ignorance of the language. This Englishwoman, the real occupant of the room, had insisted on going without a guide. She had left just before daybreak two days before—the porter had seen her start—and… she had not returned! The route was difficult and dangerous, yet not impossible for a skilled climber, even a solitary one. And the Englishwoman was an experienced mountaineer. Also, she was self-willed, careless of advice, bored by warnings, self-confident to a degree. Queer, moreover; for she kept entirely to herself, and sometimes remained in her room with locked doors, admitting no one, for days together: a "crank," evidently, of the first water.

This much Minturn gathered clearly enough from the porter's

talk while his luggage was brought in and the room set to rights; further, too, that the search party had gone out and *might*, of course, return at any moment. In which case—Thus the room was empty, yet still hers. "If Monsieur did not object—if the risk he ran of having to turn out suddenly in the night—" It was the loquacious porter who furnished the details that made the transaction questionable; and Minturn dismissed the loquacious porter as soon as possible, and prepared to get into the hastily arranged bed and snatch all the hours of sleep he could before he was turned out.

At first, it must be admitted, he felt uncomfortable—distinctly uncomfortable. He was in some one else's room. He had really no right to be there. It was in the nature of an unwarrantable intrusion; and while he unpacked he kept looking over his shoulder as though some one were watching him from the corners. Any moment, it seemed, he would hear a step in the passage, a knock would come at the door, the door would open, and there he would see this vigorous Englishwoman looking him up and down with anger. Worse still—he would hear her voice asking him what he was doing in her room—her bedroom. Of course, he had an adequate explanation, but still—!

Then, reflecting that he was already half undressed, the humour of it flashed for a second across his mind, and he laughed—*quietly*. And at once, after that laughter, under his breath, came the sudden sense of tragedy he had felt before. Perhaps, even while he smiled, her body lay broken and cold upon those awful heights, the wind of snow playing over her hair, her glazed eyes staring sightless up to the stars... It made him shudder. The sense of this woman whom he had never seen, whose name even he did not know, became extraordinarily real. Almost he could imagine that she was somewhere in the room with him, hidden, observing all he did.

He opened the door softly to put his boots outside, and

when he closed it again he turned the key. Then he finished unpacking and distributed his few things about the room. It was soon done; for, in the first place, he had only a small Gladstone and a knapsack, and secondly, the only place where he could spread his clothes was the sofa. There was no chest of drawers, and the cupboard, an unusually large and solid one, was locked. The Englishwoman's things had evidently been hastily put away in it. The only sign of her recent presence was a bunch of faded *Alpenrosen* standing in a glass jar upon the washhand stand. This, and a certain faint perfume, were all that remained. In spite, however, of these very slight evidences, the whole room was pervaded with a curious sense of occupancy that he found exceedingly distasteful. One moment the atmosphere seemed subtly charged with a "just left" feeling; the next it was a queer awareness of "still here" that made him turn cold and look hurriedly behind him.

Altogether, the room inspired him with a singular aversion, and the strength of this aversion seemed the only excuse for his tossing the faded flowers out of the window, and then hanging his mackintosh upon the cupboard door in such a way as to screen it as much as possible from view. For the sight of that big, ugly cupboard, filled with the clothing of a woman who might then be beyond any further need of covering,—thus his imagination insisted on picturing it—touched in him a startled sense of the Incongruous that did not stop there, but crept through his mind gradually till it merged somehow into a sense of a rather grotesque horror. At any rate, the sight of that cupboard was offensive, and he covered it almost instinctively. Then, turning out the electric light, he got into bed.

But the instant the room was dark he realised that it was more than he could stand; for, with the blackness, there came a sudden rush of cold that he found it hard to explain. And the odd thing was that, when he lit the candle beside his bed, he noticed that his hand trembled.

This, of course, was too much. His imagination was taking liberties and must be called to heel. Yet the way he called it to order was significant, and its very deliberateness betrayed a mind that has already admitted fear. And fear, once in, is difficult to dislodge. He lay there upon his elbow in bed and carefully took note of all the objects in the room—with the intention, as it were, of taking an inventory of everything his senses perceived, then drawing a line, adding them up finally, and saying with decision, "That's all the room contains! I've counted every single thing. There is nothing more. *Now*—I may sleep in peace!"

And it was during this absurd process of enumerating the furniture of the room that the dreadful sense of distressing lassitude came over him that made it difficult even to finish counting. It came swiftly, yet with an amazing kind of violence that overwhelmed him softly and easily with a sensation of enervating weariness hard to describe. And its first effect was to banish fear. He no longer possessed enough energy to feel really afraid or nervous. The cold remained, but the alarm vanished. And into every corner of his usually vigorous personality crept the insidious poison of a *muscular* fatigue—at first—that in a few seconds, it seemed, translated itself into *spiritual* inertia. A sudden consciousness of the foolishness, the crass futility, of life, of effort, of fighting—of all that makes life worth living, shot into every fibre of his being, and left him utterly weak. A spirit of black pessimism that was not even vigorous enough to assert itself, invaded the secret chambers of his heart...

Every picture that presented itself to his mind came dressed in grey shadows: those bored and sweating horses toiling up the ascent to—nothing! that hard-faced landlady taking so much trouble to let her desire for gain conquer her sense of morality—for a few francs! That gold-braided porter, so talkative, fussy, energetic, and so anxious to tell all he knew! What was the use of them all? And for himself, what in the world was the good of all the labour and drudgery he went through in that preparatory school where he was junior master? What could it lead to? Wherein lay the value of so much uncertain toil, when the ultimate secrets of life were hidden and no one knew the final goal? How foolish was effort, discipline, work! How vain was pleasure! How trivial the noblest life!...

With a fearful jump that nearly upset the candle Minturn pulled himself together. Such vicious thoughts were usually so remote from his normal character that the sudden vile invasion produced a swift reaction. Yet, only for a moment. Instantly, again, the black depression descended upon him like a wave. His work—it could lead to nothing but the dreary labour of a small headmastership after all—seemed as vain and foolish as his holiday in the Alps. What an idiot he had been, to be sure, to come out with a knapsack merely to work himself into a state of exhaustion climbing over toilsome mountains that led to nowhere—resulted in nothing. A dreariness of the grave possessed him. Life was a ghastly fraud! Religion childish humbug! Everything was merely a trap—a trap of death; a coloured toy that Nature used as a decoy! But a decoy for what? For nothing! There was no meaning in anything. The only *real* thing was—*death*. And the happiest people were those who found it soonest.

Then why wait for it to come?

He sprang out of bed, thoroughly frightened. This was horrible. Surely mere physical fatigue could not produce a world so black, an outlook so dismal, a cowardice that struck with such sudden hopelessness at the very roots of life? For, normally, he was cheerful and strong, full of the tides of healthy living; and this appalling lassitude swept the very basis of his personality into nothingness and the desire for death. It was like the development of a Secondary Personality. He had read, of course, how certain persons who suffered shocks developed thereafter entirely different characteristics, memory, tastes, and so forth. It had all rather frightened him. Though scientific men vouched for it, it was hardly to be believed. Yet here was a similar thing taking place in his own consciousness. He was, beyond question, experiencing all the mental variations of—*someone else*! It was un-moral. It was awful. It was—well, after all, at the same time, it was uncommonly interesting.

And this interest he began to feel was the first sign of his returning normal Self. For to feel interest is to live, and to love life.

He sprang into the middle of the room—then switched on the electric light. And the first thing that struck his eye was—the big cupboard.

"Hallo! There's that—beastly cupboard!" he exclaimed to himself, involuntarily, yet aloud. It held all the clothes, the swinging skirts and coats and summer blouses of the dead woman. For he knew now—somehow or other—that she *was* dead...

At that moment, through the open windows, rushed the sound of falling water, bringing with it a vivid realisation of the desolate, snow-swept heights. He saw her—positively *saw* her!—lying where she had fallen, the frost upon her cheeks, the snow-dust eddying about her hair and eyes, her broken limbs pushing against the lumps of ice. For a moment the sense of spiritual lassitude—of the emptiness of life—vanished before this picture of broken effort—of a small human force battling pluckily, yet in vain, against the impersonal and pitiless Potencies of Inanimate Nature—and he found himself again, his normal self. Then, instantly, returned again that terrible sense of cold, nothingness, emptiness...

And he found himself standing opposite the big cupboard where her clothes were. He wanted to see those clothes—things she had used and worn. Quite close he stood, almost touching it. The next second he had touched it. His knuckles struck upon the wood.

Why he knocked is hard to say. It was an instinctive movement probably. Something in his deepest self dictated it—ordered it. He knocked at the door. And the dull sound upon the wood into the stillness of that room brought—horror. Why it should have done so he found it as hard to explain to himself as why he should have felt impelled to knock. The fact remains that when he heard the faint reverberation inside the cupboard, it brought with it so vivid a realisation of the woman's presence that he stood there shivering upon the floor with a dreadful sense of anticipation: he almost expected to hear an answering knock from within—the rustling of the hanging skirts perhaps—or, worse still, to see the locked door slowly open towards him.

And from that moment, he declares that in some way or other he must have partially lost control of himself, or at least of his better judgment; for he became possessed by such an overmastering desire to tear open that cupboard door and see the clothes within, that he tried every key in the room in the vain effort to unlock it, and then, finally, before he quite realised what he was doing—rang the bell!

But, having rung the bell for no obvious or intelligent reason at two o'clock in the morning, he then stood waiting in the middle of the floor for the servant to come, conscious for the first time that something outside his ordinary self had pushed him towards the act. It was almost like an internal voice that directed him...and thus, when at last steps came down the passage and he faced the cross and sleepy chambermaid, amazed at being summoned at such an hour, he found no difficulty in the matter of what he should say. For the same power that insisted he should open the cupboard door also impelled him to utter words over which he apparently had no control.

"It's not *you* I rang for!" he said with decision and impatience, "I want a man. Wake the porter and send him up to me at once—hurry! I tell you, hurry—!"

And when the girl had gone, frightened at his earnestness, Minturn realised that the words surprised himself as much as they surprised her. Until they were out of his mouth he had not known what exactly he was saying. But now he understood that some force foreign to his own personality was using his mind and organs. The black depression that had possessed him a few moments before was also part of it. The powerful mood of this vanished woman had somehow momentarily taken possession of him—communicated, possibly, by the atmosphere of things in the room still belonging to her. But even now, when the porter, without coat or collar, stood beside him in the room, he did not understand *why* he insisted, with a positive fury admitting no denial, that the key of that cupboard must be found and the door instantly opened.

The scene was a curious one. After some perplexed whispering with the chambermaid at the end of the passage, the porter managed to find and produce the key in question. Neither he nor the girl knew clearly what this excited Englishman was up to, or why he was so passionately intent upon opening the cupboard at two o'clock in the morning. They watched him with an air of wondering what was going to happen next. But something of his curious earnestness, even of his late fear, communicated itself to them, and the sound of the key grating in the lock made them both jump.

They held their breath as the creaking door swung slowly open. All heard the clatter of that other key as it fell against the wooden floor—within. The cupboard had been locked *from the inside*. But it was the scared housemaid, from her position in the corridor, who first saw—and with a wild scream fell crashing against the bannisters.

The porter made no attempt to save her. The schoolmaster and himself made a simultaneous rush towards the door, now wide open. They, too, had seen.

There were no clothes, skirts or blouses on the pegs, but, all by itself, from an iron hook in the centre, they saw the body of the Englishwoman hanging by the neck, the head bent horribly forwards, the tongue protruding. Jarred by the movement of unlocking, the body swung slowly round to face them... Pinned upon the inside of the door was a hotel envelope with the following words pencilled in straggling writing:

"Tired—unhappy—hopelessly depressed... I cannot face life any longer... All is black. I must put an end to it... I meant to do it on the mountains, but was afraid. I slipped back to my room unobserved. This way is easiest and best..."

2

THE BOARDED WINDOW

Ambrose Bierce

In 1830, only a few miles away from what is now the great city of Cincinnati, lay an immense and almost unbroken forest. The whole region was sparsely settled by people of the frontier—restless souls who no sooner had hewn fairly habitable homes out of the wilderness and attained to that degree of prosperity which to-day we should call indigence than impelled by some mysterious impulse of their nature they abandoned all and pushed farther westward, to encounter new perils and privations in the effort to regain the meagre comforts which they had voluntarily renounced. Many of them had already forsaken that region for the remoter settlements, but among those remaining was one who had been of those first arriving. He lived alone in a house of logs surrounded on all sides by the great forest, of whose gloom and silence he seemed a part, for no one had ever known him to smile nor speak a needless word. His simple wants were supplied by the sale or barter of skins of wild animals in the river town, for not a thing did he grow upon the land which, if needful, he might have claimed by right of undisturbed possession. There were evidences of "improvement"—a few acres of ground immediately about the house had once been cleared of its trees, the decayed stumps of which were half concealed by the new growth that had been suffered to repair the ravage wrought by the ax. Apparently the man's zeal for agriculture had burned with a failing flame, expiring in penitential ashes.

The little log house, with its chimney of sticks, its roof

of warping clapboards weighted with traversing poles and its "chinking" of clay, had a single door and, directly opposite, a window. The latter, however, was boarded up—nobody could remember a time when it was not. And none knew why it was so closed; certainly not because of the occupant's dislike of light and air, for on those rare occasions when a hunter had passed that lonely spot the recluse had commonly been seen sunning himself on his doorstep if heaven had provided sunshine for his need. I fancy there are few persons living to-day who ever knew the secret of that window, but I am one, as you shall see.

The man's name was said to be Murlock. He was apparently seventy years old, actually about fifty. Something besides years had had a hand in his aging. His hair and long, full beard were white, his gray, lustreless eyes sunken, his face singularly seamed with wrinkles which appeared to belong to two intersecting systems. In figure he was tall and spare, with a stoop of the shoulders—a burden bearer. I never saw him; these particulars I learned from my grandfather, from whom also I got the man's story when I was a lad. He had known him when living near by in that early day.

One day Murlock was found in his cabin, dead. It was not a time and place for coroners and newspapers, and I suppose it was agreed that he had died from natural causes or I should have been told, and should remember. I know only that with what was probably a sense of the fitness of things the body was buried near the cabin, alongside the grave of his wife, who had preceded him by so many years that local tradition had retained hardly a hint of her existence. That closes the final chapter of this true story—excepting, indeed, the circumstance that many years afterward, in company with an equally intrepid spirit, I penetrated to the place and ventured near enough to the ruined cabin to throw a stone against it, and ran away to avoid the ghost which every well-informed boy thereabout knew haunted the spot. But there is an earlier chapter—that supplied by my grandfather.

When Murlock built his cabin and began laying sturdily about with his ax to hew out a farm—the rifle, meanwhile, his means of support—he was young, strong and full of hope. In that eastern country whence he came he had married, as was the fashion, a young woman in all ways worthy of his honest devotion, who shared the dangers and privations of his lot with a willing spirit and light heart. There is no known record of her name; of her charms of mind and person tradition is silent and the doubter is at liberty to entertain his doubt; but God forbid that I should share it! Of their affection and happiness there is abundant assurance in every added day of the man's widowed life; for what but the magnetism of a blessed memory could have chained that venturesome spirit to a lot like that?

One day Murlock returned from gunning in a distant part of the forest to find his wife prostrate with fever, and delirious. There was no physician within miles, no neighbor; nor was she in a condition to be left, to summon help. So he set about the task of nursing her back to health, but at the end of the third day she fell into unconsciousness and so passed away, apparently, with never a gleam of returning reason.

From what we know of a nature like his we may venture to sketch in some of the details of the outline picture drawn by my grandfather. When convinced that she was dead, Murlock had sense enough to remember that the dead must be prepared for burial. In performance of this sacred duty he blundered now and again, did certain things incorrectly, and others which he did correctly were done over and over. His occasional failures to accomplish some simple and ordinary act filled him with astonishment, like that of a drunken man who wonders at the suspension of familiar natural laws. He was surprised, too, that he did not weep—surprised and a little ashamed; surely it is unkind not to weep for the dead. "To-morrow," he said aloud, "I shall have to make the coffin and dig the grave; and then I shall miss her, when she is no longer in sight; but now—she is dead, of course, but it is all right—it must be all right, somehow. Things cannot be so bad as they seem."

He stood over the body in the fading light, adjusting the hair and putting the finishing touches to the simple toilet, doing all mechanically, with soulless care. And still through his consciousness ran an undersense of conviction that all was right—that he should have her again as before, and everything explained. He had had no experience in grief; his capacity had not been enlarged by use. His heart could not contain it all, nor his imagination rightly conceive it. He did not know he was so hard struck; that knowledge would come later, and never go. Grief is an artist of powers as various as the instruments upon which he plays his dirges for the dead, evoking from some the sharpest, shrillest notes, from others the low, grave chords that throb recurrent like the slow beating of a distant drum. Some natures it startles; some it stupefies. To one it comes like the stroke of an arrow, stinging all the sensibilities to a keener life; to another as the blow of a bludgeon, which in crushing benumbs. We may conceive Murlock to have been that way affected, for (and here we are upon surer ground than that of conjecture) no sooner had he finished his pious work than, sinking into a chair by the side of the table upon which the body lay, and noting how white the profile showed in the deepening gloom, he laid his arms upon the table's edge, and dropped his face into them, tearless yet and unutterably weary. At that moment came in through the open window a long, wailing sound like the cry of a lost child in the far deeps of the darkening wood! But the man did not move. Again, and nearer than before, sounded that unearthly cry upon his failing sense. Perhaps it was a wild beast; perhaps it was a dream. For Murlock was asleep.

Some hours later, as it afterward appeared, this unfaithful

watcher awoke and lifting his head from his arms intently listened—he knew not why. There in the black darkness by the side of the dead, recalling all without a shock, he strained his eyes to see—he knew not what. His senses were all alert, his breath was suspended, his blood had stilled its tides as if to assist the silence. Who—what had waked him, and where was it?

Suddenly the table shook beneath his arms, and at the same moment he heard, or fancied that he heard, a light, soft step—another—sounds as of bare feet upon the floor!

He was terrified beyond the power to cry out or move. Perforce he waited—waited there in the darkness through seeming centuries of such dread as one may know, yet live to tell. He tried vainly to speak the dead woman's name, vainly to stretch forth his hand across the table to learn if she were there. His throat was powerless, his arms and hands were like lead. Then occurred something most frightful. Some heavy body seemed hurled against the table with an impetus that pushed it against his breast so sharply as nearly to overthrow him, and at the same instant he heard and felt the fall of something upon the floor with so violent a thump that the whole house was shaken by the impact. A scuffling ensued, and a confusion of sounds impossible to describe. Murlock had risen to his feet. Fear had by excess forfeited control of his faculties. He flung his hands upon the table. Nothing was there!

There is a point at which terror may turn to madness; and madness incites to action. With no definite intent, from no motive but the wayward impulse of a madman, Murlock sprang to the wall, with a little groping seized his loaded rifle, and without aim discharged it. By the flash which lit up the room with a vivid illumination, he saw an enormous panther dragging the dead woman toward the window, its teeth fixed in her throat! Then there were darkness blacker than before, and silence; and when he returned to consciousness the sun was high and the wood vocal with songs of birds.

The body lay near the window, where the beast had left it when frightened away by the flash and report of the rifle. The clothing was deranged, the long hair in disorder, the limbs lay anyhow. From the throat, dreadfully lacerated, had issued a pool of blood not yet entirely coagulated. The ribbon with which he had bound the wrists was broken; the hands were tightly clenched. Between the teeth was a fragment of the animal's ear.

3

THE OVAL PORTRAIT

Edgar Allen Poe

The château into which my valet had ventured to make forcible entrance, rather than permit me, in my desperately wounded condition, to pass a night in the open air, was one of those piles of commingled gloom and grandeur which have so long frowned among the Appennines, not less in fact than in the fancy of Mrs. Radcliffe. To all appearance it had been temporarily and very lately abandoned. We established ourselves in one of the smallest and least sumptuously furnished apartments. It lay in a remote turret of the building. Its decorations were rich, yet tattered and antique. Its walls were hung with tapestry and bedecked with manifold and multiform armorial trophies, together with an unusually great number of very spirited modern paintings in frames of rich golden arabesque. In these paintings, which depended from the walls not only in their main surfaces, but in very many nooks which the bizarre architecture of the château rendered necessary—in these paintings my incipient delirium, perhaps, had caused me to take deep interest; so that I bade Pedro to close the heavy shutters of the room—since it was already night—to light the tongues of a tall candelabrum which stood by the head of my bed, and to throw open far and wide the fringed curtains of black velvet which enveloped the bed itself. I wished all this done that I might resign myself, if not to sleep, at least alternately to the contemplation of these pictures, and the perusal of a small volume which had been found upon the pillow, and which purported to criticise and describe them.

Long, long I read—and devoutly, devotedly I gazed. Rapidly and gloriously the hours flew by and the deep midnight came. The position of the candelabrum displeased me, and outreaching my hand with difficulty, rather than disturb my slumbering valet, I placed it so as to throw its rays more fully upon the book.

But the action produced an effect altogether unanticipated. The rays of the numerous candles (for there were many) now fell within a niche of the room which had hitherto been thrown into deep shade by one of the bed-posts. I thus saw in vivid light a picture all unnoticed before. It was the portrait of a young girl just ripening into womanhood. I glanced at the painting hurriedly, and then closed my eyes. Why I did this was not at first apparent even to my own perception. But while my lids remained thus shut, I ran over in my mind my reason for so shutting them. It was an impulsive movement to gain time for thought—to make sure that my vision had not deceived me—to calm and subdue my fancy for a more sober and more certain gaze. In a very few moments I again looked fixedly at the painting.

That I now saw aright I could not and would not doubt; for the first flashing of the candles upon that canvas had seemed to dissipate the dreamy stupor which was stealing over my senses, and to startle me at once into waking life.

The portrait, I have already said, was that of a young girl. It was a mere head and shoulders, done in what is technically termed a vignette manner; much in the style of the favorite heads of Sully. The arms, the bosom, and even the ends of the radiant hair melted imperceptibly into the vague yet deep shadow which formed the back-ground of the whole. The frame was oval, richly gilded and filigreed in Moresque. As a thing of art nothing could be more admirable than the painting itself. But it could have been neither the execution of the work, nor the immortal beauty of the countenance, which had so suddenly and so vehemently moved me. Least of all, could it have been that my fancy, shaken from its half slumber, had mistaken the head for that of a living person. I saw at once that the peculiarities of the design, of the vignetting, and of the frame, must have instantly dispelled such idea—must have prevented even its momentary entertainment. Thinking earnestly upon these points, I remained, for an hour perhaps, half sitting, half reclining, with my vision riveted upon the portrait. At length, satisfied with the true secret of its effect, I fell back within the bed. I had found the spell of the picture in an absolute life-likeliness of expression, which, at first startling, finally confounded, subdued, and appalled me. With deep and reverent awe I replaced the candelabrum in its former position. The cause of my deep agitation being thus shut from view, I sought eagerly the volume which discussed the paintings and their histories. Turning to the number which designated the oval portrait, I there read the vague and quaint words which follow:

"She was a maiden of rarest beauty, and not more lovely than full of glee. And evil was the hour when she saw, and loved, and wedded the painter. He, passionate, studious, austere, and having already a bride in his Art; she a maiden of rarest beauty, and not more lovely than full of glee; all light and smiles, and frolicsome as the young fawn; loving and cherishing all things; hating only the Art which was her rival; dreading only the pallet and brushes and other untoward instruments which deprived her of the countenance of her lover. It was thus a terrible thing for this lady to hear the painter speak of his desire to portray even his young bride. But she was humble and obedient, and sat meekly for many weeks in the dark, high turret-chamber where the light dripped upon the pale canvas only from overhead. But he, the painter, took glory in his work, which went on from hour to hour, and from day to day. And he was a passionate, and wild, and moody man, who became lost in reveries; so that he would not see that the light which fell so ghastly in that lone turret withered the health and the spirits of his bride, who pined visibly to all but him. Yet she smiled on and still on, uncomplainingly, because she saw that the painter (who had high renown) took a fervid and burning pleasure in his task, and wrought day and night to depict her who so loved him, yet who grew daily more dispirited and weak. And in sooth some who beheld the portrait spoke of its resemblance in low words, as of a mighty marvel, and a proof not less of the power of the painter than of his deep love for her whom he depicted so surpassingly well. But at length, as the labor drew nearer to its conclusion, there were admitted none into the turret; for the painter had grown wild with the ardor of his work, and turned his eyes from canvas merely, even to regard the countenance of his wife. And he would not see that the tints which he spread upon the canvas were drawn from the cheeks of her who sate beside him. And when many weeks had passed, and but little remained to do, save one brush upon the mouth and one tint upon the eye, the spirit of the lady again flickered up as the flame within the socket of the lamp. And then the brush was given, and then the tint was placed; and, for one moment, the painter stood entranced before the work which he had wrought; but in the next, while he yet gazed, he grew tremulous and very pallid, and aghast, and crying with a loud voice, 'This is indeed Life itself!' turned suddenly to regard his beloved:—She was dead!"

4

THE INCUBUS

Hamilton Craigie

Fear beset Gerald Marston at the very moment of his entry into the chamber—an intense, gripping horror which laid an icy hand upon his forehead and fingers of a damp coldness about his heart.

It was as if one invisible from within had reached forth to make him prisoner to its atmosphere, which, heightened physically by the slimy walls, the velvet darkness, and the ceaseless, slow dripping of liquid upon stone, chilled his soul with a nameless foreboding, a daunting menace of unutterable dread.

And yet that Something, as he told himself, was behind him—his victim, the man whom he had killed.

Even now It walked, rather, upon the surface of the oily night, felt, but unseen, driving him forward inexorably, pitilessly—so that now he stood in the entrance to this lesser blackness, his huge bulk shaking in an anguish of uncertainty but one degree removed from the panic which had ridden him until, at length, distraught and near to madness, he had stumbled into this subterranean oubliette in his frantic flight.

It seemed a week since he, together with Professor Pillsbury, had descended into this whispering labyrinth of tombs—long galleries of Aztec construction vying in completeness with the catacombs of early Rome—sinuous corridors crossing and re-crossing in a maze of underground warrens of apparently interminable extent.

It had been the Professor himself, an archaeologist whose

devotion to his calling amounted almost to an obsession, who had suggested the exploration—nay, insisted on it—nor had he, in his singleness of purpose, remembered that it had been Marston, his friend, who had, as it were, with a very triumph of casualness, implanted in his mind the first tiny seed of suggestion.

Scarcely a month before Marston had felicitated his friend upon the latter's engagement to Lucille Westley, beautiful and imperious, but there had been death in his heart. Perhaps, however, he had fancied, with the perverted hope which had grown in his heart like a green and pallid flame of lust, that, given his chance, he might have possessed this incomparable creature for his own.

And so, like a destroying fire, his obsession had mounted until, with the cunning of his twisted brain, he had evolved a plan, or, rather, deep within his consciousness, had spawned a thought: foul, slimy, furtive—even to himself half-born—an abortion, in truth, and yet...

As they had passed from the clean sunlight into the Stygian darkness of the cavern, somehow, unbidden, there had arisen in Marston's mind an echo of the classroom—a fugitive whisper which, he could have sworn, took on suddenly the form and substance of mocking speech: "*Facilis decensus Averni,*" it whispered in his ear, as in a dim current of the whispering wind.

Marston had brought with him a ball of stout twine as a necessary precaution in threading the uncharted deeps of the underground corridors. This he had knotted firmly in a clove hitch (for Marston had been a sailor). There could have been no fear of its working loose, and less danger of its fraying out against the rough walls of the passageways, since at all times it would be loosely held. Like a thin snake, it spread itself behind them, and like a snake...

The accident had been impossible to foresee. He had *known*

that it could not happen; and yet...

The Professor, leading the way with lantern held well aloft, had exclaimed aloud at the vivid beauty of a stalactite in his path, adjacent to a broad, deep ledge some three feet in height.

"Ah, Gerald!" he had cried. "It is *alive*—it writhes with motion—observe how it has grown, layer upon layer of smooth perfection! And the ledge—a perfect replica of an ancient sarcophagus! Look—"

But he was destined never to complete the speech.

For with the words he stumbled—a bight of the line snaked out to coil around his ankle—tottered, even as from behind him something moved, flashed, descended upon his head—something cold and hard. He fell, with a sodden crash, face downward in the mold.

And with his fall the lantern crashed to the floor of the cavern, sputtered a moment feebly in a brief spark of life, and then died abruptly. And at the feet of Marston that which had been sentient, alive, now lay still and motionless in the dust.

Marston stood for a moment, with groping fingers extended into the void about him; his head sang, his eyes blurred. The velvet black became suddenly, as it were, endowed with life and movement, mysterious, whispering. Near at hand there sounded abruptly a horrible, fetid panting—a gross intake of whistling breath which, in a sudden, overmastering panic, he did not recognize as his own labored breathing.

"God!" he cried, insanely, and then, in panic-struck terror at the sound of his voice, fell silent and stood shivering like a frightened horse.

With fumbling fingers he felt in his pockets and produced a box of matches, finally, after many attempts, lighting one which he held tremblingly above his head. He did not glance at the figure at his feet, but over and beyond it, where his shadow, monstrous and grotesque, seemed flung headforemost into a shallow niche, within which there rested a flat slab of rock perhaps three feet in height.

To his distorted imagination the sudden suggestion seemed filled with a vague menace—as if the brooding shadow of death had reached forth to touch, to summon, to beckon with an imperious, chill finger there in that stifling abode of changeless dark.

Abruptly, as the quick flame ate downward to his fingertips, he made a short, backward step—stumbled—and the box fell from his nerveless hand, the match winked out, and at one stride the dominion of the dark enveloped him.

He bent swiftly, with frantic fingers searching in the mold, scratching, clawing in a fever of anxiety.

He found—nothing. Then, as if impelled from behind by an inexorable Force, he began to run, stumbling, falling, bruising himself against the sharp, unseen angles of the passageway along which he fled...

Time had merged into an eternity of physical pain and mental torture, of corroding fear which left him in a sweat of agony as he fared onward in his blundering flight. The sense of direction which in the pitch blackness renders the familiar outlines of one's very bed-chamber strangely distorted—this had become confused in his first headlong rush away from the scene of that which was branded upon his heart in letters of fire.

Now, in his warped and twisted brain the germ of a thought grew, expanded, flowered abruptly in an insane cacophony of sound.

A laugh, reedy, discordant, cackling echoed in his ears, beginning in a low chuckle, then rising all about him in a furious stridor of sound. It was as if the demons of the place were welcoming him to their midst as one worthy of their company.

Again he fell prone, groveling in the mold in an ecstasy of terror at the unrecognizable mouthings which issued from his throat. But even as his insanity peopled the void about him with shapes of terror, in especial the hideous Shape which he knew even now followed him, he got somehow to his feet, arose, and lurched headlong into a recess in the rocky corridor, which would have been familiar could he have but beheld it even in the brief flaring of a match.

It was then that he heard the ceaseless, slow dripping that smote him afresh with an indescribable, crawling fear, beside which his previous insane panic had been as nothing. For a moment he heard also a gibbering—a squeaking, a rustle which with his coming ceased abruptly in a faint shadow of sound. For the moment, he could have sworn that a slinking, furtive, Something, unbelievably swift, had brushed past his leg, touched him lightly as with the faint, fugitive contact of a dead, wind-blown leaf.

That slow, continuous dripping—too well he knew its meaning, or thought that he did. And in the same breath he became aware of the place in which he stood—*recognized* it for what it was even in the enveloping blackness.

At any other time he would have known that measured dripping for what it was: the curiously suggestive rhythm of the stalactite's slow *drip-drip*, like the sluggish dripping of blood.

In his headlong flight, cleaving an unimagined depth of Cimmerian darkness, through which it seemed he was breathing the oily tide of a dim nightmare of viscid flood, all sense of direction had been completely lost.

Now, as he stood, within this fearsome catacomb, of a sudden he stumbled, knelt, put forward a groping hand, and then recoiled with a windy shriek—as his shaking fingers encountered the *clammy surface of a human face!*

He had returned, willy nilly, as it seemed, to the body of his victim. It was the face of Pillsbury, cold, clammy, silent, unresponsive.

Doomed! He was doomed, then, to kneel there, in that groping blackness of this frightful charnel—alone, yet prisoner to that silent figure—forever to hear that ceaseless dripping, regular as the beating of a heart, of a heart that was stilled forever, yet strangely pulsing in its slow *drip-drip*—inexorable, insistent, ever louder, as it seemed—rising in a veritable thunder against the low-hung curtain of the dark.

Trembling, urging his will by the severest effort he had ever known, in a sudden lucid interval he passed an exploring hand over the rigid outlines of the body, which lay, as upon a bier, on a sort of rocky shelf, perhaps three feet in height, just level with his shoulders as he bent before it. But it had not been there before! When he had left it in his overmastering panic *it had been lying, face downward in the mold!*

But it did not occur to him to question its position; the strange significance of the fact affected him not at all, for, curiously enough, with the contact there came a measure of reassurance: the Thing which had been Pillsbury, his friend—the Thing which he had left behind—had not been following him; it had existed merely in his coward imagination. Or, if it had hunted him through the maze of corridors, it was now returned to its chosen resting-place. There it was, under his hand!

It was absurd to think that he had been followed, for dead men did not walk, save in dreams, and he had returned to prove that it lay where he had left it, silent, cold, incapable of movement without volition.

On his hands and knees, his questing fingers, tracing the rigid outline of the limbs, came suddenly upon a length of line, knotted about the ankle. *Ah!*

Feverishly he felt about him in the blackness, clawing forward on hands and knees. Yes, the line ran clear, unbroken, *away* from the niche. He was saved!

In his sudden revulsion, he gave way to primitive emotion—

he chuckled, moaned, cried, wept, laughed in a horrible travesty of mirth.

Like a drowning man, he seized upon it with clutching fingers as if by some sudden magic he might be drawn, on the instant, out of this labyrinth of black terror which was eating into his soul with the corroding bite of an acid. For at the other end of that thin thread lay sunlight and life and liberty. He held that within his shaking grasp which was in truth a life-line, a tenuous yet certain means of safety, of escape from a death, the grisly face of which had but a moment before leered at him out of the tomblike depths.

In his eagerness to be gone, he straightened from his kneeling posture with a convulsive movement, his fingers holding the line, jerked it violently, and, before he could rise, there came a rustle, a thud, and a suffocating weight descended upon his back. As he fell, face downward in the mold, he squeaked like a rat as, out of the dark, two hands went round his neck and clawlike talons encircled his throat.

Curiously alive they seemed, and yet—with his own hand he had accounted for that life. It was not possible—no, it could not be!—it was unthinkable...

For a space he lay, inert, passive, but, notwithstanding his terror, his fingers still clutching the line, spread out before him in the blackness. Presently, when his panic had somewhat abated, when he found that he was still alive, unharmed, by slow stages of tremendous effort he rose to his knees, tottering under the Incubus upon his back.

Now that he knew what it was, after an interval he attempted to disengage the fingers about his neck, but he could not. He found that grip rigid, unyielding. Like a bar of iron, it resisted his utmost efforts.

It was as if a Will, implacable, inexorable, had informed those stiffened talons with purpose; it was as if the last sentient effort of an Intelligence had, by some supernatural quality, *bequeathed* to those fingers a message, a command to be performed. *Rigor mortis*—that was it—the unbreakable hold of those implacable fingers: Pillsbury's vengeful fingers, reaching out, even after death, in a dreadful cincture of doom!

But Marston rose slowly to his feet, staggering, swaying beneath that frightful burden whose fingers wrenched by a superhuman effort from his neck, bit into his shoulders like hooks of steel.

"God!" he mumbled, again, in an unconscious travesty—a hideous burlesque of supplication.

It was the end, then. Weakened as he was, his nerves a jangle of discordant wires, his mind a chaos of bemused and frantic thought, he stood, helpless, swaying, foredone, beaten, trapped by the insensate clay of his own making.

No longer a man but a beast, his brain wiped free of every thought but the blind, unreasoning impulse to live, like an animal he drew, from some unsuspected physical reservoir within him, the strength to proceed.

Tottering, swaying, he reverted to the brute, and, with the dumb, inhuman impulsion of the brute, roweling even his apelike strength to superhuman effort, he continued to advance, falling at times, and rising as with the last spent effort of a runner at the tape, yet somehow going on and on, feeling his way along that thin thread whose other end, miles distant, centuries away, stretched into the ether of Heaven!

In a nightmare of suffocating blackness, shot through at times with the red fires of the Pit, he fared onward, and now he saw, with a sudden, agonized return to the perception of the human, that those fires were all about him. They were Eyes, venomous, hateful, red with the lust of unholy anticipation...

He heard about him the slither of gaunt bodies, the patter of innumerable feet—rats they were, but of an unconscionable size, huge and voracious, such as infested this underground kingdom of the dead.

While he moved he knew that they would not attack him. While he lived, even without movement, he believed that he was safe.

But why had they refrained from that which he had given them to feast upon, the Thing which even now flapped about him, the inanimate yet strangely animate shell which he had transformed at a stroke from life to death, its legs striking against his as he moved, as if to urge him onward, rowel him forward as in a race with death?

The sounds that he had heard, the squeaks, the gibbers—as of ghouls disturbed at a ghastly rendezvous—could there have been any significance in these? Somewhere he had heard of drunken miners, asleep in the deep levels of coal, brought to a sudden, horrid awakening by cold lips nuzzling cheek or neck, but his brain considered this dully, if at all.

An odd hallucination began to possess him; dimly he dreamed that his dreadful burden was alive, but unconscious, insentient. But he knew that it was an hallucination.

He would make no immediate effort to rid himself of the Thing he carried—not now, at any rate. When he became stronger he would bury it, hide it. Years might pass—perhaps a chance party might discover in one of the innumerable corridors a moldering skeleton—but the body of his guilt would be a *corpus delicti*—there could be no conviction without evidence, and no murder without a victim produced as of due process of law.

But in a moment it seemed this thought gave place to the overmastering panic terror of escape. Instinct alone held him to his course. If there had been light one might have seen the foam which gathered on his lips, the glassy stare of his eyes.

Again he fell, and this time he fancied that the narrowing circle had drawn nearer. Even to his dulled brain he was aware of an intelligent rapacity in those burning eyes, an anticipation which sprang from *knowledge*.

Somehow, once more, he rose upright, after a multiplied agony of straining effort, but he felt, deep within his consciousness, that he was but a puppet in the hands of a ruthless fate, doomed to wander forever under his detestable load.

Of a sudden, also, an illumination, like a fiery sword, cut through the dulled functioning of his intelligence: the beast that was Marston reeled with the suggestion that penetrated the surface of his physical coma.

What if the line he followed led, not into the clean brightness of the outer air, but, by some frightful mischance, still farther into the womb of the hills, deeper and deeper into oblivion, down and down into the uttermost hell of one's imagining?

In the flux and reflux of images which had taken the place of coherent thought he saw all this, he felt it to be a possibility, and with the terror of the brute he strove once more to rid himself of this insensate tyrant, this incubus which rode him, roweling his sides with grotesquely dangling feet, spurring him on in a mad welter of fear and pain from which he could not escape.

But it was useless. Try as he would, he could not disengage that grip of steel, and thewed mightily as he was, he found that every last ounce of his great strength was needed to go on. He was just weak enough to render futile any effort to dislodge those clinging fingers, and just strong enough to continue his progress, like a mole in the dark—and that was all.

He must go on and on until flesh and blood could endure no more, the victim of his own contriving, the veritable bond-slave of his passionate soul. And when at length he should fall, no more to rise, then would come, not swift oblivion, but death, indeed, lingering, horrible, unthinkable, even for a beast...

Time had ceased, feeling had ceased; thought remained only in the faint spark which glowed somewhere within him, flickering now, glowing at the core of his being even as about him there narrowed the fell circle of the blazing eyes.

Slap—slap—shuffle—slap... With the infinite slowness of exhaustion, his feet moved, dragged, went forward, while ever at his back those other lifeless feet rose and fell in a grotesque travesty of life, of movement, spurring forward his all but fainting soul.

Dimly he perceived that the floor upon which he moved had taken an upward trend; he felt the line go suddenly taut; then, abruptly, before him, for a single instant, a pale glimmer flickered and died as from dim leagues of distance.

Summoning the last remnant of his strength, he began to run, or thought that he did, but in reality he moved by inches, and by inches the faint glimmer grew, expanded, broadened to a luminous grayness.

Stumbling, slipping, swaying from side to side, the sight of that pale shadow of the day intoxicated him with a feverish exultation, despite the weakness which seemed to dissolve his being to water. He was saved.

By a last, titanic effort, a tremendous wrenching of the will, he fell rather than staggered into the outer air—beheld, with lack-lustre eyes, the ring of faces about him, all staring eyes and white lips and working faces.

Then he sank abruptly to his knees as eager hands relieved him of his burden. He heard voices, meaningless, yet filled with meaning...

He fell instantaneously down a long stairway to the deep, enveloping mercy of unconsciousness.

Presently, after a timeless interval, he opened his eyes, and then closed them again, blinking owlishly at the strong sunlight. He heard a voice, incoherent, babbling, which, after a moment, he recognized as his own:

"The stalactite—it was the stalactite that killed him, I tell you... It was an accident—an *accident*..."

He rolled his eyes wildly from right to left; and at what he saw a strangled, mad cry of sudden comprehension—of understanding—issued from his throat ere the thick veil of a retributive insanity descended upon him forever:

"*The rats...* knew..."

Before him, his face death-white, his hands scarred from the rough stone up which he had clawed to the rocky shelf, a clean bandage about his forehead, was the face of Pillsbury. In that brief instant, like a lightning flash, illumination seared into the brain of Marston, and, by its very white-hot intensity, shriveled it to the dust of a gibbering madness:

The drunken sleep of the miners...

The nibbling of the rats... Pillsbury's awakening to consciousness... His instinctive, *upward* effort to escape to the ledge from which, with the half-conscious, and then wholly conscious grip that would not be denied, he had fallen upon Marston...

Potential murderer that he was, Marston himself, by a poetic irony of justice, had been the unwitting savior of his intended victim!

5

JUNGLE DEATH

Artemus Calloway

The very atmosphere seemed surcharged with mystery—danger—death.

Even the clear blue sky above seemed to shrink away from The Tropical Gem Plantation as from a thing accursed. Out in the muddy waters of the Ulua, apparently as lifeless as a water-soaked log, a sleepy-eyed crocodile waited—waited as if he, too, sensed impending calamity for the creatures on shore and intended being at hand to assert his rights should the threatened catastrophe bring food for his kind.

All this impressed Bart Condon, standing in the protecting shade of the softly rustling banana jungle, eyes focused on the busy scene across the river, brain busy with the disquieting events of the past few weeks.

Bart Condon was troubled. Here was something he knew not how to fight, because it was something he could not see. Until recently, he had thought himself fairly familiar with Honduras and the trials of a plantation manager there, but this was something new—something which hid in the shadows and struck when one was not looking.

First there had been the matter of the cistern water in the laborers' quarters. Some one had poisoned it—not in a manner to cause death, but illness. Condon had been mystified by the epidemic which descended upon the place until the plantation physician made an examination of the water. Then he was the more at sea. Who could have done this—and why?

Close upon this trouble came whispers—rumors that the place was bewitched. More than a dozen of the more superstitious blacks and half blacks slipped away. And their places had been hard to fill.

Then had come the fires, starting no one knew when or how. Once a manacca shack, in which a sick man lived, burned; and he was brought out half-stifled, scorched and raving about the devils that infested the place.

Other things occurred. And there was more whispering, more dissatisfaction.

And then had come death. A partly devoured body had been found lodged against a mud bar in the river. The work of crocodiles, Condon had thought, until examination disclosed the fact that there was a bullet in the man's brain. And then he knew that the crocodiles had profited from the work of a murderer.

And now all the plantation laborers threatened to leave. Somehow Condon felt that he could not blame them, though he knew that their desertion meant his ruin.

The activity along the river bank increased. The crocodile moved slowly downstream. Simultaneously with the arrival of a noisy fruit train on Condon's side of the river, another chugged into view on the opposite shore.

As soon as the trains came to a stop natives commenced transferring bananas from the cars to the fruit racks at the water's edge; here they would later be picked up by the river boat of the big fruit company which purchased the output of many Ulua River plantations, afterward shipping the bananas to the States on its own steamers.

Condon saw George Armstrong standing to the right of the train across the river, and, for some unknown reason he disliked the man more than ever. There was no real reason why he should dislike and distrust Armstrong. Yet he did dislike him, and never, from the first moment his eyes rested upon the man, had he trusted him. For two years now Condon had known the manager of the Royal Palm Plantation Company, and for that length of time some instinct had whispered that the other would be a dangerous foe.

True, Armstrong had always evinced the greatest friendliness, frequently coming across the river, which separated the plantations, to visit Condon. And occasionally—when common courtesy demanded—Condon had returned the visits.

Bart Condon had been in Honduras one year longer than Armstrong, and this year's experience as manager of the plantation of which he was majority stockholder had taught him many things of value, which he had passed on to the newcomer. But Armstrong's company was stronger financially than Condon's, and was desirous of expanding. So, for three months now, Armstrong had been trying to buy the Tropical Gem. And for nearly that length of time the Tropical Gem had been having trouble.

But it was only this morning that Condon had first commenced wondering what connection, if any, there might be between Armstrong's desire for the Tropical Gem and the trouble which had come to that plantation. Of course such thoughts were silly. Unworthy. He should be ashamed of himself... And yet...

Standing where he was, in the shelter of the tall banana plants which at a distance resembled a forest of green trees, Condon knew Armstrong had not seen him. And for some reason, which he himself did not understand, he did not want the other man to see him this morning.

Bart Condon turned and slowly made his way from the river to a trail about two hundred yards away. There he paused to watch some men cutting fruit which would be carried by mule cart to the river, the railroad being employed only for the longer hauls.

Finally he turned to his pony, fastened to a young avacado

tree, mounted and rode away. Twenty minutes later he was at plantation headquarters.

An hour after reaching headquarters Condon was sitting at his office desk, a slender young native opposite him. This man—Juan Hernandez—one of Condon's foremen, possessed intelligence above the average. He was one of the very few natives of that section of Honduras who boasted pure Spanish blood, but at the same time he understood thoroughly the mixed breeds in whose veins there flowed the blood of African, Indian, Chinese and others, to say nothing of the full-blood negroes from Jamaica, Barbadoes, and elsewhere.

Once facing Hernandez, Condon lost no time in getting to the subject:

"The men—they are very much upset?"

Hernandez nodded.

"They are, Mr. Condon," he replied in perfect English, thanks to a States education. "They are whispering that there is a curse upon the plantation; that you are the cause of it; that the spirits are displeased with you, and I don't know what else. They——"

Hernandez hesitated. Then:

"Why, they are even beginning to blame you for the death of that man found in the river, although they don't know, as we do, that someone shot him."

Condon frowned. "Somehow I suspect as much. But you are sure your information—what you tell me is correct?"

Hernandez nodded. "I am positive of it. Further than that I feel that I have discovered what is behind it all. You know you told me a week ago to look into it——"

"Yes?"

"It is voodooism. A witch doctor who lives in the jungle is behind the trouble here. And a white man is behind the witch doctor!"

Condon started. "You mean—?"

For a moment Hernandez said nothing, staring at the desk before him. Then:

"Armstrong!"

Condon's hands twitched nervously. "How do you know—or suspect—this, Hernandez?"

"I am positive, Mr. Condon. I have a man working under me whom I trust implicitly. He is an Indian—one of those commonly known as a Mosquito Indian—they live down on the Mosquito Coast, you know———"

"Yes. Go on. What about him?"

"Well, he is a very intelligent fellow. Not a drop of black blood in his veins. Of course, many of the Indians in this country have their own superstitious beliefs, but not so this man. For years he has worked around foreigners—those ideas, if he ever had them, have been supplanted by those of civilization.

"This man told me that the witch doctor—an old dried-up black fellow, no telling how old he is—has been coming to the plantation. He was here the night before the water was poisoned. He has been here since. And lately the laborers have been going to see him—holding ceremonies and that sort of thing.

"And tonight———" Hernandez lowered his voice—"they go again! They are to be there at ten o'clock. The witch doctor is going to tell them that their lives are not safe on this plantation as long as you have anything to do with it. Tomorrow they will leave. And no other laborers will come here. Then—Armstrong thinks he can buy you out. You see, with Armstrong in charge, the curse will be removed."

Condon secured a box of cigars from his desk, handed it to Hernandez, found a box of matches, lighted a cigar himself.

"*Hmm!* Pretty clever scheme. But—Oh! hang it, Hernandez, do you suppose this *can* be correct?"

Hernandez regarded his cigar thoughtfully. "I *know* it is!"

"Well———"

"Just a moment, please, Mr. Condon. There is one chance for us—only one. That is to discredit the witch doctor. Once the superstitious mixed breeds and blacks find that he is not infallible, that there is something more powerful than he, they will lose confidence in him. They will believe nothing he has told them. But until that is done the case is hopeless. You see, many of the men working here were raised on superstition—on voodooism. The blacks brought it from Africa, and their descendants in this and the other nearby countries cling to it. And, as I have said, we have them here from many places."

"How are we to discredit the witch doctor?"

Hernandez smiled. "Armstrong visits him at eight o'clock this evening, to pay half the price for running the laborers away from here. He is to pay the other half when they are gone. Of course, he has paid something all along for the various little jobs, but this is the big one—the big money job."

"What on earth would that old fellow want with money?"

Hernandez laughed. "Square-faced gin. He stays soaked all the time. But I have a plan——"

"But how," interrupted Condon, "did your man learn all this?"

"By pretending to believe in voodooism—and by watching. He has attended the ceremonies with the others. And he has followed Armstrong there when the witch doctor was alone. That is how he learned of the poisoned water. He has heard nothing there about the murder of the native, but I am sure there is a connection there somewhere if we can find it."

Hernandez made a significant gesture.

"You don't know the confidence those people have in that old fellow. He has a pond there in front of his cave. A natural sort of pond. Been there for centuries, I suppose, and it is full of crocodiles. Sacrifices to these crocodiles have been hinted at— but of course I couldn't swear to that. I do know, however, that the laborers here are blind enough in their belief of him to do anything he might tell them."

Condon's face was wrinkled in thought. "But your plan?"

Hernandez leaned nearer. "Listen..."

Seven-thirty o'clock that evening found Bart Condon, Juan Hernandez and the Indian of whom Condon had been told concealed on the side of the little jungle hill above the witch doctor's cave. Almost at his doorway was the pond of which Hernandez had spoken. An occasional *swish* of the water told of life in it. Just in front of the cave, squatted on the ground beside a faint brush fire, was the witch doctor, an old, shriveled, dried-up, gray-headed black.

"We can hear from this place?" Condon whispered.

"Yes," replied Hernandez, "but be quiet. He might hear you."

Back in the jungle, monkeys chattered. Baboons howled nearby. A macaw set up a shrill shrieking. Once Condon heard the helpless, hopeless cry of some small animal as it met the death of the jungle. Some beast of the tropics slipped past them. Bart Condon gripped his revolver.

And then they heard somebody approaching. Down a little trail—the same trail which Condon had traveled part of the way—a man was coming. A few moments later Armstrong was standing before the witch doctor's fire.

With every nerve on edge, Condon watched. Armstrong and the witch doctor, both now seated before the blaze, wasted no time on inconsequential talk.

Armstrong was speaking in Spanish: "You understand exactly what you are to tell those people when they come here tonight."

"I do."

"Very well. Here is half the money. You will receive as much more—provided you get Condon's laborers away tomorrow—and keep them and all others away."

The witch doctor nodded. "They will be away before tomorrow. When they leave here they will be afraid to return to the man Condon's plantation."

"They won't even return for their things?"

The old man laughed shrilly. "They will believe everything on that plantation accursed when I have finished with them and will never desire to see their things again. I intended telling them that they must leave tomorrow. Now I have decided to have them leave tonight. It is better so."

Again the witch doctor laughed.

"But——" and now there was something in his voice Condon had not detected there before—"there is more money to come to me, Senor."

Armstrong's tone was impatient. "You get that when the laborers have quit the plantation."

The old man chuckled. "But I mean other money."

"What other money?"

"The money for keeping your secret about the man you shot!"

George Armstrong jumped to his feet. "You're crazy! I shot no man."

The witch doctor also was on his feet. "But you did, Senor, I saw you! I don't blame you for what you did. The fellow saw you coming from here and he might have been suspicious. I, also, would have killed him, but you did the job for me. And now you will pay me for keeping the secret."

The witch doctor's words seemed to madden the manager of the Royal Palm Plantation. Straight at the old man's throat he sprang. They fought like wild animals. The witch doctor, for all his frailness, possessed enormous strength.

Suddenly Hernandez caught Condon's arm: "Look! Down the trail!" he whispered.

Condon looked. Then he gasped in amazement. The trail was filled, as far as he could see, with men.

Suddenly Condon's attention was brought back to the struggle by a scream of terror, which burst from Armstrong's lips. And then, locked in embrace, the plantation manager and the witch doctor disappeared in the crocodile pool.

There was a sudden rush—horrid grunts—the crushing of bones—and Condon imagined he could see the water redden. Armstrong and the witch doctor were no more.

Then, from Condon's laborers in the trail, came cries of denunciation. "He is no witch doctor! He fought with the white man and was eaten by crocodiles—he who told us that he could destroy white men by pointing his finger at them. He told us that the crocodiles could not harm him."

Unafraid of that which was now no mystery, some of the bolder ones advanced to the fire. One picked up some gold pieces, which the witch doctor had dropped. Another found Armstrong's purse.

They turned and rejoined their companions. Five minutes later the entire party had passed out of hearing.

Hernandez touched Condon on the shoulder. "We can go now. And our troubles are over. The men will remain on the plantation perfectly satisfied."

"But I don't understand," said Condon slowly, rising to his feet and rubbing his cramped legs, "why they came so early. I thought they were to get here at ten o'clock."

"So Armstrong and the witch doctor thought," laughed Hernandez. "But the message was carried by our friend here—and he asked my advice before delivering it. And he made the hour earlier so they would find Armstrong here. That alone would have destroyed their confidence in the witch doctor, for he is supposed to have nothing to do with white men."

Hernandez smiled.

"They were told, although this man professed not to believe it, that there was a report to the effect that Armstrong had bought the witch doctor—had paid him to betray them. That is why they understood everything so readily when they saw the end of the fight."

"Voodooism," said Condon thoughtfully, "loses its strength when it mixes up with white men."

6

THE HIDEOUS FACE
A Grim Tale of Frightful Revenge

Victor Johns

Marseilles, one hears while traveling through Europe, is the most vicious town in France.

Whether or not this ancient seaport, whose history reaches deep into the shadows of antiquity, is deserving of a criticism so sweeping and so condemnatory, I do not know. Such, at any rate, is the reputation it suffers among travelers.

All roads in Marseilles lead to La Cannebière, a street of splendid cafés. Being a sort of hyphen that connects the waterfront with the fashionable hotels and shops of the Rue Noailles, it swarms with a curious blend of dregs and pickings. Up from the Quai de la Fraternité come sailors hungry for the pleasures a few hours' shore leave will offer; Algerian troops, on their way to Africa, jostle English soldiers back from India; adventurers and *le monde élégant*, pausing in flight to or from the Riviera, and the inevitable Magdalens, spatter its length with color and charge it with restlessness.

Late one afternoon last winter I drifted through this famous thoroughfare, looking for a place among the tables that edge its pavements. It had become my habit to sit for half an hour before dinner somewhere along the street, drink an appetizer, and expect the crowd to entertain me. The rows of iron chairs were filled with earlier comers, who sat contentedly behind their *apéritifs* or cups of chocolate, but at last, in front of the Café de l'Univers, I found a vacant back row table, which I quickly possessed. With a glass of *vermouth cassis* on the table beside me, I yielded to the lure of seaport excitement.

My thoughts were soon interrupted, however, by an American voice asking in French if the other chair at my table was taken. I turned to assure the gentleman it was not, that he was in no way intruding—and I looked into the face of Lawrence Bainridge.

"Hello, Bayard," was his casual greeting. A bit too casual, I thought, considering the fact we had not seen each other for nearly two years.

I, contrariwise, must fairly have gasped, "Good Lord! What are you doing here?" for, as he swung the unoccupied chair about and sat down, he said,

"Well, what's so strange about meeting me on La Cannebière?"

There was nothing strange about it; and I wondered at the amazement which so energetically had voiced itself. A rich, itinerant artist, Lawrence had zig-zagged several times around the world to paint unknown by-ways and hidden corners. Astonishment at meeting him in Marseilles was therefore absurd. Also; I felt he might construe my lack of *savoir faire* as a blunt refusal to play up to his well-known and fondly-cherished reputation as a globe trotter. He was childish in certain respects—artists are.

The waiter quickly fetched a champagne cocktail and a package of English cigarettes. The cocktail Lawrence downed in a gulp and called for more. The second he drank with more restraint.

Though I had not seen him since two summers before—at Land's End, an isolated village in Massachusetts—our conversation was rambling and disjointed, like that of incompatible strangers who find no ease in silence. This annoyed me, for our similarity of tastes, I felt, should more than outweigh the separation.

As the late afternoon merged into early evening, the mistral blew its cold and sinister breath out to the Mediterranean. We drank steadily, Lawrence all the while jibing at me for clinging to so impotent a mixture as vermouth, currant juice and seltzer. He had reached his fifth cocktail, but through the exercise of will, apparently, was still sober. Nevertheless, he worried me.

Furtively, almost defensively, Lawrence sat in his chair. I reacted to his attitude by bracing myself against an intangible, though imminent, danger which thickened the atmosphere. He breathed jerkily, emitting from time to time a sharp clicking sound, as though part of his breathing mechanism had suddenly refused to function. Quivers ran through his body and ended in a twitch.

But he spoke with a crisp enunciation, and so precisely that each word seemed to have been scoured and weighed before utterance. On not a syllable was the checkrein loosened. I sensed a splendid effort at self-control.

I suddenly recalled the wild absurdity of Lawrence's recent work. In Paris, three months before, I had gone to his exhibition at the Vendome Galleries and left the place convinced that Lawrence Bainridge had gone stark mad.

"Flowers, *Messieurs?*" A flower girl, her wicker tray heaped with heavy-scented blossoms, paused before us. "No? Ah, *Messieurs*, but one little rose apiece—for luck!" she said.

Then she picked up a red rose bud and pinned it to the lapel of Lawrence's coat.

"*Ugh!* Take it away!" he screamed. "I can't stand it!" He tore the flower from his coat and hurled it into the gutter.

"Lawrence!" I reproved, "You're drunk."

"No, I'm not drunk," he protested. Contrition had subdued his voice. "But—I can't stand—the smell—of roses."

Thinking to avoid a scene, I suggested we take a walk. He said it might be a good idea, first, though, he would fill his cigarette case. A subterfuge, I told myself, to regain composure, and an obvious one. Lawrence had never been obvious.

At that moment there passed before us on the sidewalk such a ghastly thing that my scalp tingled and the flesh on my legs seemed to shrivel and fall away.

It was a man whose face was like a hideous mask; the left side—young and unblemished; but the right half—so mutilated that description would nauseate. Fair was divided from foul by a line running down the exact center of forehead, nose and chin.

My exclamation of horror drew Lawrence's attention to the repellent sight. At that moment the gruesome thing turned full upon us.

Lawrence fumbled with his cigarettes; the case fell from his trembling hands and clattered to the pavement. Quickly he reached down, but did not straighten up again until after the man—a sailor, to judge from his rolling gait, though he wore no uniform—had gone.

"Poor soul," I said. "How his fingers must ache to choke the life from the *Boche* responsible for that."

Lawrence made no reply. He was drained of blood. He sat rigid, petrified.

"In Paris and London," I continued, "one sees hundreds of *mutilés*—the war's driftwood—and I have trained myself to look unflinchingly into their eyes. But"—I glanced in the direction the sailor had disappeared—"my histronic ability would fail me there."

Still Lawrence made no move or sound. That he was profoundly touched I knew, for a sensitiveness, abnormal in its refinement, had been his lifelong curse. It had prevented his marriage to a young woman in whom were combined, he thought at one time, all the qualities that appeal to a man of esthetic temperament.

In his studio, one afternoon, they were planning for the wedding. Lawrence recalled a newly-acquired *object d'art* and took it from a cabinet. The treasure was an exquisite bit of ancient Egyptian glass, a spherulate bowl, so delicate of line and so ethereally opalescent of color that it always made me think of a bubble poised to float away.

I can imagine how he carried it across the room—with that caressing touch of velvet-tipped fingers peculiar to artists. The young woman, in order to examine it closely, grabbed the bowl and proceeded to paw it as a prospector might a bit of rock. Lawrence said afterward that had she struck him he could not have been more shocked. He broke the engagement that afternoon.

"Come, drink up, man!" I urged. "Stop looking as though you'd seen a ghost."

"Things other than ghosts can haunt one," he answered in a pinched tone.

We ordered drinks again, with misgivings on my part, for I felt the trembling man opposite me already had had too much. He sat slumped in his chair, shoulders hunched forward, and stared straight before him. Reminiscent or speculative, I could not tell.

Then he began to tell me a story that explained many things. His words were no longer crisp; he now spoke in a heavy, monotonous way, with many pauses, pressing his hands together in a gesture of anguish.

"The odor of that rose," he said, "and the sight—I can't stand the smell of roses! Not since two summers ago. I met a Portuguese sailor on the Wharf one day—you know—in that damn place—Land's End. Had planned a canvas, and all summer had been looking for a model—a type.

"A Portuguese Apollo he was—but a Portuguese devil, too. Didn't find that out till later. I stopped him and asked would he pose. Conceited swine! From his smile I knew it was vanity, not industry, that made him accept."

A venomous hate wove its way through Lawrence's phrases. He continued:

"Well—he called at my studio—the next afternoon—and I started the picture. He was a find. Dramatic. An inspiration.

"During the rest periods Pedro—that was his name—would lie on the floor and talk about himself while I made tea. God! How vain he was! Boasted of his success with women—his affairs. They were many. Quite plausible. He spurned the Bay and its fishing, and shipped on merchant-men. The ports of the world were his hunting ground, he said. Swashbuckling bully!"

To hear Lawrence speak so bitterly of Land's End and one of its people was puzzling, for the extraordinary note sounded in that small New England town by its so-called foreign settlement, descendants of Portuguese fishermen who came over some seventy years ago and settled along the New England coast, had appealed strongly to his artistic appreciation two years before. He had looked upon these natives as gentle, lovable folk, but to me their black eyes, heavy-lidded and drowsy, had always suggested smoldering fires, not dreams; their excessive tranquillity I thought crafty, hinting of vendettas.

Lawrence picked up the thread of his story:

"One afternoon Pedro began talking about a Portuguese funeral in town that day. A friend of his had died. I dislike funerals—corpses and such—even the mention of them. Always have. Told him to shut up. Instead, he began to tell of an interrupted funeral in Singapore he once had seen. Spared no details. Losing patience and temper, I flung a tube of paint which struck him on the head. He was furious. I told him I was sorry.

"'Pedro,' I explained, 'ever since I can remember, things connected with death have been the only things I've feared. I have never in my life been in a cemetery—and I have never seen a dead body. Just to hear of them brings out a cold sweat.' Pedro laughed and said cemeteries—or dead bodies—couldn't hurt one."

This phase of Lawrence's susceptibility I had not known. And then his pictures in Paris danced before me. What had Pedro to do with them? What had Pedro to do with the change in my friend? But I asked no questions lest I rouse Lawrence to a stubborn silence.

I found myself fidgeting about, peering suddenly into the crowd as if to catch the gaze of hypnotic eyes. Once I saw the *mutilé* standing across the street beside a kiosk, watching Lawrence, or so I imagined, with ferocious intensity. My *vis-a-vis* and his emotional recoils had by that time become agitating companions.

Yet, in truth, there was much in his surroundings to breed thoughts of adventure, even crime. Wharf loungers and apaches were slinking among the well-dressed shoppers who drifted down from the region above. Fringing the port, only a hundred meters distant, were the dark, twisting streets of a district noted for its nefarious habits and avoided by the wary; rumors of tourists who had wandered alone at night into that abyss of lawlessness, reappearing days later on the tide, skulls crushed and pockets empty, were far too numerous to pass unheeded. Out beyond the harbor the Château d'If clung to its rocks, guarding well grim secrets of a tragic past.

But to return to Lawrence.

"To blot out the Singapore funeral," he said, "I painted quickly. Makes me concentrate. Got so interested I stopped only on account of bad light. Put on my hat and left the studio—with Pedro—for a walk. Fresh air clears the brain. Must have been exhausted, for I walked along without seeing. Just followed Pedro, I suppose. A bend in the road—and I woke up—galvanized with terror.

"Before me stood the entrance to a graveyard. The stones bristled ghostly in the twilight. I halted—alert."

The stem of the glass, which Lawrence nervously had been twirling, broke, and his unfinished cocktail spilled upon the table.

"I couldn't go on—on through that forest of spectral marble. Pedro continued to walk. Was some distance ahead before he noticed I had stopped. He turned and told me to come along. I refused. He laughed—a derisive laugh—then spit out a single word—'*Coward!*'

"I've been through jungles in India. Gone deep into China where no white man had ever been. Know Calcutta—Port Said—explored the worst slums of the world—and I had never been called a coward before.

"'You don't understand, Pedro—I *can't*, I *can't* go on!' He laughed again—like a hyena.

"'Yes,' Pedro said, a coward. How they will laugh—when I tell!'

"Had never been called that before—you know. I began walking forward—slowly. My legs trembled, but I walked. Passed through the gate.

"'That's right,' Pedro said. 'There's nothing to be afraid of.'

"'No—nothing,' I answered, my jaws chattering.

"Then Pedro said, 'I'm going to the grave of my friend who was buried today and say a prayer, take a rose from his grave and dry it—to carry in a little bag—always—for good luck. No harm comes then. *You'll* take a rose, too.'

"I saw a large mound of flowers. The air was strong with perfume. Roses... We reached the grave. Pedro stopped, knelt down and said a prayer. Shadows under the trees were black and the leaves rattled like bones. I wanted to run—but I stood beside Pedro—and shivered. Pedro took a rose from the grave and put it in his pocket. Then he took another, got up and offered it to me.

"'No!' I cried, drawing away. 'I won't touch it!'

"Pedro said, 'You've got to be cured.' He pointed to a large flat stone lying flat on the ground beside him, and explained:

"'Over a hundred years ago—you can see the date when it's

light—a funny man had this grave made. Built it like a cistern. Brick walls. Look!' and he slid the stone to one side. Pedro was strong.

"I refused to look. Kept my eyes on the path. A gust of wind blew my hat against Pedro, and it fell to the ground.

"As I stooped to pick it up, he pushed me—*into the grave!*"

The horror of this piece of perversity got me.

"Lawrence!" I exclaimed. "You don't mean it!"

"Yes," he answered, in that new tone, so flat and spiritless. "I sank into something—soft... Pedro's laugh sounded far away, and he closed up the grave—with the stone.

"My throat was in a vice. Couldn't make a sound. Tried to gather strength for one big scream—then something somewhere in me snapped. '*Tsing!*' it went, soft and little.

"Don't know how long I was there. It seemed an eternity. I lived on—with the dead man—and crawling things. I don't know. There may have been nothing at all. At last I saw a rift above—the night sky—and Pedro reached down to pull me out.

"When he came the next afternoon I told him I must rest for several days. My nerves were bad. All night I lay awake—and thought—and planned. At daybreak I fell asleep. In the afternoon I went to Boston.

"Three days later, back in Land's End, I settled my accounts. All but one. Told the neighbors I was leaving for New York next day. Gave instructions to have my things packed and shipped to me there.

"Pedro came as usual in the afternoon. I worked as though nothing had happened. He got tired and lay on the floor. I boiled some water for tea. Very, very carefully I made that tea.

"'What kind of tea is this?' Pedro asked. 'It tastes so queer.'

"'A new kind,' I told him.

"He drank, then lay back—asleep.

"From a shelf of etching materials I took a bottle. The liquid inside was clear. So harmless it looked! Poured some into a cup. Filled the cup with water, then knelt down beside the sleeping Pedro—dipped a feather into the liquid—and painted half his handsome face. Nitric acid—bites deep...

"Pedro's groans were silenced with a gag. More tea for rest and sleep.

"The streets that night were empty as I half carried, half dragged Pedro to the shanty where he lived alone. I threw him on the bed and looked without pity on his face.

"No—there was nothing—to be afraid of, I told him. But Pedro didn't hear.

"Don Juan's career was finished. Apollo had become repulsive. My last debt was paid.

"I packed two bags and caught the early train. That afternoon I said 'Good-bye' to the islands of Boston Harbor as I steamed out for England."

Several minutes dragged past before either of us moved.

"Come, let's go," was all I could find to say.

I took Lawrence to his hotel and left him at the entrance with a promise to call the following morning. Unable to keep the appointment, I went around during the afternoon. He was not in his room and could not be located.

Deciding to take one last look about the Old Port before leaving for Paris that night, I strolled down the Rue Noailles, through La Cannebière and the Quai de la Fraternité, into the Quai de Rive Neuve, where a group of excited men were gathered at the water's edge. As I reached the crowd two sailors with grappling hooks were laying a dripping corpse on the pavement. It was the body of Lawrence Bainridge.

The right side of his face was slashed and crushed into a shapeless mass—but the left half was untouched and fair.

7

A CASE OF EAVESDROPPING

Algernon Blackwood

Jim Shorthouse was the sort of fellow who always made a mess of things. Everything with which his hands or mind came into contact issued from such contact in an unqualified and irremediable state of mess. His college days were a mess: he was twice rusticated. His schooldays were a mess: he went to half a dozen, each passing him on to the next with a worse character and in a more developed state of mess. His early boyhood was the sort of mess that copy-books and dictionaries spell with a big "M," and his babyhood—ugh! was the embodiment of howling, yowling, screaming mess.

At the age of forty, however, there came a change in his troubled life, when he met a girl with half a million in her own right, who consented to marry him, and who very soon succeeded in reducing his most messy existence into a state of comparative order and system.

Certain incidents, important and otherwise, of Jim's life would never have come to be told here but for the fact that in getting into his "messes" and out of them again he succeeded in drawing himself into the atmosphere of peculiar circumstances and strange happenings. He attracted to his path the curious adventures of life as unfailingly as meat attracts flies, and jam wasps. It is to the meat and jam of his life, so to speak, that he owes his experiences; his after-life was all pudding, which attracts nothing but greedy children. With marriage the interest of his life ceased for all but one person, and his path became regular as the sun's instead of erratic as a comet's.

The first experience in order of time that he related to me shows that somewhere latent behind his disarranged nervous system there lay psychic perceptions of an uncommon order. About the age of twenty-two—I think after his second rustication—his father's purse and patience had equally given out, and Jim found himself stranded high and dry in a large American city. High and dry! And the only clothes that had no holes in them safely in the keeping of his uncle's wardrobe.

Careful reflection on a bench in one of the city parks led him to the conclusion that the only thing to do was to persuade the city editor of one of the daily journals that he possessed an observant mind and a ready pen, and that he could "do good work for your paper, sir, as a reporter." This, then, he did, standing at a most unnatural angle between the editor and the window to conceal the whereabouts of the holes.

"Guess we'll have to give you a week's trial," said the editor, who, ever on the lookout for good chance material, took on shoals of men in that way and retained on the average one man per shoal. Anyhow it gave Jim Shorthouse the wherewithal to sew up the holes and relieve his uncle's wardrobe of its burden.

Then he went to find living quarters; and in this proceeding his unique characteristics already referred to—what theosophists would call his Karma—began unmistakably to assert themselves, for it was in the house he eventually selected that this sad tale took place.

There are no "diggings" in American cities. The alternatives for small incomes are grim enough—rooms in a boarding-house where meals are served, or in a room-house where no meals are served—not even breakfast. Rich people live in palaces, of course, but Jim had nothing to do with "sich-like." His horizon was bounded by boarding-houses and room-houses; and, owing to the necessary irregularity of his meals and hours, he took the latter.

It was a large, gaunt-looking place in a side street, with dirty windows and a creaking iron gate, but the rooms were large, and the one he selected and paid for in advance was on the top floor. The landlady looked gaunt and dusty as the house, and quite as old. Her eyes were green and faded, and her features large.

"Waal," she twanged, with her electrifying Western drawl, "that's the room, if you like it, and that's the price I said. Now, if you want it, why, just say so; and if you don't, why, it don't hurt me any."

Jim wanted to shake her, but he feared the clouds of long-accumulated dust in her clothes, and as the price and size of the room suited him, he decided to take it.

"Anyone else on this floor?" he asked.

She looked at him queerly out of her faded eyes before she answered.

"None of my guests ever put such questions to me before," she said; "but I guess you're different. Why, there's no one at all but an old gent that's stayed here every bit of five years. He's over thar," pointing to the end of the passage.

"Ah! I see," said Shorthouse feebly. "So I'm alone up here?"

"Reckon you are, pretty near," she twanged out, ending the conversation abruptly by turning her back on her new "guest," and going slowly and deliberately downstairs.

The newspaper work kept Shorthouse out most of the night. Three times a week he got home at 1 a.m., and three times at 3 a.m. The room proved comfortable enough, and he paid for a second week. His unusual hours had so far prevented his meeting any inmates of the house, and not a sound had been heard from the "old gent" who shared the floor with him. It seemed a very quiet house.

One night, about the middle of the second week, he came home tired after a long day's work. The lamp that usually stood all night in the hall had burned itself out, and he had to stumble upstairs in the dark. He made considerable noise in doing so, but nobody seemed to be disturbed. The whole house was utterly quiet, and probably everybody was asleep. There were no lights under any of the doors. All was in darkness. It was after two o'clock.

After reading some English letters that had come during the day, and dipping for a few minutes into a book, he became drowsy and got ready for bed. Just as he was about to get in between the sheets, he stopped for a moment and listened. There rose in the night, as he did so, the sound of steps somewhere in the house below. Listening attentively, he heard that it was somebody coming upstairs—a heavy tread, and the owner taking no pains to step quietly. On it came up the stairs, tramp, tramp, tramp—evidently the tread of a big man, and one in something of a hurry.

At once thoughts connected somehow with fire and police flashed through Jim's brain, but there were no sounds of voices with the steps, and he reflected in the same moment that it could only be the old gentleman keeping late hours and tumbling upstairs in the darkness. He was in the act of turning out the gas and stepping into bed, when the house resumed its former stillness by the footsteps suddenly coming to a dead stop immediately outside his own room.

With his hand on the gas, Shorthouse paused a moment before turning it out to see if the steps would go on again, when he was startled by a loud knocking on his door. Instantly, in obedience to a curious and unexplained instinct, he turned out the light, leaving himself and the room in total darkness.

He had scarcely taken a step across the room to open the door, when a voice from the other side of the wall, so close it almost sounded in his ear, exclaimed in German, "Is that you, father? Come in."

The speaker was a man in the next room, and the knocking,

after all, had not been on his own door, but on that of the adjoining chamber, which he had supposed to be vacant.

Almost before the man in the passage had time to answer in German, "Let me in at once," Jim heard someone cross the floor and unlock the door. Then it was slammed to with a bang, and there was audible the sound of footsteps about the room, and of chairs being drawn up to a table and knocking against furniture on the way. The men seemed wholly regardless of their neighbour's comfort, for they made noise enough to waken the dead.

"Serves me right for taking a room in such a cheap hole," reflected Jim in the darkness. "I wonder whom she's let the room to!"

The two rooms, the landlady had told him, were originally one. She had put up a thin partition—just a row of boards—to increase her income. The doors were adjacent, and only separated by the massive upright beam between them. When one was opened or shut the other rattled.

With utter indifference to the comfort of the other sleepers in the house, the two Germans had meanwhile commenced to talk both at once and at the top of their voices. They talked emphatically, even angrily. The words "Father" and "Otto" were freely used. Shorthouse understood German, but as he stood listening for the first minute or two, an eavesdropper in spite of himself, it was difficult to make head or tail of the talk, for neither would give way to the other, and the jumble of guttural sounds and unfinished sentences was wholly unintelligible. Then, very suddenly, both voices dropped together; and, after a moment's pause, the deep tones of one of them, who seemed to be the "father," said, with the utmost distinctness—

"You mean, Otto, that you refuse to get it?"

There was a sound of someone shuffling in the chair before the answer came. "I mean that I don't know how to get it. It is so much, father. It is *too* much. A part of it—"

"A part of it!" cried the other, with an angry oath, "a part of it, when ruin and disgrace are already in the house, is worse than useless. If you can get half you can get all, you wretched fool. Half-measures only damn all concerned."

"You told me last time—" began the other firmly, but was not allowed to finish. A succession of horrible oaths drowned his sentence, and the father went on, in a voice vibrating with anger—

"You know she will give you anything. You have only been married a few months. If you ask and give a plausible reason you can get all we want and more. You can ask it temporarily. All will be paid back. It will re-establish the firm, and she will never know what was done with it. With that amount, Otto, you know I can recoup all these terrible losses, and in less than a year all will be repaid. But without it... You must get it, Otto. Hear me, you must. Am I to be arrested for the misuse of trust moneys? Is our honoured name to be cursed and spat on?" The old man choked and stammered in his anger and desperation.

Shorthouse stood shivering in the darkness and listening in spite of himself. The conversation had carried him along with it, and he had been for some reason afraid to let his neighbourhood be known. But at this point he realised that he had listened too long and that he must inform the two men that they could be overheard to every single syllable. So he coughed loudly, and at the same time rattled the handle of his door. It seemed to have no effect, for the voices continued just as loudly as before, the son protesting and the father growing more and more angry. He coughed again persistently, and also contrived purposely in the darkness to tumble against the partition, feeling the thin boards yield easily under his weight, and making a considerable noise in so doing. But the voices went on unconcernedly, and louder than ever. Could it be possible they had not heard?

By this time Jim was more concerned about his own sleep than the morality of overhearing the private scandals of his neighbours, and he went out into the passage and knocked smartly at their door. Instantly, as if by magic, the sounds ceased. Everything dropped into utter silence. There was no light under the door and not a whisper could be heard within. He knocked again, but received no answer.

"Gentlemen," he began at length, with his lips close to the keyhole and in German, "please do not talk so loud. I can overhear all you say in the next room. Besides, it is very late, and I wish to sleep."

He paused and listened, but no answer was forthcoming. He turned the handle and found the door was locked. Not a sound broke the stillness of the night except the faint swish of the wind over the skylight and the creaking of a board here and there in the house below. The cold air of a very early morning crept down the passage, and made him shiver. The silence of the house began to impress him disagreeably. He looked behind him and about him, hoping, and yet fearing, that something would break the stillness. The voices still seemed to ring on in his ears; but that sudden silence, when he knocked at the door, affected him far more unpleasantly than the voices, and put strange thoughts in his brain—thoughts he did not like or approve.

Moving stealthily from the door, he peered over the banisters into the space below. It was like a deep vault that might conceal in its shadows anything that was not good. It was not difficult to fancy he saw an indistinct moving to-and-fro below him. Was that a figure sitting on the stairs peering up obliquely at him out of hideous eyes? Was that a sound of whispering and shuffling down there in the dark halls and forsaken landings? Was it something more than the inarticulate murmur of the night?

The wind made an effort overhead, singing over the skylight, and the door behind him rattled and made him start. He turned to go back to his room, and the draught closed the door slowly in his face as if there were someone pressing against it from the other side. When he pushed it open and went in, a hundred shadowy forms seemed to dart swiftly and silently back to their corners and hiding-places. But in the adjoining room the sounds had entirely ceased, and Shorthouse soon crept into bed, and left the house with its inmates, waking or sleeping, to take care of themselves, while he entered the region of dreams and silence.

Next day, strong in the common sense that the sunlight brings, he determined to lodge a complaint against the noisy occupants of the next room and make the landlady request them to modify their voices at such late hours of the night and morning. But it so happened that she was not to be seen that day, and when he returned from the office at midnight it was, of course, too late.

Looking under the door as he came up to bed he noticed that there was no light, and concluded that the Germans were not in. So much the better. He went to sleep about one o'clock, fully decided that if they came up later and woke him with their horrible noises he would not rest till he had roused the landlady and made her reprove them with that authoritative twang, in which every word was like the lash of a metallic whip.

However, there proved to be no need for such drastic measures, for Shorthouse slumbered peacefully all night, and his dreams—chiefly of the fields of grain and flocks of sheep on the far-away farms of his father's estate—were permitted to run their fanciful course unbroken.

Two nights later, however, when he came home tired out, after a difficult day, and wet and blown about by one of the wickedest storms he had ever seen, his dreams—always of the fields and sheep—were not destined to be so undisturbed.

He had already dozed off in that delicious glow that follows the removal of wet clothes and the immediate snuggling under warm blankets, when his consciousness, hovering on the borderland between sleep and waking, was vaguely troubled by a sound that rose indistinctly from the depths of the house, and, between the gusts of wind and rain, reached his ears with an accompanying sense of uneasiness and discomfort. It rose on the night air with some pretence of regularity, dying away again in the roar of the wind to reassert itself distantly in the deep, brief hushes of the storm.

For a few minutes Jim's dreams were coloured only—tinged, as it were, by this impression of fear approaching from somewhere insensibly upon him. His consciousness, at first, refused to be drawn back from that enchanted region where it had wandered, and he did not immediately awaken. But the nature of his dreams changed unpleasantly. He saw the sheep suddenly run huddled together, as though frightened by the neighbourhood of an enemy, while the fields of waving corn became agitated as though some monster were moving uncouthly among the crowded stalks. The sky grew dark, and in his dream an awful sound came somewhere from the clouds. It was in reality the sound downstairs growing more distinct.

Shorthouse shifted uneasily across the bed with something like a groan of distress. The next minute he awoke, and found himself sitting straight up in bed—listening. Was it a nightmare? Had he been dreaming evil dreams, that his flesh crawled and the hair stirred on his head?

The room was dark and silent, but outside the wind howled dismally and drove the rain with repeated assaults against the rattling windows. How nice it would be—the thought flashed through his mind—if all winds, like the west wind, went down with the sun! They made such fiendish noises at night, like the crying of angry voices. In the daytime they had such a different sound. If only——

Hark! It was no dream after all, for the sound was

momentarily growing louder, and its cause was coming up the stairs. He found himself speculating feebly what this cause might be, but the sound was still too indistinct to enable him to arrive at any definite conclusion.

The voice of a church clock striking two made itself heard above the wind. It was just about the hour when the Germans had commenced their performance three nights before. Shorthouse made up his mind that if they began it again he would not put up with it for very long. Yet he was already horribly conscious of the difficulty he would have of getting out of bed. The clothes were so warm and comforting against his back. The sound, still steadily coming nearer, had by this time become differentiated from the confused clamour of the elements, and had resolved itself into the footsteps of one or more persons.

"The Germans, hang 'em!" thought Jim. "But what on earth is the matter with me? I never felt so queer in all my life."

He was trembling all over, and felt as cold as though he were in a freezing atmosphere. His nerves were steady enough, and he felt no diminution of physical courage, but he was conscious of a curious sense of malaise and trepidation, such as even the most vigorous men have been known to experience when in the first grip of some horrible and deadly disease. As the footsteps approached this feeling of weakness increased. He felt a strange lassitude creeping over him, a sort of exhaustion, accompanied by a growing numbness in the extremities, and a sensation of dreaminess in the head, as if perhaps the consciousness were leaving its accustomed seat in the brain and preparing to act on another plane. Yet, strange to say, as the vitality was slowly withdrawn from his body, his senses seemed to grow more acute.

Meanwhile the steps were already on the landing at the top of the stairs, and Shorthouse, still sitting upright in bed, heard a heavy body brush past his door and along the wall outside, almost immediately afterwards the loud knocking of someone's knuckles on the door of the adjoining room.

Instantly, though so far not a sound had proceeded from within, he heard, through the thin partition, a chair pushed back and a man quickly cross the floor and open the door.

"Ah! it's you," he heard in the son's voice. Had the fellow, then, been sitting silently in there all this time, waiting for his father's arrival? To Shorthouse it came not as a pleasant reflection by any means.

There was no answer to this dubious greeting, but the door was closed quickly, and then there was a sound as if a bag or parcel had been thrown on a wooden table and had slid some distance across it before stopping.

"What's that?" asked the son, with anxiety in his tone.

"You may know before I go," returned the other gruffly. Indeed his voice was more than gruff: it betrayed ill-suppressed passion.

Shorthouse was conscious of a strong desire to stop the conversation before it proceeded any further, but somehow or other his will was not equal to the task, and he could not get out of bed. The conversation went on, every tone and inflexion distinctly audible above the noise of the storm.

In a low voice the father continued. Jim missed some of the words at the beginning of the sentence. It ended with: "...but now they've all left, and I've managed to get up to you. You know what I've come for." There was distinct menace in his tone.

"Yes," returned the other; "I have been waiting."

"And the money?" asked the father impatiently.

No answer.

"You've had three days to get it in, and I've contrived to stave off the worst so far—but to-morrow is the end."

No answer.

"Speak, Otto! What have you got for me? Speak, my son; for God's sake, tell me."

There was a moment's silence, during which the old man's vibrating accents seemed to echo through the rooms. Then came in a low voice the answer—

"I have nothing."

"Otto!" cried the other with passion, "nothing!"

"I can get nothing," came almost in a whisper.

"You lie!" cried the other, in a half-stifled voice. "I swear you lie. Give me the money."

A chair was heard scraping along the floor. Evidently the men had been sitting over the table, and one of them had risen. Shorthouse heard the bag or parcel drawn across the table, and then a step as if one of the men was crossing to the door.

"Father, what's in that? I must know," said Otto, with the first signs of determination in his voice. There must have been an effort on the son's part to gain possession of the parcel in question, and on the father's to retain it, for between them it fell to the ground. A curious rattle followed its contact with the floor. Instantly there were sounds of a scuffle. The men were struggling for the possession of the box. The elder man with oaths, and blasphemous imprecations, the other with short gasps that betokened the strength of his efforts. It was of short duration, and the younger man had evidently won, for a minute later was heard his angry exclamation.

"I knew it. Her jewels! You scoundrel, you shall never have them. It is a crime."

The elder man uttered a short, guttural laugh, which froze Jim's blood and made his skin creep. No word was spoken, and for the space of ten seconds there was a living silence. Then the air trembled with the sound of a thud, followed immediately by a groan and the crash of a heavy body falling over on to the table. A second later there was a lurching from the table on to the floor and against the partition that separated the rooms. The bed quivered an instant at the shock, but the unholy spell was lifted from his soul and Jim Shorthouse sprang out of bed and across the floor in a single bound. He knew that ghastly murder had been done—the murder by a father of his son.

With shaking fingers but a determined heart he lit the gas, and the first thing in which his eyes corroborated the evidence of his ears was the horrifying detail that the lower portion of the partition bulged unnaturally into his own room. The glaring paper with which it was covered had cracked under the tension and the boards beneath it bent inwards towards him. What hideous load was behind them, he shuddered to think.

All this he saw in less than a second. Since the final lurch against the wall not a sound had proceeded from the room, not even a groan or a foot-step. All was still but the howl of the wind, which to his ears had in it a note of triumphant horror.

Shorthouse was in the act of leaving the room to rouse the house and send for the police—in fact his hand was already on the door-knob—when something in the room arrested his attention. Out of the corner of his eyes he thought he caught sight of something moving. He was sure of it, and turning his eyes in the direction, he found he was not mistaken.

Something was creeping slowly towards him along the floor. It was something dark and serpentine in shape, and it came from the place where the partition bulged. He stooped down to examine it with feelings of intense horror and repugnance, and he discovered that it was moving toward him from the other side of the wall. His eyes were fascinated, and for the moment he was unable to move. Silently, slowly, from side to side like a thick worm, it crawled forward into the room beneath his frightened eyes, until at length he could stand it no longer and stretched out his arm to touch it. But at the instant of contact he withdrew his hand with a suppressed scream. It was sluggish—and it was warm! and he saw that his fingers were stained with living crimson.

A second more, and Shorthouse was out in the passage with

his hand on the door of the next room. It was locked. He plunged forward with all his weight against it, and, the lock giving way, he fell headlong into a room that was pitch dark and very cold. In a moment he was on his feet again and trying to penetrate the blackness. Not a sound, not a movement. Not even the sense of a presence. It was empty, miserably empty!

Across the room he could trace the outline of a window with rain streaming down the outside, and the blurred lights of the city beyond. But the room was empty, appallingly empty; and so still. He stood there, cold as ice, staring, shivering listening. Suddenly there was a step behind him and a light flashed into the room, and when he turned quickly with his arm up as if to ward off a terrific blow he found himself face to face with the landlady. Instantly the reaction began to set in.

It was nearly three o'clock in the morning, and he was standing there with bare feet and striped pyjamas in a small room, which in the merciful light he perceived to be absolutely empty, carpetless, and without a stick of furniture, or even a window-blind. There he stood staring at the disagreeable landlady. And there she stood too, staring and silent, in a black wrapper, her head almost bald, her face white as chalk, shading a sputtering candle with one bony hand and peering over it at him with her blinking green eyes. She looked positively hideous.

"Waal?" she drawled at length, "I heard yer right enough. Guess you couldn't sleep! Or just prowlin' round a bit—is that it?"

The empty room, the absence of all traces of the recent tragedy, the silence, the hour, his striped pyjamas and bare feet—everything together combined to deprive him momentarily of speech. He stared at her blankly without a word.

"Waal?" clanked the awful voice.

"My dear woman," he burst out finally, "there's been something awful—" So far his desperation took him, but no farther. He positively stuck at the substantive.

"Oh! there hasn't been nothin'," she said slowly still peering at him. "I reckon you've only seen and heard what the others did. I never can keep folks on this floor long. Most of 'em catch on sooner or later—that is, the ones that's kind of quick and sensitive. Only you being an Englishman I thought you wouldn't mind. Nothin' really happens; it's only thinkin' like."

Shorthouse was beside himself. He felt ready to pick her up and drop her over the banisters, candle and all.

"Look there," he said, pointing at her within an inch of her blinking eyes with the fingers that had touched the oozing blood; "look there, my good woman. Is that only thinking?"

She stared a minute, as if not knowing what he meant.

"I guess so," she said at length.

He followed her eyes, and to his amazement saw that his fingers were as white as usual, and quite free from the awful stain that had been there ten minutes before. There was no sign of blood. No amount of staring could bring it back. Had he gone out of his mind? Had his eyes and ears played such tricks with him? Had his senses become false and perverted? He dashed past the landlady, out into the passage, and gained his own room in a couple of strides. Whew!...the partition no longer bulged. The paper was not torn. There was no creeping, crawling thing on the faded old carpet.

"It's all over now," drawled the metallic voice behind him. "I'm going to bed again."

He turned and saw the landlady slowly going downstairs again, still shading the candle with her hand and peering up at him from time to time as she moved. A black, ugly, unwholesome object, he thought, as she disappeared into the darkness below, and the last flicker of her candle threw a queer-shaped shadow along the wall and over the ceiling.

Without hesitating a moment, Shorthouse threw himself into

his clothes and went out of the house. He preferred the storm to the horrors of that top floor, and he walked the streets till daylight. In the evening he told the landlady he would leave next day, in spite of her assurances that nothing more would happen.

"It never comes back," she said—"that is, not after he's killed."

Shorthouse gasped.

"You gave me a lot for my money," he growled.

"Waal, it aren't my show," she drawled. "I'm no spirit medium. You take chances. Some'll sleep right along and never hear nothin'. Others, like yourself, are different and get the whole thing."

"Who's the old gentleman?—does he hear it?" asked Jim.

"There's no old gentleman at all," she answered coolly. "I just told you that to make you feel easy like in case you did hear anythin'. You were all alone on the floor."

"Say now," she went on, after a pause in which Shorthouse could think of nothing to say but unpublishable things, "say now, do tell, did you feel sort of cold when the show was on, sort of tired and weak, I mean, as if you might be going to die?"

"How can I say?" he answered savagely; "what I felt God only knows."

"Waal, but He won't tell," she drawled out. "Only I was wonderin' how you really did feel, because the man who had that room last was found one morning in bed—"

"In bed?"

"He was dead. He was the one before you. Oh! You don't need to get rattled so. You're all right. And it all really happened, they do say. This house used to be a private residence some twenty-five years ago, and a German family of the name of Steinhardt lived here. They had a big business in Wall Street, and stood 'way up in things."

"Ah!" said her listener.

"Oh yes, they did, right at the top, till one fine day it all bust and the old man skipped with the boodle—"

"Skipped with the boodle?"

"That's so," she said; "got clear away with all the money, and the son was found dead in his house, committed soocide it was thought. Though there was some as said he couldn't have stabbed himself and fallen in that position. They said he was murdered. The father died in prison. They tried to fasten the murder on him, but there was no motive, or no evidence, or no somethin'. I forget now."

"Very pretty," said Shorthouse.

"I'll show you somethin' mighty queer any-ways," she drawled, "if you'll come upstairs a minute. I've heard the steps and voices lots of times; they don't pheaze me any. I'd just as lief hear so many dogs barkin'. You'll find the whole story in the newspapers if you look it up—not what goes on here, but the story of the Germans. My house would be ruined if they told all, and I'd sue for damages."

They reached the bedroom, and the woman went in and pulled up the edge of the carpet where Shorthouse had seen the blood soaking in the previous night.

"Look thar, if you feel like it," said the old hag. Stooping down, he saw a dark, dull stain in the boards that corresponded exactly to the shape and position of the blood as he had seen it.

That night he slept in a hotel, and the following day sought new quarters. In the newspapers on file in his office after a long search he found twenty years back the detailed story, substantially as the woman had said, of Steinhardt & Co.'s failure, the absconding and subsequent arrest of the senior partner, and the suicide, or murder, of his son Otto. The landlady's room-house had formerly been their private residence.

8

THE MEZZOTINT

M.R. James

Some time ago I believe I had the pleasure of telling you the story of an adventure which happened to a friend of mine by the name of Dennistoun, during his pursuit of objects of art for the museum at Cambridge.

He did not publish his experiences very widely upon his return to England; but they could not fail to become known to a good many of his friends, and among others to the gentleman who at that time presided over an art museum at another University. It was to be expected that the story should make a considerable impression on the mind of a man whose vocation lay in lines similar to Dennistoun's, and that he should be eager to catch at any explanation of the matter which tended to make it seem improbable that he should ever be called upon to deal with so agitating an emergency. It was, indeed, somewhat consoling to him to reflect that he was not expected to acquire ancient MSS. for his institution; that was the business of the Shelburnian Library. The authorities of that institution might, if they pleased, ransack obscure corners of the Continent for such matters. He was glad to be obliged at the moment to confine his attention to enlarging the already unsurpassed collection of English topographical drawings and engravings possessed by his museum. Yet, as it turned out, even a department so homely and familiar as this may have its dark corners, and to one of these Mr. Williams was unexpectedly introduced.

Those who have taken even the most limited interest in the

acquisition of topographical pictures are aware that there is one London dealer whose aid is indispensable to their researches. Mr. J.W. Britnell publishes at short intervals very admirable catalogues of a large and constantly changing stock of engravings, plans, and old sketches of mansions, churches, and towns in England and Wales. These catalogues were, of course, the ABC of his subject to Mr. Williams: but as his museum already contained an enormous accumulation of topographical pictures, he was a regular, rather than a copious, buyer; and he rather looked to Mr. Britnell to fill up gaps in the rank and file of his collection than to supply him with rarities.

Now, in February of last year there appeared upon Mr. Williams's desk at the museum a catalogue from Mr. Britnell's emporium, and accompanying it was a typewritten communication from the dealer himself. This letter ran as follows:

"DEAR SIR,

"We beg to call your attention to No. 978 in our accompanying catalogue, which we shall be glad to send on approval.

"Yours faithfully,
"J.W. BRITNELL."

To turn to No. 978 in the accompanying catalogue was with Mr. Williams (as he observed to himself) the work of a moment, and in the place indicated he found the following entry:

978.—*Unknown*. Interesting mezzotint: View of a manor-house, early part of the century. 15 by 10 inches; black frame. £2 2s.

It was not specially exciting, and the price seemed high. However, as Mr. Britnell, who knew his business and his customer, seemed to set store by it, Mr. Williams wrote a postcard asking for the article to be sent on approval, along with some other engravings and sketches which appeared in the same catalogue. And so he passed without much excitement of anticipation to the ordinary labours of the day.

A parcel of any kind always arrives a day later than you expect it, and that of Mr. Britnell proved, as I believe the right phrase goes, no exception to the rule. It was delivered at the museum by the afternoon post of Saturday, after Mr. Williams had left his work, and it was accordingly brought round to his rooms in college by the attendant, in order that he might not have to wait over Sunday before looking through it and returning such of the contents as he did not propose to keep. And here he found it when he came in to tea, with a friend.

The only item with which I am concerned was the rather large, black-framed mezzotint of which I have already quoted the short description given in Mr. Britnell's catalogue. Some more details of it will have to be given, though I cannot hope to put before you the look of the picture as clearly as it is present to my own eye. Very nearly the exact duplicate of it may be seen in a good many old inn parlours, or in the passages of undisturbed country mansions at the present moment. It was a rather indifferent mezzotint, and an indifferent mezzotint is, perhaps, the worst form of engraving known. It presented a full-face view of a not very large manor-house of the last century, with three rows of plain sashed windows with rusticated masonry about them, a parapet with balls or vases at the angles, and a small portico in the centre. On either side were trees, and in front a considerable expanse of lawn. The legend A.W.F. sculpsit was engraved on the narrow margin; and there was no further inscription. The whole thing gave the impression that it was the work of an amateur. What in the world Mr. Britnell could mean by affixing the price of £2 2s. to such an object was more than Mr. Williams could imagine. He turned it over with a good deal of contempt; upon the back was a paper label, the left-hand half of which had been torn off. All that remained were the ends of two lines of writing: the first had the letters—*ngley Hall*; the second,—*ssex*.

It would, perhaps, be just worth while to identify the place represented, which he could easily do with the help of a gazetteer, and then he would send it back to Mr. Britnell, with some remarks reflecting upon the judgement of that gentleman.

He lighted the candles, for it was now dark, made the tea, and supplied the friend with whom he had been playing golf (for I believe the authorities of the University I write of indulge in that pursuit by way of relaxation); and tea was taken to the accompaniment of a discussion which golfing persons can imagine for themselves, but which the conscientious writer has no right to inflict upon any non-golfing persons.

The conclusion arrived at was that certain strokes might have been better, and that in certain emergencies neither player had experienced that amount of luck which a human being has a right to expect. It was now that the friend—let us call him Professor Binks—took up the framed engraving, and said:

"What's this place, Williams?"

"Just what I am going to try to find out," said Williams, going to the shelf for a gazetteer. "Look at the back. Somethingley Hall, either in Sussex or Essex. Half the name's gone, you see. You don't happen to know it, I suppose?"

"It's from that man Britnell, I suppose, isn't it?" said Binks. "Is it for the museum?"

"Well, I think I should buy it if the price was five shillings," said Williams; "but for some unearthly reason he wants two guineas for it. I can't conceive why. It's a wretched engraving, and there aren't even any figures to give it life."

"It's not worth two guineas, I should think," said Binks; "but I don't think it's so badly done. The moonlight seems rather good to me; and I should have thought there were figures, or at least a figure, just on the edge in front."

"Let's look," said Williams. "Well, it's true the light is rather cleverly given. Where's your figure? Oh yes! Just the head, in the very front of the picture."

And indeed there was—hardly more than a black blot on the extreme edge of the engraving—the head of a man or woman, a good deal muffled up, the back turned to the spectator, and looking towards the house.

Williams had not noticed it before.

"Still," he said, "though it's a cleverer thing than I thought, I can't spend two guineas of museum money on a picture of a place I don't know."

Professor Binks had his work to do, and soon went; and very nearly up to Hall time Williams was engaged in a vain attempt to identify the subject of his picture. "If the vowel before the ng had only been left, it would have been easy enough," he thought; "but as it is, the name may be anything from Guestingley to Langley, and there are many more names ending like this than I thought; and this rotten book has no index of terminations."

Hall in Mr. Williams's college was at seven. It need not be dwelt upon; the less so as he met there colleagues who had been playing golf during the afternoon, and words with which we have no concern were freely bandied across the table—merely golfing words, I would hasten to explain.

I suppose an hour or more to have been spent in what is called common-room after dinner. Later in the evening some few retired to Williams's rooms, and I have little doubt that whist was played and tobacco smoked. During a lull in these operations Williams picked up the mezzotint from the table without looking at it, and handed it to a person mildly interested in art, telling him where it had come from, and the other particulars which we already know.

The gentleman took it carelessly, looked at it, then said, in a tone of some interest:

"It's really a very good piece of work, Williams; it has quite a feeling of the romantic period. The light is admirably managed, it seems to me, and the figure, though it's rather too grotesque, is somehow very impressive."

"Yes, isn't it?" said Williams, who was just then busy giving whisky-and-soda to others of the company, and was unable to come across the room to look at the view again.

It was by this time rather late in the evening, and the visitors were on the move. After they went Williams was obliged to write a letter or two and clear up some odd bits of work. At last, some time past midnight, he was disposed to turn in, and he put out his lamp after lighting his bedroom candle. The picture lay face upwards on the table where the last man who looked at it had put it, and it caught his eye as he turned the lamp down. What he saw made him very nearly drop the candle on the floor, and he declares now that if he had been left in the dark at that moment he would have had a fit. But, as that did not happen, he was able to put down the light on the table and take a good look at the picture. It was indubitable—rankly impossible, no doubt, but absolutely certain. In the middle of the lawn in front of the unknown house there was a figure where no figure had been at five o'clock that afternoon. It was crawling on all-fours towards the house, and it was muffled in a strange black garment with a white cross on the back.

I do not know what is the ideal course to pursue in a situation of this kind. I can only tell you what Mr. Williams did. He took the picture by one corner and carried it across the passage to a second set of rooms which he possessed. There he locked it up in a drawer, sported the doors of both sets of rooms, and retired to bed; but first he wrote out and signed an account of the extraordinary change which the picture had undergone since it had come into his possession.

Sleep visited him rather late; but it was consoling to reflect that the behaviour of the picture did not depend upon his own unsupported testimony. Evidently the man who had looked at it the night before had seen something of the same kind as he had, otherwise he might have been tempted to think that something gravely wrong was happening either to his eyes or his mind. This possibility being fortunately precluded, two matters awaited him on the morrow. He must take stock of the picture very carefully, and call in a witness for the purpose, and he must make a determined effort to ascertain what house it was that was represented. He would therefore ask his neighbour Nisbet to breakfast with him, and he would subsequently spend a morning over the gazetteer.

Nisbet was disengaged, and arrived about 9.30. His host was not quite dressed, I am sorry to say, even at this late hour. During breakfast nothing was said about the mezzotint by Williams, save that he had a picture on which he wished for Nisbet's opinion. But those who are familiar with University life can picture for themselves the wide and delightful range of subjects over which the conversation of two Fellows of Canterbury College is likely to extend during a Sunday morning breakfast. Hardly a topic was left unchallenged, from golf to lawn-tennis. Yet I am bound to say that Williams was rather distraught; for his interest naturally centred in that very strange picture which was now reposing, face downwards, in the drawer in the room opposite.

The morning pipe was at last lighted, and the moment had arrived for which he looked. With very considerable—almost tremulous—excitement he ran across, unlocked the drawer, and, extracting the picture—still face downwards—ran back, and put it into Nisbet's hands.

"Now," he said, "Nisbet, I want you to tell me exactly what you see in that picture. Describe it, if you don't mind, rather minutely. I'll tell you why afterwards."

"Well," said Nisbet, "I have here a view of a country-house—English, I presume—by moonlight."

"Moonlight? You're sure of that?"

"Certainly. The moon appears to be on the wane, if you wish for details, and there are clouds in the sky."

"All right. Go on. I'll swear," added Williams in an aside, "there was no moon when I saw it first."

"Well, there's not much more to be said," Nisbet continued. "The house has one—two—three rows of windows, five in each row, except at the bottom, where there's a porch instead of the middle one, and—"

"But what about figures?" said Williams, with marked interest.

"There aren't any," said Nisbet; "but—"

"What! No figure on the grass in front?"

"Not a thing."

"You'll swear to that?"

"Certainly I will. But there's just one other thing."

"What?"

"Why, one of the windows on the ground-floor—left of the door—is open."

"Is it really so? My goodness! he must have got in," said Williams, with great excitement; and he hurried to the back of the sofa on which Nisbet was sitting, and, catching the picture from him, verified the matter for himself.

It was quite true. There was no figure, and there was the open window. Williams, after a moment of speechless surprise, went to the writing-table and scribbled for a short time. Then he brought two papers to Nisbet, and asked him first to sign one—it was his own description of the picture, which you have just heard—and then to read the other which was Williams's statement written the night before.

"What can it all mean?" said Nisbet.

"Exactly," said Williams. "Well, one thing I must do—or

three things, now I think of it. I must find out from Garwood"—this was his last night's visitor—"what he saw, and then I must get the thing photographed before it goes further, and then I must find out what the place is."

"I can do the photographing myself," said Nisbet, "and I will. But, you know, it looks very much as if we were assisting at the working out of a tragedy somewhere. The question is, has it happened already, or is it going to come off? You must find out what the place is. Yes," he said, looking at the picture again, "I expect you're right: he has got in. And if I don't mistake there'll be the devil to pay in one of the rooms upstairs."

"I'll tell you what," said Williams: "I'll take the picture across to old Green" (this was the senior Fellow of the College, who had been Bursar for many years). "It's quite likely he'll know it. We have property in Essex and Sussex, and he must have been over the two counties a lot in his time.

"Quite likely he will," said Nisbet; "but just let me take my photograph first. But look here, I rather think Green isn't up today. He wasn't in Hall last night, and I think I heard him say he was going down for the Sunday."

"That's true, too," said Williams; "I know he's gone to Brighton. Well, if you'll photograph it now, I'll go across to Garwood and get his statement, and you keep an eye on it while I'm gone. I'm beginning to think two guineas is not a very exorbitant price for it now."

In a short time he had returned, and brought Mr. Garwood with him. Garwood's statement was to the effect that the figure, when he had seen it, was clear of the edge of the picture, but had not got far across the lawn. He remembered a white mark on the back of its drapery, but could not have been sure it was a cross. A document to this effect was then drawn up and signed, and Nisbet proceeded to photograph the picture.

"Now what do you mean to do?" he said. "Are you going to

sit and watch it all day?"

"Well, no, I think not," said Williams. "I rather imagine we're meant to see the whole thing. You see, between the time I saw it last night and this morning there was time for lots of things to happen, but the creature only got into the house. It could easily have got through its business in the time and gone to its own place again; but the fact of the window being open, I think, must mean that it's in there now. So I feel quite easy about leaving it. And, besides, I have a kind of idea that it wouldn't change much, if at all, in the daytime. We might go out for a walk this afternoon, and come in to tea, or whenever it gets dark. I shall leave it out on the table here, and sport the door. My skip can get in, but no one else."

The three agreed that this would be a good plan; and, further, that if they spent the afternoon together they would be less likely to talk about the business to other people; for any rumour of such a transaction as was going on would bring the whole of the Phasmatological Society about their ears.

We may give them a respite until five o'clock.

At or near that hour the three were entering Williams's staircase. They were at first slightly annoyed to see that the door of his rooms was unsported; but in a moment it was remembered that on Sunday the skips came for orders an hour or so earlier than on weekdays. However, a surprise was awaiting them. The first thing they saw was the picture leaning up against a pile of books on the table, as it had been left, and the next thing was Williams's skip, seated on a chair opposite, gazing at it with undisguised horror. How was this? Mr. Filcher (the name is not my own invention) was a servant of considerable standing, and set the standard of etiquette to all his own college and to several neighbouring ones, and nothing could be more alien to his practice than to be found sitting on his master's chair, or appearing to take any particular notice of his master's furniture or pictures. Indeed, he seemed to feel this himself. He started violently when the three men were in the room, and got up with a marked effort. Then he said:

"I ask your pardon, sir, for taking such a freedom as to set down."

"Not at all, Robert," interposed Mr. Williams. "I was meaning to ask you some time what you thought of that picture."

"Well, sir, of course I don't set up my opinion again yours, but it ain't the pictur I should 'ang where my little girl could see it, sir."

"Wouldn't you, Robert? Why not?"

"No, sir. Why, the pore child, I recollect once she see a Door Bible, with pictures not 'alf what that is, and we 'ad to set up with her three or four nights afterwards, if you'll believe me; and if she was to ketch a sight of this skelinton here, or whatever it is, carrying off the pore baby, she would be in a taking. You know 'ow it is with children; 'ow nervish they git with a little thing and all. But what I should say, it don't seem a right pictur to be laying about, sir, not where anyone that's liable to be startled could come on it. Should you be wanting anything this evening, sir? Thank you, sir."

With these words the excellent man went to continue the round of his masters, and you may be sure the gentlemen whom he left lost no time in gathering round the engraving. There was the house, as before, under the waning moon and the drifting clouds. The window that had been open was shut, and the figure was once more on the lawn: but not this time crawling cautiously on hands and knees. Now it was erect and stepping swiftly, with long strides, towards the front of the picture. The moon was behind it, and the black drapery hung down over its face so that only hints of that could be seen, and what was visible made the spectators profoundly thankful that they could see no more than a white dome-like forehead and a few straggling hairs. The head was bent down, and the arms were tightly clasped over an object which could be dimly seen and identified as a child, whether dead or living it was not possible to say. The legs of the appearance alone could be plainly discerned, and they were horribly thin.

From five to seven the three companions sat and watched the picture by turns. But it never changed. They agreed at last that it would be safe to leave it, and that they would return after Hall and await further developments.

When they assembled again, at the earliest possible moment, the engraving was there, but the figure was gone, and the house was quiet under the moonbeams. There was nothing for it but to spend the evening over gazetteers and guide-books. Williams was the lucky one at last, and perhaps he deserved it. At 11.30 p.m. he read from Murray's *Guide to Essex* the following lines:

16½ miles, *Anningley*. The church has been an interesting building of Norman date, but was extensively classicized in the last century. It contains the tomb of the family of Francis, whose mansion, Anningley Hall, a solid Queen Anne house, stands immediately beyond the churchyard in a park of about 80 acres. The family is now extinct, the last heir having disappeared mysteriously in infancy in the year 1802. The father, Mr. Arthur Francis, was locally known as a talented amateur engraver in mezzotint. After his son's disappearance he lived in complete retirement at the Hall, and was found dead in his studio on the third anniversary of the disaster, having just completed an engraving of the house, impressions of which are of considerable rarity.

This looked like business, and, indeed, Mr. Green on his return at once identified the house as Anningley Hall.

"Is there any kind of explanation of the figure, Green?" was the question which Williams naturally asked.

"I don't know, I'm sure, Williams. What used to be said in the place when I first knew it, which was before I came up here, was just this: old Francis was always very much down on these poaching fellows, and whenever he got a chance he used to get a man whom he suspected of it turned off the estate, and by degrees he got rid of them all but one. Squires could do a lot of things then that they daren't think of now. Well, this man that was left was what you find pretty often in that country—the last remains of a very old family. I believe they were Lords of the Manor at one time. I recollect just the same thing in my own parish."

"What, like the man in *Tess o' the Durbervilles?*" Williams put in.

"Yes, I dare say; it's not a book I could ever read myself. But this fellow could show a row of tombs in the church there that belonged to his ancestors, and all that went to sour him a bit; but Francis, they said, could never get at him—he always kept just on the right side of the law—until one night the keepers found him at it in a wood right at the end of the estate. I could show you the place now; it marches with some land that used to belong to an uncle of mine. And you can imagine there was a row; and this man Gawdy (that was the name, to be sure—Gawdy; I thought I should get it—Gawdy), he was unlucky enough, poor chap! to shoot a keeper. Well, that was what Francis wanted, and grand juries—you know what they would have been then—and poor Gawdy was strung up in double-quick time; and I've been shown the place he was buried in, on the north side of the church— you know the way in that part of the world: anyone that's been hanged or made away with themselves, they bury them that side. And the idea was that some friend of Gawdy's—not a relation, because he had none, poor devil! he was the last of his line: kind of *spes ultima gentis*—must have planned to get hold of Francis's boy and put an end to *his* line, too. I don't know—it's rather an out-of-the-way thing for an Essex poacher to think of—but, you know, I should say now it looks more as if old Gawdy had managed the job himself. Booh! I hate to think of it! have some whisky, Williams!"

The facts were communicated by Williams to Dennistoun, and by him to a mixed company, of which I was one, and the Sadducean Professor of Ophiology another. I am sorry to say that the latter, when asked what he thought of it, only remarked: "Oh, those Bridgeford people will say anything"—a sentiment which met with the reception it deserved.

I have only to add that the picture is now in the Ashleian Museum; that it has been treated with a view to discovering whether sympathetic ink has been used in it, but without effect; that Mr. Britnell knew nothing of it save that he was sure it was uncommon; and that, though carefully watched, it has never been known to change again.

9

THE BLACK CAT

Edgar Allen Poe

For the most wild, yet most homely narrative which I am about to pen, I neither expect nor solicit belief. Mad indeed would I be to expect it, in a case where my very senses reject their own evidence. Yet, mad am I not—and very surely do I not dream. But to-morrow I die, and to-day I would unburthen my soul. My immediate purpose is to place before the world, plainly, succinctly, and without comment, a series of mere household events. In their consequences, these events have terrified—have tortured—have destroyed me. Yet I will not attempt to expound them. To me, they have presented little but horror—to many they will seem less terrible than *barroques*. Hereafter, perhaps, some intellect may be found which will reduce my phantasm to the common-place—some intellect more calm, more logical, and far less excitable than my own, which will perceive, in the circumstances I detail with awe, nothing more than an ordinary succession of very natural causes and effects.

From my infancy I was noted for the docility and humanity of my disposition. My tenderness of heart was even so conspicuous as to make me the jest of my companions. I was especially fond of animals, and was indulged by my parents with a great variety of pets. With these I spent most of my time, and never was so happy as when feeding and caressing them. This peculiarity of character grew with my growth, and in my manhood, I derived from it one of my principal sources of pleasure. To those who have cherished an affection for a faithful and sagacious dog, I need hardly be at the trouble of explaining the nature or the intensity of the gratification thus derivable. There is something in the unselfish and self-sacrificing love of a brute, which goes directly to the heart of him who has had frequent occasion to test the paltry friendship and gossamer fidelity of mere *Man*.

I married early, and was happy to find in my wife a disposition not uncongenial with my own. Observing my partiality for domestic pets, she lost no opportunity of procuring those of the most agreeable kind. We had birds, gold-fish, a fine dog, rabbits, a small monkey, and *a cat*.

This latter was a remarkably large and beautiful animal, entirely black, and sagacious to an astonishing degree. In speaking of his intelligence, my wife, who at heart was not a little tinctured with superstition, made frequent allusion to the ancient popular notion, which regarded all black cats as witches in disguise. Not that she was ever *serious* upon this point—and I mention the matter at all for no better reason than that it happens, just now, to be remembered.

Pluto—this was the cat's name—was my favorite pet and playmate. I alone fed him, and he attended me wherever I went about the house. It was even with difficulty that I could prevent him from following me through the streets.

Our friendship lasted, in this manner, for several years, during which my general temperament and character—through the instrumentality of the Fiend Intemperance—had (I blush to confess it) experienced a radical alteration for the worse. I grew, day by day, more moody, more irritable, more regardless of the feelings of others. I suffered myself to use intemperate language to my wife. At length, I even offered her personal violence. My pets, of course, were made to feel the change in my disposition. I not only neglected, but ill-used them. For Pluto, however, I still retained sufficient regard to restrain me from maltreating him, as I made no scruple of maltreating the rabbits, the monkey, or even the dog, when by accident, or through affection, they came in my way. But my disease grew upon me—for what disease is like Alcohol!—and at length even Pluto, who was now becoming old, and consequently somewhat peevish—even Pluto began to experience the effects of my ill temper.

One night, returning home, much intoxicated, from one of my haunts about town, I fancied that the cat avoided my presence. I seized him; when, in his fright at my violence, he inflicted a slight wound upon my hand with his teeth. The fury of a demon instantly possessed me. I knew myself no longer. My original soul seemed, at once, to take its flight from my body and a more than fiendish malevolence, gin-nurtured, thrilled every fibre of my frame. I took from my waistcoat-pocket a pen-knife, opened it, grasped the poor beast by the throat, and deliberately cut one of its eyes from the socket! I blush, I burn, I shudder, while I pen the damnable atrocity.

When reason returned with the morning—when I had slept off the fumes of the night's debauch—I experienced a sentiment half of horror, half of remorse, for the crime of which I had been guilty; but it was, at best, a feeble and equivocal feeling, and the soul remained untouched. I again plunged into excess, and soon drowned in wine all memory of the deed.

In the meantime the cat slowly recovered. The socket of the lost eye presented, it is true, a frightful appearance, but he no longer appeared to suffer any pain. He went about the house as usual, but, as might be expected, fled in extreme terror at my approach. I had so much of my old heart left, as to be at first grieved by this evident dislike on the part of a creature which had once so loved me. But this feeling soon gave place to irritation. And then came, as if to my final and irrevocable overthrow, the spirit of PERVERSENESS. Of this spirit philosophy takes no account. Yet I am not more sure that my soul lives, than I am that perverseness is one of the primitive impulses of the human heart—one of the indivisible primary faculties, or sentiments, which give direction to the character of Man. Who has not, a hundred times, found himself committing a vile or a silly action, for no other reason than because he knows he should *not*? Have we not a perpetual inclination, in the teeth of our best judgment, to violate that which is *Law*, merely because we understand it to be such? This spirit of perverseness, I say, came to my final overthrow. It was this unfathomable longing of the soul to *vex itself*—to offer violence to its own nature—to do wrong for the wrong's sake only—that urged me to continue and finally to consummate the injury I had inflicted upon the unoffending brute. One morning, in cool blood, I slipped a noose about its neck and hung it to the limb of a tree;—hung it with the tears streaming from my eyes, and with the bitterest remorse at my heart;—hung it because I knew that it had loved me, and *because* I felt it had given me no reason of offence;—hung it *because* I knew that in so doing I was committing a sin—a deadly sin that would so jeopardize my immortal soul as to place it—if such a thing were possible—even beyond the reach of the infinite mercy of the Most Merciful and Most Terrible God.

On the night of the day on which this cruel deed was done, I was aroused from sleep by the cry of fire. The curtains of my bed were in flames. The whole house was blazing. It was with great difficulty that my wife, a servant, and myself, made our escape from the conflagration. The destruction was complete. My entire worldly wealth was swallowed up, and I resigned myself thenceforward to despair.

I am above the weakness of seeking to establish a sequence of cause and effect, between the disaster and the atrocity. But I am detailing a chain of facts—and wish not to leave even a possible link imperfect. On the day succeeding the fire, I visited the ruins. The walls, with one exception, had fallen in. This exception was found in a compartment wall, not very thick, which stood about the middle of the house, and against which had rested the head of my bed. The plastering had here, in great measure, resisted the action of the fire—a fact which I attributed to its having been recently spread. About this wall a dense crowd were collected, and many persons seemed to be examining a particular portion of it with very minute and eager attention. The words "Strange!" "Singular!" and other similar expressions, excited my curiosity. I approached and saw, as if graven in *bas relief* upon the white surface, the figure of a gigantic *cat*. The impression was given with an accuracy truly marvellous. There was a rope about the animal's neck.

When I first beheld this apparition—for I could scarcely regard it as less—my wonder and my terror were extreme. But at length reflection came to my aid. The cat, I remembered, had been hung in a garden adjacent to the house. Upon the alarm of fire, this garden had been immediately filled by the crowd—by some one of whom the animal must have been cut from the tree and thrown, through an open window, into my chamber. This had probably been done with the view of arousing me from sleep. The falling of other walls had compressed the victim of my cruelty into the substance of the freshly-spread plaster; the lime of which, with the flames, and the *ammonia* from the carcass, had then accomplished the portraiture as I saw it.

Although I thus readily accounted to my reason, if not altogether to my conscience, for the startling fact just detailed, it did not the less fail to make a deep impression upon my fancy. For months I could not rid myself of the phantasm of the cat; and, during this period, there came back into my spirit a half-sentiment that seemed, but was not, remorse. I went so far as to regret the loss of the animal, and to look about me, among the vile haunts which I now habitually frequented, for another pet of the same species, and of somewhat similar appearance, with which to supply its place.

One night as I sat, half stupefied, in a den of more than infamy, my attention was suddenly drawn to some black object, reposing upon the head of one of the immense hogsheads of gin, or of rum, which constituted the chief furniture of the apartment. I had been looking steadily at the top of this hogshead for some minutes, and what now caused me surprise was the fact that I had not sooner perceived the object thereupon. I approached it, and touched it with my hand. It was a black cat—a very large one—fully as large as Pluto, and closely resembling him in every respect but one. Pluto had not a white hair upon any portion of his body; but this cat had a large, although indefinite splotch of white, covering nearly the whole region of the breast. Upon my touching him, he immediately arose, purred loudly, rubbed against my hand, and appeared delighted with my notice. This, then, was the very creature of which I was in search. I at once offered to purchase it of the landlord; but this person made no claim to it—knew nothing of it—had never seen it before.

I continued my caresses, and, when I prepared to go home, the animal evinced a disposition to accompany me. I permitted it to do so; occasionally stooping and patting it as I proceeded. When it reached the house it domesticated itself at once, and became immediately a great favorite with my wife.

For my own part, I soon found a dislike to it arising within me. This was just the reverse of what I had anticipated; but—I know not how or why it was—its evident fondness for myself rather disgusted and annoyed. By slow degrees, these feelings of disgust and annoyance rose into the bitterness of hatred. I avoided the creature; a certain sense of shame, and the remembrance of my former deed of cruelty, preventing me from physically abusing it. I did not, for some weeks, strike, or otherwise violently ill use it; but gradually—very gradually—I came to look upon it with unutterable loathing, and to flee silently from its odious presence, as from the breath of a pestilence.

What added, no doubt, to my hatred of the beast, was the discovery, on the morning after I brought it home, that, like Pluto, it also had been deprived of one of its eyes. This circumstance, however, only endeared it to my wife, who, as I have already said, possessed, in a high degree, that humanity of feeling which had once been my distinguishing trait, and the source of many of my simplest and purest pleasures.

With my aversion to this cat, however, its partiality for myself seemed to increase. It followed my footsteps with a pertinacity which it would be difficult to make the reader comprehend. Whenever I sat, it would crouch beneath my chair, or spring upon my knees, covering me with its loathsome caresses. If I arose to walk it would get between my feet and thus nearly throw me down, or, fastening its long and sharp claws in my dress, clamber, in this manner, to my breast. At such times, although I longed to destroy it with a blow, I was yet withheld from so doing, partly by a memory of my former crime, but chiefly—let me confess it at once—by absolute *dread* of the beast.

This dread was not exactly a dread of physical evil—and yet I should be at a loss how otherwise to define it. I am almost ashamed to own—yes, even in this felon's cell, I am almost ashamed to own—that the terror and horror with which the animal inspired me, had been heightened by one of the merest chimaeras it would be possible to conceive. My wife had called my attention, more than once, to the character of the mark of white hair, of which I have spoken, and which constituted the sole visible difference between the strange beast and the one I had destroyed. The reader will remember that this mark, although large, had been originally very indefinite; but, by slow degrees—degrees nearly imperceptible, and which for a long time my reason struggled to reject as fanciful—it had, at length, assumed a rigorous distinctness of outline. It was now the representation of an object that I shudder to name—and for this, above all, I loathed, and dreaded, and would have rid myself of the monster *had I dared*—it was now, I say, the image of a hideous—of a ghastly thing—of the GALLOWS!—oh, mournful and terrible engine of horror and of crime—of agony and of death!

And now was I indeed wretched beyond the wretchedness of mere Humanity. And *a brute beast*—whose fellow I had contemptuously destroyed—*a brute beast* to work out for *me*—for me a man, fashioned in the image of the High God—so much of insufferable woe! Alas! neither by day nor by night knew I the blessing of rest any more! During the former the creature left me no moment alone, and in the latter I started hourly from dreams of unutterable fear to find the hot breath of *the thing* upon my face, and its vast weight—an incarnate nightmare that I had no power to shake off—incumbent eternally upon my *heart!*

Beneath the pressure of torments such as these, the feeble remnant of the good within me succumbed. Evil thoughts became my sole intimates—the darkest and most evil of thoughts. The moodiness of my usual temper increased to hatred of all things and of all mankind; while, from the sudden, frequent, and ungovernable outbursts of a fury to which I now blindly abandoned myself, my uncomplaining wife, alas, was the most usual and the most patient of sufferers.

One day she accompanied me, upon some household errand, into the cellar of the old building which our poverty compelled us to inhabit. The cat followed me down the steep stairs, and, nearly throwing me headlong, exasperated me to madness. Uplifting an axe, and forgetting, in my wrath, the childish dread which had hitherto stayed my hand, I aimed a blow at the animal which, of course, would have proved instantly fatal had it descended as I wished. But this blow was arrested by the hand of my wife. Goaded, by the interference, into a rage more than demoniacal, I withdrew my arm from her grasp and buried the axe in her brain. She fell dead upon the spot, without a groan.

This hideous murder accomplished, I set myself forthwith, and with entire deliberation, to the task of concealing the body. I knew that I could not remove it from the house, either by day or by night, without the risk of being observed by the neighbors. Many projects entered my mind. At one period I thought of cutting the corpse into minute fragments, and destroying them by fire. At another, I resolved to dig a grave for it in the floor of the cellar. Again, I deliberated about casting it in the well in the yard—about packing it in a box, as if merchandise, with the usual arrangements, and so getting a porter to take it from the house. Finally I hit upon what I considered a far better expedient than either of these. I determined to wall it up in the cellar—as the monks of the middle ages are recorded to have walled up their victims.

For a purpose such as this the cellar was well adapted. Its walls were loosely constructed, and had lately been plastered throughout with a rough plaster, which the dampness of the atmosphere had prevented from hardening. Moreover, in one of the walls was a projection, caused by a false chimney, or fireplace, that had been filled up, and made to resemble the red of the cellar. I made no doubt that I could readily displace the bricks at this point, insert the corpse, and wall the whole up as before, so that no eye could detect any thing suspicious. And in this calculation I was not deceived. By means of a crow-bar I easily dislodged the bricks, and, having carefully deposited the body against the inner wall, I propped it in that position, while, with little trouble, I re-laid the whole structure as it originally stood. Having procured mortar, sand, and hair, with every possible precaution, I prepared a plaster which could not be distinguished from the old, and with this I very carefully went over the new brickwork. When I had finished, I felt satisfied that all was right. The wall did not present the slightest appearance of having been disturbed. The rubbish on the floor was picked up with the minutest care. I looked around triumphantly, and said to myself: "Here at least, then, my labor has not been in vain."

My next step was to look for the beast which had been the cause of so much wretchedness; for I had, at length, firmly resolved to put it to death. Had I been able to meet with it, at the moment, there could have been no doubt of its fate; but it appeared that the crafty animal had been alarmed at the violence of my previous anger, and forebore to present itself in my present mood. It is impossible to describe, or to imagine, the deep, the blissful sense of relief which the absence of the detested creature occasioned in my bosom. It did not make its appearance during the night; and thus for one night at least, since its introduction into the house, I soundly and tranquilly slept; aye, slept even with the burden of murder upon my soul!

The second and the third day passed, and still my tormentor came not. Once again I breathed as a freeman. The monster, in terror, had fled the premises forever! I should behold it no more! My happiness was supreme! The guilt of my dark deed disturbed me but little. Some few inquiries had been made, but these had been readily answered. Even a search had been instituted—but of course nothing was to be discovered. I looked upon my future felicity as secured.

Upon the fourth day of the assassination, a party of the police came, very unexpectedly, into the house, and proceeded again to make rigorous investigation of the premises. Secure, however, in the inscrutability of my place of concealment, I felt no embarrassment whatever. The officers bade me accompany them in their search. They left no nook or corner unexplored. At length, for the third or fourth time, they descended into the cellar. I quivered not in a muscle. My heart beat calmly as that of one who slumbers in innocence. I walked the cellar from end to end. I folded my arms upon my bosom, and roamed easily to and fro. The police were thoroughly satisfied and prepared to depart. The glee at my heart was too strong to be restrained. I burned to say if but one word, by way of triumph, and to render doubly sure their assurance of my guiltlessness.

"Gentlemen," I said at last, as the party ascended the steps, "I delight to have allayed your suspicions. I wish you all health, and a little more courtesy. By the bye, gentlemen, this—this is a very well-constructed house." (In the rabid desire to say something easily, I scarcely knew what I uttered at all.)—"I may say an *excellently* well-constructed house. These walls—are you going, gentlemen?—these walls are solidly put together;" and here, through the mere phrenzy of bravado, I rapped heavily, with a cane which I held in my hand, upon that very portion of the brick-work behind which stood the corpse of the wife of my bosom.

But may God shield and deliver me from the fangs of the Arch-Fiend! No sooner had the reverberation of my blows sunk into silence, than I was answered by a voice from within the tomb!—by a cry, at first muffled and broken, like the sobbing of a child, and then quickly swelling into one long, loud, and continuous scream, utterly anomalous and inhuman—a howl—a wailing shriek, half of horror and half of triumph, such as might have arisen only out of hell, conjointly from the throats of the damned in their agony and of the demons that exult in the damnation.

Of my own thoughts it is folly to speak. Swooning, I staggered to the opposite wall. For one instant the party upon the stairs remained motionless, through extremity of terror and of awe. In the next, a dozen stout arms were toiling at the wall. It fell bodily. The corpse, already greatly decayed and clotted with gore, stood erect before the eyes of the spectators. Upon its head, with red extended mouth and solitary eye of fire, sat the hideous beast whose craft had seduced me into murder, and whose informing voice had consigned me to the hangman. I had walled the monster up within the tomb!

10

PRESENT AT A HANGING

Ambrose Bierce

An old man named Daniel Baker, living near Lebanon, Iowa, was suspected by his neighbors of having murdered a peddler who had obtained permission to pass the night at his house. This was in 1853, when peddling was more common in the Western country than it is now, and was attended with considerable danger. The peddler with his pack traversed the country by all manner of lonely roads, and was compelled to rely upon the country people for hospitality. This brought him into relation with queer characters, some of whom were not altogether scrupulous in their methods of making a living, murder being an acceptable means to that end. It occasionally occurred that a peddler with diminished pack and swollen purse would be traced to the lonely dwelling of some rough character and never could be traced beyond. This was so in the case of "old man Baker," as he was always called. (Such names are given in the western "settlements" only to elderly persons who are not esteemed; to the general disrepute of social unworth is affixed the special reproach of age.) A peddler came to his house and none went away—that is all that anybody knew.

Seven years later the Rev. Mr. Cummings, a Baptist minister well known in that part of the country, was driving by Baker's farm one night. It was not very dark: there was a bit of moon somewhere above the light veil of mist that lay along the earth. Mr. Cummings, who was at all times a cheerful person, was whistling a tune, which he would occasionally interrupt to speak a word of friendly encouragement to his horse. As he came to a little bridge across a dry ravine he saw the figure of a man standing upon it, clearly outlined against the gray background of a misty forest. The man had something strapped on his back and carried a heavy stick—obviously an itinerant peddler. His attitude had in it a suggestion of abstraction, like that of a sleepwalker. Mr. Cummings reined in his horse when he arrived in front of him, gave him a pleasant salutation and invited him to a seat in the vehicle—"if you are going my way," he added. The man raised his head, looked him full in the face, but neither answered nor made any further movement. The minister, with good-natured persistence, repeated his invitation. At this the man threw his right hand forward from his side and pointed downward as he stood on the extreme edge of the bridge. Mr. Cummings looked past him, over into the ravine, saw nothing unusual and withdrew his eyes to address the man again. He had disappeared. The horse, which all this time had been uncommonly restless, gave at the same moment a snort of terror and started to run away. Before he had regained control of the animal the minister was at the crest of the hill a hundred yards along. He looked back and saw the figure again, at the same place and in the same attitude as when he had first observed it. Then for the first time he was conscious of a sense of the supernatural and drove home as rapidly as his willing horse would go.

On arriving at home he related his adventure to his family, and early the next morning, accompanied by two neighbors, John White Corwell and Abner Raiser, returned to the spot. They found the body of old man Baker hanging by the neck from one of the beams of the bridge, immediately beneath the spot where the apparition had stood. A thick coating of dust, slightly dampened by the mist, covered the floor of the bridge, but the only footprints were those of Mr. Cummings' horse.

In taking down the body the men disturbed the loose, friable earth of the slope below it, disclosing human bones already nearly uncovered by the action of water and frost. They were identified as those of the lost peddler. At the double inquest the coroner's jury found that Daniel Baker died by his own hand while suffering from temporary insanity, and that Samuel Morritz was murdered by some person or persons to the jury unknown.

11

DAGON

H.P. Lovecraft

I am writing this under an appreciable mental strain, since by tonight I shall be no more. Penniless, and at the end of my supply of the drug which alone makes life endurable, I can bear the torture no longer; and shall cast myself from this garret window into the squalid street below. Do not think from my slavery to morphine that I am a weakling or a degenerate. When you have read these hastily scrawled pages you may guess, though never fully realise, why it is that I must have forgetfulness or death.

It was in one of the most open and least frequented parts of the broad Pacific that the packet of which I was supercargo fell a victim to the German sea-raider. The great war was then at its very beginning, and the ocean forces of the Hun had not completely sunk to their later degradation; so that our vessel was made a legitimate prize, whilst we of her crew were treated with all the fairness and consideration due us as naval prisoners. So liberal, indeed, was the discipline of our captors, that five days after we were taken I managed to escape alone in a small boat with water and provisions for a good length of time.

When I finally found myself adrift and free, I had but little idea of my surroundings. Never a competent navigator, I could only guess vaguely by the sun and stars that I was somewhat south of the equator. Of the longitude I knew nothing, and no island or coast-line was in sight. The weather kept fair, and for uncounted days I drifted aimlessly beneath the scorching sun;

waiting either for some passing ship, or to be cast on the shores of some habitable land. But neither ship nor land appeared, and I began to despair in my solitude upon the heaving vastnesses of unbroken blue.

The change happened whilst I slept. Its details I shall never know; for my slumber, though troubled and dream-infested, was continuous. When at last I awaked, it was to discover myself half sucked into a slimy expanse of hellish black mire which extended about me in monotonous undulations as far as I could see, and in which my boat lay grounded some distance away.

Though one might well imagine that my first sensation would be of wonder at so prodigious and unexpected a transformation of scenery, I was in reality more horrified than astonished; for there was in the air and in the rotting soil a sinister quality which chilled me to the very core. The region was putrid with the carcasses of decaying fish, and of other less describable things which I saw protruding from the nasty mud of the unending plain. Perhaps I should not hope to convey in mere words the unutterable hideousness that can dwell in absolute silence and barren immensity. There was nothing within hearing, and nothing in sight save a vast reach of black slime; yet the very completeness of the stillness and homogeneity of the landscape oppressed me with a nauseating fear.

The sun was blazing down from a sky which seemed to me almost black in its cloudless cruelty; as though reflecting the inky marsh beneath my feet. As I crawled into the stranded boat I realised that only one theory could explain my position. Through some unprecedented volcanic upheaval, a portion of the ocean floor must have been thrown to the surface, exposing regions which for innumerable millions of years had lain hidden under unfathomable watery depths. So great was the extent of the new land which had risen beneath me, that I could not detect the faintest noise of the surging ocean, strain my ears as I might. Nor were there any sea-fowl to prey upon the dead things.

For several hours I sat thinking or brooding in the boat, which lay upon its side and afforded a slight shade as the sun moved across the heavens. As the day progressed, the ground lost some of its stickiness, and seemed likely to dry sufficiently for travelling purposes in a short time. That night I slept but little, and the next day I made for myself a pack containing food and water, preparatory to an overland journey in search of the vanished sea and possible rescue.

On the third morning I found the soil dry enough to walk upon with ease. The odour of the fish was maddening; but I was too much concerned with graver things to mind so slight an evil, and set out boldly for an unknown goal. All day I forged steadily westward, guided by a far-away hummock which rose higher than any other elevation on the rolling desert. That night I encamped, and on the following day still travelled toward the hummock, though that object seemed scarcely nearer than when I had first espied it. By the fourth evening I attained the base of the mound which turned out to be much higher than it had appeared from a distance, an intervening valley setting it out in sharper relief from the general surface. Too weary to ascend, I slept in the shadow of the hill.

I know not why my dreams were so wild that night; but ere the waning and fantastically gibbous moon had risen far above the eastern plain, I was awake in a cold perspiration, determined to sleep no more. Such visions as I had experienced were too much for me to endure again. And in the glow of the moon I saw how unwise I had been to travel by day. Without the glare of the parching sun, my journey would have cost me less energy; indeed, I now felt quite able to perform the ascent which had deterred me at sunset. Picking up my pack, I started for the crest of the eminence.

I have said that the unbroken monotony of the rolling plain was a source of vague horror to me; but I think my horror was greater when I gained the summit of the mound and looked down the other side into an immeasurable pit or canyon, whose black recesses the moon had not yet soard high enough to illuminate. I felt myself on the edge of the world; peering over the rim into a fathomless chaos of eternal night. Through my terror ran curious reminiscences of *Paradise Lost*, and of Satan's hideous climb through the unfashioned realms of darkness.

As the moon climbed higher in the sky, I began to see that the slopes of the valley were not quite so perpendicular as I had imagined. Ledges and outcroppings of rock afforded fairly easy foot-holds for a descent, whilst after a drop of a few hundred feet, the declivity became very gradual. Urged on by an impulse which I cannot definitely analyse, I scrambled with difficulty down the rocks and stood on the gentler slope beneath, gazing into the Stygian deeps where no light had yet penetrated.

All at once my attention was captured by a vast and singular object on the opposite slope, which rose steeply about an hundred yards ahead of me; an object that gleamed whitely in the newly bestowed rays of the ascending moon. That it was merely a gigantic piece of stone, I soon assured myself; but I was conscious of a distinct impression that its contour and position were not altogether the work of Nature. A closer scrutiny filled me with sensations I cannot express; for despite its enormous magnitude, and its position in an abyss which had yawned at the bottom of the sea since the world was young, I perceived beyond a doubt that the strange object was a well-shaped monolith whose massive bulk had known the workmanship and perhaps the worship of living and thinking creatures.

Dazed and frightened, yet not without a certain thrill of the scientist's or archaeologist's delight, I examined my surroundings more closely. The moon, now near the zenith, shone weirdly and vividly above the towering steeps that hemmed in the chasm, and revealed the fact that a far-flung body of water flowed at the bottom, winding out of sight in both directions, and almost lapping my feet as I stood on the slope. Across the chasm, the wavelets washed the base of the Cyclopean monolith; on whose surface I could now trace both inscriptions and crude sculptures. The writing was in a system of hieroglyphics unknown to me, and unlike anything I had ever seen in books; consisting for the most part of conventionalised aquatic symbols such as fishes, eels, octopi, crustaceans, molluscs, whales, and the like. Several characters obviously represented marine things which are unknown to the modern world, but whose decomposing forms I had observed on the ocean-risen plain.

It was the pictorial carving, however, that did most to hold me spellbound. Plainly visible across the intervening water on account of their enormous size, were an array of bas-reliefs whose subjects would have excited the envy of Doré. I think that these things were supposed to depict men—at least, a certain sort of men; though the creatures were shown disporting like fishes in waters of some marine grotto, or paying homage at some monolithic shrine which appeared to be under the waves as well. Of their faces and forms I dare not speak in detail; for the mere remembrance makes me grow faint. Grotesque beyond the imagination of a Poe or a Bulwer, they were damnably human in general outline despite webbed hands and feet, shockingly wide and flabby lips, glassy, bulging eyes, and other features less pleasant to recall. Curiously enough, they seemed to have been chiselled badly out of proportion with their scenic background; for one of the creatures was shown in the act of killing a whale represented as but little larger than himself. I remarked, as I say, their grotesqueness and strange size, but in a moment decided that they were merely the imaginary gods of some primitive fishing or seafaring tribe; some tribe whose last descendant had perished eras before the first ancestor of the Piltdown or Neanderthal Man was born. Awestruck at this unexpected glimpse into a past beyond the conception of the most daring anthropologist, I stood musing whilst the moon cast queer reflections on the silent channel before me.

Then suddenly I saw it. With only a slight churning to mark its rise to the surface, the thing slid into view above the dark waters. Vast, Polyphemus-like, and loathsome, it darted like a stupendous monster of nightmares to the monolith, about which it flung its gigantic scaly arms, the while it bowed its hideous head and gave vent to certain measured sounds. I think I went mad then.

Of my frantic ascent of the slope and cliff, and of my delirious journey back to the stranded boat, I remember little. I believe I sang a great deal, and laughed oddly when I was unable to sing. I have indistinct recollections of a great storm some time after I reached the boat; at any rate, I know that I heard peals of thunder and other tones which Nature utters only in her wildest moods.

When I came out of the shadows I was in a San Francisco hospital; brought thither by the captain of the American ship which had picked up my boat in mid-ocean. In my delirium I had said much, but found that my words had been given scant attention. Of any land upheaval in the Pacific, my rescuers knew nothing; nor did I deem it necessary to insist upon a thing which I knew they could not believe. Once I sought out a celebrated ethnologist, and amused him with peculiar questions regarding the ancient Philistine legend of Dagon, the Fish-God; but soon perceiving that he was hopelessly conventional, I did not press my inquiries.

It is at night, especially when the moon is gibbous and waning, that I see the thing. I tried morphine; but the drug has given only transient surcease, and has drawn me into its clutches as a hopeless slave. So now I am to end it all, having written a full account for the information or the contemptuous amusement of my fellow-men. Often I ask myself if it could not all have been a pure phantasm—a mere freak of fever as I lay sun-stricken and raving in the open boat after my escape from the German man-of-war. This I ask myself, but ever does there come before me a hideously vivid vision in reply. I cannot think of the deep sea without shuddering at the nameless things that may at this very moment be crawling and floundering on its slimy bed, worshipping their ancient stone idols and carving their own detestable likenesses on submarine obelisks of water-soaked granite. I dream of a day when they may rise above the billows to drag down in their reeking talons the remnants of puny, war-exhausted mankind—of a day when the land shall sink, and the dark ocean floor shall ascend amidst universal pandemonium.

The end is near. I hear a noise at the door, as of some immense slippery body lumbering against it. It shall not find me. God, that hand! The window! The window!

12

THE VOICE IN THE NIGHT

William Hope Hodgson

It was a dark, starless night. We were becalmed in the northern Pacific. Our exact position I do not know; for the sun had been hidden during the course of a weary, breathless week, by a thin haze which had seemed to float above us, about the height of our mastheads, at whiles descending and shrouding the surrounding sea.

With there being no wind, we had steadied the tiller, and I was the only man on deck. The crew, consisting of two men and a boy, were sleeping forward in their den, while Will—my friend, and the master of our little craft—was aft in his bunk on the port side of the little cabin.

Suddenly, from out of the surrounding darkness, there came a hail:

"Schooner, ahoy!"

The cry was so unexpected that I gave no immediate answer, because of my surprise.

It came again—a voice curiously throaty and inhuman, calling from somewhere upon the dark sea away on our port broadside:

"Schooner, ahoy!"

"Hullo!" I sang out, having gathered my wits somewhat. "What are you? What do you want?"

"You need not be afraid," answered the queer voice, having probably noticed some trace of confusion in my tone. "I am only an old—man."

The pause sounded odd, but it was only afterward that it

came back to me with any significance.

"Why don't you come alongside, then?" I queried somewhat snappishly, for I liked not his hinting at my having been a trifle shaken.

"I—I—can't. It wouldn't be safe. I—" The voice broke off, and there was silence.

"What do you mean?" I asked, growing more and more astonished. "What's not safe? Where are you?"

I listened for a moment, but there came no answer. And then, a sudden indefinite suspicion, of I knew not what, coming to me, I stepped swiftly to the binnacle and took out the lighted lamp. At the same time, I knocked on the deck with my heel to waken Will. Then I was back at the side, throwing the yellow funnel of light out into the silent immensity beyond our rail. As I did so, I heard a slight muffled cry, and then the sound of a splash, as though someone had dipped oars abruptly. Yet I cannot say with certainty that I saw anything; save, it seemed to me, that with the first flash of the light there had been something upon the waters, where now there was nothing.

"Hullo, there!" I called. "What foolery is this?"

But there came only the indistinct sounds of a boat being pulled away into the night.

Then I heard Will's voice from the direction of the after scuttle:

"What's up, George?"

"Come here, Will!" I said.

"What is it?" he asked, coming across the deck.

I told him the queer thing that had happened. He put several questions; then, after a moment's silence, he raised his hands to his lips and hailed:

"Boat, ahoy!"

From a long distance away there came back to us a faint reply, and my companion repeated his call. Presently, after a short period of silence, there grew on our hearing the muffled sound of oars, at which Will hailed again.

This time there was a reply: "Put away the light."

"I'm damned if I will," I muttered; but Will told me to do as the voice bade, and I shoved it down under the bulwarks.

"Come nearer," he said, and the oar strokes continued. Then, when apparently some half dozen fathoms distant, they again ceased.

"Come alongside!" exclaimed Will. "There's nothing to be frightened of aboard here."

"Promise that you will not show the light?"

"What's to do with you," I burst out, "that you're so infernally afraid of the light?"

"Because—" began the voice, and stopped short.

"Because what?" I asked quickly.

Will put his hand on my shoulder. "Shut up a minute, old man," he said in a low voice. "Let me tackle him."

He leaned more over the rail. "See here, mister," he said, "this is a pretty queer business, you coming upon us like this, right out in the middle of the blessed Pacific. How are we to know what sort of a hanky-panky trick you're up to? You say there's only one of you. How are we to know, unless we get a squint at you—eh? What's your objection to the light, anyway?"

As he finished, I heard the noise of the oars again, and then the voice came; but now from a greater distance, and sounding extremely hopeless and pathetic.

"I am sorry—sorry! I would not have troubled you, only I am hungry, and—so is she."

The voice died away, and the sound of the oars, dipping irregularly, was borne to us.

"Stop!" sang out Will. "I don't want to drive you away. Come back! We'll keep the light hidden if you don't like it."

He turned to me. "It's a damned queer rig, this; but I think there's nothing to be afraid of?"

There was a question in his tone, and I replied, "No, I think the poor devil's been wrecked around here, and gone crazy."

The sound of the oars drew nearer.

"Shove that lamp back in the binnacle," said Will; then he leaned over the rail and listened. I replaced the lamp and came back to his side. The dipping of the oars ceased some dozen yards distant.

"Won't you come alongside now?" asked Will in an even voice. "I have had the lamp put back in the binnacle."

"I—I cannot," replied the voice. "I dare not come nearer. I dare not even pay you for the— the provisions."

"That's all right," said Will, and hesitated. "You're welcome to as much grub as you can take—" Again he hesitated.

"You are very good!" exclaimed the voice. "May God, who understands everything, reward you—" It broke off huskily.

"The—the lady?" said Will abruptly. "Is she—"

"I have left her behind upon the island," came the voice.

"What island?" I cut in.

"I know not its name," returned the voice. "I would to God—" it began, and checked itself as suddenly.

"Could we not send a boat for her?" asked Will at this point.

"No!" said the voice, with extraordinary emphasis. "My God! No!" There was a moment's pause; then it added, in a tone which seemed a merited reproach:

"It was because of our want I ventured—because her agony tortured me."

"I am a forgetful brute!" exclaimed Will. "Just wait a minute, whoever you are, and I will bring you up something at once."

In a couple of minutes he was back again, and his arms were full of various edibles. He paused at the rail.

"Can't you come alongside for them?" he asked.

"No—I dare not," replied the voice, and it seemed to me

that in its tones I detected a note of stifled craving, as though the owner hushed a mortal desire. It came to me then in a flash that the poor old creature out there in the darkness was suffering for actual need for that which Will held in his arms; and yet, because of some unintelligible dread, refraining from dashing to the side of our schooner and receiving it. And with the lightning-like conviction there came the knowledge that the Invisible was not mad, but sanely facing some intolerable horror.

"Damn it, Will!" I said, full of many feelings, over which predominated a vast sympathy. "Get a box. We must float off the stuff to him in it."

This we did, propelling it away from the vessel, out into the darkness, by means of a boat hook.

In a minute a slight cry from the Invisible came to us, and we knew that he had secured the box.

A little later he called out a farewell to us, and so heartful a blessing that I am sure we were the better for it. Then, without more ado, we heard the ply of oars across the darkness.

"Pretty soon off," remarked Will, with perhaps just a little sense of injury.

"Wait," I replied. "I think somehow he'll come back. He must have been badly needing that food."

"And the lady," said Will. For a moment he was silent; then he continued:

"It's the queerest thing ever I've tumbled across since I've been fishing."

"Yes," I said, and fell to pondering.

And so the time slipped away—an hour, another, and still Will stayed with me; for the queer adventure had knocked all desire for sleep out of him.

The third hour was three parts through when we heard again the sound of oars across the silent ocean.

"Listen!" said Will, a low note of excitement in his voice.

"He's coming, just as I thought," I muttered.

The dipping of the oars grew nearer, and I noted that the strokes were firmer and longer. The food had been needed.

They came to a stop a little distance off the broadside, and the queer voice came again to us through the darkness:

"Schooner, ahoy!"

"That you?" asked Will.

"Yes," replied the voice. "I left you suddenly, but—but there was great need."

"The lady?" questioned Will.

"The—lady is grateful now on earth. She will be more grateful soon in—in heaven."

Will began to make some reply, in a puzzled voice, but became confused and broke off. I said nothing. I was wondering at the curious pauses, and apart from my wonder, I was full of a great sympathy.

The voice continued:

"We—she and I, have talked, as we shared the result of God's tenderness and yours—"

Will interposed; but without coherence.

"I beg of you not to—to belittle your deed of Christian charity this night," said the voice. "Be sure that it has not escaped His notice."

It stopped, and there was a full minute's silence. Then it came again:

"We have spoken together upon that which—which has befallen us. We had thought to go out, without telling anyone of the terror which has come into our—lives. She is with me in believing that tonight's happenings are under a special ruling, and that it is God's wish that we should tell to you all that we have suffered since—since—"

"Yes?" said Will softly.

"Since the sinking of the Albatross."

"Ah!" I exclaimed involuntarily. "She left Newcastle for 'Frisco some six months ago, and hasn't been heard of since."

"Yes" answered the voice. "But some few degrees to the North of the line, she was caught in a terrible storm and dismasted. When the calm came, it was found that she was leaking badly, and presently, it falling to a calm, the sailors took to the boats, leaving—leaving a young lady—my fiancée—and myself upon the wreck.

"We were below, gathering together a few of our belongings, when they left. They were entirely callous, through fear, and when we came up upon the decks, we saw them only as small shapes afar off upon the horizon. Yet we did not despair, but set to work and constructed a small raft. Upon this we put such few matters as it would hold, including a quantity of water and some ship's biscuit. Then, the vessel being very deep in the water, we got ourselves onto the raft and pushed off.

"It was later that I observed we seemed to be in the way of some tide or current, which bore us from the ship at an angle, so that in the course of three hours, by my watch, her hull became invisible to our sight, her broken masts remaining in view for a somewhat longer period. Then, toward evening, it grew misty, and so through the night. The next day we were still encompassed by the mist, the weather remaining quiet.

"For four days we drifted through this strange haze, until, on the evening of the fourth day, there grew upon our ears the murmur of breakers at a distance. Gradually it became plainer, and somewhat after midnight, it appeared to sound upon either hand at no very great space. The raft was raised upon a swell several times, and then we were in smooth water, and the noise of the breakers was behind.

"When the morning came, we found that we were in a sort of great lagoon, but of this we noticed little at the time; for close before us, through the enshrouding mist, loomed the hull of a large sailing vessel. With one accord we fell upon our knees and thanked God, for we thought that here was an end to our perils. We had much to learn.

"The raft drew near to the ship, and we shouted on them to take us aboard; but none answered. Presently the raft touched against the side of the vessel, and seeing a rope hanging downward, I seized it and began to climb. Yet I had much ado to make my way up, because of a kind of gray, lichenous fungus that had seized upon the rope and blotched the side of the ship lividly.

"I reached the rail and clambered over it, onto the deck. Here I saw that the decks were covered in great patches with the gray masses, some of them rising into nodules several feet in height; but at the time I thought less of this matter than of the possibility of there being people aboard the ship. I shouted, but none answered. Then I went to the door below the poop deck. I opened it and peered in. There was a great smell of staleness, so that I knew in a moment that nothing living was within, and with the knowledge, I shut the door quickly, for I felt suddenly lonely.

"I went back to the side where I had scrambled up. My—my sweetheart was still sitting quietly upon the raft. Seeing me look down, she called up to know whether there were any aboard the ship. I replied that the vessel had the appearance of having been long deserted, but that if she would wait a little, I would see whether there was anything in the shape of a ladder by which she could ascend to the deck. Then we would make a search through the vessel together. A little later, on the opposite side of the decks, I found a rope side ladder. This I carried across, and a minute afterward she was beside me.

"Together we explored the cabins and apartments in the afterpart of the ship, but nowhere was there any sign of life. Here and there, within the cabins themselves, we came across odd patches of that queer fungus; but this, as my sweetheart said, could be cleansed away.

"In the end, having assured ourselves that the after portion of the vessel was empty, we picked our ways to the bows, between the ugly gray nodules of that strange growth; and here we made a further search, which told us that there was indeed none aboard but ourselves.

"This being now beyond any doubt, we returned to the stern of the ship and proceeded to make ourselves as comfortable as possible. Together we cleared out and cleaned two of the cabins, and after that I made examination whether there was anything eatable in the ship. This I soon found was so, and thanked God for His goodness. In addition to this I discovered a fresh-water pump, and having fixed it, I found the water drinkable, though somewhat unpleasant to the taste.

"For several days we stayed aboard the ship without attempting to get to the shore. We were busily engaged in making the place habitable. Yet even thus early we became aware that our lot was even less to be desired than might have been imagined; for though, as a first step, we scraped away the odd patches of growth that studded the floors and walls of the cabins and saloon, yet they returned almost to their original size within the space of twenty-four hours, which not only discouraged us but gave us a feeling of vague unease.

"Still we would not admit ourselves beaten, so set to work afresh, and not only scraped away the fungus but soaked the places where it had been with carbolic, a canful of which I had found in the pantry. Yet by the end of the week the growth had returned in full strength, and in addition it had spread to other places, as though our touching it had allowed germs from it to travel elsewhere.

"On the seventh morning, my sweetheart woke to find a small patch of it growing on her pillow, close to her face. At that, she came to me, as soon as she could get her garments upon her. I was in the galley at the time, lighting the fire for breakfast."

"'Come here, John,' she said, and led me aft. When I saw the thing upon her pillow I shuddered, and then and there we agreed to go right out of the ship and see whether we could not fare to make ourselves more comfortable ashore.

"Hurriedly we gathered together our few belongings, and even among these I found that the fungus had been at work, for one of her shawls had a little lump of it growing near one edge. I threw the whole thing over the side without saying anything to her.

"The raft was still alongside, but it was too clumsy to guide, and I lowered down a small boat that hung across the stern, and in this we made our way to the shore. Yet as we drew near to it, I became gradually aware that here the vile fungus, which had driven us from the ship, was growing riot. In places it rose into horrible, fantastic mounds, which seemed almost to quiver, as with a quiet life, when the wind blew across them. Here and there it took on the forms of vast fingers, and in others it just spread out flat and smooth and treacherous. Odd places, it appeared as grotesque stunted trees, extraordinarily kinked and gnarled—the whole quaking vilely at times.

"At first it seemed to us that there was no single portion of the surrounding shore which was not hidden beneath the masses of the hideous lichen; yet in this I found we were mistaken, for somewhat later, coasting along the shore at a little distance, we descried a smooth white patch of what appeared to be fine sand, and there we landed. It was not sand. What it was I do not know.

All that I have observed is that upon it the fungus will not grow; while everywhere else, save where the sandlike earth wanders oddly, pathwise, amid the gray desolation of the lichen, there is nothing but that loathsome grayness.

"It is difficult to make you understand how cheered we were to find one place that was absolutely free from the growth, and here we deposited our belongings. Then we went back to the ship for such things as it seemed to us we should need. Among other matters, I managed to bring ashore with me one of the ship's sails. With it I constructed two small tents, which, though exceedingly rough-shaped, served the purposes for which they were intended. In these we lived and stored our various necessities, and thus for a matter of some four weeks all went smoothly and without particular unhappiness. Indeed, I may say with much happiness—for—we were together.

"It was on the thumb of her right hand that the growth first showed. It was only a small circular spot, much like a little gray mole. My God! How the fear leaped to my heart when she showed me the place. We cleansed it, between us, washing it with carbolic and water. In the morning of the following day she showed her hand to me again. The gray warty thing had returned. For a little while we looked at one another in silence. Then, still wordless, we started again to remove it. In the midst of the operation she spoke suddenly."

"'What's that on the side of your face, dear?' Her voice was sharp with anxiety. I put my hand up to feel.

"'There! Under the hair by your ear. A little to the front a bit.' My finger rested upon the place, and then I knew.

"'Let us get your thumb done first,' I said. And she submitted, only because she was afraid to touch me until it was cleansed. I finished washing and disinfecting her thumb, and then she turned to my face. After it was finished we sat together and talked awhile of many things; for there had come into our lives sudden, very terrible thoughts. We were, all at once, afraid of something worse than death. We spoke of loading the boat with provisions and water and making our way out onto the sea; yet we were helpless, for many causes, and—and the growth had attacked us already. We decided to stay. God would do with us what was His will. We would wait.

"A month, two months, three months passed and the places

grew somewhat, and there had come others. Yet we fought so strenuously with the fear that its headway was but slow, comparatively speaking.

"Occasionally we ventured off to the ship for such stores as we needed. There we found that the fungus grew persistently. One of the nodules on the main deck soon became as high as my head.

"We had now given up all thought or hope of leaving the island. We had realized that it would be unallowable to go among healthy humans with the thing from which we were suffering.

"With this determination and knowledge in our minds we knew that we should have to husband our food and water; for we did not know, at that time, but that we should possibly live for many years.

"This reminds me that I have told you that I am an old man. Judged by years this is not so. But—but—"

He broke off, then continued somewhat abruptly:

"As I was saying, we knew that we should have to use care in the matter of food. But we had no idea then how little food there was left of which to take care. It was a week later that I made the discovery that all the other bread tanks—which I had supposed full—were empty, and that (beyond odd tins of vegetables and meat, and some other matters) we had nothing on which to depend but the bread in the tank which I had already opened.

"After learning this I bestirred myself to do what I could, and set to work at fishing in the lagoon; but with no success. At this I was somewhat inclined to feel desperate, until the thought came to me to try outside the lagoon, in the open sea.

"Here, at times, I caught odd fish, but so infrequently that they proved of but little help in keeping us from the hunger which threatened. It seemed to me that our deaths were likely to come by hunger, and not by the growth of the thing which had seized upon our bodies.

"We were in this state of mind when the fourth month wore

out. Then I made a very horrible discovery. One morning, a little before midday, I came off from the ship with a portion of the biscuits which were left. In the mouth of her tent I saw my sweetheart sitting, eating something.

"'What is it, my dear?' I called out as I leaped ashore. Yet, on hearing my voice, she seemed confused, and, turning, slyly threw something toward the edge of the little clearing. It fell short, and a vague suspicion having arisen within me, I walked across and picked it up. It was a piece of the gray fungus.

"As I went to her with it in my hand, she turned deadly pale; then a rose red.

"I felt strangely dazed and frightened.

"'My dear! My dear!' I said, and could say no more. Yet at my words she broke down and cried bitterly. Gradually, as she calmed, I got from her the news that she had tried it the preceding day, and—and liked it. I got her to promise on her knees not to touch it again, however great our hunger. After she had promised, she told me that the desire for it had come suddenly, and that until the moment of desire, she had experienced nothing toward it but the most extreme repulsion.

"Later in the day, feeling strangely restless and much shaken with the thing which I had discovered, I made my way along one of the twisted paths—formed by the white, sandlike substance—which led among the fungoid growth. I had, once before, ventured along there, but not to any great distance. This time, being involved in perplexing thought, I went much farther than hitherto.

"Suddenly I was called to myself by a queer hoarse sound on my left. Turning quickly, I saw that there was movement among an extraordinarily shaped mass of fungus close to my elbow. It was swaying uneasily, as though it possessed life of its own. Abruptly, as I stared, the thought came to me that the thing had a grotesque resemblance to the figure of a distorted human creature. Even as the fancy flashed into my brain, there was a slight, sickening noise of tearing, and I saw that one of the branchlike arms was detaching itself from the surrounding masses, and coming toward me. The head of the thing, a shapeless gray ball, inclined in my direction. I stood stupidly, and the vile arm brushed across my face. I gave out a frightened cry and ran back a few paces. There was a sweetish taste upon my lips where the thing had touched me. I licked them, and was immediately filled with an inhuman desire. I turned and seized a mass of the fungus. Then more, and—more. I was insatiable. In the midst of devouring, the remembrance of the morning's discovery swept into my amazed brain. It was sent by God. I dashed the fragment I held to the ground. Then, utterly wretched and feeling a dreadful guiltiness, I made my way back to the encampment.

"I think she knew, by some marvelous intuition which love must have given, so soon as she set eyes on me. Her quiet sympathy made it easier for me, and I told her of my sudden weakness, yet omitted to mention the extraordinary thing which had gone before. I desired to spare her all unnecessary terror.

"But for myself I had added an intolerable knowledge, to breed an incessant terror in my brain; for I doubted not that I had seen the end of one of these men who had come to the island in the ship in the lagoon; and in that monstrous ending I had seen our own.

"Thereafter we kept from the abominable food, though the desire for it had entered into our blood. Yet our dreary punishment was upon us; for day by day, with monstrous rapidity, the fungoid growth took hold of our poor bodies. Nothing we could do would check it materially, and so—and so—we who had been human became—Well, it matters less each day. Only—only we had been man and maid!

"And day by day the fight is more dreadful to withstand the hunger-lust for the terrible lichen.

"A week ago we ate the last of the biscuit, and since that time I have caught three fish. I was out here fishing tonight when your schooner drifted upon me out of the mist. I hailed you. You know the rest, and may God, out of His great heart, bless you for your goodness to a—a couple of poor outcast souls."

There was the dip of an oar—another. Then the voice came again, and for the last time, sounding through the slight surrounding mist, ghostly and mournful.

"God bless you! Good-bye!"

"Good-bye," we shouted together hoarsely, our hearts full of many emotions I glanced about me. I became aware that the dawn was upon us.

The sun flung a stray beam across the hidden sea, pierced the mist dully, and lit up the receding boat with a gloomy fire. Indistinctly I saw something nodding between the oars. I thought of a sponge—a great, gray nodding sponge. The oars continued to ply. They were gray—as was the boat—and my eyes searched a moment vainly for the conjunction of hand and oar. My gaze flashed back to the—head. It nodded forward as the oars went backward for the stroke. Then the oars were dipped, the boat shot out of the patch of light, and the—the thing went nodding into the mist.

13

COUNT MAGNUS

M.R. James

By what means the papers out of which I have made a connected story came into my hands is the last point which the reader will learn from these pages. But it is necessary to prefix to my extracts from them a statement of the form in which I possess them.

They consist, then, partly of a series of collections for a book of travels, such a volume as was a common product of the forties and fifties. Horace Marryat's "Journal of a Residence in Jutland and the Danish Isles" is a fair specimen of the class to which I allude. These books usually treated of some unknown district on the Continent. They were illustrated with woodcuts or steel plates. They gave details of hotel accommodation, and of means of communication, such as we now expect to find in any well-regulated guide-book, and they dealt largely in reported conversations with intelligent foreigners, racy innkeepers, and garrulous peasants. In a word, they were chatty.

Begun with the idea of furnishing material for such a book, my papers as they progressed assumed the character of a record of one single personal experience, and this record was continued up to the very eve, almost, of its termination.

The writer was a Mr. Wraxall. For my knowledge of him I have to depend entirely on the evidence his writings afford, and from these I deduce that he was a man past middle age, possessed of some private means, and very much alone in the world. He had, it seems, no settled abode in England, but was a denizen of hotels and boarding-houses. It is probable that he entertained the idea of settling down at some future time which never came; and I think it also likely that the Pantechnicon fire in the early seventies must have destroyed a great deal that would have thrown light on his antecedents, for he refers once or twice to property of his that was warehoused at that establishment.

It is further apparent that Mr. Wraxall had published a book, and that it treated of a holiday he had once taken in Brittany. More than this I cannot say about his work, because a diligent search in bibliographical works has convinced me that it must have appeared either anonymously or under a pseudonym.

As to his character, it is not difficult to form some superficial opinion. He must have been an intelligent and cultivated man. It seems that he was near being a Fellow of his college at Oxford—Brasenose, as I judge from the Calendar. His besetting fault was pretty clearly that of over-inquisitiveness, possibly a good fault in a traveller, certainly a fault for which this traveller paid dearly enough in the end.

On what proved to be his last expedition, he was plotting another book. Scandinavia, a region not widely known to Englishmen forty years ago, had struck him as an interesting field. He must have alighted on some old books of Swedish history or memoirs, and the idea had struck him that there was room for a book descriptive of travel in Sweden, interspersed with episodes from the history of some of the great Swedish families. He procured letters of introduction, therefore, to some persons of quality in Sweden, and set out thither in the early summer of 1863.

Of his travels in the North there is no need to speak, nor of his residence of some weeks in Stockholm. I need only mention that some *savant* resident there put him on the track of an important collection of family papers belonging to the proprietors of an ancient manor-house in Vestergothland, and obtained for him permission to examine them.

The manor-house, or *herrgård*, in question is to be called Råbäck (pronounced something like Roebeck), though that is not its name. It is one of the best buildings of its kind in all the country, and the picture of it in Dahlenberg's *Suecia antiqua et moderna*, engraved in 1694, shows it very much as the tourist may see it today. It was built soon after 1600, and is, roughly speaking, very much like an English house of that period in respect of material—red-brick with stone facings—and style. The man who built it was a scion of the great house of De la Gardie, and his descendants possess it still. De la Gardie is the name by which I will designate them when mention of them becomes necessary.

They received Mr. Wraxall with great kindness and courtesy, and pressed him to stay in the house as long as his researches lasted. But, preferring to be independent, and mistrusting his powers of conversing in Swedish, he settled himself at the village inn, which turned out quite sufficiently comfortable, at any rate during the summer months. This arrangement would entail a short walk daily to and from the manor-house of something under a mile. The house itself stood in a park, and was protected—we should say grown up—with large old timber. Near it you found the walled garden, and then entered a close wood fringing one of the small lakes with which the whole country is pitted. Then came the wall of the demesne, and you climbed a steep knoll—a knob of rock lightly covered with soil—and on the top of this stood the church, fenced in with tall dark trees. It was a curious building to English eyes. The nave and aisles were low, and filled with pews and galleries. In the western gallery stood the handsome old organ, gaily painted, and with silver pipes. The ceiling was flat, and had been adorned by a seventeenth-century artist with a strange and hideous "Last Judgement", full of lurid flames, falling cities, burning ships, crying souls, and brown and smiling demons. Handsome brass coronæ hung from the roof; the pulpit was like a doll's-house covered with little painted wooden cherubs and saints; a stand with three hour-glasses was hinged to the preacher's desk. Such sights as these may be seen in many a church in Sweden now, but what distinguished this one was an addition to the original building. At the eastern end of the north aisle the builder of the manor-house had erected a mausoleum for himself and his family. It was a largish eight-sided building, lighted by a series of oval windows, and it had a domed roof, topped by a kind of pumpkin-shaped object rising into a spire, a form in which Swedish architects greatly delighted. The roof was of copper externally, and was painted black, while the walls, in common with those of the church, were staringly white. To this mausoleum there was no access from the church. It had a portal and steps of its own on the northern side.

Past the churchyard the path to the village goes, and not more than three or four minutes bring you to the inn door.

On the first day of his stay at Råbäck Mr. Wraxall found the church door open, and made those notes of the interior which I have epitomized. Into the mausoleum, however, he could not make his way. He could by looking through the keyhole just descry that there were fine marble effigies and sarcophagi of copper, and a wealth of armorial ornament, which made him very anxious to spend some time in investigation.

The papers he had come to examine at the manor-house proved to be of just the kind he wanted for his book. There were family correspondence, journals, and account-books of the earliest owners of the estate, very carefully kept and clearly written, full of amusing and picturesque detail. The first De la Gardie appeared in them as a strong and capable man. Shortly after the building of the mansion there had been a period of distress in the district, and the peasants had risen and attacked several châteaux and done some damage. The owner of Råbäck took a leading part in supressing the trouble, and there was reference to executions of ring-leaders and severe punishments inflicted with no sparing hand.

The portrait of this Magnus de la Gardie was one of the best in the house, and Mr. Wraxall studied it with no little interest after his day's work. He gives no detailed description of it, but I gather that the face impressed him rather by its power than by its beauty or goodness; in fact, he writes that Count Magnus was an almost phenomenally ugly man.

On this day Mr. Wraxall took his supper with the family, and walked back in the late but still bright evening.

"I must remember," he writes, "to ask the sexton if he can let me into the mausoleum at the church. He evidently has access to it himself, for I saw him tonight standing on the steps, and, as I thought, locking or unlocking the door."

I find that early on the following day Mr. Wraxall had some conversation with his landlord. His setting it down at such length as he does surprised me at first; but I soon realized that the papers I was reading were, at least in their beginning, the materials for the book he was meditating, and that it was to have been one of those quasi-journalistic productions which admit of the introduction of an admixture of conversational matter.

His object, he says, was to find out whether any traditions of Count Magnus de la Gardie lingered on in the scenes of that gentleman's activity, and whether the popular estimate of him were favourable or not. He found that the Count was decidedly not a favourite. If his tenants came late to their work on the days which they owed to him as Lord of the Manor, they were set on the wooden horse, or flogged and branded in the manor-house yard. One or two cases there were of men who had occupied lands which encroached on the lord's domain, and whose houses had been mysteriously burnt on a winter's night, with the whole family inside. But what seemed to dwell on the innkeeper's mind most—for he returned to the subject more than once—was that the Count had been on the Black Pilgrimage, and had brought something or someone back with him.

You will naturally inquire, as Mr. Wraxall did, what the Black Pilgrimage may have been. But your curiosity on the point must remain unsatisfied for the time being, just as his did. The landlord was evidently unwilling to give a full answer, or indeed any answer, on the point, and, being called out for a moment, trotted out with obvious alacrity, only putting his head in at the door a few minutes afterwards to say that he was called away to Skara, and should not be back till evening.

So Mr. Wraxall had to go unsatisfied to his day's work at the manor-house. The papers on which he was just then engaged soon put his thoughts into another channel, for he had to occupy himself with glancing over the correspondence between Sophia Albertina in Stockholm and her married cousin Ulrica Leonora at Råbäck in the years 1705-1710. The letters were of exceptional interest from the light they threw upon the culture of that period in Sweden, as anyone can testify who has read the full edition of them in the publications of the Swedish Historical Manuscripts Commission.

In the afternoon he had done with these, and after returning the boxes in which they were kept to their places on the shelf, he proceeded, very naturally, to take down some of the volumes nearest to them, in order to determine which of them had best be his principal subject of investigation next day. The shelf he had hit upon was occupied mostly by a collection of accountbooks in the writing of the first Count Magnus. But one among them was not an account-book, but a book of alchemical and other tracts in another sixteenth-century hand. Not being very familiar with alchemical literature, Mr. Wraxall spends much space which he might have spared in setting out the names and beginnings of the various treatises: The book of the Phœnix, book of the Thirty Words, book of the Toad, book of Miriam, Turba philosophorum, and so forth; and then he announces with a good deal of circumstance his delight at finding, on a leaf originally left blank near the middle of the book, some writing of Count Magnus himself headed "Liber nigræ peregrinationis". It is true that only a few lines were written, but there was quite enough to show that the landlord had that morning been referring to a belief at least as old as the time of Count Magnus, and probably shared by him. This is the English of what was written:

"If any man desires to obtain a long life, if he would obtain a faithful messenger and see the blood of his enemies, it is necessary that he should first go into the city of Chorazin, and there salute the prince..." Here there was an erasure of one word, not very thoroughly done, so that Mr. Wraxall felt pretty sure that he was right in reading it as *aëris* ("of the air"). But there was no more of the text copied, only a line in Latin: "Quære reliqua hujus materiei inter secretiora" (See the rest of this matter among the more private things).

It could not be denied that this threw a rather lurid light upon the tastes and beliefs of the Count; but to Mr. Wraxall, separated from him by nearly three centuries, the thought that he might have added to his general forcefulness alchemy, and to alchemy something like magic, only made him a more picturesque figure; and when, after a rather prolonged contemplation of his picture in the hall, Mr. Wraxall set out on his homeward way, his mind was full of the thought of Count Magnus. He had no eyes for his surroundings, no perception of the evening scents of the woods or the evening light on the lake; and when all of a sudden he pulled up short, he was astonished to find himself already at the gate of the churchyard, and within a few minutes of his dinner. His eyes fell on the mausoleum.

"Ah," he said, "Count Magnus, there you are. I should dearly like to see you."

"Like many solitary men," he writes, "I have a habit of talking to myself aloud; and, unlike some of the Greek and Latin particles, I do not expect an answer. Certainly, and perhaps fortunately in this case, there was neither voice nor any that regarded: only the woman who, I suppose, was cleaning up the church, dropped some metallic object on the floor, whose clang startled me. Count Magnus, I think, sleeps sound enough."

That same evening the landlord of the inn, who had heard Mr. Wraxall say that he wished to see the clerk or deacon (as he would be called in Sweden) of the parish, introduced him to that official in the inn parlour. A visit to the De la Gardie tomb-house was soon arranged for the next day, and a little general conversation ensued.

Mr. Wraxall, remembering that one function of Scandinavian deacons is to teach candidates for Confirmation, thought he would refresh his own memory on a Biblical point.

"Can you tell me," he said, "anything about Chorazin?"

The deacon seemed startled, but readily reminded him how that village had once been denounced.

"To be sure," said Mr. Wraxall; "it is, I suppose, quite a ruin now?"

"So I expect," replied the deacon. "I have heard some of our old priests say that Antichrist is to be born there; and there are tales—"

"Ah! what tales are those?" Mr. Wraxall put in.

"Tales, I was going to say, which I have forgotten," said the deacon; and soon after that he said good night.

The landlord was now alone, and at Mr. Wraxall's mercy; and that inquirer was not inclined to spare him.

"Herr Nielsen," he said, "I have found out something about the Black Pilgrimage. You may as well tell me what you know. What did the Count bring back with him?"

Swedes are habitually slow, perhaps, in answering, or perhaps the landlord was an exception. I am not sure; but Mr. Wraxall notes that the landlord spent at least one minute in looking at him before he said anything at all. Then he came close up to his guest, and with a good deal of effort he spoke:

"Mr. Wraxall, I can tell you this one little tale, and no more—not any more. You must not ask anything when I have done. In my grandfather's time—that is, ninety-two years ago—there were two men who said: 'The Count is dead; we do not care for him. We will go tonight and have a free hunt in his wood'—the long wood on the hill that you have seen behind Råbäck. Well, those that heard them say this, they said: 'No, do not go; we are sure you will meet with persons walking who should not be walking. They should be resting, not walking.' These men laughed. There were no forestmen to keep the wood, because no one wished to live there. The family were not here at the house. These men could do what they wished.

"Very well, they go to the wood that night. My grandfather was sitting here in this room. It was the summer, and a light night. With the window open, he could see out to the wood, and hear.

"So he sat there, and two or three men with him, and they listened. At first they hear nothing at all; then they hear someone—you know how far away it is—they hear someone scream, just as if the most inside part of his soul was twisted out of him. All of them in the room caught hold of each other, and they sat so for three-quarters of an hour. Then they hear someone else, only about three hundred ells off. They hear him laugh out loud: it was not one of those two men that laughed, and, indeed, they have all of them said that it was not any man at all. After that they hear a great door shut.

"Then, when it was just light with the sun, they all went to the priest. They said to him:

"'Father, put on your gown and your ruff, and come to bury these men, Anders Bjornsen and Hans Thorbjorn.'

"You understand that they were sure these men were dead. So they went to the wood—my grandfather never forgot this. He said they were all like so many dead men themselves. The priest, too, he was in a white fear. He said when they came to him:

"'I heard one cry in the night, and I heard one laugh afterwards. If I cannot forget that, I shall not be able to sleep again.'

"So they went to the wood, and they found these men on the edge of the wood. Hans Thorbjorn was standing with his back against a tree, and all the time he was pushing with his hands—pushing something away from him which was not there. So he was not dead. And they led him away, and took him to the house at Nykjoping, and he died before the winter; but he went on pushing with his hands. Also Anders Bjornsen was there; but he was dead. And I tell you this about Anders Bjornsen, that he was once a beautiful man, but now his face was not there, because the flesh of it was sucked away off the bones. You understand that? My grandfather did not forget that. And they laid him on the bier which they brought, and they put a cloth over his head, and the priest walked before; and they began to sing the psalm for the dead as well as they could. So, as they were singing the end of the first verse, one fell down, who was carrying the head of the bier, and the others looked back, and they saw that the cloth had fallen off, and the eyes of Anders Bjornsen were looking up, because there was nothing to close over them. And this they could not bear. Therefore the priest laid the cloth upon him, and sent for a spade, and they buried him in that place."

The next day Mr. Wraxall records that the deacon called for him soon after his breakfast, and took him to the church and mausoleum. He noticed that the key of the latter was hung on a nail just by the pulpit, and it occurred to him that, as the church door seemed to be left unlocked as a rule, it would not be difficult for him to pay a second and more private visit to the monuments if there proved to be more of interest among them than could be digested at first. The building, when he entered it, he found not unimposing. The monuments, mostly large erections of the seventeenth and eighteenth centuries, were dignified if luxuriant, and the epitaphs and heraldry were copious. The central space of the domed room was occupied by three copper sarcophagi, covered with finely-engraved ornament. Two of them had, as is commonly the case in Denmark and Sweden, a large metal crucifix on the lid. The third, that of Count Magnus, as it appeared, had, instead of that, a full-length effigy engraved upon it, and round the edge were several bands of similar ornament representing various scenes. One was a battle, with cannon belching out smoke, and walled towns, and troops of pikemen. Another showed an execution. In a third, among trees, was a man running at full speed, with flying hair and outstretched hands. After him followed a strange form; it would be hard to say whether the artist had intended it for a man, and was unable to give the requisite similitude, or whether it was intentionally made as monstrous as it looked. In view of the skill with which the rest of the drawing was done, Mr. Wraxall felt inclined to adopt the latter idea. The figure was unduly short, and was for the most part muffled in a hooded garment which swept the ground. The only part of the form which projected from that shelter was not shaped like any hand or arm. Mr. Wraxall compares it to the tentacle of a devil-fish, and continues: "On seeing this, I said to myself, 'This, then, which is evidently an allegorical representation of some kind—a fiend pursuing a hunted soul—may be the origin of the story of Count Magnus and his mysterious companion. Let us see how the huntsman is pictured: doubtless it will be a demon blowing his horn.'" But, as it turned out, there was no such sensational figure, only the semblance of a cloaked man on a hillock, who stood leaning on a stick, and watching the hunt with an interest which the engraver had tried to express in his attitude.

Mr. Wraxall noted the finely-worked and massive steel padlocks—three in number—which secured the sarcophagus. One of them, he saw, was detached, and lay on the pavement. And then, unwilling to delay the deacon longer or to waste his own working-time, he made his way onward to the manor-house.

"It is curious," he notes, "how, on retracing a familiar path, one's thoughts engross one to the absolute exclusion of surrounding objects. Tonight, for the second time, I had entirely failed to notice where I was going (I had planned a private visit to the tomb-house to copy the epitaphs), when I suddenly, as it were, awoke to consciousness, and found myself (as before) turning in at the churchyard gate, and, I believe, singing or chanting some such words as, 'Are you awake, Count Magnus? Are you asleep, Count Magnus?' and then something more which I have failed to recollect. It seemed to me that I must have been behaving in this nonsensical way for some time."

He found the key of the mausoleum where he had expected to find it, and copied the greater part of what he wanted; in fact, he stayed until the light began to fail him.

"I must have been wrong," he writes, "in saying that one of the padlocks of my Count's sarcophagus was unfastened; I see tonight that two are loose. I picked both up, and laid them carefully on the window-ledge, after trying unsuccessfully to close them. The remaining one is still firm, and, though I take it to be a spring lock, I cannot guess how it is opened. Had I succeeded in undoing it, I am almost afraid I should have taken the liberty of opening the sarcophagus. It is strange, the interest I feel in the personality of this, I fear, somewhat ferocious and grim old noble."

The day following was, as it turned out, the last of Mr. Wraxall's stay at Råbäck. He received letters connected with certain investments which made it desirable that he should return to England; his work among the papers was practically done, and travelling was slow. He decided, therefore, to make his farewells, put some finishing touches to his notes, and be off.

These finishing touches and farewells, as it turned out, took more time than he had expected. The hospitable family insisted on his staying to dine with them—they dined at three—and it was verging on half past six before he was outside the iron gates of Råbäck. He dwelt on every step of his walk by the lake, determined to saturate himself, now that he trod it for the last time, in the sentiment of the place and hour. And when he reached the summit of the churchyard knoll, he lingered for many minutes, gazing at the limitless prospect of woods near and distant, all dark beneath a sky of liquid green. When at last he turned to go, the thought struck him that surely he must bid farewell to Count Magnus as well as the rest of the De la Gardies. The church was but twenty yards away, and he knew where the key of the mausoleum hung. It was not long before he was standing over the great copper coffin, and, as usual, talking to himself aloud. "You may have been a bit of a rascal in your time, Magnus," he was saying, "but for all that I should like to see you, or, rather—"

"Just at that instant," he says, "I felt a blow on my foot. Hastily enough I drew it back, and something fell on the pavement with a clash. It was the third, the last of the three padlocks which had fastened the sarcophagus. I stooped to pick it up, and—Heaven is my witness that I am writing only the bare truth—before I had raised myself there was a sound of metal hinges creaking, and I distinctly saw the lid shifting upwards. I may have behaved like a coward, but I could not for my life stay for one moment. I was outside that dreadful building in less time than I can write—almost as quickly as I could have said—the words; and what frightens me yet more, I could not turn the key in the lock. As I sit here in my room noting these facts, I ask myself (it was not twenty minutes ago) whether that noise of creaking metal continued, and I cannot tell whether it did or not. I only know that there was something more than I have written that alarmed me, but whether it was sound or sight I am not able to remember. What is this that I have done?"

Poor Mr. Wraxall! He set out on his journey to England on the next day, as he had planned, and he reached England in safety; and yet, as I gather from his changed hand and inconsequent jottings, a broken man. One of several small note-books that have come to me with his papers gives, not a key to, but a kind of inkling of, his experiences. Much of his journey was made by canal-boat, and I find not less than six painful attempts to enumerate and describe his fellow-passengers. The entries are of this kind:

"24. Pastor of village in Skåne. Usual black coat and soft black hat.

"25. Commercial traveller from Stockholm going to Trollhättan. Black cloak, brown hat.

"26. Man in long black cloak, broad-leafed hat, very old-fashioned.'

This entry is lined out, and a note added: "Perhaps identical with No. 13. Have not yet seen his face." On referring to No. 13, I find that he is a Roman priest in a cassock.

The net result of the reckoning is always the same. Twenty-eight people appear in the enumeration, one being always a man in a long black cloak and broad hat, and another a "short figure in dark cloak and hood". On the other hand, it is always noted that only twenty-six passengers appear at meals, and that the man in the cloak is perhaps absent, and the short figure is certainly absent.

On reaching England, it appears that Mr. Wraxall landed at Harwich, and that he resolved at once to put himself out of the reach of some person or persons whom he never specifies, but whom he had evidently come to regard as his pursuers. Accordingly he took a vehicle—it was a closed fly—not trusting the railway and drove across country to the village of Belchamp St. Paul. It was about nine o'clock on a moonlight August night when he neared the place. He was sitting forward, and looking out of the window at the fields and thickets—there was little else to be seen—racing past him. Suddenly he came to a cross-road. At the corner two figures were standing motionless; both were in dark cloaks; the taller one wore a hat, the shorter a hood. He had no time to see their faces, nor did they make any motion that he could discern. Yet the horse shied violently and broke into a gallop, and Mr. Wraxall sank back into his seat in something like desperation. He had seen them before.

Arrived at Belchamp St. Paul, he was fortunate enough to find a decent furnished lodging, and for the next twenty-four hours he lived, comparatively speaking, in peace. His last notes were written on this day. They are too disjointed and ejaculatory to be given here in full, but the substance of them is clear enough. He is expecting a visit from his pursuers—how or when he knows not—and his constant cry is "What has he done?" and "Is there no hope?" Doctors, he knows, would call him mad, policemen would laugh at him. The parson is away. What can he do but lock his door and cry to God?

People still remembered last year at Belchamp St. Paul how a strange gentleman came one evening in August years back; and how the next morning but one he was found dead, and there was an inquest; and the jury that viewed the body fainted, seven of 'em did, and none of 'em wouldn't speak to what they see, and the verdict was visitation of God; and how the people as kep' the 'ouse moved out that same week, and went away from that part. But they do not, I think, know that any glimmer of light has ever been thrown, or could be thrown, on the mystery. It so happened that last year the little house came into my hands as part of a legacy. It had stood empty since 1863, and there seemed no prospect of letting it; so I had it pulled down, and the papers of which I have given you an abstract were found in a forgotten cupboard under the window in the best bedroom.

14

THE WERE-WOLF

H.B. Marryatt

My father was not born, or originally a resident, in the Hartz Mountains; he was the serf of an Hungarian nobleman, of great possessions, in Transylvania; but, although a serf, he was not by any means a poor or illiterate man. In fact, he was rich, and his intelligence and respectability were such, that he had been raised by his lord to the stewardship; but, whoever may happen to be born a serf, a serf must he remain, even though he become a wealthy man; such was the condition of my father. My father had been married for about five years; and, by his marriage, had three children—my eldest brother Cæsar, myself (Hermann), and a sister named Marcella. Latin is still the language spoken in that country; and that will account for our high-sounding names. My mother was a very beautiful woman, unfortunately more beautiful than virtuous: she was seen and admired by the lord of the soil; my father was sent away upon some mission; and, during his absence, my mother, flattered by the attentions, and won by the assiduities, of this nobleman, yielded to his wishes. It so happened that my father returned very unexpectedly, and discovered the intrigue. The evidence of my mother's shame was positive: he surprised her in the company of her seducer! Carried away by the impetuosity of his feelings, he watched the opportunity of a meeting taking place between them, and murdered both his wife and her seducer. Conscious that, as a serf, not even the provocation which he had received would be allowed as a justification of his conduct, he hastily collected together what money he could lay his hands upon, and, as we were then in the depth of winter, he put his horses to the sleigh, and taking his children with him, he set off in the middle of the night, and was far away before the tragical circumstance had transpired. Aware that he would be pursued, and that he had no chance of escape if he remained in any portion of his native country (in which the authorities could lay hold of him), he continued his flight without intermission until he had buried himself in the intricacies and seclusion of the Hartz Mountains. Of course, all that I have now told you I learned afterwards. My oldest recollections are knit to a rude, yet comfortable cottage, in which I lived with my father, brother, and sister. It was on the confines of one of those vast forests which cover the northern part of Germany; around it were a few acres of ground, which, during the summer months, my father cultivated, and which, though they yielded a doubtful harvest, were sufficient for our support. In the winter we remained much in doors, for, as my father followed the chase, we were left alone, and the wolves, during that season, incessantly prowled about. My father had purchased the cottage, and land about it, of one of the rude foresters, who gain their livelihood partly by hunting, and partly by burning charcoal, for the purpose of smelting the ore from the neighbouring mines; it was distant about two miles from any other habitation. I can call to mind the whole landscape now: the tall pines which rose up on the mountain above us, and the wide expanse of forest beneath, on the topmost boughs and heads of whose trees we looked down from our cottage, as the mountain below us rapidly descended into the distant valley. In summer time the prospect was beautiful; but during the severe winter, a more desolate scene could not well be imagined.

I said that, in the winter, my father occupied himself with the chase; every day he left us, and often would he lock the door, that we might not leave the cottage. He had no one to assist him, or to take care of us—indeed, it was not easy to find a female servant who would live in such a solitude; but, could he have found one, my father would not have received her, for he had imbibed a horror of the sex, as a difference of his conduct toward us, his two boys, and my poor little sister, Marcella, evidently proved. You may suppose we were sadly neglected; indeed, we suffered much, for my father, fearful that we might come to some harm, would not allow us fuel, when he left the cottage; and we were obliged, therefore, to creep under the heaps of bears'-skins, and there to keep ourselves as warm as we could until he returned in the evening, when a blazing fire was our delight. That my father chose this restless sort of life may appear strange, but the fact was that he could not remain quiet; whether from remorse for having committed murder, or from the misery consequent on his change of situation, or from both combined, he was never happy unless he was in a state of activity. Children, however, when left much to themselves, acquire a thoughtfulness not common to their age. So it was with us; and during the short cold days of winter we would sit silent, longing for the happy hours when the snow would melt, and the leaves burst out, and the birds begin their songs, and when we should again be set at liberty.

Such was our peculiar and savage sort of life until my brother Cæsar was nine, myself seven, and my sister five, years old, when the circumstances occurred on which is based the extraordinary narrative which I am about to relate.

One evening my father returned home rather later than usual; he had been unsuccessful, and, as the weather was very severe, and many feet of snow were upon the ground, he was not only very cold, but in a very bad humour. He had brought in wood, and we were all three of us gladly assisting each other in blowing on the embers to create the blaze, when he caught poor little Marcella by the arm and threw her aside; the child fell, struck her mouth, and bled very much. My brother ran to raise her up.

Accustomed to ill usage, and afraid of my father, she did not dare to cry, but looked up in his face very piteously. My father drew his stool nearer to the hearth, muttered something in abuse of women, and busied himself with the fire, which both my brother and I had deserted when our sister was so unkindly treated. A cheerful blaze was soon the result of his exertions; but we did not, as usual, crowd round it. Marcella, still bleeding, retired to a corner, and my brother and I took our seats beside her, while my father hung over the fire gloomily and alone. Such had been our position for about half-an-hour, when the howl of a wolf, close under the window of the cottage, fell on our ears. My father started up, and seized his gun; the howl was repeated, he examined the priming, and then hastily left the cottage, shutting the door after him. We all waited (anxiously listening), for we thought that if he succeeded in shooting the wolf, he would return in a better humour; and although he was harsh to all of us, and particularly so to our little sister, still we loved our father, and loved to see him cheerful and happy, for what else had we to look up to? And I may here observe, that perhaps there never were three children who were fonder of each other; we did not, like other children, fight and dispute together; and if, by chance, any disagreement did arise between my elder brother and me, little Marcella would run to us, and kissing us both, seal, through her entreaties, the peace between us. Marcella was a lovely, amiable child; I can recall her beautiful features even now—Alas! poor little Marcella.

We waited for some time, but the report of the gun did not reach us, and my elder brother then said, "Our father has followed the wolf, and will not be back for some time. Marcella, let us wash the blood from your mouth, and then we will leave this corner, and go to the fire and warm ourselves."

We did so, and remained there until near midnight, every minute wondering, as it grew later, why our father did not return.

We had no idea that he was in any danger, but we thought that he must have chased the wolf for a very long time. "I will look out and see if father is coming," said my brother Cæsar, going to the door. "Take care," said Marcella, "the wolves must be about now, and we cannot kill them, brother." My brother opened the door very cautiously, and but a few inches; he peeped out.—"I see nothing," said he, after a time, and once more he joined us at the fire. "We have had no supper," said I, for my father usually cooked the meat as soon as he came home; and during his absence we had nothing but the fragments of the preceding day.

"And if our father comes home after his hunt, Cæsar," said Marcella, "he will be pleased to have some supper; let us cook it for him and for ourselves." Cæsar climbed upon the stool, and reached down some meat—I forget now whether it was venison or bear's meat; but we cut off the usual quantity, and proceeded to dress it, as we used to do under our father's superintendence. We were all busied putting it into the platters before the fire, to await his coming, when we heard the sound of a horn. We listened—there was a noise outside, and a minute afterwards my father entered, ushering in a young female, and a large dark man in a hunter's dress.

Perhaps I had better now relate, what was only known to me many years afterwards. When my father had left the cottage, he perceived a large white wolf about thirty yards from him; as soon as the animal saw my father, it retreated slowly, growling and snarling. My father followed; the animal did not run, but always kept at some distance; and my father did not like to fire until he was pretty certain that his ball would take effect: thus they went on for some time, the wolf now leaving my father far behind, and then stopping and snarling defiance at him, and then again, on his approach, setting off at speed.

Anxious to shoot the animal (for the white wolf is very rare), my father continued the pursuit for several hours, during which he continually ascended the mountain.

You must know that there are peculiar spots on those mountains which are supposed, and, as my story will prove, truly supposed, to be inhabited by the evil influences; they are well known to the huntsmen, who invariably avoid them. Now, one of these spots, an open space in the pine forests above us, had been pointed out to my father as dangerous on that account. But, whether he disbelieved these wild stories, or whether, in his eager pursuit of the chase, he disregarded them, I know not; certain, however, it is that he was decoyed by the white wolf to this open space, when the animal appeared to slacken her speed. My father approached, came close up to her, raised his gun to his shoulder, and was about to fire, when the wolf suddenly disappeared. He thought that the snow on the ground must have dazzled his sight, and he let down his gun to look for the beast—but she was gone; how she could have escaped over the clearance, without his seeing her, was beyond his comprehension. Mortified at the ill success of his chase, he was about to retrace his steps, when he heard the distant sound of a horn. Astonishment at such a sound—at such an hour—in such a wilderness, made him forget for the moment his disappointment, and he remained riveted to the spot. In a minute the horn was blown a second time, and at no great distance; my father stood still, and listened: a third time it was blown. I forget the term used to express it, but it was the signal which, my father well knew, implied that the party was lost in the woods. In a few minutes more my father beheld a man on horseback, with a female seated on the crupper, enter the cleared space, and ride up to him. At first, my father called to mind the strange stories which he had heard of the supernatural beings who were said to frequent these mountains; but the nearer approach of the parties satisfied him that they were mortals like himself. As soon as they came up to him, the man who guided the horse accosted him. "Friend Hunter, you are out late, the better fortune for us: we have ridden far, and are in fear of our lives, which are eagerly sought after. These mountains have enabled us to elude our pursuers; but if we find not shelter and refreshment, that will avail us little, as we must perish from hunger and the inclemency of the night. My daughter, who rides behind me, is now more dead than alive—say, can you assist us in our difficulty?"

"My cottage is some few miles distant," replied my father, "but I have little to offer you besides a shelter from the weather; to the little I have you are welcome. May I ask whence you come?"

"Yes, friend, it is no secret now; we have escaped from Transylvania, where my daughter's honour and my life were equally in jeopardy!"

This information was quite enough to raise an interest in my father's heart. He remembered his own escape: he remembered the loss of his wife's honour, and the tragedy by which it was wound up. He immediately, and warmly, offered all the assistance which he could afford them.

"There is no time to be lost, then, good sir," observed the horseman; "my daughter is chilled with the frost, and cannot hold out much longer against the severity of the weather."

"Follow me," replied my father, leading the way towards his home.

"I was lured away in pursuit of a large white wolf," observed my father; "it came to the very window of my hut, or I should not have been out at this time of night."

"The creature passed by us just as we came out of the wood," said the female in a silvery tone.

"I was nearly discharging my piece at it," observed the hunter; "but since it did us such good service, I am glad that I allowed it to escape."

In about an hour and a half, during which my father walked at a rapid pace, the party arrived at the cottage, and, as I said before, came in.

"We are in good time, apparently," observed the dark hunter, catching the smell of the roasted meat, as he walked to the fire and surveyed my brother and sister, and myself. "You have young cooks here, Mynheer." "I am glad that we shall not have to wait," replied my father. "Come, mistress, seat yourself by the fire; you require warmth after your cold ride." "And where can I put up my horse, Mynheer?" observed the huntsman. "I will take care of him," replied my father, going out of the cottage door.

The female must, however, be particularly described. She was young, and apparently twenty years of age. She was dressed in a travelling dress, deeply bordered with white fur, and wore a cap of white ermine on her head. Her features were very beautiful, at least I thought so, and so my father has since declared. Her hair was flaxen, glossy and shining, and bright as a mirror; and her mouth, although somewhat large when it was open, showed the most brilliant teeth I have ever beheld. But there was something about her eyes, bright as they were, which made us children afraid; they were so restless, so furtive; I could not at that time tell why, but I felt as if there was cruelty in her eye; and when she beckoned us to come to her, we approached her with fear and trembling. Still she was beautiful, very beautiful. She spoke kindly to my brother and myself, patted our heads, and caressed us; but Marcella would not come near her; on the contrary, she slunk away, and hid herself in the bed, and would not wait for the supper, which half an hour before she had been so anxious for.

My father, having put the horse into a close shed, soon returned, and supper was placed upon the table. When it was over, my father requested that the young lady would take possession of his bed, and he would remain at the fire, and sit up with her father. After some hesitation on her part, this arrangement was agreed to, and I and my brother crept into the other bed with Marcella, for we had as yet always slept together.

But we could not sleep; there was something so unusual, not

only in seeing strange people, but in having those people sleep at the cottage, that we were bewildered. As for poor little Marcella, she was quiet, but I perceived that she trembled during the whole night, and sometimes I thought that she was checking a sob. My father had brought out some spirits, which he rarely used, and he and the strange hunter remained drinking and talking before the fire. Our ears were ready to catch the slightest whisper—so much was our curiosity excited.

"You said you came from Transylvania?" observed my father.

"Even so, Mynheer," replied the hunter. "I was a serf to the noble house of——; my master would insist upon my surrendering up my fair girl to his wishes; it ended in my giving him a few inches of my hunting-knife."

"We are countrymen, and brothers in misfortune," replied my father, taking the huntsman's hand, and pressing it warmly.

"Indeed! Are you, then, from that country?"

"Yes; and I too have fled for my life. But mine is a melancholy tale."

"Your name?" inquired the hunter.

"Krantz."

"What! Krantz of—I have heard your tale; you need not renew your grief by repeating it now. Welcome, most welcome, Mynheer, and, I may say, my worthy kinsman. I am your second cousin, Wilfred of Barnsdorf," cried the hunter, rising up and embracing my father.

They filled their horn mugs to the brim, and drank to one another, after the German fashion. The conversation was then carried on in a low tone; all that we could collect from it was, that our new relative and his daughter were to take up their abode in our cottage, at least for the present. In about an hour they both fell back in their chairs, and appeared to sleep.

"Marcella, dear, did you hear?" said my brother in a low tone.

"Yes," replied Marcella, in a whisper; "I heard all. Oh! brother,

I cannot bear to look upon that woman—I feel so frightened."

My brother made no reply, and shortly afterwards we were all three fast asleep.

When we awoke the next morning, we found that the hunter's daughter had risen before us. I thought she looked more beautiful than ever. She came up to little Marcella and caressed her; the child burst into tears, and sobbed as if her heart would break.

But, not to detain you with too long a story, the huntsman and his daughter were accommodated in the cottage. My father and he went out hunting daily, leaving Christina with us. She performed all the household duties; was very kind to us children; and, gradually, the dislike even of little Marcella wore away. But a great change took place in my father; he appeared to have conquered his aversion to the sex, and was most attentive to Christina. Often, after her father and we were in bed, would he sit up with her, conversing in a low tone by the fire. I ought to have mentioned, that my father and the huntsman Wilfred, slept in another portion of the cottage, and that the bed which he formerly occupied, and which was in the same room as ours, had been given up to the use of Christina. These visitors had been about three weeks at the cottage, when, one night, after we children had been sent to bed, a consultation was held. My father had asked Christina in marriage, and had obtained both her own consent and that of Wilfred; after this a conversation took place, which was, as nearly as I can recollect, as follows:

"You may take my child, Mynheer Krantz, and my blessing with her, and I shall then leave you and seek some other habitation—it matters little where."

"Why not remain here, Wilfred?"

"No, no, I am called elsewhere; let that suffice, and ask no more questions. You have my child."

"I thank you for her, and will duly value her; but there is one difficulty."

"I know what you would say; there is no priest here in this wild country: true, neither is there any law to bind; still must some ceremony pass between you, to satisfy a father. Will you consent to marry her after my fashion? if so, I will marry you directly."

"I will," replied my father.

"Then take her by the hand. Now, Mynheer, swear."

"I swear," repeated my father.

"By all the spirits of the Hartz Mountains——"

"Nay, why not by Heaven?" interrupted my father.

"Because it is not my humour," rejoined Wilfred; "if I prefer that oath, less binding perhaps, than another, surely you will not thwart me."

"Well, be it so then; have your humour. Will you make me swear by that in which I do not believe?"

"Yet many do so, who in outward appearance are Christians," rejoined Wilfred; "say, will you be married, or shall I take my daughter away with me?"

"Proceed," replied my father, impatiently.

"I swear by all the spirits of the Hartz Mountains, by all their power for good or for evil, that I take Christina for my wedded wife; that I will ever protect her, cherish her, and love her; that my hand shall never be raised against her to harm her."

My father repeated the words after Wilfred.

"And if I fail in this, my vow, may all the vengeance of the spirits fall upon me and upon my children; may they perish by the vulture, by the wolf, or other beasts of the forest; may their flesh be torn from their limbs, and their bones blanch in the wilderness; all this I swear."

My father hesitated, as he repeated the last words; little Marcella could not restrain herself, and as my father repeated the last sentence, she burst into tears. This sudden interruption appeared to discompose the party, particularly my father; he spoke harshly to the child, who controlled her sobs, burying her face under the bed-clothes.

Such was the second marriage of my father. The next morning, the hunter Wilfred mounted his horse and rode away.

My father resumed his bed, which was in the same room as ours; and things went on much as before the marriage, except that our new mother-in-law did not show any kindness towards us; indeed, during my father's absence, she would often beat us, particularly little Marcella, and her eyes would flash fire, as she looked eagerly upon the fair and lovely child.

One night, my sister awoke me and my brother.

"What is the matter?" said Cæsar.

"She has gone out," whispered Marcella.

"Gone out!"

"Yes, gone out at the door, in her night-clothes," replied the child; "I saw her get out of bed, look at my father to see if he slept, and then she went out at the door."

What could induce her to leave her bed, and all undressed to go out, in such bitter wintry weather, with the snow deep on the ground, was to us incomprehensible; we lay awake, and in about an hour we heard the growl of a wolf, close under the window.

"There is a wolf," said Cæsar, "she will be torn to pieces."

"Oh, no!" cried Marcella.

In a few minutes afterwards our mother-in-law appeared; she was in her night-dress, as Marcella had stated. She let down the latch of the door, so as to make no noise, went to a pail of water, and washed her face and hands, and then slipped into the bed where my father lay.

We all three trembled, we hardly knew why, but we resolved to watch the next night: we did so—and not only on the ensuing night, but on many others, and always at about the same hour, would our mother-in-law rise from her bed, and leave the cottage—and after she was gone, we invariably heard the growl of a wolf under our window, and always saw her, on her return, wash herself before she retired to bed. We observed, also, that she seldom sat down to meals, and that when she did, she appeared to eat with dislike; but when the meat was taken down, to be prepared for dinner, she would often furtively put a raw piece into her mouth.

My brother Cæsar was a courageous boy; he did not like to speak to my father until he knew more. He resolved that he would follow her out, and ascertain what she did. Marcella and I endeavoured to dissuade him from this project; but he would not be controlled, and, the very next night he lay down in his clothes, and as soon as our mother-in-law had left the cottage, he jumped up, took down my father's gun, and followed her.

You may imagine in what a state of suspense Marcella and I remained, during his absence. After a few minutes, we heard the report of a gun. It did not awaken my father, and we lay trembling with anxiety. In a minute afterwards we saw our mother-in-law enter the cottage—her dress was bloody. I put my hand to Marcella's mouth to prevent her crying out, although I was myself in great alarm. Our mother-in-law approached my father's bed, looked to see if he was asleep, and then went to the chimney, and blew up the embers into a blaze.

"Who is there?" said my father, waking up.

"Lie still, dearest," replied my mother-in-law, "it is only me; I have lighted the fire to warm some water; I am not quite well."

My father turned round and was soon asleep; but we watched our mother-in-law. She changed her linen, and threw the garments she had worn into the fire; and we then perceived that her right leg was bleeding profusely, as if from a gun-shot wound. She bandaged it up, and then dressing herself, remained before the fire until the break of day.

Poor little Marcella, her heart beat quick as she pressed me to her side—so indeed did mine. Where was our brother, Cæsar?

How did my mother-in-law receive the wound unless from his gun? At last my father rose, and then, for the first time I spoke, saying, "Father, where is my brother, Cæsar?"

"Your brother!" exclaimed he, "why, where can he be?"

"Merciful Heaven! I thought as I lay very restless last night," observed our mother-in-law, "that I heard somebody open the latch of the door; and, dear me, husband, what has become of your gun?"

My father cast his eyes up above the chimney, and perceived that his gun was missing. For a moment he looked perplexed, then seizing a broad axe, he went out of the cottage without saying another word.

He did not remain away from us long: in a few minutes he returned, bearing in his arms the mangled body of my poor brother; he laid it down, and covered up his face.

My mother-in-law rose up, and looked at the body, while Marcella and I threw ourselves by its side wailing and sobbing bitterly.

"Go to bed again, children," said she sharply. "Husband," continued she, "your boy must have taken the gun down to shoot a wolf, and the animal has been too powerful for him. Poor boy! He has paid dearly for his rashness."

My father made no reply; I wished to speak—to tell all—but Marcella, who perceived my intention, held me by the arm, and looked at me so imploringly, that I desisted.

My father, therefore, was left in his error; but Marcella and I, although we could not comprehend it, were conscious that our mother-in-law was in some way connected with my brother's death.

That day my father went out and dug a grave, and when he laid the body in the earth, he piled up stones over it, so that the wolves should not be able to dig it up. The shock of this catastrophe was to my poor father very severe; for several days he never went to the chase, although at times he would utter bitter anathemas and vengeance against the wolves.

But during this time of mourning on his part, my mother-in-law's nocturnal wanderings continued with the same regularity as before.

At last, my father took down his gun, to repair to the forest; but he soon returned, and appeared much annoyed.

"Would you believe it, Christina, that the wolves—perdition to the whole race—have actually contrived to dig up the body of my poor boy, and now there is nothing left of him but his bones?"

"Indeed!" replied my mother-in-law. Marcella looked at me, and I saw in her intelligent eye all she would have uttered.

"A wolf growls under our window every night, father," said I.

"Aye, indeed?—why did you not tell me, boy?—wake me the next time you hear it."

I saw my mother-in-law turn away; her eyes flashed fire, and she gnashed her teeth.

My father went out again, and covered up with a larger pile of stones the little remnants of my poor brother which the wolves had spared. Such was the first act of the tragedy.

The spring now came on: the snow disappeared, and we were permitted to leave the cottage; but never would I quit, for one moment, my dear little sister, to whom, since the death of my brother, I was more ardently attached than ever; indeed I was afraid to leave her alone with my mother-in-law, who appeared to have a particular pleasure in ill-treating the child. My father was now employed upon his little farm, and I was able to render him some assistance.

Marcella used to sit by us while we were at work, leaving my mother-in-law alone in the cottage. I ought to observe that, as the spring advanced, so did my mother decrease her nocturnal rambles, and that we never heard the growl of the wolf under the window after I had spoken of it to my father.

One day, when my father and I were in the field, Marcella being with us, my mother-in-law came out, saying that she was going into the forest, to collect some herbs my father wanted, and that Marcella must go to the cottage and watch the dinner. Marcella went, and my mother-in-law soon disappeared in the forest, taking a direction quite contrary to that in which the cottage stood, and leaving my father and I, as it were, between her and Marcella.

About an hour afterwards we were startled by shrieks from the cottage, evidently the shrieks of little Marcella. "Marcella has burnt herself, father," said I, throwing down my spade. My father threw down his, and we both hastened to the cottage. Before we could gain the door, out darted a large white wolf, which fled with the utmost celerity. My father had no weapon; he rushed into the cottage, and there saw poor little Marcella expiring; her body was dreadfully mangled, and the blood pouring from it had formed a large pool on the cottage floor. My father's first intention had been to seize his gun and pursue, but he was checked by this horrid spectacle; he knelt down by his dying child, and burst into tears: Marcella could just look kindly on us for a few seconds, and then her eyes were closed in death.

My father and I were still hanging over my poor sister's body, when my mother-in-law came in. At the dreadful sight she expressed much concern, but she did not appear to recoil from the sight of blood, as most women do.

"Poor child!" said she, "it must have been that great white wolf which passed me just now, and frightened me so—she's quite dead, Krantz."

"I know it—I know it!" cried my father in agony.

I thought my father would never recover from the effects of this second tragedy: he mourned bitterly over the body of his sweet child, and for several days would not consign it to its grave, although frequently requested by my mother-in-law to do so.

At last he yielded, and dug a grave for her close by that of my poor brother, and took every precaution that the wolves should not violate her remains.

I was now really miserable, as I lay alone in the bed which I had formerly shared with my brother and sister. I could not help thinking that my mother-in-law was implicated in both their deaths, although I could not account for the manner; but I no longer felt afraid of her: my little heart was full of hatred and revenge.

The night after my sister had been buried, as I lay awake, I perceived my mother-in-law get up and go out of the cottage. I waited for some time, then dressed myself, and looked out through the door, which I half-opened. The moon shone bright, and I could see the spot where my brother and my sister had been buried; and what was my horror, when I perceived my mother-in-law busily removing the stones from Marcella's grave.

She was in her white night-dress, and the moon shone full upon her. She was digging with her hands, and throwing away the stones behind her with all the ferocity of a wild beast. It was some time before I could collect my senses and decide what I should do. At last, I perceived that she had arrived at the body, and raised it up to the side of the grave. I could bear it no longer; I ran to my father and awoke him.

"Father! father!" cried I, "dress yourself, and get your gun."

"What!" cried my father, "the wolves are there, are they?"

He jumped out of bed, threw on his clothes, and in his anxiety did not appear to perceive the absence of his wife. As soon as he was ready, I opened the door, he went out, and I followed him.

Imagine his horror, when (unprepared as he was for such a sight) he beheld, as he advanced towards the grave, not a wolf, but his wife, in her night-dress, on her hands and knees, crouching by the body of my sister, and tearing off large pieces of the flesh, and devouring them with all the avidity of a wolf. She was too busy to be aware of our approach. My father dropped his gun, his hair stood on end; so did mine; he breathed heavily, and then his breath for a time stopped. I picked up the gun and put it into his hand. Suddenly he appeared as if concentrated rage had restored him to double vigour; he levelled his piece, fired, and with a loud shriek, down fell the wretch whom he had fostered in his bosom.

"God of Heaven!" cried my father, sinking down upon the earth in a swoon, as soon as he had discharged his gun.

I remained some time by his side before he recovered. "Where am I?" said he, "what has happened?—Oh!—yes, yes! I recollect now. Heaven forgive me!"

He rose and we walked up to the grave; what again was our astonishment and horror to find that instead of the dead body of my mother-in-law, as we expected, there was lying over the remains of my poor sister, a large, white she wolf.

"The white wolf!" exclaimed my father, "the white wolf which decoyed me into the forest—I see it all now—I have dealt with the spirits of the Hartz Mountains."

For some time my father remained in silence and deep thought. He then carefully lifted up the body of my sister, replaced it in the grave, and covered it over as before, having struck the head of the dead animal with the heel of his boot, and raving like a madman. He walked back to the cottage, shut the door, and threw himself on the bed; I did the same, for I was in a stupor of amazement.

Early in the morning we were both roused by a loud knocking at the door, and in rushed the hunter Wilfred.

"My daughter!—man—my daughter!—where is my daughter!" cried he in a rage.

"Where the wretch, the fiend, should be, I trust," replied my father, starting up and displaying equal choler; "where she should be—in hell!—Leave this cottage or you may fare worse."

"Ha-ha!" replied the hunter, "would you harm a potent spirit of the Hartz Mountains? Poor mortal, who must needs wed a were wolf."

"Out, demon! I defy thee and thy power."

"Yet shall you feel it; remember your oath—your solemn oath—never to raise your hand against her to harm her."

"I made no compact with evil spirits."

"You did; and if you failed in your vow, you were to meet the vengeance of the spirits. Your children were to perish by the vulture, the wolf——"

"Out, out, demon!"

"And their bones blanch in the wilderness. Ha!-ha!"

My father, frantic with rage, seized his axe, and raised it over Wilfred's head to strike.

"All this I swear," continued the huntsman, mockingly.

The axe descended; but it passed through the form of the hunter, and my father lost his balance, and fell heavily on the floor.

"Mortal!" said the hunter, striding over my father's body, "we have power over those only who have committed murder. You have been guilty of a double murder—you shall pay the penalty attached to your marriage vow. Two of your children are gone; the third is yet to follow—and follow them he will, for your oath is registered. Go—it were kindness to kill thee—your punishment is—that you live!"

15

WHAT WAS IT?
A Mystery

Fitz-James O'Brien

It is, I confess, with considerable diffidence that I approach the strange narrative which I am about to relate. The events which I purpose detailing are of so extraordinary and unheard-of a character that I am quite prepared to meet with an unusual amount of incredulity and scorn. I accept all such beforehand. I have, I trust, the literary courage to face unbelief. I have, after mature consideration, resolved to narrate, in as simple and straightforward a manner as I can compass, some facts that passed under my observation in the month of July last, and which, in the annals of the mysteries of physical science, are wholly unparalleled.

I live at No.—Twenty-sixth Street, in this city. The house is in some respects a curious one. It has enjoyed for the last two years the reputation of being haunted. It is a large and stately residence, surrounded by what was once a garden, but which is now only a green inclosure used for bleaching clothes. The dry basin of what has been a fountain, and a few fruit-trees, ragged and unpruned, indicate that this spot, in past days, was a pleasant, shady retreat, filled with fruits and flowers and the sweet murmur of waters.

The house is very spacious. A hall of noble size leads to a vast spiral staircase winding through its center, while the various apartments are of imposing dimensions. It was built some fifteen or twenty years since by Mr. A——, the well-known New York merchant, who five years ago threw the commercial world into convulsions by a stupendous bank fraud. Mr. A——, as every one knows, escaped to Europe, and died not long after of a broken heart. Almost immediately after the news of his decease reached this country, and was verified, the report spread in Twenty-sixth Street that No.—— was haunted. Legal measures had dispossessed the widow of its former owner, and it was inhabited merely by a care taker and his wife, placed there by the house agent into whose hands it had passed for purposes of renting or sale. These people declared that they were troubled with unnatural noises. Doors were opened without any visible agency. The remnants of furniture scattered through the various rooms were, during the night, piled one upon the other by unknown hands. Invisible feet passed up and down the stairs in broad daylight, accompanied by the rustle of unseen silk dresses, and the gliding of viewless hands along the massive balusters. The care taker and his wife declared that they would live there no longer. The house agent laughed, dismissed them, and put others in their place. The noises and supernatural manifestations continued. The neighborhood caught up the story, and the house remained untenanted for three years. Several persons negotiated for it; but somehow, always before the bargain was closed, they heard the unpleasant rumors, and declined to treat any further.

It was in this state of things that my landlady—who at that time kept a boarding-house in Bleecker Street, and who wished to move farther up town—conceived the bold idea of renting No.—— Twenty-sixth Street. Happening to have in her house rather a plucky and philosophical set of boarders, she laid down her scheme before us, stating candidly everything she had heard respecting the ghostly qualities of the establishment to which she wished to remove us. With the exception of two timid persons,—a sea captain and a returned Californian, who immediately gave notice that they would leave,—all of Mrs. Moffat's guests declared that they would accompany her in her chivalric incursion into the abode of spirits.

Our removal was effected in the month of May, and we were all charmed with our new residence. The portion of Twenty-sixth Street where our house is situated—between Seventh and Eighth Avenues—is one of the pleasantest localities in New York. The gardens back of the houses, running down nearly to the Hudson, form, in the summer time, a perfect avenue of verdure. The air is pure and invigorating, sweeping, as it does, straight across the river from the Weehawken heights, and even the ragged garden which surrounded the house on two sides, although displaying on washing days rather too much clothesline, still gave us a piece of greensward to look at, and a cool retreat in the summer evenings, where we smoked our cigars in the dusk, and watched the fireflies flashing their dark-lanterns in the long grass.

Of course we had no sooner established ourselves at No.— than we began to expect the ghosts. We absolutely awaited their advent with eagerness. Our dinner conversation was supernatural. One of the boarders, who had purchased Mrs. Crowe's "Night Side of Nature" for his own private delectation, was regarded as a public enemy by the entire household for not having bought twenty copies. The man led a life of supreme wretchedness while he was reading this volume. A system of espionage was established, of which he was the victim. If he incautiously laid the book down for an instant and left the room, it was immediately seized and read aloud in secret places to a select few. I found myself a person of immense importance, it having leaked out that I was tolerably well versed in the history of supernaturalism, and had once written a story, entitled "The Pot of Tulips," for Harper's Monthly, the foundation of which was a ghost. If a table or a wainscot panel happened to warp when we were assembled in the large drawing-room, there was an instant silence, and every one was prepared for an immediate clanking of chains and a spectral form.

After a month of psychological excitement, it was with the utmost dissatisfaction that we were forced to acknowledge that nothing in the remotest degree approaching the supernatural had manifested itself. Once the black butler asseverated that his candle had been blown out by some invisible agency while he was undressing himself for the night; but as I had more than once discovered this colored gentleman in a condition when one candle must have appeared to him like two, I thought it possible that, by going a step farther in his potations, he might have reversed his phenomenon, and seen no candle at all where he ought to have beheld one.

Things were in this state when an incident took place so awful and inexplicable in its character that my reason fairly reels at the bare memory of the occurrence. It was the tenth of July. After dinner was over I repaired with my friend, Dr. Hammond, to the garden to smoke my evening pipe. The Doctor and myself found ourselves in an unusually metaphysical mood. We lit our large meerschaums, filled with fine Turkish tobacco; we paced to and fro, conversing. A strange perversity dominated the currents of our thought. They would not flow through the sun-lit channels into which we strove to divert them. For some unaccountable reason they constantly diverged into dark and lonesome beds, where a continual gloom brooded. It was in vain that, after our old fashion, we flung ourselves on the shores of the East, and talked of its gay bazaars, of the splendors of the time of Haroun, of harems and golden palaces. Black afreets continually arose from the depths of our talk, and expanded, like the one the fisherman released from the copper vessel, until they blotted everything bright from our vision. Insensibly, we yielded to the occult force that swayed us, and indulged in gloomy speculation. We had talked some time upon the proneness of the human mind to mysticism, and the almost universal love of the Terrible, when Hammond suddenly said to me, "What do you consider to be the greatest element of Terror?"

The question, I own, puzzled me. That many things were terrible, I knew. Stumbling over a corpse in the dark; beholding, as I once did, a woman floating down a deep and rapid river, with wildly lifted arms, and awful, upturned face, uttering, as she sank, shrieks that rent one's heart, while we, the spectators, stood frozen at a window which overhung the river at a height of sixty feet, unable to make the slightest effort to save her, but dumbly watching her last supreme agony and her disappearance. A shattered wreck, with no life visible, encountered floating listlessly on the ocean, is a terrible object, for it suggests a huge terror, the proportions of which are veiled. But it now struck me for the first time that there must be one great and ruling embodiment of fear, a King of Terrors to which all others must succumb. What might it be? To what train of circumstances would it owe its existence?

"I confess, Hammond," I replied to my friend, "I never considered the subject before. That there must be one Something more terrible than any other thing, I feel. I cannot attempt, however, even the most vague definition."

"I am somewhat like you, Harry," he answered. "I feel my capacity to experience a terror greater than anything yet conceived by the human mind,—something combining in fearful and unnatural amalgamation hitherto supposed incompatible elements. The calling of the voices in Brockden Brown's novel of 'Wieland' is awful; so is the picture of the Dweller of the Threshold, in Bulwer's 'Zanoni'; but," he added, shaking his head gloomily, "there is something more horrible still than these."

"Look here, Hammond," I rejoined, "let us drop this kind of talk, for Heaven's sake!"

"I don't know what's the matter with me to-night," he replied, "but my brain is running upon all sorts of weird and awful thoughts. I feel as if I could write a story like Hoffman to night, if I were only master of a literary style."

"Well, if we are going to be Hoffmanesque in our talk, I'm off to bed. How sultry it is! Good night, Hammond."

"Good night, Harry. Pleasant dreams to you."

"To you, gloomy wretch, afreets, ghouls, and enchanters."

We parted, and each sought his respective chamber. I undressed quickly and got into bed, taking with me, according to my usual custom, a book, over which I generally read myself to sleep. I opened the volume as soon as I had laid my head upon the pillow, and instantly flung it to the other side of the room. It was Goudon's "History of Monsters"—a curious French work, which I had lately imported from Paris, but which, in the state of mind I had then reached, was anything but an agreeable companion. I resolved to go to sleep at once; so, turning down my gas until nothing but a little blue point of light glimmered on the top of the tube, I composed myself to rest.

The room was in total darkness. The atom of gas that still remained lighted did not illuminate a distance of three inches round the burner. I desperately drew my arm across my eyes, as if to shut out even the darkness, and tried to think of nothing. It was in vain. The confounded themes touched on by Hammond in the garden kept obtruding themselves on my brain. I battled against them. I erected ramparts of would-be blankness of intellect to keep them out. They still crowded upon me. While I was lying still as a corpse, hoping that by a perfect physical inaction I should hasten mental repose, an awful incident occurred. A Something dropped, as it seemed, from the ceiling, plumb upon my chest, and the next instant I felt two bony hands encircling my throat, endeavoring to choke me.

I am no coward, and am possessed of considerable physical strength. The suddenness of the attack, instead of stunning me, strung every nerve to its highest tension. My body acted from instinct, before my brain had time to realize the terrors of my position. In an instant I wound two muscular arms around the creature, and squeezed it, with all the strength of despair, against my chest. In a few seconds the bony hands that had fastened on my throat loosened their hold, and I was free to breathe once more. Then commenced a struggle of awful intensity. Immersed in the most profound darkness, totally ignorant of the nature of the Thing by which I was so suddenly attacked, finding my grasp slipping every moment, by reason, it seemed to me, of the entire nakedness of my assailant, bitten with sharp teeth in the shoulder, neck, and chest, having every moment to protect my throat against a pair of sinewy, agile hands, which my utmost efforts could not confine— these were a combination of circumstances to combat which required all the strength and skill and courage that I possessed.

At last, after a silent, deadly, exhausting struggle, I got my assailant under by a series of incredible efforts of strength. Once pinned, with my knee on what I made out to be its chest, I knew that I was victor. I rested for a moment to breathe. I heard the creature beneath me panting in the darkness, and felt the violent throbbing of a heart. It was apparently as exhausted as I was; that was one comfort. At this moment I remembered that I usually placed under my pillow, before going to bed, a large yellow silk pocket handkerchief, for use during the night. I felt for it instantly; it was there. In a few seconds more I had, after a fashion, pinioned the creature's arms.

I now felt tolerably secure. There was nothing more to be done but to turn on the gas, and, having first seen what my midnight assailant was like, arouse the household. I will confess to being actuated by a certain pride in not giving the alarm before; I wished to make the capture alone and unaided.

Never losing my hold for an instant, I slipped from the bed to the floor, dragging my captive with me. I had but a few steps to make to reach the gas-burner; these I made with the greatest caution, holding the creature in a grip like a vice. At last I got within arm's-length of the tiny speck of blue light which told me where the gas-burner lay. Quick as lightning I released my grasp with one hand and let on the full flood of light. Then I turned to look at my captive.

I cannot even attempt to give any definition of my sensations the instant after I turned on the gas. I suppose I must have shrieked with terror, for in less than a minute afterward my room was crowded with the inmates of the house. I shudder now as I think of that awful moment. I saw nothing! Yes; I had one arm firmly clasped round a breathing, panting, corporeal shape, my other hand gripped with all its strength a throat as warm, and apparently fleshly, as my own; and yet, with this living substance in my grasp, with its body pressed against my own, and all in the bright glare of a large jet of gas, I absolutely beheld nothing! Not even an outline,—a vapor!

I do not, even at this hour, realize the situation in which I found myself. I cannot recall the astounding incident thoroughly. Imagination in vain tries to compass the awful paradox.

It breathed. I felt its warm breath upon my cheek. It struggled fiercely. It had hands. They clutched me. Its skin was smooth, like my own. There it lay, pressed close up against me, solid as stone,—and yet utterly invisible!

I wonder that I did not faint or go mad on the instant. Some wonderful instinct must have sustained me; for, absolutely, in place of loosening my hold on the terrible Enigma, I seemed to gain an additional strength in my moment of horror, and tightened my grasp with such wonderful force that I felt the creature shivering with agony.

Just then Hammond entered my room at the head of the household. As soon as he beheld my face—which, I suppose, must have been an awful sight to look at—he hastened forward, crying, "Great heaven, Harry! what has happened?"

"Hammond! Hammond!" I cried, "come here. Oh! this is awful! I have been attacked in bed by something or other, which I have hold of; but I can't see it—I can't see it!"

Hammond, doubtless struck by the unfeigned horror expressed in my countenance, made one or two steps forward with an anxious yet puzzled expression. A very audible titter burst from the remainder of my visitors. This suppressed laughter made me furious. To laugh at a human being in my position! It was the worst species of cruelty. Now, I can understand why the appearance of a man struggling violently, as it would seem, with an airy nothing, and calling for assistance against a vision, should have appeared ludicrous. Then, so great was my rage against the mocking crowd that had I the power I would have stricken them dead where they stood.

"Hammond! Hammond!" I cried again, despairingly, "for God's sake come to me. I can hold the—the Thing but a short while longer. It is overpowering me. Help me! Help me!"

"Harry," whispered Hammond, approaching me, "you have been smoking too much."

"I swear to you, Hammond, that this is no vision," I answered, in the same low tone. "Don't you see how it shakes my whole frame with its struggles? If you don't believe me, convince yourself. Feel it,—touch it."

Hammond advanced and laid his hand on the spot I indicated. A wild cry of horror burst from him. He had felt it!

In a moment he had discovered somewhere in my room a long piece of cord, and was the next instant winding it and knotting it about the body of the unseen being that I clasped in my arms.

"Harry," he said, in a hoarse, agitated voice, for, though he preserved his presence of mind, he was deeply moved, "Harry, it's all safe now. You may let go, old fellow, if you're tired. The Thing can't move."

I was utterly exhausted, and I gladly loosed my hold.

Hammond stood holding the ends of the cord that bound the Invisible, twisted round his hand, while before him, self-supporting as it were, he beheld a rope laced and interlaced, and stretching tightly round a vacant space. I never saw a man look so thoroughly stricken with awe. Nevertheless his face expressed all the courage and determination which I knew him to possess. His lips, although white, were set firmly, and one could perceive at a glance that, although stricken with fear, he was not daunted.

The confusion that ensued among the guests of the house who were witnesses of this extraordinary scene between Hammond and myself,—who beheld the pantomime of binding this struggling Something,—who beheld me almost sinking from physical exhaustion when my task of jailer was over—the confusion and terror that took possession of the bystanders, when they saw all this, was beyond description. The weaker ones fled from the apartment. The few who remained clustered near the door, and could not be induced to approach Hammond and his Charge. Still incredulity broke out through their terror. They had not the courage to satisfy themselves, and yet they doubted. It was in vain that I begged of some of the men to come near and convince themselves by touch of the existence in that room of a living being which was invisible. They were incredulous, but did not dare to undeceive themselves. How could a solid, living, breathing body be invisible, they asked. My reply was this. I gave a sign to Hammond, and both of us—conquering our fearful repugnance to touch the invisible creature—lifted it from the ground, manacled as it was, and took it to my bed. Its weight was about that of a boy of fourteen.

"Now, my friends," I said, as Hammond and myself held the creature suspended over the bed, "I can give you self-evident proof that here is a solid, ponderable body which, nevertheless, you cannot see. Be good enough to watch the surface of the bed attentively."

I was astonished at my own courage in treating this strange event so calmly; but I had recovered from my first terror, and felt a sort of scientific pride in the affair which dominated every other feeling.

The eyes of the bystanders were immediately fixed on my bed. At a given signal Hammond and I let the creature fall. There was the dull sound of a heavy body alighting on a soft mass. The timbers of the bed creaked. A deep impression marked itself distinctly on the pillow, and on the bed itself. The crowd who witnessed this gave a sort of low, universal cry, and rushed from the room. Hammond and I were left alone with our Mystery.

We remained silent for some time, listening to the low, irregular breathing of the creature on the bed, and watching the rustle of the bedclothes as it impotently struggled to free itself from confinement. Then Hammond spoke.

"Harry, this is awful."

"Aye, awful."

"But not unaccountable."

"Not unaccountable! What do you mean? Such a thing has never occurred since the birth of the world. I know not what to think, Hammond. God grant that I am not mad, and that this is not an insane fantasy!"

"Let us reason a little, Harry. Here is a solid body which we touch, but which we cannot see. The fact is so unusual that it strikes us with terror. Is there no parallel, though, for such a phenomenon? Take a piece of pure glass. It is tangible and transparent. A certain chemical coarseness is all that prevents its being so entirely transparent as to be totally invisible. It is not theoretically impossible, mind you, to make a glass which shall not reflect a single ray of light—a glass so pure and homogeneous in its atoms that the rays from the sun shall pass through it as they do through the air, refracted but not reflected. We do not see the air, and yet we feel it."

"That's all very well, Hammond, but these are inanimate substances. Glass does not breathe, air does not breathe. This thing has a heart that palpitates,—a will that moves it—lungs that play, and inspire and respire."

"You forget the strange phenomena of which we have so often heard of late," answered the Doctor, gravely. "At the meetings called 'spirit circles,' invisible hands have been thrust into the hands of those persons round the table—warm, fleshly hands that seemed to pulsate with mortal life."

"What? Do you think, then, that this thing is—"

"I don't know what it is," was the solemn reply; "but please the gods I will, with your assistance, thoroughly investigate it."

We watched together, smoking many pipes, all night long, by the bedside of the unearthly being that tossed and panted until it was apparently wearied out. Then we learned by the low, regular breathing that it slept.

The next morning the house was all astir. The boarders congregated on the landing outside my room, and Hammond and myself were lions. We had to answer a thousand questions as to the state of our extraordinary prisoner, for as yet not one person in the house except ourselves could be induced to set foot in the apartment.

The creature was awake. This was evidenced by the convulsive manner in which the bedclothes were moved in its efforts to escape. There was something truly terrible in beholding, as it were, those second-hand indications of the terrible writhings and agonized struggles for liberty which themselves were invisible.

Hammond and myself had racked our brains during the long night to discover some means by which we might realize the shape and general appearance of the Enigma. As well as we could make out by passing our hands over the creature's form, its outlines and lineaments were human. There was a mouth; a round, smooth head without hair; a nose, which, however, was little elevated above the cheeks; and its hands and feet felt like those of a boy. At first we thought of placing the being on a smooth surface and tracing its outline with chalk, as shoemakers trace the outline of the foot. This plan was given up as being of no value. Such an outline would give not the slightest idea of its conformation.

A happy thought struck me. We would take a cast of it in plaster of Paris. This would give us the solid figure, and satisfy all our wishes. But how to do it? The movements of the creature would disturb the setting of the plastic covering, and distort the mold. Another thought. Why not give it chloroform? It had respiratory organs—that was evident by its breathing. Once reduced to a state of insensibility, we could do with it what we would. Doctor X—was sent for; and after the worthy physician had recovered from the first shock of amazement, he proceeded to administer the chloroform. In three minutes afterward we were enabled to remove the fetters from the creature's body, and a well-known modeler of this city was busily engaged in covering the invisible form with the moist clay. In five minutes more we had a mold, and before evening a rough fac simile of the mystery. It was shaped like a man,—distorted, uncouth, and horrible, but still a man. It was small, not over four feet and some inches in height, and its limbs revealed a muscular development that was unparalleled. Its face surpassed in hideousness anything I had ever seen. Gustave Doré, or Callot, or Tony Johannot, never conceived anything so horrible. There is a face in one of the latter's illustrations to "Un Voyage où il vous plaira," which somewhat approaches the countenance of this creature, but does not equal it. It was the physiognomy of what I should have fancied a ghoul to be. It looked as if it was capable of feeding on human flesh.

Having satisfied our curiosity, and bound every one in the house to secrecy, it became a question what was to be done with our Enigma. It was impossible that we should keep such a horror in our house; it was equally impossible that such an awful being should be let loose upon the world. I confess that I would have gladly voted for the creature's destruction. But who would shoulder the responsibility? Who would undertake the execution of this horrible semblance of a human being? Day after day this question was deliberated gravely. The boarders all left the house. Mrs. Moffat was in despair, and threatened Hammond and myself with all sorts of legal penalties if we did not remove the Horror. Our answer was, "We will go if you like, but we decline taking this creature with us. Remove it yourself if you please. It appeared in your house. On you the responsibility rests." To this there was, of course, no answer. Mrs. Moffat could not obtain for love or money a person who would even approach the Mystery.

The most singular part of the transaction was that we were entirely ignorant of what the creature habitually fed on. Everything in the way of nutriment that we could think of was placed before it, but was never touched. It was awful to stand by, day after day, and see the clothes toss, and hear the hard breathing, and know that it was starving.

Ten, twelve days, a fortnight passed, and it still lived. The pulsations of the heart, however, were daily growing fainter, and had now nearly ceased altogether. It was evident that the creature was dying for want of sustenance. While this terrible life struggle was going on, I felt miserable. I could not sleep of nights. Horrible as the creature was, it was pitiful to think of the pangs it was suffering.

At last it died. Hammond and I found it cold and stiff one morning in the bed. The heart had ceased to beat, the lungs to inspire. We hastened to bury it in the garden. It was a strange funeral, the dropping of that viewless corpse into the damp hole. The cast of its form I gave to Dr. X——, who keeps it in his museum in Tenth Street.

As I am on the eve of a long journey from which I may not return, I have drawn up this narrative of an event the most singular that has ever come to my knowledge.

Note.— It was rumored that the proprietors of a well-known museum in this city had made arrangements with Dr. X—to exhibit to the public the singular cast which Mr. Escott deposited with him. So extraordinary a history cannot fail to attract universal attention.

16

THE MASQUE OF THE RED DEATH

Edgar Allen Poe

The "Red Death" had long devastated the country. No pestilence had ever been so fatal, or so hideous. Blood was its Avatar and its seal—the redness and the horror of blood. There were sharp pains, and sudden dizziness, and then profuse bleeding at the pores, with dissolution. The scarlet stains upon the body and especially upon the face of the victim, were the pest ban which shut him out from the aid and from the sympathy of his fellow-men. And the whole seizure, progress and termination of the disease, were the incidents of half an hour.

But the Prince Prospero was happy and dauntless and sagacious. When his dominions were half depopulated, he summoned to his presence a thousand hale and light-hearted friends from among the knights and dames of his court, and with these retired to the deep seclusion of one of his castellated abbeys. This was an extensive and magnificent structure, the creation of the prince's own eccentric yet august taste. A strong and lofty wall girdled it in. This wall had gates of iron. The courtiers, having entered, brought furnaces and massy hammers and welded the bolts. They resolved to leave means neither of ingress or egress to the sudden impulses of despair or of frenzy from within. The abbey was amply provisioned. With such precautions the courtiers might bid defiance to contagion. The external world could take care of itself. In the meantime it was folly to grieve, or to think. The prince had provided all the appliances of pleasure. There were buffoons, there were improvisatori, there were ballet-dancers, there were musicians, there was Beauty, there was wine. All these and security were within. Without was the "Red Death."

It was toward the close of the fifth or sixth month of his seclusion, and while the pestilence raged most furiously abroad, that the Prince Prospero entertained his thousand friends at a masked ball of the most unusual magnificence.

It was a voluptuous scene, that masquerade. But first let me tell of the rooms in which it was held. There were seven—an imperial suite. In many palaces, however, such suites form a long and straight vista, while the folding doors slide back nearly to the walls on either hand, so that the view of the whole extent is scarcely impeded. Here the case was very different; as might have been expected from the duke's love of the *bizarre*. The apartments were so irregularly disposed that the vision embraced but little more than one at a time. There was a sharp turn at every twenty or thirty yards, and at each turn a novel effect. To the right and left, in the middle of each wall, a tall and narrow Gothic window looked out upon a closed corridor which pursued the windings of the suite. These windows were of stained glass whose color varied in accordance with the prevailing hue of the decorations of the chamber into which it opened. That at the eastern extremity was hung, for example, in blue—and vividly blue were its windows. The second chamber was purple in its ornaments and tapestries, and here the panes were purple. The third was green throughout, and so were the casements. The fourth was furnished and lighted with orange—the fifth with white—the sixth with violet. The seventh apartment was closely shrouded in black velvet tapestries that hung all over the ceiling and down the walls, falling in heavy folds upon a carpet of the same material and hue. But in this chamber only, the color of the windows failed to correspond with the decorations. The panes here were scarlet—a deep blood color. Now in no one of the seven apartments was there any lamp or candelabrum, amid the profusion of golden ornaments that lay scattered to and fro or depended from the roof. There was no light of any kind emanating from lamp or candle within the suite of chambers. But in the corridors that followed the suite, there stood, opposite to each window, a heavy tripod, bearing a brazier of fire that projected its rays through the tinted glass and so glaringly illumined the room. And thus were produced a multitude of gaudy and fantastic appearances. But in the western or black chamber the effect of the fire-light that streamed upon the dark hangings through the blood-tinted panes, was ghastly in the extreme, and produced so wild a look upon the countenances of those who entered, that there were few of the company bold enough to set foot within its precincts at all.

It was in this apartment, also, that there stood against the western wall, a gigantic clock of ebony. Its pendulum swung to and fro with a dull, heavy, monotonous clang; and when the minute-hand made the circuit of the face, and the hour was to be stricken, there came from the brazen lungs of the clock a sound which was clear and loud and deep and exceedingly musical, but of so peculiar a note and emphasis that, at each lapse of an hour, the musicians of the orchestra were constrained to pause, momentarily, in their performance, to hearken to the sound; and thus the waltzers perforce ceased their evolutions; and there was a brief disconcert of the whole gay company; and, while the chimes of the clock yet rang, it was observed that the giddiest grew pale, and the more aged and sedate passed their hands over their brows as if in confused reverie or meditation. But when the echoes had fully ceased, a light laughter at once pervaded the assembly; the musicians looked at each other and smiled as if at their own nervousness and folly, and made whispering vows, each to the other, that the next chiming of the clock should produce in them no similar emotion; and then, after the lapse of sixty minutes, (which embrace three thousand and six hundred seconds of the Time that flies,) there came yet another chiming of the clock, and then were the same disconcert and tremulousness and meditation as before.

But, in spite of these things, it was a gay and magnificent revel. The tastes of the duke were peculiar. He had a fine eye for colors and effects. He disregarded the *decora* of mere fashion. His plans were bold and fiery, and his conceptions glowed with barbaric lustre. There are some who would have thought him mad. His followers felt that he was not. It was necessary to hear and see and touch him to be sure that he was not.

He had directed, in great part, the moveable embellishments of the seven chambers, upon occasion of this great fête; and it was his own guiding taste which had given character to the masqueraders. Be sure they were grotesque. There were much glare and glitter and piquancy and phantasm—much of what has been since seen in "Hernani." There were arabesque figures with unsuited limbs and appointments. There were delirious fancies such as the madman fashions. There was much of the beautiful, much of the wanton, much of the *bizarre*, something of the terrible, and not a little of that which might have excited disgust. To and fro in the seven chambers there stalked, in fact, a multitude of dreams. And these—the dreams—writhed in and about, taking hue from the rooms, and causing the wild music of the orchestra to seem as the echo of their steps. And, anon, there strikes the ebony clock which stands in the hall of the velvet. And then, for a moment, all is still, and all is silent save the voice of the clock. The dreams are stiff-frozen as they stand. But the echoes of the chime die away—they have endured but an instant—and a light, half-subdued laughter floats after them as they depart. And now again the music swells, and the dreams live, and writhe to and fro more merrily than ever, taking hue from the many-tinted windows through which stream the rays from the tripods. But to the chamber which lies most westwardly of the seven, there are now none of the maskers who venture; for the night is waning away; and there flows a ruddier light through the blood-colored panes; and the blackness of the sable drapery appals; and to him whose foot falls upon the sable carpet, there comes from the near clock of ebony a muffled peal more solemnly emphatic than any which reaches *their* ears who indulge in the more remote gaieties of the other apartments.

But these other apartments were densely crowded, and in them beat feverishly the heart of life. And the revel went whirlingly on, until at length there commenced the sounding of midnight upon the clock. And then the music ceased, as I have told; and the evolutions of the waltzers were quieted; and there was an uneasy cessation of all things as before. But now there were twelve strokes to be sounded by the bell of the clock; and thus it happened, perhaps, that more of thought crept, with more of time, into the meditations of the thoughtful among those who revelled. And thus, too, it happened, perhaps, that before the last echoes of the last chime had utterly sunk into silence, there were many individuals in the crowd who had found leisure to become aware of the presence of a masked figure which had arrested the attention of no single individual before. And the rumor of this new presence having spread itself whisperingly around, there arose at length from the whole company a buzz, or murmur, expressive of disapprobation and surprise—then, finally, of terror, of horror, and of disgust.

In an assembly of phantasms such as I have painted, it may well be supposed that no ordinary appearance could have excited such sensation. In truth the masquerade license of the night was nearly unlimited; but the figure in question had out-Heroded Herod, and gone beyond the bounds of even the prince's indefinite decorum. There are chords in the hearts of the most reckless which cannot be touched without emotion. Even with the utterly lost, to whom life and death are equally jests, there are matters of which no jest can be made. The whole company, indeed, seemed now deeply to feel that in the costume and bearing of the stranger neither wit nor propriety existed. The figure was tall and gaunt, and shrouded from head to foot in the habiliments of the grave. The mask which concealed the visage was made so nearly to resemble the countenance of a stiffened corpse that the closest scrutiny must have had difficulty in detecting the cheat. And yet all this might have been endured, if not approved, by the mad revellers around. But the mummer had gone so far as to assume the type of the Red Death. His vesture was dabbled in blood—and his broad brow, with all the features of the face, was besprinkled with the scarlet horror.

When the eyes of Prince Prospero fell upon this spectral image (which with a slow and solemn movement, as if more fully to sustain its *role*, stalked to and fro among the waltzers) he was seen to be convulsed, in the first moment with a strong shudder either of terror or distaste; but, in the next, his brow reddened with rage.

"Who dares?" he demanded hoarsely of the courtiers who stood near him—"who dares insult us with this blasphemous mockery? Seize him and unmask him—that we may know whom we have to hang at sunrise, from the battlements!"

It was in the eastern or blue chamber in which stood the Prince Prospero as he uttered these words. They rang throughout the seven rooms loudly and clearly—for the prince was a bold and robust man, and the music had become hushed at the waving of his hand.

It was in the blue room where stood the prince, with a group of pale courtiers by his side. At first, as he spoke, there was a slight rushing movement of this group in the direction of the intruder, who at the moment was also near at hand, and now, with deliberate and stately step, made closer approach to the speaker. But from a certain nameless awe with which the mad assumptions of the mummer had inspired the whole party, there were found none who put forth hand to seize him; so that, unimpeded, he passed within a yard of the prince's person; and, while the vast assembly, as if with one impulse, shrank from the centres of the rooms to the walls, he made his way uninterruptedly, but with the same solemn and measured step which had distinguished him from the first, through the blue chamber to the purple—through the purple to the green—through the green to the orange—through this again to the white—and even thence to the violet, ere a decided movement had been made to arrest him. It was then, however, that the Prince Prospero, maddening with rage and the shame of his own momentary cowardice, rushed hurriedly through the six chambers, while none followed him on account of a deadly terror that had seized upon all. He bore aloft a drawn dagger, and had approached, in rapid impetuosity, to within three or four feet of the retreating figure, when the latter, having attained the extremity of the velvet apartment, turned suddenly and confronted his pursuer. There was a sharp cry—and the dagger dropped gleaming upon the sable carpet, upon which, instantly afterwards, fell prostrate in death the Prince Prospero. Then, summoning the wild courage of despair, a throng of the revellers at once threw themselves into the black apartment, and, seizing the mummer, whose tall figure stood erect and motionless within the shadow of the ebony clock, gasped in unutterable horror at finding the grave-cerements and corpse-like mask which they handled with so violent a rudeness, untenanted by any tangible form.

And now was acknowledged the presence of the Red Death. He had come like a thief in the night. And one by one dropped the revellers in the blood-bedewed halls of their revel, and died each in the despairing posture of his fall. And the life of the ebony clock went out with that of the last of the gay. And the flames of the tripods expired. And Darkness and Decay and the Red Death held illimitable dominion over all.

17

THE HALL OF THE DEAD
A Strange Tale

Francis D. Grierson

"You have good nerves?" asked Professor Julius March, with a somewhat cynical smile.

Annette Grey shrugged her shoulders.

"People who work for their living," she replied, "cannot afford nerves."

The Professor nodded.

"There is something in that," he answered, thoughtfully. "At the same time, I must make the position clear to you. As you are aware, I am an Egyptologist, and in my house here I have many queer things. Some people dislike the idea of working among mummies and——"

Annette interrupted him with a deprecating gesture.

"Believe me," she said, "that sort of thing does not affect me in the least. As your secretary, I am prepared to work where and when you like."

"My former secretary—" the professor began, and paused.

"Your former secretary disappeared," said the girl. "Of course I know that; you will remember that I applied for the vacancy after reading about her in the paper. I do not propose to disappear; the terms you offer are too good."

She smiled faintly, and the Egyptologist shrewdly eyed her.

"Well," he said at last, "your qualifications and education appear to recommend you for the work I should want you to do. It is secretarial work in the broadest sense of the term—from typing my notes (when you have learned to decipher my abominably bad handwriting) to looking up references in the British Museum, or—should occasion arise—accompanying me on a flying visit to Egypt. I give you fair warning that I shall work you hard, but, apart from the salary and board, which I have already named, you will not find me ungenerous if you prove yourself valuable."

"Then I may consider myself engaged?"

March bowed.

"Certainly," he replied. "You will probably learn presently," he added, in his cynical way, "that I am regarded as an eccentric person, and somewhat of a hard taskmaster—"

"I prefer to form my own opinion," said Annette quietly.

Again he smiled. It was not a pleasant smile.

So Annette Grey took up her residence in the rambling old house on the outskirts of London in which Professor Julius March had gradually accumulated relics of ancient Egypt that were regarded with respect by the curators of some of the greatest museums in the world.

There were those who hinted that the Professor had not always been scrupulous in the methods he adopted to secure his rarer curios; but March laughed at such stories when anyone had the hardihood to repeat them to him, openly attributing them to the jealousy of less fortunate rivals. Wealthy and profoundly learned, he had become known as one of the greatest Egyptologists of his day.

Annette studied her new employer with the patience characteristic of her nature, and she found the study an interesting as well as a useful one. March, for the most part, was reserved and silent, but he was capable of bursts of extraordinary excitement. He devoted himself, with an almost religious fervor, to the pursuit which he had made his life study, and the few friends he possessed—for he was not a popular man—were almost all brother archeologists.

Tall and thin, with black eyes peering through large tortoise-shell-rimmed spectacles, his gray hair tumbled in a shaggy mass over his broad forehead, he had a habit of thrusting his square chin aggressively forward when he spoke. His long, graceful fingers moved in nervous sympathy with what he was saying, and he would spring from his chair and walk rapidly up and down with catlike steps that reminded Annette of a panther ceaselessly pacing to and fro behind the bars of its cage.

Possessed of great endurance, he would sit for hours at a stretch poring over an ancient papyrus, disdaining food and sleep. Then, plunging into a cold bath, he would emerge glowing, eat an enormous meal and set off for a long walk, indifferent as to whether it happened to be day or the middle of the night.

When March first asked her whether or not she had good nerves, Annette had supposed him to be referring to the disappearance of Beatrice Vane, his former assistant. Beatrice, a beautiful girl just budding into the maturity of womanhood, had vanished utterly, leaving her clothes and other possessions behind her, but no clue as to where she had gone. March, with his lawyer, Henry Sturges, had sought the assistance of the police, and every effort had been made to trace the missing girl, but without success.

Attorney Sturges, who had recommended Beatrice Vane to Professor March, had been the girl's guardian. An orphan, she had been left a small annual income, the capital of which was under Sturges' control as trustee. She had received a good education, and the lawyer had procured her employment with Julius March in order that she might occupy her time and at the same time supplement the scanty income which declining financial conditions had left her.

March spoke highly of her work, and was more affected by

her disappearance than many, who saw only the cynicism of the man, would have believed. He feared, Annette supposed, that his new secretary would think it unlucky to step into the shoes of the girl who had vanished so mysteriously, and she hastened to disabuse his mind of any such idea.

But Annette soon found that there existed an additional reason for his question. The old house, she found, was divided into two parts. In one, the smaller of the two, lived March and his staff. A bachelor, he was looked after by an elderly housekeeper, one or two maids, a chauffeur and a confidential valet, who had been with him for years. These people attended to what he called the "domesticities" of the place.

The larger part of the house was consecrated to his hobby, and had been, indeed, altered and partially reconstructed to suit his unusual requirements. Into this Egypt in miniature the servants were sternly forbidden to penetrate. There March would bury himself amid his mummies and papyri, and sometimes, in his morose moods, even his secretary was forbidden access.

Annette had a comfortably-furnished sitting-room of her own, and a little room furnished as an office, but a great part of her work, she found, was to be done in the room which March grimly called the "Hall of the Dead."

It was, indeed, an apartment in which only a girl of strong nerves could have worked without glancing fearfully over her shoulder. Floored with black-and-white marble, alternated in a curious pattern, it was dimly lit by a lamp swung from the roof by bronze chains. To afford the stronger light necessary for the study of ancient inscriptions, a smaller lamp stood on each of two small tables, the incongruous effect of their electric wiring being mitigated by their antique shape. These lamps, however, illuminated only their immediate neighborhood, leaving the greater part of the huge room in semi-obscurity.

Round the room were placed at regular intervals mummies

and mummy-cases, whose grave immobility seemed but a mask which they could tear off at will, descending to move about the hall with measured steps and to converse on topics that had been of living importance to a long-dead civilization.

In the center of the hall stood a great stone table, curiously grooved and hollowed, and between the mummies were placed objects of metal and earthenware, the uses of which Annette could only guess.

In this strange room March would pass hour after hour. Annette soon learned to understand and accommodate herself to his methods. The sharp sound of an electric bell in her room would bring her to the Hall of the Dead, notebook and pencil in hand. The heavy door, controlled by an automatic mechanism, would roll back as she approached, closing silently behind her as she entered and took her seat, without a word, at one of the smaller tables.

Acknowledging her presence only by a gesture, March would stride up and down the room with his quick tread, pausing now and again to examine a document or to apply a magnifying glass to the inscription on a mummy-case, muttering to himself as he resumed his rapid pacing. Suddenly, without warning, he would commence to dictate, in sharp, staccato sentences, admirably lucid and without a superfluous word.

He would cease as suddenly as he had begun, and for perhaps half an hour, or longer, he would remain buried in thought, resuming his dictation as unexpectedly as he had ceased, but without ever losing the sequence of his ideas.

Sometimes this would go on for hours. On such occasions he would recollect himself suddenly, glance at the ancient water-clock on its carved pedestal, and dismiss Annette with a word of apology for his forgetfulness.

Once an incident occurred which revealed yet another side of this man's complex character.

Annette had received a lengthy piece of dictation, and had been at work in her office for nearly an hour, transcribing her notes. She was a competent writer of shorthand, but some of the technical expressions which March used were quite unfamiliar, and she did not care to interrupt him, preferring to wait until he had finished before asking him any questions. On this occasion it had seemed fairly plain sailing, but toward the end of her notes she came across a sign the significance of which completely baffled her.

Finding that the context was of no assistance, and not wishing to delay the work, which she knew the Professor required as quickly as possible, she resolved to consult him.

It was the first time she had visited the Hall of the Dead unbidden, and she was uncertain how to attract his attention from outside, for there was no knocker or bell on the great door. The mechanism which controlled it, however, either did not depend on the person inside, or could be so set as to work independently, for as she reached the threshold some concealed spring was put into operation and the door opened before her as usual. Still standing on the threshold, she was about to enter, when she stopped as though turned into stone.

Inside the hall she saw Julius March kneeling before one of the mummy-cases—the mummy-case of a woman. His head rested against the knees of the image, and his body was shaken by great sobs.

Amazed, moved by the strange sight, Annette turned and fled to her own room. Behind her the door of the Hall of the Dead swung noiselessly into its frame.

A week later, Annette entered the little-used drawing-room of Professor March's house shortly before seven o'clock in the evening, and sat down near the bright fire ready to receive his guests. For March was giving one of his rare dinner-parties.

A few moments later the door opened, and the servant

ushered in Attorney Sturges and a friend of his, a pleasant, rather simple-looking man named Sims.

"I fear we are a little early, Miss Grey," said Sturges, when he had presented his friend.

"Not at all," Annette replied easily. "Professor March asked me to make his excuses to you; he was detained at the British Museum and only arrived a few minutes ago. He is dressing, and will be down in a few minutes. Meanwhile, I must play hostess."

"And most adequately," murmured Sturges, with old-fashioned courtesy.

Then, as the door closed behind the servant, he spoke rapidly:

"We came a little early on purpose," he explained. "You are prepared, Miss Vane?"

"Quite," said the girl calmly.

"Good. Inspector Sims agrees with me that if we are ever to discover the mystery of your sister's disappearance, it will be tonight. Sims has been practising his part, and does it admirably."

The Scotland Yard man smiled.

"I think I can play it," he said. "And I congratulate you, Miss Vane, on the way you have handled the matter. This idea is an excellent one, and I admit I should never have thought of it myself. I hope, too," he went on, without the slightest alteration in his tone, as a step sounded outside and the door opened, "that Professor March will not deny me a peep at the wonderful treasures he keeps here."

"Why, of course not," cried March heartily, as he entered the room. "I caught your last words, Mr. Sims," he went on, "—for I am sure you are Sturges' psychic friend—and I shall be delighted to show you round my little museum. Well, Sturges, I must apologize to you both for keeping you waiting like this; but you have been in good hands."

He bowed courteously to Annette.

"It is very good of you, Mr. Sims," he went on, "to come

and visit a recluse like this. Sturges has told me of your powers of necromancy, and I confess I am hoping to see something very wonderful."

The words were polite and were uttered with perfect civility, but the old lawyer laughed gently.

"It's no good, March," he said; "you cannot quite get the true ring. You scientific fellows always scoff at the unseen, and decline to believe anything that cannot be set down in writing, like an algebraic equation."

"Not at all," replied the Professor, with sudden gravity. "On the contrary, my researches have convinced me that there are mysteries to which, if we only had the clue—but we'll talk of that later," he added, with a sudden change of tone. "My first duty, as your host, is to feed you; come and help me perform the sacred rite of hospitality."

Laughing, he opened the door and bowed Annette to the head of the little procession to the dining-room, where they were presently seated round a candle-lit table of richly-polished mahogany.

It was a strange dinner-party, at which two, at least, of the diners found it difficult to appreciate the sallies of the host. Mr. Sims, however, expanded under the influence of the Professor's geniality. March was in unusually high spirits, for he had just succeeded in translating a hieroglyphic inscription which had defeated the Museum authorities, and he devoted himself to the sport of drawing out his psychic guest with a delicate irony which, to do him justice, never passed the bounds of good taste.

The innocent Mr. Sims responded to this subtle flattery with a readiness which delighted the Professor, and even Annette and the lawyer could not refrain from smiling at the naïveté with which Sims played his part.

At last the dinner drew to a close, and March rose.

"I am not going to let you off, Mr. Sims," he said. "I am eager to learn something of the methods of the modern spiritualists, for I admit I am more familiar with those of the past. But I think we ought to have a more suitable atmosphere for the *seance*," he added, chuckling. "Miss Grey, I hope you will not leave us? I think my Egyptian room would form an admirable background for Mr. Sims' experiments."

Annette smiled, with something of an effort, and led the way to the Hall of the Dead.

Despite himself, Sims could not repress an exclamation of awe at the sight of the great, gloomy room, with its solemn figures and mysterious shadows.

The Professor rubbed his hands, well pleased at the effect he had produced.

"Now, Mr. Sims," he said, "here is a carved chair on which a Pharaoh once sat. Enthrone yourself there. We will sit, metaphorically, at your feet, and listen to what you are pleased to tell us."

Sims bowed, but did not return the Professor's smile. Gravely he seated himself in the heavy wooden chair, rested his elbow on one of the quaintly-carved arms, and let his head sink onto his hand. The others grouped themselves near and waited, in a heavy silence.

Sensitive to impressions, the Professor's gay mood faded gradually into a tense expectancy that made his long fingers work nervously. He startled as Sims' voice broke the silence sharply.

"I am aware, Professor March," said Sims in a hard, level tone that startled his hearers, "that you are a skeptic."

The Professor murmured something, but Sims went on, without heeding him.

"I feel tonight that I am going to prove to you that I can see things that are hidden..."

He paused, and again the silence was broken only by the sound of heavy breathing. As suddenly as before, Sims spoke again:

"Listen!" he said. "I see a great room, half lit by a lamp in the roof. There is a brighter light near a table in the center of the room. It is a stone table, such as was used in ancient Egypt by the embalmers."

The Professor drew in his breath with a sharp gasp, but the voice went steadily on:

"Beside the table I see a man. He is bending over something—something white. It is the body of a woman—"

"*Stop*, damn you!" screamed the Professor; and Sims, springing from his chair, took something from the pocket of his dinner-jacket.

The Professor laughed discordantly—the laugh of a madman.

"Put up your pistol," he cried. "You will not need it. I don't know who you are, and, damn you, I don't care! Do you hear that? *I don't care!* Listen, all of you; listen, I say! Today I have completed my task; I have learned the secret which I have sought so patiently. I am going to join my Princess, my Hora."

He ceased, and threw his arms out in a great gesture to the mummy-case in front of which he had been standing. Huge drops of sweat stood out on his forehead, and he tore open his linen collar with a madman's strength. But it was in a controlled, almost tender voice that he went on:

"Listen to me, and I will tell you a wonderful thing. Countless years ago I—I who speak to you here tonight—was a priest in Egypt. I was vowed to the service of Isis. But one day there came to the temple, where I ministered, a woman. A woman? Nay, a goddess! A being of such beauty that my heart leaped within me at the sight of her loveliness.

"She was the Princess Hora. We loved. Ten thousand words could say no more. But an evil fate tore her from me; the Pharaoh had seen her, and coveted her. Sooner than lie in his foul embrace she plunged a dagger into her white bosom..."

He paused, and for a few moments covered his face with his

hands, his shoulders quivering. Then he tore his hands away and stretched them once more toward the painted image that looked so calmly down at him.

"Hora, my Hora!" he cried passionately. "I have sought thee for centuries, through age after age. And now, at last thou hast come to me—and gone again. But only for a little while, a few brief moments, for I follow thee tonight."

Again he paused, and again he resumed, mastering his emotion:

"She came to me here, here in this house, where I have labored so long, striving to regain my knowledge of that past which is sometimes so clear, and sometimes, O Isis, so terribly dark! She came to me, my beautiful Hora; came clad in the garb of today, bearing the name of Beatrice."

A low sob broke from Annette, but he went on, unheeding:

"I told you, Hora, I *tried* to tell you—but your eyes were filmed by the gods. You could not understand... You spurned me. Then it was that I understood that for us there could be only one way. One touch of this little knife, steeped in a poison so deadly that your soul had flown ere your body had fallen into my arms.

"Tenderly I bathed you and poured into your veins the secret essences that keep the flesh firm and fair as in life, and bore you to the tomb where you sit, waiting for me. But in another world, Hora, you wait for me, a thousand times more beautiful, and knowing that I, your lover, have sought you and found you at last. Hora, *I come!*"

With a wild cry, he raised the little dagger which he had drawn from his pocket. Sims sprang forward, but before he could reach him Professor Julius March had buried it in his heart. Hardly had the blade touched his flesh than he swayed, stumbled and crashed down at the feet of the mummy-case.

For a moment the others gazed at the prostrate form. Then Inspector Sims sprang forward and fumbled with trembling fingers at the fastenings of the mummy-case. Suddenly the front fell forward, and Annette uttered a terrible cry.

In the case, thus revealed, sat the girl who had been Beatrice Vane. She was nude, the chaste beauty of her lovely form standing out against the dark interior of the case. So wonderfully had the madman done his work that no scar marred the grace of the firm bosom, the long, rounded limbs, the head set proudly on the ivory neck. She sat as might have sat the Princess Hora, had she so wished, beside the Pharaoh himself on his Egyptian throne.

Sims drew back and bowed his head reverently as Annette, stumbling forward, laid her head on her dead sister's knees in a grief too terrible for tears.

18

THE GRAVE
A Story of Stark Terror

Orville R. Emerson

The end of this story was first brought to my attention when Fromwiller returned from his trip to Mount Kemmel, with a very strange tale indeed and one extremely hard to believe.

But I believed it enough to go back to the Mount with "From" to see if we could discover anything more. And after digging for awhile at the place where "From's" story began, we made our way into an old dugout that had been caved in, or at least where all the entrances had been filled with dirt, and there we found, written on German correspondence paper, a terrible story.

We found the story on Christmas day, 1918, while making the trip in the colonel's machine from Watou, in Flanders, where our regiment was stationed. Of course, you have heard of Mount Kemmel in Flanders: more than once it figured in newspaper reports as it changed hands during some of the fiercest fighting of the war. And when the Germans were finally driven from this point of vantage, in October, 1918, a retreat was started which did not end until it became a race to see who could get into Germany first.

The advance was so fast that the victorious British and French forces had no time to bury their dead; and, terrible as it may seem to those who have not seen it, in December of that year one could see the rotting corpses of the unburied dead scattered here and there over the top of Mount Kemmel. It was a place of ghastly sights and sickening odors. And it was there that we found this tale.

With the chaplain's help, we translated the story, which follows:

"For two weeks I have been buried alive! For two weeks I have not seen daylight, nor heard the sound of another person's voice. Unless I can find something to do, besides this everlasting digging, I shall go mad. So I shall write. As long as my candles last, I will pass part of the time each day in setting down on paper my experiences.

"Not that I need to do this in order to remember them. God knows that when I get out the first thing I shall do will be to try to forget them! But if I should *not* get out!...

"I am an Ober-lieutenant in the Imperial German Army. Two weeks ago my regiment was holding Mount Kemmel in Flanders. We were surrounded on three sides and subjected to a terrific artillery fire, but on account of the commanding position we were ordered to hold the Mount to the last man. Our engineers, however, had made things very comfortable. Numerous deep dugouts had been constructed, and in them we were comparatively safe from shell-fire.

"Many of these had been connected by passageways so that there was a regular little underground city, and the majority of the garrison never left the protection of the dugouts. But even under these conditions our casualties were heavy. Lookouts had to be maintained above ground, and once in a while a direct hit by one of the huge railway guns would even destroy some of the dugouts.

"A little over two weeks ago—I can't be sure, because I have lost track of the exact number of days—the usual shelling was increased a hundred fold. With about twenty others, I was sleeping in one of the shallower dugouts. The tremendous increase in shelling awakened me with a start, and my first impulse was to go at once into a deeper dugout, which was connected to the one I was in by an underground passageway.

"It was a smaller dugout, built a few feet lower than the one I was in. It had been used as a sort of a storeroom and no one was supposed to sleep there. But it seemed safer to me, and, alone, I crept into it. A thousand times since I have wished I had taken another man with me. But my chances for doing it were soon gone.

"I had hardly entered the smaller dugout when there was a tremendous explosion behind me. The ground shook as if a mine had exploded below us. Whether that was indeed the case, or whether some extra large caliber explosive shell had struck the dugout behind me, I never knew.

"After the shock of the explosion had passed I went back to the passageway. When about half-way along it, I found the timbers above had fallen, allowing the earth to settle, and my way was effectually blocked.

"So I returned to the dugout and waited alone through several hours of terrific shelling. The only other entrance to the dugout I was in was the main entrance from the trench above, and all those who had been above ground had gone into dugouts long before this. So I could not expect anyone to enter while the shelling continued; and when it ceased there would surely be an attack.

"As I did not want to be killed by a grenade thrown down the entrance; I remained awake in order to rush out at the first signs of cessation of the bombardment and join what comrades there might be left on the hill.

"After about six hours of the heavy bombardment, all sound above ground seemed to cease. Five minutes went by, then ten; surely the attack was coming. I rushed to the stairway leading out to the air. I took a couple of strides up the stairs. There was a blinding flash and a deafening explosion.

"I felt myself falling. Then darkness swallowed everything."

"How long I lay unconscious in the dugout I never knew.

"But after what seemed like a long time, I practically grew conscious of a dull ache in my left arm. I could not move it. I opened my eyes and found only darkness. I felt pain and a stiffness all over my body.

"Slowly I rose, struck a match, found a candle and lit it and looked at my watch. It had stopped. I did not know how long I had remained there unconscious. All noise of bombardment had ceased. I stood and listened for some time, but could hear no sound of any kind.

"My gaze fell on the stairway entrance. I started in alarm. The end of the dugout, where the entrance was, was half filled with dirt.

"I went over and looked closer. The entrance was completely filled with dirt at the bottom, and no light of any kind could be seen from above. I went to the passageway to the other dugout, although I remembered it had caved in. I examined the fallen timbers closely. Between two of them I could feel a slight movement of air. Here was an opening to the outside world.

"I tried to move the timbers, as well as I could with one arm, only to precipitate a small avalanche of dirt which filled the crack. Quickly I dug at the dirt until again I could feel the movement of air. This might be the only place where I could obtain fresh air.

"I was convinced that it would take some little work to open up either of the passageways, and I began to feel hungry. Luckily, there was a good supply of canned foods and hard bread, for the officers had kept their rations stored in this dugout. I also found a keg of water and about a dozen bottles of wine, which I discovered to be very good. After I had relieved my appetite and finished one of the bottles of wine, I felt sleepy and, although my left arm pained me considerably, I soon dropped off to sleep.

"The time I have allowed myself for writing is up, so I will stop for today. After I have performed my daily task of digging tomorrow, I shall again write. Already my mind feels easier. Surely help will come soon. At any rate, within two more weeks I shall have liberated myself. Already I am half way up the stairs. And my rations will last that long. I have divided them so they will."

"Yesterday I did not feel like writing after I finished my digging. My arm pained me considerably. I guess I used it too much.

"But today I was more careful with it, and it feels better. And I am worried again. Twice today big piles of earth caved in, where the timbers above were loose, and each time as much dirt fell into the passageway as I can remove in a day. Two days more before I can count on getting out by myself.

"The rations will have to be stretched out some more. The daily amount is already pretty small. But I shall go on with my account.

"From the time I became conscious I started my watch, and since then I have kept track of the days. On the second day I took stock of the food, water, wood, matches, candles, etc., and found a plentiful supply for two weeks at least. At that time I did not look forward to a stay of more than a few days in my prison.

"Either the enemy or ourselves will occupy the hill I told myself, because it is such an important position. And whoever now holds the hill will be compelled to dig in deeply in order to hold it.

"So to my mind it was only a matter of a few days until either the entrance or the passageway would be cleared, and my only doubts were as to whether it would be friends or enemies that would discover me. My arm felt better, although I could not use it much, and so I spent the day in reading an old newspaper which I found among the food supplies, and in waiting for help to come. What fool I was! If I had only worked from the start, I would be just that many days nearer deliverance.

"On the third day I was annoyed by water, which began dripping from the roof and seeping in at the sides of the dugout. I cursed that muddy water, then, as I have often cursed such dugout nuisances before, but it may be that I shall yet bless that water and it shall save my life.

"But it certainly made things uncomfortable; so I spent the day in moving my bunk, food and water supplies, candles, etc., up into the passageway. For a space of about ten feet it was unobstructed, and, being slightly higher than the dugout, was dryer and more comfortable. Besides, the air was much better here, as I had found that practically all my supply of fresh air came in through the crack between the timbers, and I thought maybe the rats wouldn't bother me so much at night. Again I spent the balance of the day simply in waiting for help.

"It was not until well into the fourth day that I really began to feel uneasy. It suddenly became impressed on my consciousness that I had not heard the sound of a gun, or felt the earth shake from the force of a concussion, since the fatal shell that had filled the entrance. What was the meaning of the silence? Why did I hear no sounds of fighting? It was as still as the grave.

"What a horrible death to die! Buried Alive! A panic of fear swept over me. But my will and reason reasserted itself. In time, I should be able to dig myself out by my own efforts. It would take time but it could be done.

"So, although I could not use my left arm as yet, I spent the rest of that day and all of the two following days in digging dirt from the entrance and carrying it back into the far corner of the dugout.

"On the seventh day after regaining consciousness I was tired and stiff from my unwanted exertions of the three previous days. I could see by this time that it was a matter of weeks—two or three, at least—before I could hope to liberate myself. I might be rescued at an earlier date, but, without outside aid, it would take probably three more weeks of labor before I could dig my way out.

"Already dirt had caved in from the top, where the timbers had sprung apart, and I could repair the damage to the roof of the stairway only in a crude way with one arm. But my left arm was much better. With a day's rest, I would be able to use it pretty well. Besides, I must conserve my energy. So I spent the seventh day in rest and prayer for my speedy release from a living grave.

"I also reapportioned my food on the basis of three more weeks. It made the daily portions pretty small, especially as the digging was strenuous work. There was a large supply of candles, so that I had plenty of light for my work. But the supply of water bothered me. Almost half of the small keg was gone in the first week. I decided to drink only once a day.

"The following six days were all days of feverish labor, light eating and even lighter drinking. But, despite all my efforts, only a quarter of the keg was left at the end of two weeks. And the horror of the situation grew on me. My imagination would not be quiet. I would picture to myself the agonies to come, when I would have even less food and water than at present. My mind would run on and on—to death by starvation—to the finding of my emaciated body by those who would eventually open up the dugout—even to their attempts to reconstruct the story of my end.

"And, adding to my physical discomfort, were the swarming vermin infesting the dugout and my person. A month had gone by since I had had a bath, and I could not now spare a drop of water even to wash my face. The rats had become so bold that I had to leave a candle burning all night in order to protect myself in my sleep.

"Partly to relieve my mind, I started to write this tale of my experiences. It did act as a relief at first, but now, as I read it over, the growing terror of this awful place grips me. I would cease writing, but some impulse urges me to write each day."

"Three weeks have passed since I was buried in this living tomb.

"Today I drank the last drop of water in the keg. There is a pool of stagnant water on the dugout floor—dirty, slimy and alive with vermin—always standing there, fed by drippings from the roof. As yet I cannot bring myself to touch it.

"Today I divided up my food supply for another week. God knows the portions were already small enough! But there have been so many cave-ins recently that I can never finish clearing the entrance in another week.

"Sometimes I feel that I shall never clear it. But I *must*! I can never bear to die here. I must will myself to escape, and *I shall escape*!

"Did not the captain often say that the will to win was half the victory? I shall rest no more. Every waking hour must be spent in removing the treacherous dirt.

"Even my writing must cease."

"Oh, god! I am afraid, *afraid*!

"I must write to relieve my mind. Last night I went to sleep at nine by my watch. At twelve I woke to find myself in the dark, frantically digging with my bare hands at the hard sides of the dugout. After some trouble I found a candle and lit it.

"The whole dugout was upset. My food supplies were lying in the mud. The box of candles had been spilled. My finger nails were broken and bloody from clawing at the ground.

"The realization dawned upon me that I had been out of my head. And then came the fear—dark, raging fear—fear of insanity. I have been drinking the stagnant water from the floor for days. I do not know how many.

"I have only about one meal left, but I must save it."

"I had a meal today. For three days I have been without food.

"But today I caught one of the rats that infest the place. He was a big one, too. Gave me a bad bite, but I killed him. I feel lots better today. Have had some bad dreams lately, but they don't bother me now.

"That rat was tough, though. Think I'll finish this digging and go back to my regiment in a day or two."

"Heaven have mercy! I must be out of my head half the time now.

"I have absolutely no recollection of having written that last entry. And I feel feverish and weak.

"If I had my strength, I think I could finish clearing the entrance in a day or two. But I can only work a short time at a stretch.

"I am beginning to give up hope."

"Wild spells come on me oftener now. I awake tired out from exertions, which I cannot remember.

"Bones of rats, picked clean, are scattered about, yet I do not remember eating them. In my lucid moments I don't seem to be able to catch them, for they are too wary and I am too weak.

"I get some relief by chewing the candles, but I dare not eat them all. I am afraid of the dark, I am afraid of the rats, but worst of all is the hideous fear of myself.

"My mind is breaking down. I must escape soon, or I will be little better than a wild animal. Oh, God, send help! I am going mad!"

"Terror, desperation, despair—is this the end?"

"For a long time I have been resting.

"I have had a brilliant idea. Rest brings back strength. The longer a person rests the stronger they should get. I have been resting a long time now. Weeks or months, I don't know which. So I must be very strong. I feel strong. My fever has left me. So listen! There is only a little dirt left in the entrance way. I am going out and crawl through it. Just like a mole. Right out into the sunlight. I feel much stronger than a mole. So this is the end of my little tale. A sad tale, but one with a happy ending. Sunlight! A very happy ending."

And that was the end of the manuscript. There only remains to tell Fromwiller's tale.

At first, I didn't believe it. But now I do. I put it down, though, just as Fromwiller told it to me, and you can take it or leave it as you choose.

"Soon after we were billeted at Watou," said Fromwiller, "I decided to go out and see Mount Kemmel. I had heard that things were rather gruesome out there, but I was really not prepared for the conditions that I found. I had seen unburied dead around Roulers and in the Argonne, but it had been almost two months since the fighting on Mount Kemmel and there were still many unburied dead. But there was another thing that I had never seen, and that was the *buried living*!

"As I came up to the highest point of the Mount, I was attracted by a movement of loose dirt on the edge of a huge shell hole. The dirt seemed to be falling in to a common center, as if the dirt below was being removed. As I watched, suddenly I was horrified to see a long, skinny human arm emerge from the ground.

"It disappeared, drawing back some of the earth with it. There was a movement of dirt over a larger area, and the arm reappeared, together with a man's head and shoulders. He pulled himself up out of the very ground, as it seemed, shook the dirt from his body like a huge, gaunt dog, and stood erect. I never want to see such another creature!

"Hardly a strip of clothing was visible, and, what little there was, was so torn and dirty that it was impossible to tell what kind it had been. The skin was drawn tightly over the bones, and there was a vacant stare in the protruding eyes. It looked like a corpse that had lain in the grave a long time.

"This apparition looked directly at me, and yet did not appear to see me. He looked as if the light bothered him. I spoke, and a look of fear came over his face. He seemed filled with terror.

"I stepped toward him, shaking loose a piece of barbed wire which had caught in my puttees. Quick as a flash, he turned and started to run from me.

"For a second I was too astonished to move. Then I started to follow him. In a straight line he ran, looking neither to the right or left. Directly ahead of him was a deep and wide trench. He was running straight toward it. Suddenly it dawned on me that he did not see it.

"I called out, but it seemed to terrify him all the more, and with one last lunge he stepped into the trench and fell. I heard his body strike the other side of the trench and fell with a splash into the water at the bottom.

"I followed and looked down into the trench. There he lay, with his head bent back in such a position that I was sure his neck was broken. He was half in and half out of the water, and as I looked at him I could scarcely believe what I had seen. Surely he looked as if he had been dead as long as some of the other corpses, scattered over the hillside. I turned and left him as he was.

"Buried while living, I left him unburied when dead."

19

THE GHOUL AND THE CORPSE

G.A. Wells

This is Chris Bonner's tale, not mine. Please remember that. I positively will not stand sponsor for it. I used to have a deal of faith in Chris Bonner's veracity, but that is a thing of the past. He is a liar; a liar without conscience. I as good as told him so to his face. I wonder what kind of fool he thinks I am!

Attend, now, and you shall hear that remarkable tale he told me. It was, and is, a lie. I shall always think so.

He came marching into my igloo up there at Aurora Bay. That is in Alaska, you know, on the Arctic sea. I had been in the back-country trading for pelts for a New York concern, and due to bad luck I didn't reach the coast until the third day after the last steamer out had gone. And there I was marooned for the winter, without chance of getting out until spring, with a few dozen ignorant Indians for companions. Thank heaven I had plenty of white man's grub in tins!

As I said, here came Chris Bonner marching in on me the same as you would go down the block a few doors to call on a neighbor.

"And where the devil did you drop in from?" I demanded, helping him off with his stiff parka.

"Down there," he answered, jerking an elbow toward the south. "Let's have something to eat, MacNeal. I'm hungry as hell. Look at the pack, will you!"

I had already looked at the pack he had cast off his shoulders to the fur-covered floor of the igloo. It was as lean as a starved hound. I heated a can of beef bouillon and some beans, and made a pot of coffee over the blubber-fat fire that served for both heat and light, and put these and some crackers before my guest. He tore into his meal wolfishly.

"Now a pipe and some tobac, MacNeal," he ordered, pushing the empty dishes aside.

I gave him one of my pipes and my tobacco-pouch. He filled and lighted up. He seemed to relish the smoke; I imagined he hadn't had one for some time. He sat silent for a while staring into the flickering flame.

"Say, MacNeal," he spoke at length; "what do you know about a theory that says once on a time this old world of ours revolved on its axis in a different plane? I've heard it said the earth tipped up about seventy degrees. What d'you know about it?"

That was a queer thing for Chris Bonner to ask. He was simon-pure prospector and I had never known him to get far away from the subject of mining and prospecting. He had been hunting gold from Panama to the Arctic Circle for the past thirty years.

"No more than you do, probably," I answered his question. "I've heard of that theory, too. I'd say it is any man's guess."

"This theory holds that the North Pole used to be where the Equator is now," he said. "Do you believe that?"

"I don't know anything about it, Chris," I replied. "But I do know that they have found things up this way that are now generally recognized as being peculiarly tropical in nature."

"What, for instance?"

"Palms and ferns, a species of parrot, saber-tooth tigers; and also mastodons, members of the elephant family. All fossils and parts of skeletons, you understand."

"No human beings, MacNeal? Any skeletons or fossils of those up this way?"

"Never heard of it. Prehistoric people are being found in England and France, however."

"Huh," he said.

He pondered, puffing at his pipe, his eyes on the fire. He looked perplexed about something.

"Look here, MacNeal," he said suddenly. "Say a man dies. He's dead, ain't he?"

"No doubt of it," I laughed, wondering.

"Couldn't come to life again, eh?"

"Hardly. Not if he were really dead. I've heard of cases of suspended animation. The heart, apparently, quits beating for one, two or possibly ten minutes. It doesn't in fact, though; it's simply that its beating can't be detected. When a man's heart stops beating he's dead."

Bonner nodded.

"'Suspended animation,'" he muttered, more to himself than to me. "That must be it. That's the only thing that'll explain it; nothing else will. If it could cover a period of ten minutes, why not a period of twenty or even a hundred thousand years—"

"If you'd like to turn in and get some rest, Chris, I'll fix you up," I broke in.

He caught the significance of my tone and grinned.

"You think I'm crazy, eh?" he said. "I'm not. It's a wonder, though, considering what I've seen and what I—here, let me show you something!"

He thrust a hand into his lean pack and brought forth an object that at first glance I thought to be a butcher's knife.

He handed it to me and I at once saw that it was not a butcher's knife as I knew such knives. It was a curious sort of knife, and one for which a collector of the antique would have paid good money.

It was a very dark color, almost black; corroded, it seemed to me, as if it had lain for a long time in a damp cellar. It was in one piece, the handle about five inches long and the blade perhaps ten inches. Both edges of the blade were sharp and the end was pointed like a dagger. And it certainly wasn't steel. I scratched one side of the blade with my thumb nail and exposed a creamy yellow under the veneer of black.

"Part of that's blood you scraped away, MacNeal," Bonner said. "Now what's that knife made of?"

I examined the yellow spot closely. The knife was made of ivory. Not the kind of ivory I was acquainted with, however; it was a very much coarser grain than any ivory I had ever seen.

"That came out of a mastodon's tusk, MacNeal," Bonner said.

I looked at him. He was nodding, seriously. He apparently believed what he said, at any rate.

"Nice curio, Chris," I commented, handing the thing back to him. "Heirloom, no doubt. Picked it up in one of the Indian villages, eh?"

He did not speak at once. He sat puffing, looking at the fire. Once he puckered his brows in a deep frown. I waited.

"I've been prospecting, as usual," he said at length. "Down there around the headquarters of the Tukuvuk. It's an awful place; nobody ever goes there. The Indians tell me the spirits of the dead live there. I can believe it; it's an ideal place for imps and devils. And I was right through the heart of it. I believe I'm the first. No matter how I got there; I came up from the south last summer. You see, I had an idea there was gold in that country.

"The place where I finally settled down was in a little valley on one of the branches of the Tukuvuk between two ranges of hills running from five hundred to maybe three thousand feet high. Messy-looking place, it was; all littered up, as if the Lord had a few sizable chunks of stuff left over and just threw 'em down there to be out of the way.

"But the gold was there; I could almost smell it. I'd been getting some mighty nice color in my pan; that's what made me decide to stay there. I got there about the middle of July, and

I spent the rest of the summer sinking holes in the edge of the creek and along the benches above. What I found indicated that there was a mighty rich vein of the yellow metal thereabouts, with one end of it laying in a pocket of the stuff. If I could locate that pocket, I thought, I'd have the United States treasury backed off the map. But I wasn't able to run the pocket down by taking bearings from my holes, because the holes didn't line up in any particular direction.

"What with my interest in trying to get a line on that pocket, I didn't notice that the season was getting late. But I'd brought in enough grub to last the winter through, so that didn't matter. Just the same it was up to me to get some sort of shelter over my head, so I hustled up a one-room shack about twelve by twelve I cut from the timber on the slopes with my hand-ax. Nothing fancy, but tight enough. I put in a fireplace and cut and stacked a lot of wood outside.

"That done, winter was on me; I simply couldn't resist the temptation to have one more try at finding the pocket that spewed the yellow metal all around there. As I said, I got no information from the holes sunk, and it was pure guesswork. I guessed I'd find my pocket on the side of a certain hill, about two hundred feet above creek level. A glacier flowed down the side of that hill through a little gulley, and my idea was that the ice ground away at the pocket and brought the metal down to the creek, and the creek scattered it. This theory was borne out to some extent by the fact that my best showings of color always came from a point a little below the conjunction of the creek and glacier.

"It was snowing the morning I took my pan and shovel and started up the side of the hill, keeping to the edge of the glacier. It wasn't much of a glacier for size; say, about fifteen feet wide. I could see it winding up the side of the hill until it went out of sight through a cleft about a thousand feet up. Fed by a lake up there, probably.

"I had climbed the hill maybe a hundred feet, following the edge of the glacier, when I caught sight of a dark blotch in the edge of the ice. It was about two feet under the surface. I brushed away the film of snow to have a look. The ice was as clear as a crystal, of a blue color. And what d'you think, MacNeal? It was a man's body!"

He paused and gave me a quick glance. He wanted to see how I took that, I presume.

"The body of a man," he went on. "And the queerest-looking man I ever saw in my life. He was lying on his belly and I didn't get a look at the front of him just then, but I knew it was a man all right. He was covered all over with long hair like a—well, like a bear, say. Not a stitch of clothes."

"What did you do?" I asked.

"Why, I was that surprised I let my pan and shovel drop and stared at the damn thing with the eyes near popping out of my head. What would anybody do, finding a hair-covered thing like that frozen in a glacier? I won't deny I was a bit scared, MacNeal.

"Well, I stood there staring at the thing for I don't know how long. It didn't occur to me, then, to ask myself how the thing got there. Certainly the idea of fossils or prehistoric men didn't enter my head. I didn't think much about anything; I just stood there gaping.

"You know me, MacNeal; I guess I'm pretty soft-hearted in some respects. I'd stop to bury a dead dog I found in the road. I knew I wouldn't rest easy until I'd cut that thing out of the glacier and given it decent burial. Moreover, I didn't want it where I'd be seeing it when I went to work on that hillside in the spring; and it would surely be there in the spring, because I imagine that glacier didn't move an inch a year.

"So I went back to the shack and got my ax, and with none too good a heart for the job turned to and made the chips fly. It took me about three hours to get the thing out of the glacier.

You see, as I came down to it I went slow; I don't care to hack even a dead man.

"Say, MacNeal, can you imagine what it meant to me, digging a corpse out of a glacier down there on the side of a hill in that devil-ridden country? No, you can't, and that's the truth. You'd have to go through it to know. It was hell. I don't want any more of it in mine. Nor what followed, either."

"What was that?" I asked when he deliberated.

"You'll hear," he answered, and went on: "I got the thing out at last, little chunks of ice clinging to it, and dragged it ashore, if a glacier has a shore. It froze me to look at the thing with those little chunks of ice sticking to the long hair. Once, at Dawson, I'd seen a man pulled out of the Yukon, ice clinging to him. That was different, though; at Dawson there was a crowd to sort of buck a man up. I turned the thing over on its back to see what it looked like in front."

"Well?" said I.

"You've seen apes, MacNeal?"

"This thing looked like that?" I countered, beginning to connect up his first queer questions with what he was telling me. "You don't mean it, Chris!"

"I'm telling you," he nodded solemnly. "An ape man, that's what it was. More man than ape, if you ask me. For instance, the face was flatter than an ape's, and the forehead and chin were more pronounced. The nose was flat, but it wasn't an ape's nose. And the hands and feet were like those of a man. Oh, it was a man, all right. The thing that convinced me, I think, was the knife gripped in its hand."

"The knife you have there?" I inquired.

"This very knife," he answered.

"What then, Chris?" I urged him to go on.

"I had a good look at that thing and started for my shack. Yes, MacNeal, I ran, and I'm not ashamed to say so. It scared me.

Ugliest thing I ever saw. Eyes wide open, glaring and glinting, and the thick lips parted to show the nastiest set of fangs I ever saw in the mouth of man or beast. Why, I tell you the damned thing looked *alive*! No wonder I scooted. You would have done the same. Anybody would.

"Back in the shack, I sat down on my bunk to think it over. And it was while I sat there trying to puzzle it out that I remembered that theory about the earth tipping over. That gave me a hint of what I had run up against. Of course, I'd heard about fossils and parts of the skeletons of prehistoric men being found. Had I found, not a fossil or part of a skeleton, but the prehistoric man himself? That knocked the wind out of me. If that were the case my name would go down in history and I would be asked to give lectures before scientific societies and such. Consider it, MacNeal.

"I tell you, I couldn't quite grasp the thing. It was incredible. There I was in this year of our Lord, with the intact corpse of a man who had lived God only knows how many centuries ago. That body, understand, could well be the key to the mystery of the origin of mankind. It might possibly settle the Darwinian theory forever, one way or the other. It was a pretty serious business for me, don't you see?

"Well, I decided to preserve the thing until I could get out and make a report of the find. But how to preserve it? Of course if I had left it in the glacier it would have kept indefinitely, like a side of beef in cold storage. I was afraid to put it back in the hole in the glacier and freeze it in again with water I carried from the creek; the creek water might exert some chemical action that would ruin the thing. And if I let it lay where it was the snow would cover it, form a warm blanket, and probably cause it to decompose, then I'd have nothing left but the skeleton. I wanted to save the thing just as I'd found it; maybe the scientists would find a way to embalm it.

"I finally hit on the plan of keeping it in an ice pack. That would turn the trick until the weather took on the job. It hadn't turned bitter cold yet. I tell you, it was a nasty job keeping that thing iced with chunks I chopped from the glacier, and to make it worse the weather stayed moderate for a couple of weeks. Then, suddenly, the mercury in my little thermometer went down with a rush and it got stinging cold. I carried the thing to the shack and stood it up against the wall outside where it couldn't be covered with snow, and lashed it there.

"Can you imagine me going to sleep in my bunk in the shack every night after that, with that thing standing against the wall outside not two feet away? Of course you can't. It frazzled my nerves, and more than once I was tempted to cut a hole in the ice on the creek and chuck the damn thing in where I'd never see it again. But no, I had to save it for the scientists and get my name in history; that idea got to be an obsession with me. I knew well enough that if ever I told people the tale I'm telling you now, without some proof of it, I'd get laughed at."

"No doubt of it," I sneered.

"The days went by," he continued, ignoring my sneer, "and more and more that thing outside kept getting on my nerves. The sun went south, and from one day to another I never saw it. The never-ending night was bad enough, but when you add the northern lights and the howling of the wolves you've got a condition that breaks a man if he's not careful. Furthermore, there was that ugly-looking devil outside to think about.

"I was thinking about that thing constantly, and got so I couldn't sleep. If I shut my eyes I'd see it, anyhow, and if I went to sleep I'd have a nightmare over it. Now and then I'd go out and stand there in the starlight or the aurora looking at it. It fascinated me, yet the sight of the thing gave me the creeps. Finally I began taking a club or my rifle along when I went to look at it; got afraid the thing would come alive and try to murder me with that knife.

"And that's the way of things for maybe three months and more. My thoughts all the time on that thing outside.

"Well, that couldn't go on, you know. One morning I woke up with the worst headache a man ever had. I thought my head would split wide open. My blood was like molten iron flowing through my veins. I knew what it was. *Fever.* I had thought and worried about that thing outside until it got me, and I was in for a brain-storm. I was as weak as a cat, but managed to build up a good fire and pack my bunk with all the blankets and furs I had and crawl in. I only hoped I wouldn't freeze to death when the fire went out.

"I no sooner got all set in the bunk than things let go; I went completely off. I can't say positively what happened for a few days after that. Seems like I remember, though, periods when I was semi-rational. I think once I got up to put more wood on the fire. Another time I saw that thing standing in the doorway grinning at me like the devil it was. I shot at it with my rifle and later found a bullet in the door. My shooting couldn't have been a delusion, at any rate. But the door was still fastened against the wolves and there were no tracks in the snow outside."

Bonner paused to light his pipe, and then went on:

"I don't know exactly how long I was out of my head. I'd wound my watch before I crawled into the bunk the first time, and I half remember I wound it again when I got up to put wood on the fire, and it was pretty well run down. It goes forty hours without winding, yet when my head cleared it had stopped. I must have been off my nut about four days.

"Well, you can lay your bottom dollar I'd had enough of prehistoric men hanging around the shack by that time. Let the scientists be damned; I was determined to get rid of that thing the quickest way possible. The quickest way, I thought, would be to get the corpse warm so it would decompose rapidly, then I'd put it outside where the wolves and ravens would pick the bones clean. The scientists would have to be satisfied with the skeleton.

"So I made a big fire in the fireplace and got the shack good and hot, then went out and brought in the corpse. I got sick at the stomach on that job, but that was the only way. I didn't have the heart to leave the thing outside and build a fire over it out there. I try to respect the dead, even if the corpse is that of a man who had been dead several thousand years and looked more like an animal than a human being.

"I laid the thing on the floor before the fireplace, then sat down on the bunk to wait. I watched it pretty close, because, being dead so long, I thought when it got warm and started to decompose it would go like butter; I didn't want the shack to be all smelled up with the stink of it. Probably half an hour went by, then all of a sudden *I saw the thing quiver—*"

"Your brain-storm returning," I interposed.

"Wait," said Bonner sharply. "It quivered; not much, but enough to notice. That sort of got me, then I reasoned that anything thawing out like that would naturally quiver a little. Maybe another fifteen or twenty minutes passed, then one of the legs moved. Jerked, sort of. It startled me. Remember, there I was down there in those hills alone with that thing. I was pretty susceptible to weird influences, understand. Anyhow, the leg moved, and—"

"It sat up and asked for a drink of water." I could not help putting in. Bonner continued, paying no attention to my sarcasm. He seemed to be talking aloud to himself:

"I watched it like a hawk for some time after that, then as I didn't see it move any more I stepped outside to get some more wood for the fire and to pull a few good breaths of cold air into my lungs. That shack was like the inside of an oven.

"When I went in again I saw that the damned thing *had*

turned over on its back.

"Turned over on its back, I say. And there was a change in the eyes, too; they had a half-awake sort of look in them; a more *alive* look, understand. And breathing! Yes, sir, *breathing*! Why the thing didn't see me when I came in and shut the door I don't know, but apparently it didn't. And, believe me or not, the hand that had held the knife was open and the knife was lying on the floor apart from the body.

"Crazy? I tell you *no*! I was as sane as I am now. I tell you I saw these things with my own two eyes; saw them just as plain as I see you now. I see you don't believe me, MacNeal. Oh, well, I don't blame you; I hardly believe it myself sometimes."

He uttered a little laugh.

"But there it was, just as I'm telling you. And I was that gone when I saw that the thing had turned over on its back that I dropped the wood I had in my arm. The crash of it on the floor brought the thing to its feet on the jump. You needn't look at me like that; I tell you it did. I take my oath it did! There it was, crouched like a panther ready for the spring, the eyes of it flashing like fire, its lips pulled back tight across the gums and the yellow fangs showing. Can you see that? No, you can't."

Bonner made an expressive gesture with one hand.

"Remarkable, but the thing hadn't seen me yet. It was looking at the fire; it was half turned toward me so I could see that. Suddenly it screamed in an outlandish gibberish and leaped to the fireplace and tried to gather in an armful of flames. I take it the thing had never seen fire before; didn't know what it was; probably imagined it some kind of wild animal. Naturally the only thing it got out of that play was burned arms and hands, and the long hair sizzled and curled. It leaped back with a snarl, spitting that funny gibberish. Talk, I guess it was; it came from way down in the belly and sounded like pigs grunting.

"I tell you, MacNeal, I was fair dazed. But I had the sense

left to try to help myself. My rifle was leaning against the bunk and I made a quick dive for it. Then, apparently, the thing saw me for the first time. The way it glared at me with those glittering eyes was a caution. I didn't stop to argue; I snatched up the rifle, cocked it and made a snap shot. The bullet caught the thing in the left breast and the blood gushed. Of course you don't believe it. But blood, I tell you, gushed from the breast of a thing that had been frozen in a glacier for thousands of years!

"Well, here it came like a cyclone. I didn't have time to shoot again. Smell? That thing smelled like carrion; almost strangled me. Maybe you know how the cage of a wild animal stinks if it ain't cleaned out for a week or two. This thing smelled like that, only worse. I can smell it yet. Lord!"

Bonner wrinkled his nose and shivered.

"But there we were at grips, the thing making those belly noises and smelling like a thousand garbage piles. It had the strength of ten men; I sensed that. It jerked the rifle from me and bent the barrel of it double with a twist of the wrists. The barrel of a thirty-eight caliber Winchester rifle—bent it as easy as you or I would bend a piece of copper wire.

"Then we were at it, fighting like a couple of wild cats all over the shack. I'm no slouch of a man myself, MacNeal, when it comes to a rough-and-tumble; but that thing handled me like a baby. I could see my finish. We threshed about the floor, me fighting like a devil, it fighting like forty devils. We kicked into the fire and out again and scattered live coals all over the place, and the shack took fire.

"I was just about gone when my hand accidentally fell on the handle of the knife the thing had dropped on the floor. I hung on to it and poked away at that thing for all I was worth, driving the blade clean up to the hilt with every punch."

"That knife?" I broke in.

"This knife," answered Bonner. "There's the dried blood on

it yet. But I think it was really the bullet that did the work. It must have cut an artery. Anyhow, the blood kept gushing out of the thing's breast; it got on my hands and made 'em slippery. I knew the thing couldn't pour out blood like that and keep going; that's what put the heart in me to keep on fighting. And, as I say, I think it was the bullet that did the work in the long run. A lucky shot, otherwise I wouldn't be here now.

"I felt the thing sagging and going limp in my hands, and its grip began to relax. I saw my chance and put up a knee and broke the grip and kicked it away. It staggered around a moment or two, clutching its breast with its bloody paws, gnashing its fangs and glaring murder at me; then it crashed down to the floor and fell smack into the flames.

"I saw plain enough there was no chance of saving the shack, so I snatched up what I could lay my hands on in the way of food and clothing and blankets, and tore out. I don't remember putting the knife in my pocket, but that's where I found it later. The shack burned down to nothing, and that thing burned with it; probably not a bone of it left. The scientists were out of luck and the mystery of mankind would remain unsolved.

"I didn't stop to investigate, of course; my job was to make tracks. I knew about this village and came on. How I got here I don't know; this is a terrible country to cross afoot in the winter. I'd turned my ten huskies adrift to shift for themselves when I reached the valley where all this happened; I didn't have the grub to keep them going. I had to walk here.

"And that's all, MacNeal. You can say what you please; I know what I saw with my own eyes and you can't change my mind about it. Suspended animation? Yes, for a period covering many centuries. It would be a mighty fine thing if we could picture what happened away back there when this old earth tipped over.

"Perhaps we'd see a man, a man that was half ape, crossing a creek with a knife in his hand on the way to murder an enemy sleeping on the opposite bank. Then suddenly the earth tipped over—climatic conditions in those days were such as to freeze things up in a flash—things are held in the grip of the ice just as the dust and lava held 'em in the days of Pompeii, and—

"Well, who's to say what happened? Anything was possible. We don't know the conditions of those days. Anyhow, here I come thousands of years later and dig a man, with a knife in his hand, out of a glacier. I heat his body in order to decompose the flesh. Instead of decomposing; he comes to life and I have to kill him. He's been hibernating in a glacier for centuries. I don't know what to think about it."

Bonner refilled and lighted his pipe, then looked at me questioningly.

"Chris," I said, "I tell you frankly that I don't believe a word you have said. You tell me you were out of your head for a few days. That accounts for it. You had the jim-jams and imagined all that, then try to spring it on me as actual fact."

He looked hurt. He looked at the knife in his hand steadily for several long moments, then thrust it toward me, his eyes boring into mine.

"Then where in hell," he demanded, "did I get this knife?"

20

THE UNKNOWN BEAST

Howard Ellis Davis

At the edge of the little settlement of Bayou le Tor lapped the slack waters from which the village had been named. A mile to the south, they lost themselves in the Mississippi Sound. Northward, they wound among somber swamps, to disappear at last into the marshes above.

Giant cypress trees crowded down to the very edge of the settlement, as if jealous of the small space of cleared land it occupied beside the bayou, and to one not accustomed to the place it seemed that an evil boding lurked forever within the depths of those overhanging, gloomy swamps.

But until the unknown Beast first made its mysterious presence felt, no harm for the people of Bayou le Tor ever had come out of those swamps, except the deadly malaria, which clutched its victims in shaking agues and burning fevers that consumed life as a woods fire might consume a strip of dried sedge grass.

Before this strange death that had come to haunt the night swamps, they shrank in helpless terror. Cows were driven in from their pastures while the sun was yet high. Mothers called in their sallow-faced children from play as soon as the shadows began to lengthen.

The first victim had been Swan Davis, an old fisherman who lived by himself on the edge of the bayou above the settlement. He had been found in the swamp, dead. At first it was thought that he had been beaten to death, he was so broken about the body.

Finally, however, it was decided he had been crushed by some mysterious, unknown force. Something had caught him and squeezed him until his bones had cracked like dry reeds.

Then the three Buntly boys, driving in a bunch of steers from the marshes, were overtaken by night on the swamp road. The cattle had been going peacefully enough, when suddenly they had become frightened and lumbered off ahead, bellowing madly. Themselves frightened at the queer behavior of the animals, the boys followed, as fast as they could on foot.

That is, two of them did; for when Jard and Peter Buntly emerged from the shadows of the swamp road, they found that their brother, Sims, was not with them.

Terror-stricken though they were, they had returned into the swamp, calling his name. When they saw nothing of him, and he did not answer their calls, they went quickly home and reported what had happened. All night long, bearing flaming torches, the men of the settlement beat up and down the swamp. Toward morning, they found the young man's body, bruised and broken, but no trace of what had killed him.

When the people of Bayou le Tor gathered to discuss the circumstances surrounding these two mysterious deaths, the negroes, and some others, declared that an evil spirit haunted the gloomy fastness to the north of the settlement, while the more conservative agreed that some creature strange to those parts, some unknown beast, was ranging the night swamps, a creature that killed for the love of killing.

Armed with shotgun and rifle, they hunted him. They set bear-traps, baited with an entire quarter of beef hung above. But no one ventured into the swamps after dark, until, one night, ten of the best men in the settlement formed a party and rode out on horseback through the swamp road.

Armed with pistol and sheath-knife, they rode, two by two, knee to knee, their horses following each other nose to tail, so that if any one of the party were attacked they all could turn and fight in a body.

Nothing happened until they were on their way back; then Walter Brandon—who, because he was one of their bravest, brought up the rear—grew careless and lagged behind. Suddenly, his horse came charging in among the others, riderless.

They could find no trace of Walter, and the other nine could only ride in and break the news to his young wife, who carried a baby at her breast.

The next day, the girl's father, old Arner Horn, secured the services of a small, battered automobile and crossed two counties to see Ed Hardin and beg that he come and deliver them from this unknown beast that, one by one, was killing the men-folk of Bayou le Tor.

In his own county Ed Hardin was a deputy sheriff, and the reputation of his prowess had traveled far. Each summer, when the fishing was best on the Sound, he came to Bayou le Tor. Each winter, he came to hunt wild turkeys in the swamps that surrounded the settlement. The people had grown to know him well, and they knew that he feared neither man, beast, nor the devil.

He returned in the automobile with Arner, bringing with him his young friend, Alex Rowe. When they reached Bayou le Tor, the news awaited them that Walter's body, which bore on it the same marks as those others who had been killed, had been found floating on the waters of the bayou, and that it was being held at the water's edge so that Ed Hardin might see for himself the nature of death which this creature inflicted upon its victims.

After he had seen, Ed Hardin came away alone, grim-mouthed. When he entered Arner's yard, it already was growing dark, the night breeze rustling in the liveoaks overhead. He went to the barn and saddled Arner's bay mare. Having led her to the front fence, he tied her there and went into the house.

In the hallway, which divided the house through the middle, he paused as he heard in the room beside him the low sobbing of a woman. Then he passed on to the room that had been assigned to him and Alex Rowe. A small kerosene lamp had been lighted and set upon the dresser, and in the light of this he was buckling on a belt holding a broad hunting-knife and a pistol when Alex burst in upon him.

"Ed Hardin," cried the young man, "what is that mare doin' at the front fence? Where be you goin'?"

"I'm goin' ter hunt that beast, Alex."

"Yer ain't goin' ter do that thing, Ed! Yer don't know what hit is. How—"

"I'm goin', Alex."

"But, Ed, hit's *night*. Wait till daylight. The last two times folks went out on the swamp road at night they was er man killed."

Broad-shouldered, sparely-made, the big deputy drew himself up to his full height and turned to gaze for a moment at his young friend.

"I'm goin' now," he said calmly.

"But, Ed, you heerd what they said 'bout the schooner up in the bayou. Hit's been layin' there fer two weeks, 'thout dealin's with nobody. You heerd what Rensie Bucker, the ole nigger what uster be er sailor, said. He said he paddled up in his dugout by that schooner an' them folks on board is India folks. He says that in their lan' they's strange beasts an' reptiles, an' that mebbe they've sot one of 'em loose in the swamp, mebbe put hit ter watch the swamp road."

"Ef hit's been sot ter watch the swamp road at night," said Ed, "that's jes wher I want ter go. I want ter meet it."

"Wait, Ed. Wait till I git holt of er hoss. I'm goin' with yer."

A soft smile played for a moment about Ed Hardin's grim mouth.

"No, Alex," he said: "I reckon I'll go by myse'f."

As he was untying the mare, those who had returned to the house gathered about him and, as Alex had done, tried to prevent his going off alone into the swamp at night.

But he swung lightly to the saddle and galloped out through the settlement, into the shadows of the giant cypress trees.

The mare was a spirited and nervous animal, and she leaped and shied as she danced among the stagnant pools that lay black in the swamp road.

In thus going out deliberately to use himself as a bait for the Unknown Beast, Ed felt that he could depend largely upon her agility and quickness to prevent being taken unawares by a sudden rush from the darkness. He drew from its holster his heavy Colt's revolver and thrust it through his belt in front, within convenient reach.

So dark was the black tunnel of the road that he could see no space in front of him, and he let the reins lie slack on the mare's neck, so that she might be undisturbed in picking her footing. And as he plunged deeper into the swamp, he experienced a lonely boding that was new to him.

Time and again, he had gone fearlessly out alone in the pursuit and capture of desperate men. Now, however, he did not know what nature of creature it was he sought, and he had to invite an attack from the darkness in order to get in touch with it.

The night was murky, almost sticky in its heaviness, and the swamp seemed strangely silent. Only the occasional call of some night bird pierced the stillness. He was familiar with the road, having traveled it frequently, and the places where violence had occurred had been described to him in detail.

A few hundred yards to the left of the road, where he now

was riding, the fisherman had met his death. He passed the place where Brandon last had been seen, and, soon after, entered the deeper recess of the swamp where the herder had been snatched into the darkness of death. Plainly, this neighborhood of violence was the creature's lurking-place.

Suddenly, the mare shied, snorted, and stood quivering, her head turned as though she saw or smelled something at the side of the road. He raised his pistol, which he now held ready cocked in his hand, and fired quickly into the darkness. As he had only one hand on the reins, it was some moments after the report before he could calm the startled animal sufficiently to proceed on his way.

Twice more, at indications of terror from his horse, guided by her forward-pointed ears, Ed Hardin fired into the black shadows at the side of the road, the discharges making lurid flashes in the darkness.

The Unknown Beast evidently was near, following him through the brush—or over the treetops. If it were on the ground, he hoped for the slender chance of killing or wounding it before it had an opportunity to attack.

After each shot, as well as he could for the plunging of the mare, he listened intently for some cry of pain, some movement of the bushes; but the silence of the shadows was unbroken. The strain was nervewracking, and he had a wild desire to whirl the mare about and speed away in mad flight. He could not urge her out of a slow, hesitating walk, and she frequently shied from one side of the road to the other, with those periodic halts of trembling fear.

Then the road ran from beneath the arches of the swamp and passed over a corduroy crossing, bordered on each side by a dense growth of titi. The mare went more quietly now, and Ed began to hope that some of his shots had taken effect. He breathed more freely, now that the branches no longer drooped overhead.

Presently, however, he found himself beneath spreading liveoaks. These, flanking the road on either side, sent their giant limbs horizontally across. He peered from side to side, his eyes straining to penetrate the gloom, each indistinct tree trunk assuming a sinister outline.

Overhead, the trees towered in cavernous depths, and suddenly, with a swish of leaves and branches, out of them dropped a great, dark object!

The frightened mare leaped forward; but the nameless creature alighted behind the saddle.

Hardin snatched out his pistol, only to find that he was unable to use it. For he had been caught in a giant embrace that pinioned his arms to his sides, an embrace against which his own great strength was powerless.

The mare ran desperately, her supple body close to the ground, her graceful neck outstretched. Out from the swamp she sped, crossing a reach of flat country, once heavily covered with pines. The timber long since had been cut, only the stumps remaining, charred by forest fires—hordes of black ghosts crowding down to the edge of the road on both sides.

It was a wild ride for the man, with death perched there behind. The great arms, wound about him, were slowly squeezing the breath from his body, and beneath that embrace he felt his ribs bend inward to the point of cracking. Desperately, he maintained his grip on the saddle with his knees.

Then, just before consciousness would have left him, he raised his legs and flung himself sideways. The saddle slipped under the mare's belly. Carried by the momentum, but with that crushing grip never relaxing, the man and the terrible creature which held him hurtled through the air.

They struck with a *thud* against a shattered stump at the side of the road, while the frightened mare sped on. The murderous creature was next the stump and at the impact its hold on Ed Hardin loosened. Having slipped from the great arms, Ed flung himself over and rolled for several feet to one side.

The pistol long since had dropped from his nerveless fingers; but he now quickly drew his hunting-knife. Expecting an immediate attack with fang and claw, he lay on his back, his feet drawn up, very much in the position a cat assumes when defending itself. He knew it would be useless to pit his strength against that of the enormous creature, and the best he could hope for was to ward off an attack with his feet and watch for an opportunity to reach and drive home the knife.

And suddenly it was looming there above him. For an instant it seemed to hesitate, then it backed slowly away. With a quick, halting motion, walking upright like a man, it began to circle about him. Its long arms swung below its knees. A round head was set on a neck so thick and short that it seemed to spring from the shoulders themselves. As it circled about him, Ed turned also, keeping his feet always presented.

Again the creature backed off, up the road. Then it turned and walked slowly away.

For a moment Ed Hardin lay watching it, unwilling to change his position. Then, tentatively, he raised himself to a sitting position.

Suddenly, as if, without looking, the creature divined his movement, it turned about, at a distance of perhaps fifty feet.

And then, with a strangely human shriek of rage, it rushed toward him.

As it came through the gloom, this maddened creature, with its uncouth, hopping run, swinging its long arms from side to side.

The man dropped back into his former position, feet raised, arm held ready to strike with the knife.

Before it reached him, it dropped forward, without in the

least pausing, and, propelled by both arms and legs, shot in a great, froglike leap through the air.

The shock, as it landed upon him, drove Ed Hardin's knees back against his chest. His right arm, held ready to strike with the knife, was pinned and twisted painfully.

The knife slipped from his hand. A long arm shot forward and talon-like fingers clutched his hair. With his legs doubled back as they were, once more he was seized in that giant embrace, and he felt that his knees were being pressed into his chest until it soon must crush in like a shattered eggshell.

Then consciousness left him.

...When his senses slowly returned, he became aware of lights flashing and horses stamping, and the sound of men's voices.

Jonas Keil was speaking, and Ed had the rare experience of hearing himself discussed after he was thought to be dead.

"—'Most on my bended knees ter git 'im not ter do it. But he said he wouldn't feel right ter let Death run loose unhindered, long as he was livin' an' with strength ter fight. An' when he rid out single-handed an' alone, the bravest man what ever drawed breath was kilt."

From his position, he judged that he had been placed on the grass at the side of the road. Near him was someone who, from an occasional quivering intake of breath, seemed to have been sobbing.

He tried to turn and see who it was, and he found that he could not so much as twitch a finger.

He heard three new arrivals come up the road, a man on horseback and two runners, the two evidently holding by the rider's stirrup leathers. The rider, as soon as he drew up, said:

"We come soon's we heerd you-all was gone ter foller Ed. Arn's bringin' the waggin. Hit'll be here terreckly; we passed hit er piece back. But Arn didn' git the straights from Cy when he come atter the waggin what hit was kilt Ed. Po' ole Ed!"

Old Rensie Bucker, the negro who once had been a sailor, speaking with the *patois* of foreign birth, replied to him:

"Hit ees Jonas, de chile-minded neegar who was shanghaed from his mammy's shack down on de point ten year back. He had de mind of er chile an' de strength ob five men, wid his beeg wide shoulders an' short neck; wid de hump on his back an' his arms hangin' mos' ter his ankles. He was gentle in dem days; but de East Indee folks tuck heem off an' dey brought heem back er beast. He's frum de schooner, by his clothes, an' dey must have sot heem on de swamp road at night ter watch an' keel.

"Dere he lies, dead. De stump 'gin which he struck when he pull Meester Ed Hardin frum his hoss had er sliver which stuck mos' through heem. Den when he fit wid Meester Ed de hurt must have killed heem, because there is no other wound."

The man beside Ed Hardin spoke, and Ed recognized him.

"Alex," he said huskily.

There was a cry of amazement. Alex called for a light. Someone else, evidently startled by the voice coming from what all had thought to be a dead man, started to run, kicked over a lantern, and was cursed roundly by the others, who were crowding up.

When the wagon arrived, he was so far recovered that, with the assistance of the others, he was able to clamber painfully in and sink to the blankets on the bottom, every joint in his body aching.

The two Buntlys had called the younger men to one side and they were whispering excitedly together. Presently the riding-horses all were tied at the side of the road, and when the wagon creaked its way homeward, Ed was accompanied only by Alex, who had refused to leave him, and by old Arner. Rensie had gone with the others.

Two days later, he was able to creep out to the front porch of Arner's little home and sit in the cool of a breeze that swept up from the bayou. After a space of silence, he asked:

"Arn, what'd them fellers do the yuther night? I can't git er peep outen 'em."

"They foun' right smart of stuff in boxes, what Rensie said was some sorter dope, bein' unloaded from the schooner. But they th'owed hit in the water."

"I ain't intrusted in no dope, Arn. I say what'd they do?"

"The leader of the gang confessed, after he'd been questioned by Rensie, an' when he saw the jig was up, anyhow. They had sot Jonas ter keep folks skeerd off the swamp road at night, by killin' whosomever come there. They was goin' ter git er truck an' haul that stuff off somewheres."

"Well, what'd the boys do?"

Reflectively, Arner stroked his short, heavy beard. He spat into the yard. Then he turned to the deputy:

"Ed," he said slowly, "yo' comin' down here, an', single-handed an' alone, huntin' out the critter what was killin' us off will be remembered an' talked about in generations ter come—when these here swamps is cleared off an' drained an' producin' corn an' taters. But sich er little matter as er schooner lyin' at the bottom of the bayou gatherin' barnacles is soon forgot, an' let's you an' me fergit that part of hit, too."

21

TWO MILITARY EXECUTIONS

Ambrose Bierce

In the spring of the year 1862 General Buell's big army lay in camp, licking itself into shape for the campaign which resulted in the victory at Shiloh. It was a raw, untrained army, although some of its fractions had seen hard enough service, with a good deal of fighting, in the mountains of Western Virginia, and in Kentucky. The war was young and soldiering a new industry, imperfectly understood by the young American of the period, who found some features of it not altogether to his liking. Chief among these was that essential part of discipline, subordination. To one imbued from infancy with the fascinating fallacy that all men are born equal, unquestioning submission to authority is not easily mastered, and the American volunteer soldier in his "green and salad days" is among the worst known. That is how it happened that one of Buell's men, Private Bennett Story Greene, committed the indiscretion of striking his officer. Later in the war he would not have done that; like Sir Andrew Aguecheek, he would have "seen him damned" first. But time for reformation of his military manners was denied him: he was promptly arrested on complaint of the officer, tried by court-martial and sentenced to be shot.

"You might have thrashed me and let it go at that," said the condemned man to the complaining witness; "that is what you used to do at school, when you were plain Will Dudley and I was as good as you. Nobody saw me strike you; discipline would not have suffered much."

"Ben Greene, I guess you are right about that," said the lieutenant. "Will you forgive me? That is what I came to see you about."

There was no reply, and an officer putting his head in at the door of the guard-tent where the conversation had occurred, explained that the time allowed for the interview had expired. The next morning, when in the presence of the whole brigade Private Greene was shot to death by a squad of his comrades, Lieutenant Dudley turned his back upon the sorry performance and muttered a prayer for mercy, in which himself was included.

A few weeks afterward, as Buell's leading division was being ferried over the Tennessee River to assist in succoring Grant's beaten army, night was coming on, black and stormy. Through the wreck of battle the division moved, inch by inch, in the direction of the enemy, who had withdrawn a little to reform his lines. But for the lightning the darkness was absolute. Never for a moment did it cease, and ever when the thunder did not crack and roar were heard the moans of the wounded among whom the men felt their way with their feet, and upon whom they stumbled in the gloom. The dead were there, too—there were dead a-plenty.

In the first faint gray of the morning, when the swarming advance had paused to resume something of definition as a line of battle, and skirmishers had been thrown forward, word was passed along to call the roll. The first sergeant of Lieutenant Dudley's company stepped to the front and began to name the men in alphabetical order. He had no written roll, but a good memory. The men answered to their names as he ran down the alphabet to G.

"Gorham."

"Here!"

"Grayrock."

"Here!"

The sergeant's good memory was affected by habit:

"Greene."

"Here!"

The response was clear, distinct, unmistakable!

A sudden movement, an agitation of the entire company front, as from an electric shock, attested the startling character of the incident. The sergeant paled and paused. The captain strode quickly to his side and said sharply:

"Call that name again."

Apparently the Society for Psychical Research is not first in the field of curiosity concerning the Unknown.

"Bennett Greene."

"Here!"

All faces turned in the direction of the familiar voice; the two men between whom in the order of stature Greene had commonly stood in line turned and squarely confronted each other.

"Once more," commanded the inexorable investigator, and once more came—a trifle tremulously—the name of the dead man:

"Bennett Story Greene."

"Here!"

At that instant a single rifle-shot was heard, away to the front, beyond the skirmish-line, followed, almost attended, by the savage hiss of an approaching bullet which passing through the line, struck audibly, punctuating as with a full stop the captain's exclamation, "What the devil does it mean?"

Lieutenant Dudley pushed through the ranks from his place in the rear.

"It means this," he said, throwing open his coat and displaying a visibly broadening stain of crimson on his breast. His knees gave way; he fell awkwardly and lay dead.

A little later the regiment was ordered out of line to relieve the congested front, and through some misplay in the game of battle was not again under fire. Nor did Bennett Greene, expert in military executions, ever again signify his presence at one.

22

THE SPECTRE BRIDE

William Harrison Ainsworth

The castle of Hernswolf, at the close of the year 1655, was the resort of fashion and gaiety. The baron of that name was the most powerful nobleman in Germany, and equally celebrated for the patriotic achievements of his sons, and the beauty of his only daughter. The estate of Hernswolf, which was situated in the centre of the Black Forest, had been given to one of his ancestors by the gratitude of the nation, and descended with other hereditary possessions to the family of the present owner. It was a castellated, gothic mansion, built according to the fashion of the times, in the grandest style of architecture, and consisted principally of dark winding corridors, and vaulted tapestry rooms, magnificent indeed in their size, but ill-suited to private comfort, from the very circumstance of their dreary magnitude. A dark grove of pine and mountain ash encompassed the castle on every side, and threw an aspect of gloom around the scene, which was seldom enlivened by the cheering sunshine of heaven.

The castle bells rung out a merry peal at the approach of a winter twilight, and the warder was stationed with his retinue on the battlements, to announce the arrival of the company who were invited to share the amusements that reigned within the walls. The Lady Clotilda, the baron's only daughter, had but just attained her seventeenth year, and a brilliant assembly was invited to celebrate the birthday. The large vaulted apartments were thrown open for the reception of the numerous guests, and the gaieties of the evening had scarcely commenced when the clock from the dungeon tower was heard to strike with unusual solemnity, and on the instant a tall stranger, arrayed in a deep suit of black, made his appearance in the ballroom. He bowed courteously on every side, but was received by all with the strictest reserve. No one knew who he was or whence he came, but it was evident from his appearance, that he was a nobleman of the first rank, and though his introduction was accepted with distrust, he was treated by all with respect. He addressed himself particularly to the daughter of the baron, and was so intelligent in his remarks, so lively in his sallies, and so fascinating in his address, that he quickly interested the feelings of his young and sensitive auditor. In fine, after some hesitation on the part of the host, who, with the rest of the company, was unable to approach the stranger with indifference, he was requested to remain a few days at the castle, an invitation which was cheerfully accepted.

The dead of the night drew on, and when all had retired to rest, the dull heavy bell was heard swinging to and fro in the grey tower, though there was scarcely a breath to move the forest trees. Many of the guests, when they met the next morning at the breakfast table, averred that there had been sounds as of the most heavenly music, while all persisted in affirming that they had heard awful noises, proceeding, as it seemed, from the apartment which the stranger at that time occupied. He soon, however, made his appearance at the breakfast circle, and when the circumstances of the preceding night were alluded to, a dark smile of unutterable meaning played round his saturnine features, and then relapsed into an expression of the deepest melancholy. He addressed his conversation principally to Clotilda, and when he talked of the different climes he had visited, of the sunny regions of Italy, where the very air breathes the fragrance of flowers, and the summer breeze sighs over a land of sweets; when he spoke to her of those delicious countries, where the smile of the day sinks into the softer beauty of the night, and the loveliness of heaven is never for an instant obscured, he drew tears of regret from the bosom of his fair auditor, and for the first time she regretted that she was yet at home.

Days rolled on, and every moment increased the fervour of the inexpressible sentiments with which the stranger had inspired her. He never discoursed of love, but he looked it in his language, in his manner, in the insinuating tones of his voice, and in the slumbering softness of his smile, and when he found that he had succeeded in inspiring her with favourable sentiments, a sneer of the most diabolical meaning spoke for an instant, and died again on his dark featured countenance. When he met her in the company of her parents, he was at once respectful and submissive, and it was only when alone with her, in her ramble through the dark recesses of the forest, that he assumed the guise of the more impassioned admirer.

As he was sitting one evening with the baron in the wainscotted apartment of the library, the conversation happened to turn upon supernatural agency. The stranger remained reserved and mysterious during the discussion, but when the baron in a jocular manner denied the existence of spirits, and satirically mocked their appearance, his eyes glowed with unearthly lustre, and his form seemed to dilate to more than its natural dimensions. When the conversation had ceased, a fearful pause of a few seconds and a chorus of celestial harmony was heard pealing through the dark forest glade. All were entranced with delight, but the stranger was disturbed and gloomy; he looked at his noble host with compassion, and something like a tear swam in his dark eye. After the lapse of a few seconds, the music died gently in the distance, and all was hushed as before. The baron soon after quitted the apartment, and was followed almost immediately by the stranger. He had not long been absent, when an awful noise, as of a person in the agonies of death, was heard, and the Baron was discovered stretched dead along the corridors. His countenance was convulsed with pain, and the grip of a human hand was visible on his blackened throat. The alarm was instantly given, the castle searched in every direction, but the stranger was seen no more. The body of the baron, in the meantime, was quietly committed to the earth, and the remembrance of the dreadful transaction, recalled but as a thing that once was.

After the departure of the stranger, who had indeed fascinated her very senses, the spirits of the gentle Clotilda evidently declined. She loved to walk early and late in the walks that he had once frequented, to recall his last words; to dwell on his sweet smile; and wander to the spot where she had once discoursed with him of love. She avoided all society, and never seemed to be happy but when left alone in the solitude of her chamber. It was then that she gave vent to her affliction in tears; and the love that the pride of maiden modesty concealed in public, burst forth in the hours of privacy. So beauteous, yet so resigned was the fair mourner, that she seemed already an angel freed from the trammels of the world, and prepared to take her flight to heaven.

As she was one summer evening rambling to the sequestered spot that had been selected as her favourite residence, a slow step advanced towards her. She turned round, and to her infinite surprise discovered the stranger. He stepped gaily to her side, and commenced an animated conversation. "You left me," exclaimed the delighted girl; "and I thought all happiness was fled from me for ever; but you return, and shall we not again be happy?"—"Happy," replied the stranger, with a scornful burst of derision, "Can I ever be happy again—can there;—but excuse the agitation, my love, and impute it to the pleasure I experience at our meeting. Oh! I have many things to tell you; aye! and many kind words to receive; is it not so, sweet one? Come, tell me truly, have you been happy in my absence? No! I see in that sunken eye, in that pallid cheek, that the poor wanderer has at least gained some slight interest in the heart of his beloved. I have roamed to other climes, I have seen other nations; I have met with other females, beautiful and accomplished, but I have met with but one angel, and she is here before me. Accept this simple offering of my affection, dearest," continued the stranger, plucking a heath-rose from its stem; "it is beautiful as the wild flowers that deck thy hair, and sweet as is the love I bear thee."—"It is sweet, indeed," replied Clotilda, "but its sweetness must wither ere night closes around. It is beautiful, but its beauty is short-lived, as the love evinced by man. Let not this, then, be the type of thy attachment; bring me the delicate evergreen, the sweet flower that blossoms throughout the year, and I will say, as I wreathe it in my hair, 'The violets have bloomed and died—the roses have flourished and decayed; but the evergreen is still young, and so is the love of heart!'—you will not—cannot desert me. I live but in you; you are my hopes, my thoughts, my existence itself: and if I lose you, I lose my all—I was but a solitary wild flower in the wilderness of nature, until you transplanted me to a more genial soil; and can you now break the fond heart you first taught to glow with passion?"—"Speak not thus," returned the stranger, "it rends my very soul to hear you; leave me—forget me—avoid me for ever—or your eternal ruin must ensue. I am a thing abandoned of God and man—and did you but see the scared heart that scarcely beats within this moving mass of deformity, you would flee me, as you would an adder in your path. Here is my heart, love, feel how cold it is; there is no pulse that betrays its emotion; for all is chilled and dead as the friends I once knew."—"You are unhappy, love, and your poor Clotilda shall stay to succour you. Think not I can abandon you in your misfortunes. No! I will wander with thee through the wide world, and be thy servant, thy slave, if thou wilt have it so. I will shield thee from the night winds, that they blow not too roughly on thy unprotected head. I will defend thee from the tempest that howls around; and though the cold world may devote thy name to scorn—though friends may fall off, and associates wither in the grave, there shall be one fond heart who shall love thee better in thy misfortune, and cherish thee, bless thee still." She ceased, and her blue eyes swam in tears, as she turned it glistening with affection towards the stranger. He averted his head from her gaze, and a scornful sneer of the darkest, the deadliest malice passed over his fine countenance. In an instant, the expression subsided; his fixed glassy eye resumed its unearthly chillness, and he turned once again to his companion. "It is the hour of sunset," he exclaimed; "the soft, the beauteous hour, when the hearts of lovers are happy, and nature smiles in unison with their feelings; but to me it will smile no longer—ere the morrow dawns I shall very far, from the house of my beloved; from the scenes where my heart is enshrined, as in a sepulchre. But must I leave thee, dearest flower of the wilderness, to be the sport of a whirlwind, the prey of the mountain blast?"—"No, we will not part,' replied the impassioned girl; "where thou goest, will I go; thy home shall be my home; and thy God shall be my God."—"Swear it, swear it," resumed the stranger, wildly grasping her by the hand; "swear to the fearful oath I shall dictate." He then desired her to kneel, and holding his right hand in a menacing attitude towards heaven, and throwing back his dark raven locks, exclaimed in a strain of bitter imprecation with the ghastly smile of an incarnate fiend, "May the curses of an offended God," he cried, "haunt thee, cling to thee for ever in the tempest and in the calm, in the day and in the night, in sickness and in sorrow, in life and in death, shouldst thou swerve from the promise thou hast here made to be mine. May the dark spirits of the damned howl in thine ears the accursed chorus of fiends—may the air rack thy bosom with the quenchless flames of hell! May thy soul be as the lazar-house of corruption, where the ghost of departed pleasure sits enshrined, as in a grave: where the hundred-headed worm never dies where the fire is never extinguished. May a spirit of evil lord it over thy brow, and proclaim, as thou passest by, 'THIS IS THE ABANDONED OF GOD AND MAN;' may fearful spectres haunt thee in the night season; may thy dearest friends drop day by day into the grave, and curse thee with their dying breath: may all that is most horrible in human nature, more solemn than language can frame, or lips can utter, may this, and more than this, be thy eternal portion, shouldst thou violate the oath that thou has taken." He ceased—hardly knowing what she did, the terrified girl acceded to the awful adjuration, and promised eternal fidelity to him who was henceforth to be her lord. "Spirits of the damned, I thank thee for thine assistance," shouted the stranger; "I have wooed my fair bride bravely. She is mine—mine for ever.—Aye, body and soul both mine; mine in life, and mine in death. What in tears, my sweet one, ere yet the honeymoon is past? Why! indeed thou hast cause for weeping: but when next we meet we shall meet to sign the nuptial bond." He then imprinted a cold salute on the cheek of his young bride, and softening down the unutterable horrors of his countenance, requested her to meet him at eight o'clock on the ensuing evening in the chapel adjoining to the castle of Hernswolf. She turned round to him with a burning sigh, as if to implore protection from himself, but the stranger was gone.

On entering the castle, she was observed to be impressed with deepest melancholy. Her relations vainly endeavoured to ascertain the cause of her uneasiness; but the tremendous oath she had sworn completely paralysed her faculties, and she was fearful of betraying herself by even the slightest intonation of her voice, or the least variable expression of her countenance. When the evening was concluded, the family retired to rest; but Clotilda, who was unable to take repose, from the restlessness of her disposition, requested to remain alone in the library that adjoined her apartment.

All was now deep midnight; every domestic had long since retired to rest, and the only sound that could be distinguished was the sullen howl of the ban-dog as he bayed, the waning moon Clotilda remained in the library in an attitude of deep meditation. The lamp that burnt on the table, where she sat, was dying away, and the lower end of the apartment was already more than half obscured. The clock from the northern angle of the castle tolled out the hour of twelve, and the sound echoed dismally in the solemn stillness of the night. Sudden the oaken door at the farther end of the room was gently lifted on its latch, and a bloodless figure, apparelled in the habiliments of the grave, advanced slowly up the apartment. No sound heralded its approach, as it moved with noiseless steps to the table where the lady was stationed. She did not at first perceive it, till she felt a death-cold hand fast grasped in her own, and heard a solemn voice whisper in her ear, "Clotilda." She looked up, a dark figure was standing beside her; she endeavoured to scream, but her voice was unequal to the exertion; her eye was fixed, as if by magic, on the form which, slowly removed the garb that concealed its countenance, and disclosed the livid eyes and skeleton shape of her father. It seemed to gaze on her with pity, an regret, and mournfully exclaimed—"Clotilda, the dresses and the servants are ready, the church bell has tolled, and the priest is at the altar, but where is the affianced bride? There is room for her in the grave, and tomorrow shall she be with me."—"Tomorrow?" faltered out the distracted girl; "the spirits of hell shall have registered it, and tomorrow must the bond be cancelled." The figure ceased—slowly retired, and was soon lost in the obscurity of distance.

The morning—evening—arrived; and already as the hall clock struck eight, Clotilda was on her road to the chapel. It was a dark, gloomy night, thick masses of dun clouds sailed across the firmament, and the roar of the winter wind echoed awfully through the forest trees. She reached the appointed place; a figure was in waiting for her—it advanced—and discovered the features of the stranger. "Why! this is well, my bride," he exclaimed, with a sneer; "and well will I repay thy fondness. Follow me." They proceeded together in silence through the winding avenues of the chapel, until they reached the adjoining cemetery. Here they paused for an instant; and the stranger, in a softened tone, said, "But one hour more, and the struggle will be over. And yet this heart of incarnate malice can feel, when it devotes so young, so pure a spirit to the grave. But it must—it must be," he proceeded, as the memory of her past love rushed on her mind; "for the fiend whom I obey has so willed it. Poor girl, I am leading thee indeed to our nuptials; but the priest will be death, thy parents the mouldering skeletons that rot in heaps around; and the witnesses to our union, the lazy worms that revel on the carious bones of the dead. Come, my young bride, the priest is impatient for his victim." As they proceeded, a dim blue light moved swiftly before them, and displayed at the extremity of the churchyard the portals of a vault. It was open, and they entered it in silence. The hollow wind came rushing through the gloomy abode of the dead; and on every side were piled the mouldering remnants of coffins, which dropped piece by piece upon the damp mud. Every step they took was on a dead body; and the bleached bones rattled horribly beneath their feet. In the centre of the vault rose a heap of unburied skeletons, whereon was seated, a figure too awful even for the darkest imagination to conceive. As they approached it, the hollow vault rung with a hellish peal of laughter; and every mouldering corpse seemed endued with unholy life. The stranger paused, and as he grasped his victim in his hand, one sigh burst from his heart—one tear glistened in his eye. It was but for an instant; the figure frowned awfully at his vacillation, and waved his gaunt hand.

The stranger advanced; he made certain mystic circles in the air, uttered unearthly words, and paused in excess of terror. On a sudden he raised his voice and wildly exclaimed—"Spouse of the spirit of darkness, a few moments are yet thine; that thou may'st know to whom thou hast consigned thyself. I am the undying spirit of the wretch who curst his Saviour on the cross. He looked at me in the closing hour of his existence, and that look hath not yet passed away, for I am curst above all on earth. I am eternally condemned to hell and I must cater for my master's taste till the world is parched as is a scroll, and the heavens and the earth have passed away. I am he of whom thou may'st have read, and of whose feats thou may'st have heard. A million souls has my master condemned me to ensnare, and then my penance is accomplished, and I may know the repose of the grave. Thou art the thousandth soul that I have damned. I saw thee in thine hour of purity, and I marked thee at once for my home. Thy father did I murder for his temerity, and permitted to warn thee of thy fate; and myself have I beguiled for thy simplicity. Ha! the spell works bravely, and thou shall soon see, my sweet one, to whom thou hast linked thine undying fortunes, for as long as the seasons shall move on their course of nature—as long as the lightning shall flash, and the thunders roll, thy penance shall be eternal. Look below! and see to what thou art destined.' She looked, the vault split in a thousand different directions; the earth yawned asunder; and the roar of mighty waters was heard. A living ocean of molten fire glowed in the abyss beneath her, and blending with the shrieks of the damned, and the triumphant shouts of the fiends, rendered horror more horrible than imagination. Ten millions of souls were writhing in the fiery flames, and as the boiling billows dashed them against the blackened rocks of adamant, they cursed with the blasphemies of despair; and each curse echoed in thunder cross the wave. The stranger rushed towards his victim. For an instant he held her over the burning vista, looked fondly in her face and wept as he were a child. This was but the impulse of a moment; again he grasped her in his arms, dashed her from him with fury; and as her last parting glance was cast in kindness on his face, shouted aloud, "not mine is the crime, but the religion that thou professest; for is it not said that there is a fire of eternity prepared for the souls of the wicked; and hast not thou incurred its torments?" She, poor girl, heard not, heeded not the shouts of the blasphemer. Her delicate form bounded from rock to rock, over billow, and over foam; as she fell, the ocean lashed itself as it were in triumph to receive her soul, and as she sunk deep in the burning pit, ten thousand voices reverberated from the bottomless abyss, "Spirit of evil! here indeed is an eternity of torments prepared for thee; for here the worm never dies, and the fire is never quenched."

23

HOW HE LEFT THE HOTEL

Louisa Baldwin

I used to work the passenger-lift in the Empire Hotel, that big block of building in lines of red and white brick like streaky bacon, that stands at the corner of—Street. I'd served my time in the army, and got my discharge with good-conduct stripes; and how I got the job was in this way. The hotel was a big company affair with a managing committee of retired officers and suchlike; gentlemen with a bit o' money in the concern, and nothing to do but fidget about it, and my late Colonel was one of 'em. He was as good-tempered a man as ever stepped when his will wasn't crossed, and when I asked him for a job, "Mole," says he, "you're the very man to work the lift at our big hotel. Soldiers are civil and businesslike, and the public like 'em only second best to sailors. We've had to give our last man the sack, and you can take his place."

I liked my work well enough and my pay, and kept my place a year, and I should have been there still if it hadn't been for a circumstance—But don't let me anticipate. Ours was a hydraulic lift. None o' them rickety things swung up like a poll parrot's cage in a well staircase that I shouldn't care to trust my neck to. It ran as smooth as oil, a child might have worked it, and safe as standing on the ground. Instead of being stuck full of advertisements like an omnibus, we'd mirrors in it, and the ladies would look at themselves, and pat their hair, and set their mouths when I was taking 'em downstairs dressed of an evening. It was a little sitting-room, with red velvet cushions to sit down on, and you'd nothing to do but get into it, and it 'ud float you up or float you down light as a bird.

All the visitors used the lift one time or another, going up or coming down. Some of them was French, and they called the lift the "*assenser*," and good enough for them in their language, no doubt; but why the Americans, that can speak English when they choose, and are always finding out ways of doing things quicker than other folks, should waste time and breath calling a lift an elevator, I can't make out.

I was in charge of the lift from noon till midnight. By that time the theatre and dining-out folks had come in, and anyone returning late walked upstairs, for my day's work was done. One of the porters worked the lift till I come on duty in the morning; but before twelve there was nothing particular going on, and not much till after two o'clock. Then it was pretty hot work with visitors going up and down constant, and the electric bell ringing you from one floor to another like a house on fire. Then came a quiet spell while dinner was on, and I'd sit down comfortable in the lift and read my paper, only I mightn't smoke. But nobody else might neither, and I had to ask furren gentlemen to please not smoke in it, it was against the rule. I hadn't so often to tell English gentlemen, they're not like furreners that seem as if their cigars was glued to their lips.

I always noticed faces as folks got into the lift, for I've sharp sight and a good memory, and none of the visitors needed to tell me twice where to take them. I knew them and I knew their floor as well as they did themselves.

It was in November that Colonel Saxby came to the Empire Hotel. I noticed him particularly, because you could see at once that he was a soldier. He was a tall, thin man about fifty, with a hawk nose, keen eyes, and a grey moustache, and walked stiff from a gun-shot wound in the knee. But what I noticed most was the scar of a sabrecut across the right side of the face. As he got into the lift to go to his room on the fourth floor, I thought what a difference there is among officers. Colonel Saxby put me in mind of a telegraph-post for height and thinness; and my old Colonel was like a barrel in uniform, but a brave soldier and a gentleman all the same. Colonel Saxby's room was number 210, just opposite the glass door leading to the lift, and every time I stopped on the fourth floor number 210 stared me in the face. The Colonel used to go up in the lift every day regular, though he never came down in it till—But I'm coming to that presently. Sometimes, when he was alone in the lift, he'd speak to me. He asked me in what regiment I'd served, and said he knew the officers in it. But I can't say he was comfortable to talk to. There was something stand-off about him, and he always seemed deep in his own thoughts. He never sat down in the lift. Whether it was empty or full he stood bolt upright under the lamp, where the light fell on his pale face and scarred cheek.

One day in February I didn't take the Colonel up in the lift, and as he was regular as clockwork I noticed it, but I supposed he'd gone away for a few days, and I thought no more about it. Whenever I stopped on the fourth floor the door of 210 was shut, and as he often left it open, I made sure the Colonel was away. At the end of a week I heard a chambermaid say that Colonel Saxby was ill; so, thinks I, that's why he hasn't been in the lift lately.

It was a Tuesday night, and I'd had an uncommonly busy time of it. It was one stream of traffic up and down, and so it went on the whole evening. It was on the strike of midnight, and I was about to put out the light in the lift, lock the door, and leave the key in the office for the man in the morning, when the electric bell rang out sharp; I looked at the dial, and saw I was wanted on the fourth floor. It struck twelve as I stepped into the lift. As I passed the second and third floors, I wondered who it was that had rung so late, and thought it must be a stranger that didn't know the rule of the house. But when I stopped at the fourth floor and flung open the door of the lift, Colonel Saxby was standing there wrapped in a military cloak. The door of his room was shut behind him, for I read the number on it. I thought he was ill in his bed, and ill enough he looked, but he had his hat on, and what could a man that had been in bed ten days want with going out on a winter midnight? I don't think he saw me, but when I'd set the lift in motion, I looked at him standing under the lamp, with the shadow of his hat hiding his eyes, and the light full on the lower part of his face, that was deadly pale, the scar on his cheek showing still paler.

"Glad to see you're better, sir," said I; but he said nothing, and I didn't like to look at him again. He stood like a statue with his cloak about him, and I was downright glad when I opened the door of the lift for him to step out in the hall. I saluted as he got out, and he went past me towards the front door.

"The Colonel wants to go out," I said to the porter who stood staring, and he opened the door and Colonel Saxby walked out into the snow.

"That's a queer go!" he said.

"It is," said I. "I don't like the Colonel's looks, he doesn't seem himself at all. He's ill enough to be in his bed, and there he is gone out on a night like this."

"Anyhow he's got a famous cloak to keep him warm. I say, supposing he's gone to a fancy ball, and got that cloak on to hide his dress," said the porter, laughing uneasily, for we both felt queerer than we cared to say, and as we spoke there came a loud ring at the door-bell.

"No more passengers for me!" I said; and I was really putting the light out this time, when Joe opened the door, and two gentlemen entered that I knew at a glance were doctors. One was tall, and the other was short and stout, and they both came to the lift.

"Sorry, gentlemen, but it's against the rule for the lift to go up after, midnight."

"Nonsense!" said the stout gentleman; "it's only just past twelve, and a matter of life and death. Take us up at once to the fourth floor," and they were in the lift like a shot; so up we went, and when I opened the door, they walked straight to number 10. A nurse came out to meet them, and the stout doctor said: "No change for the worse, I hope?"

And I heard her reply: "The patient died five minutes ago, sir."

Though I'd no business to speak, that was more than I could stand. I followed the doctors to the door and said: "There's some mistake here, gentlemen, I took the Colonel down in the lift since the clock struck twelve, and he went out."

The stout doctor said sharply: "A case of mistaken identity. It was someone else you took for the Colonel."

"Begging your pardon, gentlemen, it was the Colonel himself, and the night porter that opened the front door for him knew him as well as me. He was dressed for a night like this, with his military cloak wrapped round him."

"Step in and see for yourself," said the nurse.

I followed the doctor into the room, and there lay Colonel Saxby looking just as I had seen him a few minutes before. There he lay, dead as his forefathers, and the great cloak spread over the bed to keep him warm that would feel heat and cold no more. I never slept that night. I sat up with Joe, expecting every minute to hear the Colonel ring the front door bell. Next day, every time the bell for the lift rang sharp and sudden, the sweat broke out on me and I shook again. I felt as bad as I did the first time I was in action. Me and Joe told the manager all about it, and he said we'd been dreaming; but, said he, "Mind you don't talk about it, or the house'll be empty in a week."

The Colonel's coffin was smuggled into the house the next

night. Me and the manager and the undertaker's men took it up in the lift, and it lay right across it, and not an inch to spare. They carried it into number 210, and while I waited for them to come out again, a queer feeling came over me. Then the door opened softly, and four men carried out the long coffin straight across the passage, and set it down with its foot towards the door of the lift, and the manager looked round for me.

"I can't do it, sir," I said. "I can't take the Colonel down *again*. I took him down at midnight yesterday, and that was enough for me."

"Push it in," said the manager, speaking short and sharp, and they ran the coffin into the lift without a sound. The manager got in last, and before he closed the door he said, "Mole, you've worked this lift for the last time, it strikes me." And I had, for I wouldn't have stayed on at the Empire Hotel after what had happened, not if they'd doubled my wages; and me and the night porter left together.

24

"AND NO BIRD SINGS"

E.F. Benson

The red chimneys of the house for which I was bound were visible from just outside the station at which I had alighted, and, so the chauffeur told me, the distance was not more than a mile's walk if I took the path across the fields. It ran straight till it came to the edge of that wood yonder, which belonged to my host, and above which his chimneys were visible. I should find a gate in the paling of this wood, and a track traversing it, which debouched close to his garden. So, in this adorable afternoon of early May, it seemed a waste of time to do other than walk through meadows and woods, and I set off on foot, while the motor carried my traps.

It was one of those golden days which every now and again leak out of Paradise and drip to earth. Spring had been late in coming, but now it was here with a burst, and the whole world was boiling with the sap of life. Never have I seen such a wealth of spring flowers, or such vividness of green, or heard such melodious business among the birds in the hedgerows; this walk through the meadows was a jubilee of festal ecstasy. And best of all, so I promised myself, would be the passage through the wood newly fledged with milky green that lay just ahead. There was the gate, just facing me, and I passed through it into the dappled lights and shadows of the grass-grown track.

Coming out of the brilliant sunshine was like entering a dim tunnel; one had the sense of being suddenly withdrawn from the brightness of the spring into some subaqueous cavern. The tree-tops formed a green roof overhead, excluding the light to a remarkable degree; I moved in a world of shifting obscurity. Presently, as the trees grew more scattered, their place was taken by a thick growth of hazels, which met over the path, and then, the ground sloping downwards, I came upon an open clearing, covered with bracken and heather, and studded with birches. But though now I walked once more beneath the luminous sky, with the sunlight pouring down, it seemed to have lost its effulgence. The brightness—was it some odd optical illusion?—was veiled as if it came through crêpe. Yet there was the sun still well above the tree-tops in an unclouded heaven, but for all that the light was that of a stormy winter's day, without warmth or brilliance. It was oddly silent, too; I had thought that the bushes and trees would be ringing with the song of mating-birds, but listening, I could hear no note of any sort, neither the fluting of thrush or blackbird, nor the cheerful whirr of the chaffinch, nor the cooing wood-pigeon, nor the strident clamour of the jay. I paused to verify this odd silence; there was no doubt about it. It was rather eerie, rather uncanny, but I supposed the birds knew their own business best, and if they were too busy to sing it was their affair.

As I went on it struck me also that since entering the wood I had not seen a bird of any kind; and now, as I crossed the clearing, I kept my eyes alert for them, but fruitlessly, and soon I entered the further belt of thick trees which surrounded it. Most of them I noticed were beeches, growing very close to each other, and the ground beneath them was bare but for the carpet of fallen leaves, and a few thin bramble-bushes. In this curious dimness and thickness of the trees, it was impossible to see far to right or left of the path, and now, for the first time since I had left the open, I heard some sound of life. There came the rustle of leaves from not far away, and I thought to myself that a rabbit, anyhow, was moving. But somehow it lacked the staccato patter of a small animal; there was a certain stealthy heaviness about it, as if something much larger were stealing along and desirous of not being heard. I paused again to see what might emerge, but instantly the sound ceased. Simultaneously I was conscious of some faint but very foul odour reaching me, a smell choking and corrupt, yet somehow pungent, more like the odour of something alive rather than rotting. It was peculiarly sickening, and not wanting to get any closer to its source I went on my way.

Before long I came to the edge of the wood; straight in front of me was a strip of meadow-land, and beyond an iron gate between two brick walls, through which I had a glimpse of lawn and flower-beds. To the left stood the house, and over house and garden there poured the amazing brightness of the declining afternoon.

Hugh Granger and his wife were sitting out on the lawn, with the usual pack of assorted dogs: a Welsh collie, a yellow retriever, a fox-terrier, and a Pekinese. Their protest at my intrusion gave way to the welcome of recognition, and I was admitted into the circle. There was much to say, for I had been out of England for the last three months, during which time Hugh had settled into this little estate left him by a recluse uncle, and he and Daisy had been busy during the Easter vacation with getting into the house. Certainly it was a most attractive legacy; the house, through which I was presently taken, was a delightful little Queen Anne manor, and its situation on the edge of this heather-clad Surrey ridge quite superb. We had tea in a small panelled parlour overlooking the garden, and soon the wider topics narrowed down to those of the day and the hour. I had walked, had I, asked Daisy, from the station: did I go through the wood, or follow the path outside it?

The question she thus put to me was given trivially enough; there was no hint in her voice that it mattered a straw to her which way I had come. But it was quite clearly borne in upon me that not only she but Hugh also listened intently for my reply.

He had just lit a match for his cigarette, but held it unapplied till he heard my answer. Yes, I had gone through the wood; but now, though I had received some odd impressions in the wood, it seemed quite ridiculous to mention what they were. I could not soberly say that the sunshine there was of very poor quality, and that at one point in my traverse I had smelt a most iniquitous odour. I had walked through the wood; that was all I had to tell them.

I had known both my host and hostess for a tale of many years, and now, when I felt that there was nothing except purely fanciful stuff that I could volunteer about my experiences there, I noticed that they exchanged a swift glance, and could easily interpret it. Each of them signalled to the other an expression of relief; they told each other (so I construed their glance) that I, at any rate, had found nothing unusual in the wood, and they were pleased at that. But then, before any real pause had succeeded to my answer that I had gone through the wood, I remembered that strange absence of bird-song and birds, and as that seemed an innocuous observation in natural history, I thought I might as well mention it.

"One odd thing struck me," I began (and instantly I saw the attention of both riveted again), "I didn't see a single bird or hear one from the time I entered the wood to when I left it."

Hugh lit his cigarette.

"I've noticed that too," he said, "and it's rather puzzling. The wood is certainly a bit of primeval forest, and one would have thought that hosts of birds would have nested in it from time immemorial. But, like you, I've never heard or seen one in it. And I've never seen a rabbit there either."

"I thought I heard one this afternoon," said I. "Something was moving in the fallen beech leaves."

"Did you see it?" he asked.

I recollected that I had decided that the noise was not quite the patter of a rabbit.

"No, I didn't see it," I said, "and perhaps it wasn't one. It sounded, I remember, more like something larger."

Once again and unmistakably a glance passed between Hugh and his wife, and she rose.

"I must be off," she said. "Post goes out at seven, and I lazed all morning. What are you two going to do?"

"Something out of doors, please," said I. "I want to see the domain."

Hugh and I accordingly strolled out again with the cohort of dogs. The domain was certainly very charming; a small lake lay beyond the garden, with a reed bed vocal with warblers, and a tufted margin into which coots and moorhens scudded at our approach. Rising from the end of that was a high heathery knoll full of rabbit holes, which the dogs nosed at with joyful expectations, and there we sat for a while overlooking the wood which covered the rest of the estate. Even now in the blaze of the sun near to its setting, it seemed to be in shadow, though like the rest of the view it should have basked in brilliance, for not a cloud flecked the sky and the level rays enveloped the world in a crimson splendour. But the wood was grey and darkling. Hugh, also, I was aware, had been looking at it, and now, with an air of breaking into a disagreeable topic, he turned to me.

"Tell me," he said, "does anything strike you about that wood?"

"Yes: it seems to lie in shadow."

He frowned.

"But it can't, you know," he said. "Where does the shadow come from? Not from outside, for sky and land are on fire."

"From inside, then?" I asked

He was silent a moment.

"There's something queer about it," he said at length. "There's something there, and I don't know what it is. Daisy feels it too;

she won't ever go into the wood, and it appears that birds won't either. Is it just the fact that, for some unexplained reason, there are no birds in it that has set all our imaginations at work?"

I jumped up.

"Oh, it's all rubbish," I said. "Let's go through it now and find a bird. I bet you I find a bird."

"Sixpence for every bird you see," said Hugh.

We went down the hillside and walked round the wood till we came to the gate where I had entered that afternoon. I held it open after I had gone in for the dogs to follow. But there they stood, a yard or so away, and none of them moved.

"Come on, dogs," I said, and Fifi, the fox-terrier, came a step nearer and then with a little whine retreated again.

"They always do that," said Hugh, "not one of them will set foot inside the wood. Look!"

He whistled and called, he cajoled and scolded, but it was no use. There the dogs remained, with little apologetic grins and signallings of tails, but quite determined not to come.

"But why?" I asked.

"Same reason as the birds, I suppose, whatever that happens to be. There's Fifi, for instance, the sweetest-tempered little lady; once I tried to pick her up and carry her in, and she snapped at me. They'll have nothing to do with the wood; they'll trot round outside it and go home."

We left them there, and in the sunset light which was now beginning to fade began the passage. Usually the sense of eeriness disappears if one has a companion, but now to me, even with Hugh walking by my side, the place seemed even more uncanny than it had done that afternoon, and a sense of intolerable uneasiness, that grew into a sort of waking nightmare, obsessed me. I had thought before that the silence and loneliness of it had played tricks with my nerves; but with Hugh here it could not be that, and indeed I felt that it was not any such notion that lay at the root of this fear, but rather the conviction that there was some presence lurking there, invisible as yet, but permeating the gathered gloom. I could not form the slighted idea of what it might be, or whether it was material or ghostly; all I could diagnose of it from my own sensations was that it was evil and antique.

As we came to the open ground in the middle of the wood, Hugh stopped, and though the evening was cool I noticed that he mopped his forehead.

"Pretty nasty," he said. "No wonder the dogs don't like it. How do you feel about it?"

Before I could answer, he shot out his hand, pointing to the belt of trees that lay beyond.

"What's that?" he said in a whisper.

I followed his finger, and for one half-second thought I saw against the black of the wood some vague flicker, grey or faintly luminous. It waved as if it had been the head and forepart of some huge snake rearing itself, but it instantly disappeared, and my glimpse had been so momentary that I could not trust my impression.

"It's gone," said Hugh, still looking in the direction he had pointed; and as we stood there, I heard again what I had heard that afternoon, a rustle among the fallen beech-leaves. But there was no wind nor breath of breeze astir.

He turned to me.

"What on earth was it?" he said. "It looked like some enormous slug standing up. Did you see it?"

"I'm not sure whether I did or not," I said. "I think I just caught sight of what you saw."

"But what was it?" he said again. "Was it a real material creature, or was it—"

"Something ghostly, do you mean?" I asked.

"Something half-way between the two," he said. "I'll tell you what I mean afterwards, when we've got out of this place."

The thing, whatever it was, had vanished among the trees to the left of where our path lay, and in silence we walked across the open till we came to where it entered tunnel-like among the trees. Frankly I hated and feared the thought of plunging into that darkness with the knowledge that not so far off there was something the nature of which I could not ever so faintly conjecture, but which, I now made no doubt, was that which filled the wood with some nameless terror. Was it material, was it ghostly, or was it (and now some inkling of what Hugh meant began to form itself into my mind) some being that lay on the borderland between the two? Of all the sinister possibilities that appeared the most terrifying.

As we entered the trees again I perceived that reek, alive and yet corrupt, which I had smelt before, but now it was far more potent, and we hurried on, choking with the odour that I now guessed to be not the putrescence of decay, but the living substance of that which crawled and reared itself in the darkness of the wood where no bird would shelter. Somewhere among those trees lurked the reptilian thing that defied and yet compelled credence.

It was a blessed relief to get out of that dim tunnel into the wholesome air of the open and the clear light of evening. Within doors, when we returned, windows were curtained and lamps lit. There was a hint of frost, and Hugh put a match to the fire in his room, where the dogs, still a little apologetic, hailed us with thumpings of drowsy tails.

"And now we've got to talk," said he, "and lay our plans, for whatever it is that is in the wood, we've got to make an end of it. And, if you want to know what I think it is, I'll tell you."

"Go ahead," said I.

"You may laugh at me, if you like," he said, "but I believe it's an elemental. That's what I meant when I said it was a being half-way between the material and the ghostly. I never caught a glimpse of it till this afternoon; I only felt there was something horrible there. But now I've seen it, and it's like what spiritualists and that sort of folk describe as an elemental. A huge phosphorescent slug is what they tell us of it, which at will can surround itself with darkness."

Somehow, now safe within doors, in the cheerful light and warmth of the room, the suggestion appeared merely grotesque. Out there in the darkness of that uncomfortable wood something within me had quaked, and I was prepared to believe any horror, but now commonsense revolted.

"But you don't mean to tell me you believe in such rubbish?" I said. "You might as well say it was a unicorn. What is an elemental, anyway? Who has ever seen one except the people who listen to raps in the darkness and say they are made by their aunts?"

"What is it then?" he asked.

"I should think it is chiefly our own nerves," I said. "I frankly acknowledge I got the creeps when I went through the wood first, and I got them much worse when I went through it with you. But it was just nerves; we are frightening ourselves and each other."

"And are the dogs frightening themselves and each other?" he asked. "And the birds?"

That was rather harder to answer; in fact I gave it up.

Hugh continued.

"Well, just for the moment we'll suppose that something else, not ourselves, frightened us and the dogs and the birds," he said, "and that we did see something like a huge phosphorescent slug. I won't call it an elemental, if you object to that; I'll call it It. There's another thing, too, which the existence of It would explain."

"What's that?" I asked.

"Well, it is supposed to be some incarnation of evil, it is a corporeal form of the devil. It is not only spiritual, it is material to this extent that it can be seen bodily in form, and heard, and, as you noticed, smelt, and, God forbid, handled. It has to be kept alive by nourishment. And that explains perhaps why, every day since I have been here, I've found on that knoll we went up some half-dozen dead rabbits."

"Stoats and weasels," said I.

"No, not stoats and weasels. Stoats kill their prey and eat it. These rabbits have not been eaten; they've been drunk."

"What on earth do you mean?" I asked.

"I examined several of them. There was just a small hole in their throats, and they were drained of blood. Just skin and bones, and a sort of grey mash of fibre, like, like the fibre of an orange which has been sucked. Also there was a horrible smell lingering on them. And was the thing you had a glimpse of like a stoat or a weasel?"

There came a rattle at the handle of the door.

"Not a word to Daisy," said Hugh as she entered.

"I heard you come in," she said. "Where did you go?"

"All round the place," said I, "and came back through the wood. It is odd; not a bird did we see, but that is partly accounted for because it was dark."

I saw her eyes search Hugh's, but she found no communication there. I guessed that he was planning some attack on It next day, and he did not wish her to know that anything was afoot.

"The wood's unpopular," he said. "Birds won't go there, dogs won't go there, and Daisy won't go there. I'm bound to say I share the feeling too, but having braved its terrors in the dark I've broken the spell."

"All quiet, was it?" asked she.

"Quiet wasn't the word for it. The smallest pin could have been heard dropping half a mile off."

We talked over our plans that night after she had gone up to bed. Hugh's story about the sucked rabbits was rather horrible, and though there was no certain connection between those empty rinds of animals and what we had seen, there seemed a certain reasonableness about it. But anything, as he pointed out, which could feed like that was clearly not without its material side—ghosts did not have dinner, and if it was material it was vulnerable.

Our plans, therefore, were very simple; we were going to tramp through the wood, as one walks up partridges in a field of turnips, each with a shot-gun and a supply of cartridges. I cannot say that I looked forward to the expedition, for I hated the thought of getting into closer quarters with that mysterious denizen of the woods; but there was a certain excitement about it, sufficient to keep me awake a long time, and when I got to sleep to cause very vivid and awful dreams.

The morning failed to fulfil the promise of the clear sunset; the sky was lowering and cloudy and a fine rain was falling. Daisy had shopping-errands which took her into the little town, and as soon as she had set off we started on our business. The yellow retriever, mad with joy at the sight of guns, came bounding with us across the garden, but on our entering the wood he slunk back home again.

The wood was roughly circular in shape, with a diameter perhaps of half a mile. In the centre, as I have said, there was an open clearing about a quarter of a mile across, which was thus surrounded by a belt of thick trees and copse a couple of hundred yards in breadth. Our plan was first to walk together up the path which led through the wood, with all possible stealth, hoping to hear some movement on the part of what we had come to seek. Failing that, we had settled to tramp through the wood at the distance of some fifty yards from each other in a circular track; two or three of these circuits would cover the whole ground pretty thoroughly. Of the nature of our quarry, whether it would try to steal away from us, or possibly attack, we had no idea; it seemed, however, yesterday to have avoided us.

Rain had been falling steadily for an hour when we entered the wood; it hissed a little in the tree-tops overhead; but so thick was the cover that the ground below was still not more than damp. It was a dark morning outside; here you would say that the sun had already set and that night was falling. Very quietly we moved up the grassy path, where our footfalls were noiseless, and once we caught a whiff of that odour of live corruption; but though we stayed and listened not a sound of anything stirred except the sibilant rain over our heads. We went across the clearing and through to the far gate, and still there was no sign.

"We'll be getting into the trees then," said Hugh. "We had better start where we got that whiff of it."

We went back to the place, which was towards the middle of the encompassing trees. The odour still lingered on the windless air.

"Go on about fifty yards," he said, "and then we'll go in. If either of us comes on the track of it we'll shout to each other."

I walked on down the path till I had gone the right distance, signalled to him, and we stepped in among the trees.

I have never known the sensation of such utter loneliness. I knew that Hugh was walking parallel with me, only fifty yards away, and if I hung on my step I could faintly hear his tread among the beech leaves. But I felt as if I was quite sundered in this dim place from all companionship of man; the only live thing that lurked here was that monstrous mysterious creature of evil. So thick were the trees that I could not see more than a dozen yards in any direction; all places outside the wood seemed infinitely remote, and infinitely remote also everything that had occurred to me in normal human life. I had been whisked out of all wholesome experiences into this antique and evil place. The rain had ceased, it whispered no longer in the tree-tops, testifying that there did exist a world and a sky outside, and only a few drops from above pattered on the beech leaves.

Suddenly I heard the report of Hugh's gun, followed by his shouting voice.

"I've missed it," he shouted; "it's coming in your direction."

I heard him running towards me, the beech-leaves rustling, and no doubt his footsteps drowned a stealthier noise that was close to me. All that happened now, until once more I heard the report of Hugh's gun, happened, I suppose, in less than a minute. If it had taken much longer I do not imagine I should be telling it to-day.

I stood there then, having heard Hugh's shout, with my gun cocked, and ready to put to my shoulder, and I listened to his running footsteps. But still I saw nothing to shoot at and heard nothing. Then between two beech trees, quite close to me, I saw what I can only describe as a ball of darkness. It rolled very swiftly towards me over the few yards that separated me from it, and then, too late, I heard the dead beech-leaves rustling below it. Just before it reached me, my brain realised what it was, or what it might be, but before I could raise my gun to shoot at that nothingness, it was upon me. My gun was twitched out of my hand, and I was enveloped in this blackness, which was the very essence of corruption. It knocked me off my feet, and I sprawled flat on my back, and upon me, as I lay there, I felt the weight of this invisible assailant.

I groped wildly with my hands and they clutched something cold and slimy and hairy. They slipped off it, and next moment there was laid across my shoulder and neck something which felt like an india-rubber tube. The end of it fastened on to my neck like a snake, and I felt the skin rise beneath it. Again, with clutching hands, I tried to tear that obscene strength away from me, and as I struggled with it, I heard Hugh's footsteps close to me through this layer of darkness that hid everything.

My mouth was free, and I shouted at him.

"Here, here!" I yelled "Close to you, where it is darkest."

I felt his hands on mine, and that added strength detached from my neck that sucker that pulled at it. The coil that lay heavy on my legs and chest writhed and struggled and relaxed. Whatever it was that our four hands held, slipped out of them, and I saw Hugh standing close to me. A yard or two off, vanishing among the beech trunks, was that blackness which had poured over me. Hugh put up his gun, and with his second barrel fired at it.

The blackness dispersed, and there, wriggling and twisting like a huge worm lay what we had come to find. It was alive still, and I picked up my gun which lay by my side and fired two more barrels into it. The writhings dwindled into mere shudderings and shakings, and then it lay still.

With Hugh's help I got to my feet, and we both reloaded before going nearer. On the ground there lay a monstrous thing, half-slug, half worm. There was no head to it; it ended in a blunt point with an orifice. In colour it was grey covered with sparse black hairs; its length I suppose was some four feet, its thickness at the broadest part was that of a man's thigh, tapering towards each end. It was shattered by shot at its middle. There were stray pellets which had hit it elsewhere, and from the holes they had made there oozed not blood, but some grey viscous matter.

As we stood there some swift process of disintegration and decay began. It lost outline, it melted, it liquified, and in a minute more we were looking at a mass of stained and coagulated beech leaves. Again and quickly that liquor of corruption faded, and there lay at our feet no trace of what had been there. The overpowering odour passed away, and there came from the ground just the sweet savour of wet earth in springtime, and from above the glint of a sunbeam piercing the clouds. Then a sudden pattering among the dead leaves sent my heart into my mouth again, and I cocked my gun. But it was only Hugh's yellow retriever who had joined us.

We looked at each other.

"You're not hurt?" he said.

I held my chin up.

"Not a bit," I said. "The skin's not broken, is it?"

"No; only a round red mark. My God, what was it? What happened?"

"Your turn first," said I. "Begin at the beginning."

"I came upon it quite suddenly," he said. "It was lying coiled like a sleeping dog behind a big beech. Before I could fire, it slithered off in the direction where I knew you were. I got a snap shot at it among the trees, but I must have missed, for I heard it rustling away. I shouted to you and ran after it. There was a circle of absolute darkness on the ground, and your voice came from the middle of it. I couldn't see you at all, but I clutched at the blackness and my hands met yours. They met something else, too."

We got back to the house and had put the guns away before Daisy came home from her shopping. We had also scrubbed and brushed and washed. She came into the smoking-room.

"You lazy folk," she said. "It has cleared up, and why are you still indoors? Let's go out at once."

I got up.

"Hugh has told me you've got a dislike of the wood," I said, "and it's a lovely wood. Come and see; he and I will walk on each side of you and hold your hands. The dogs shall protect you as well."

"But not one of them will go a yard into the wood," said she.

"Oh yes, they will. At least we'll try them. You must promise to come if they do."

Hugh whistled them up, and down we went to the gate. They sat panting for it to be opened, and scuttled into the thickets in pursuit of interesting smells.

"And who says there are no birds in it?" said Daisy. "Look at that robin! Why, there are two of them. Evidently house-hunting."

25

THE OUTSIDER

H.P. Lovecraft

That night the Baron dreamt of many a wo;
And all his warrior-guests, with shade and form
Of witch, and demon, and large coffin-worm,
Were long be-nightmared.

—KEATS

Unhappy is he to whom the memories of childhood bring only fear and sadness. Wretched is he who looks back upon lone hours in vast and dismal chambers with brown hangings and maddening rows of antique books, or upon awed watches in twilight groves of grotesque, gigantic, and vine-encumbered trees that silently wave twisted branches far aloft. Such a lot the gods gave to me—to me, the dazed, the disappointed; the barren, the broken. And yet I am strangely content and cling desperately to those sere memories, when my mind momentarily threatens to reach beyond to the other.

I know not where I was born, save that the castle was infinitely old and infinitely horrible, full of dark passages and having high ceilings where the eye could find only cobwebs and shadows. The stones in the crumbling corridors seemed always hideously damp, and there was an accursed smell everywhere, as of the piled-up corpses of dead generations. It was never light, so that I used sometimes to light candles and gaze steadily at them for relief, nor was there any sun outdoors, since the terrible trees grew high above the topmost accessible tower. There was one black tower which reached above the trees into the unknown outer sky, but that was partly ruined and could not be ascended save by a well-nigh impossible climb up the sheer wall, stone by stone.

I must have lived years in this place, but I cannot measure the time. Beings must have cared for my needs, yet I cannot recall any person except myself, or anything alive but the noiseless rats and bats and spiders. I think that whoever nursed me must have been shockingly aged, since my first conception of a living person was that of somebody mockingly like myself, yet distorted, shrivelled, and decaying like the castle. To me there was nothing grotesque in the bones and skeletons that strewed some of the stone crypts deep down among the foundations. I fantastically associated these things with everyday events, and thought them more natural than the coloured pictures of living beings which I found in many of the mouldy books. From such books I learned all that I know. No teacher urged or guided me, and I do not recall hearing any human voice in all those years—not even my own; for although I had read of speech, I had never thought to try to speak aloud. My aspect was a matter equally unthought of, for there were no mirrors in the castle, and I merely regarded myself by instinct as akin to the youthful figures I saw drawn and painted in the books. I felt conscious of youth because I remembered so little.

Outside, across the putrid moat and under the dark mute trees, I would often lie and dream for hours about what I read in the books; and would longingly picture myself amidst gay crowds in the sunny world beyond the endless forests. Once I tried to escape from the forest, but as I went farther from the castle the shade grew denser and the air more filled with brooding fear; so that I ran frantically back lest I lose my way in a labyrinth of nighted silence.

So through endless twilights I dreamed and waited, though

I knew not what I waited for. Then in the shadowy solitude my longing for light grew so frantic that I could rest no more, and I lifted entreating hands to the single black ruined tower that reached above the forest into the unknown outer sky. And at last I resolved to scale that tower, fall though I might; since it were better to glimpse the sky and perish, than to live without ever beholding day.

In the dank twilight I climbed the worn and aged stone stairs till I reached the level where they ceased, and thereafter clung perilously to small footholds leading upward. Ghastly and terrible was that dead, stairless cylinder of rock; black, ruined, and deserted, and sinister with startled bats whose wings made no noise. But more ghastly and terrible still was the slowness of my progress; for climb as I might, the darkness overhead grew no thinner, and a new chill as of haunted and venerable mould assailed me. I shivered as I wondered why I did not reach the light, and would have looked down had I dared. I fancied that night had come suddenly upon me, and vainly groped with one free hand for a window embrasure, that I might peer out and above, and try to judge the height I had once attained.

All at once, after an infinity of awesome, sightless, crawling up that concave and desperate precipice, I felt my head touch a solid thing, and I knew I must have gained the roof, or at least some kind of floor. In the darkness I raised my free hand and tested the barrier, finding it stone and immovable. Then came a deadly circuit of the tower, clinging to whatever holds the slimy wall could give; till finally my testing hand found the barrier yielding, and I turned upward again, pushing the slab or door with my head as I used both hands in my fearful ascent. There was no light revealed above, and as my hands went higher I knew that my climb was for the nonce ended; since the slab was the trapdoor of an aperture leading to a level stone surface of greater circumference than the lower tower, no doubt the floor of some lofty and capacious observation chamber. I crawled through carefully, and tried to prevent the heavy slab from falling back into place, but failed in the latter attempt. As I lay exhausted on the stone floor I heard the eerie echoes of its fall, but hoped when necessary to pry it up again.

Believing I was now at prodigious height, far above the accursed branches of the wood, I dragged myself up from the floor and fumbled about for windows, that I might look for the first time upon the sky, and the moon and stars of which I had read. But on every hand I was disappointed; since all that I found were vast shelves of marble, bearing odious oblong boxes of disturbing size. More and more I reflected, and wondered what hoary secrets might abide in this high apartment so many aeons cut off from the castle below. Then unexpectedly my hands came upon a doorway, where hung a portal of stone, rough with strange chiselling. Trying it, I found it locked; but with a supreme burst of strength I overcame all obstacles and dragged it open inward. As I did so there came to me the purest ecstasy I have ever known; for shining tranquilly through an ornate grating of iron, and down a short stone passageway of steps that ascended from the newly found doorway, was the radiant full moon, which I had never before seen save in dreams and in vague visions I dared not call memories.

Fancying now that I had attained the very pinnacle of the castle, I commenced to rush up the few steps beyond the door; but the sudden veiling of the moon by a cloud caused me to stumble, and I felt my way more slowly in the dark. It was still very dark when I reached the grating—which I tried carefully and found unlocked, but which I did not open for fear of falling from the amazing height to which I had climbed. Then the moon came out.

Most demoniacal of all shocks is that of the abysmally unexpected and grotesquely unbelievable. Nothing I had before undergone could compare in terror with what I now saw; with the bizarre marvels that sight implied. The sight itself was as simple as it was stupefying, for it was merely this: instead of a dizzying prospect of treetops seen from a lofty eminence, there stretched around me on the level through the grating nothing less than *the solid ground*, decked and diversified by marble slabs and columns, and overshadowed by an ancient stone church, whose ruined spire gleamed spectrally in the moonlight.

Half unconscious, I opened the grating and staggered out upon the white gravel path that stretched away in two directions. My mind, stunned and chaotic as it was, still held the frantic craving for light; and not even the fantastic wonder which had happened could stay my course. I neither knew nor cared whether my experience was insanity, dreaming, or magic; but was determined to gaze on brilliance and gaiety at any cost. I knew not who I was or what I was, or what my surroundings might be; though as I continued to stumble along I became conscious of a kind of fearsome latent memory that made my progress not wholly fortuitous. I passed under an arch out of that region of slabs and columns, and wandered through the open country; sometimes following the visible road, but sometimes leaving it curiously to tread across meadows where only occasional ruins bespoke the ancient presence of a forgotten road. Once I swam across a swift river where crumbling, mossy masonry told of a bridge long vanished.

Over two hours must have passed before I reached what seemed to be my goal, a venerable ivied castle in a thickly wooded park, maddeningly familiar, yet full of perplexing strangeness to me. I saw that the moat was filled in, and that some of the well-known towers were demolished, whilst new wings existed to confuse the beholder. But what I observed with chief interest and delight were the open windows—gorgeously ablaze with light and sending forth sound of the gayest revelry. Advancing to one of these I looked in and saw an oddly dressed company indeed; making merry, and speaking brightly to one another. I had never, seemingly, heard human speech before and could guess only vaguely what was said. Some of the faces seemed to hold expressions that brought up incredibly remote recollections, others were utterly alien.

I now stepped through the low window into the brilliantly lighted room, stepping as I did so from my single bright moment of hope to my blackest convulsion of despair and realization. The nightmare was quick to come, for as I entered, there occurred immediately one of the most terrifying demonstrations I had ever conceived. Scarcely had I crossed the sill when there descended upon the whole company a sudden and unheralded fear of hideous intensity, distorting every face and evoking the most horrible screams from nearly every throat. Flight was universal, and in the clamour and panic several fell in a swoon and were dragged away by their madly fleeing companions. Many covered their eyes with their hands, and plunged blindly and awkwardly in their race to escape, overturning furniture and stumbling against the walls before they managed to reach one of the many doors.

The cries were shocking; and as I stood in the brilliant apartment alone and dazed, listening to their vanishing echoes, I trembled at the thought of what might be lurking near me unseen. At a casual inspection the room seemed deserted, but when I moved towards one of the alcoves I thought I detected a presence there—a hint of motion beyond the golden-arched doorway leading to another and somewhat similar room. As I approached the arch I began to perceive the presence more clearly; and then, with the first and last sound I ever uttered—a ghastly ululation that revolted me almost as poignantly as its noxious cause—I beheld in full, frightful vividness the inconceivable, indescribable, and unmentionable monstrosity which had by its simple appearance changed a merry company to a herd of delirious fugitives.

I cannot even hint what it was like, for it was a compound of all that is unclean, uncanny, unwelcome, abnormal, and detestable. It was the ghoulish shade of decay, antiquity, and dissolution; the putrid, dripping eidolon of unwholesome revelation, the awful baring of that which the merciful earth should always hide. God knows it was not of this world—or no longer of this world—yet to my horror I saw in its eaten-away and bone-revealing outlines a leering, abhorrent travesty on the human shape; and in its mouldy, disintegrating apparel an unspeakable quality that chilled me even more.

I was almost paralysed, but not too much so to make a feeble effort towards flight; a backward stumble which failed to break the spell in which the nameless, voiceless monster held me. My eyes bewitched by the glassy orbs which stared loathsomely into them, refused to close; though they were mercifully blurred, and showed the terrible object but indistinctly after the first shock. I tried to raise my hand to shut out the sight, yet so stunned were my nerves that my arm could not fully obey my will. The attempt, however, was enough to disturb my balance; so that I had to stagger forward several steps to avoid falling. As I did so I became suddenly and agonizingly aware of the nearness of the carrion thing, whose hideous hollow breathing I half fancied I could hear. Nearly mad, I found myself yet able to throw out a hand to ward off the foetid apparition which pressed so close; when in one cataclysmic second of cosmic nightmarishness and hellish accident my fingers touched the rotting outstretched paw of the monster beneath the golden arch.

I did not shriek, but all the fiendish ghouls that ride the nightwind shrieked for me as in that same second there crashed down upon my mind a single fleeting avalanche of soul-annihilating memory. I knew in that second all that had been;

I remembered beyond the frightful castle and the trees, and recognized the altered edifice in which I now stood; I recognized, most terrible of all, the unholy abomination that stood leering before me as I withdrew my sullied fingers from its own.

But in the cosmos there is balm as well as bitterness, and that balm is nepenthe. In the supreme horror of that second I forgot what had horrified me, and the burst of black memory vanished in a chaos of echoing images. In a dream I fled from that haunted and accursed pile, and ran swiftly and silently in the moonlight. When I returned to the churchyard place of marble and went down the steps I found the stone trap-door immovable; but I was not sorry, for I had hated the antique castle and the trees. Now I ride with the mocking and friendly ghouls on the night-wind, and play by day amongst the catacombs of Nephren-Ka in the sealed and unknown valley of Hadoth by the Nile. I know that light is not for me, save that of the moon over the rock tombs of Neb, nor any gaiety save the unnamed feasts of Nitokris beneath the Great Pyramid; yet in my new wildness and freedom I almost welcome the bitterness of alienage.

For although nepenthe has calmed me, I know always that I am an outsider; a stranger in this century and among those who are still men. This I have known ever since I stretched out my fingers to the abomination within that great gilded frame; stretched out my fingers and touched *a cold and unyielding surface of polished glass*.

26

THE COLD EMBRACE

Mary Elizabeth Braddon

He was an artist—such things as happened to him happen sometimes to artists.

He was a German—such things as happened to him happen sometimes to Germans.

He was young, handsome, studious, enthusiastic, metaphysical, reckless, unbelieving, heartless.

And being young, handsome and eloquent, he was beloved.

He was an orphan, under the guardianship of his dead father's brother, his uncle Wilhelm, in whose house he had been brought up from a little child; and she who loved him was his cousin—his cousin Gertrude, whom he swore he loved in return.

Did he love her? Yes, when he first swore it. It soon wore out, this passionate love; how threadbare and wretched a sentiment it became at last in the selfish heart of the student! But in its golden dawn, when he was only nineteen, and had just returned from his apprenticeship to a great painter at Antwerp, and they wandered together in the most romantic outskirts of the city at rosy sunset, by holy moonlight, or bright and joyous morning, how beautiful a dream!

They keep it a secret from Wilhelm, as he has the father's ambition of a wealthy suitor for his only child—a cold and dreary vision beside the lover's dream.

So they are betrothed; and standing side by side when the dying sun and the pale rising moon divide the heavens, he puts the betrothal ring upon her finger, the white and taper finger whose slender shape he knows so well. This ring is a peculiar one, a massive golden serpent, its tail in its mouth, the symbol of eternity; it had been his mother's, and he would know it amongst a thousand. If he were to become blind tomorrow, he could select it from amongst a thousand by the touch alone.

He places it on her finger, and they swear to be true to each other for ever and ever—through trouble and danger—sorrow and change—in wealth or poverty. Her father must needs be won to consent to their union by and by, for they were now betrothed, and death alone could part them.

But the young student, the scoffer at revelation, yet the enthusiastic adorer of the mystical, asks:

"Can death part us? I would return to you from the grave, Gertrude. My soul would come back to be near my love. And you—you, if you died before me—the cold earth would not hold you from me; if you loved me, you would return, and again these fair arms would be clasped round my neck as they are now."

But she told him, with a holier light in her deep-blue eyes than had ever shone in his—she told him that the dead who die at peace with God are happy in heaven, and cannot return to the troubled earth; and that it is only the suicide—the lost wretch on whom sorrowful angels shut the door of Paradise—whose unholy spirit haunts the footsteps of the living.

The first year of their betrothal is passed, and she is alone, for he has gone to Italy, on a commission for some rich man, to copy Raphaels, Titians, Guidos, in a gallery at Florence. He has gone to win fame, perhaps; but it is not the less bitter—he is gone!

Of course her father misses his young nephew, who has been as a son to him; and he thinks his daughter's sadness no more than a cousin should feel for a cousin's absence.

In the meantime, the weeks and months pass. The lover writes—often at first, then seldom—at last, not at all.

How many excuses she invents for him! How many times

she goes to the distant little post-office, to which he is to address his letters! How many times she hopes, only to be disappointed! How many times she despairs, only to hope again!

But real despair comes at last, and will not be put off any more. The rich suitor appears on the scene, and her father is determined. She is to marry at once. The wedding-day is fixed—the fifteenth of June.

The date seems to burn into her brain.

The date, written in fire, dances for ever before her eyes.

The date, shrieked by the Furies, sounds continually in her ears.

But there is time yet—it is the middle of May—there is time for a letter to reach him at Florence; there is time for him to come to Brunswick, to take her away and marry her, in spite of her father—in spite of the whole world.

But the days and the weeks fly by, and he does not write—he does not come. This is indeed despair which usurps her heart, and will not be put away.

It is the fourteenth of June. For the last time she goes to the little post-office; for the last time she asked the old question, and they give her for the last time the dreary answer, "No; no letter."

For the last time—for tomorrow is the day appointed for the bridal. Her father will hear no entreaties; her rich suitor will not listen to her prayers. They will not be put off a day—an hour; to-night alone is hers—this night, which she may employ as she will.

She takes another path than that which leads home; she hurries through some by-streets of the city, out on to a lonely bridge, where he and she had stood so often in the sunset, watching the rose-coloured light glow, fade, and die upon the river.

He returns from Florence. He had received her letter. That letter, blotted with tears, entreating, despairing—he had received it, but he loved her no longer. A young Florentine, who has sat to him for a model, had bewitched his fancy—that fancy which with him stood in place of a heart—and Gertrude had been half-forgotten. If she had a rich suitor, good; let her marry him; better for her, better far for himself. He had no wish to fetter himself with a wife. Had he not his art always?—his eternal bride, his unchanging mistress.

Thus he thought it wiser to delay his journey to Brunswick, so that he should arrive when the wedding was over—arrive in time to salute the bride.

And the vows—the mystical fancies—the belief in his return, even after death, to the embrace of his beloved? O, gone out of his life; melted away for ever, those foolish dreams of his boyhood.

So on the fifteenth of June he enters Brunswick, by that very bridge on which she stood, the stars looking down on her, the night before. He strolls across the bridge and down by the water's edge, a great rough dog at his heels, and the smoke from his short meerschaum-pipe curling in blue wreaths fantastically in the pure morning air. He has his sketch-book under his arm, and attracted now and then by some object that catches his artist's eye, stops to draw: a few weeds and pebbles on the river's brink—a crag on the opposite shore—a group of pollard willows in the distance. When he has done, he admires his drawing, shuts his sketch-book, empties the ashes from his pipe, refills from his tobacco-pouch, sings the refrain of a gay drinking-song, calls to his dog, smokes again, and walks on. Suddenly he opens his sketch-book again; this time that which attracts him is a group of figures: but what is it?

It is not a funeral, for there are no mourners.

It is not a funeral, but a corpse lying on a rude bier, covered with an old sail, carried between two bearers.

It is not a funeral, for the bearers are fishermen—fishermen in their everyday garb.

About a hundred yards from him they rest their burden on a bank—one stands at the head of the bier, the other throws himself down at the foot of it.

And thus they form the perfect group; he walks back two or three paces, selects his point of sight, and begins to sketch a hurried outline. He has finished it before they move; he hears their voices, though he cannot hear their words, and wonders what they can be talking of. Presently he walks on and joins them.

"You have a corpse there, my friends?" he says.

"Yes; a corpse washed ashore an hour ago."

"Drowned?"

"Yes, drowned. A young girl, very handsome."

"Suicides are always handsome," says the painter; and then he stands for a little while idly smoking and meditating, looking at the sharp outline of the corpse and the stiff folds of the rough canvas covering.

Life is such a golden holiday for him—young, ambitious, clever—that it seems as though sorrow and death could have no part in his destiny.

At last he says that, as this poor suicide is so handsome, he should like to make a sketch of her.

He gives the fishermen some money, and they offer to remove the sailcloth that covers her features.

No; he will do it himself. He lifts the rough, coarse, wet canvas from her face. What face?

The face that shone on the dreams of his foolish boyhood; the face which once was the light of his uncle's home. His cousin Gertrude—his betrothed!

He sees, as in one glance, while he draws one breath, the rigid features—the marble arms—the hands crossed on the cold bosom; and, on the third finger of the left hand, the ring which had been his mother's—the golden serpent; the ring which, if he were to become blind, he could select from a thousand others by the touch alone.

But he is a genius and a metaphysician—grief, true grief, is not for such as he. His first thought is flight—flight anywhere out of that accursed city—anywhere far from the brink of that hideous river—anywhere away from remorse—anywhere to forget.

He is miles on the road that leads away from Brunswick before he knows that he has walked a step.

It is only when his dog lies down panting at his feet that he feels how exhausted he is himself, and sits down upon a bank to rest. How the landscape spins round and round before his dazzled eyes, while his morning's sketch of the two fishermen and the canvas-covered bier glares redly at him out of the twilight.

At last, after sitting a long time by the roadside, idly playing with his dog, idly smoking, idly lounging, looking as any idle, light-hearted travelling student might look, yet all the while acting over that morning's scene in his burning brain a hundred times a minute; at last he grows a little more composed, and tries presently to think of himself as he is, apart from his cousin's suicide. Apart from that, he was no worse off than he was yesterday. His genius was not gone; the money he had earned at Florence still lined his pocket-book; he was his own master, free to go whither he would.

And while he sits on the roadside, trying to separate himself from the scene of that morning—trying to put away the image of the corpse covered with the damp canvas sail—trying to think of what he should do next, where he should go, to be farthest away from Brunswick and remorse, the old diligence coming rumbling and jingling along. He remembers it; it goes from Brunswick to Aix-la-Chapelle.

He whistles to the dog, shouts to the postillion to stop, and springs into the coupé.

During the whole evening, through the long night, though he does not once close his eyes, he never speaks a word; but when morning dawns, and the other passengers awake and begin to talk to each other, he joins in the conversation. He tells them that he is an artist, that he is going to Cologne and to Antwerp to copy Rubenses, and the great picture by Quentin Matsys, in the museum. He remembered afterwards that he talked and laughed boisterously, and that when he was talking and laughing loudest, a passenger, older and graver than the rest, opened the window near him, and told him to put his head out. He remembered the fresh air blowing in his face, the singing of the birds in his ears, and the flat fields and roadside reeling before his eyes. He remembered this, and then falling in a lifeless heap on the floor of the diligence.

It is a fever that keeps him for six long weeks on a bed at a hotel in Aix-la-Chapelle.

He gets well, and, accompanied by his dog, starts on foot for Cologne. By this time he is his former self once more. Again the blue smoke from his short meerschaum curls upwards in the morning air—again he sings some old university drinking song—again stops here and there, meditating and sketching.

He is happy, and has forgotten his cousin—and so on to Cologne.

It is by the great cathedral he is standing, with his dog at his side. It is night, the bells have just chimed the hour, and the clocks are striking eleven; the moonlight shines full upon the magnificent pile, over which the artist's eye wanders, absorbed in the beauty of form.

He is not thinking of his drowned cousin, for he has forgotten her and is happy.

Suddenly someone, something from behind him, puts two cold arms round his neck, and clasps its hands on his breast.

And yet there is no one behind him, for on the flags bathed

in the broad moonlight there are only two shadows, his own and his dog's. He turns quickly round—there is no one—nothing to be seen in the broad square but himself and his dog; and though he feels, he cannot see the cold arms clasped round his neck.

It is not ghostly, this embrace, for it is palpable to the touch—it cannot be real, for it is invisible.

He tries to throw off the cold caress. He clasps the hands in his own to tear them asunder, and to cast them off his neck. He can feel the long delicate fingers cold and wet beneath his touch, and on the third finger of the left hand he can feel the ring which was his mother's—the golden serpent—the ring which he has always said he would know among a thousand by the touch alone. He knows it now!

His dead cousin's cold arms are round his neck—his dead cousin's wet hands are clasped upon his breast. He asks himself if he is mad. "Up, Leo!" he shouts. "Up, up, boy!" and the Newfoundland leaps to his shoulders—the dog's paws are on the dead hands, and the animal utters a terrific howl, and springs away from his master.

The student stands in the moonlight, the dead arms around his neck, and the dog at a little distance moaning piteously.

Presently a watchman, alarmed by the howling of the dog, comes into the square to see what is wrong.

In a breath the cold arms are gone.

He takes the watchman home to the hotel with him and gives him money; in his gratitude he could have given the man half his little fortune.

Will it ever come to him again, this embrace of the dead?

He tries never to be alone; he makes a hundred acquaintances, and shares the chamber of another student. He starts up if he is left by himself in the public room of the inn where he is staying, and runs into the street. People notice his strange actions, and begin to think that he is mad.

But, in spite of all, he is alone once more; for one night the public room being empty for a moment, when on some idle pretence he strolls into the street, the street is empty too, and for the second time he feels the cold arms round his neck, and for the second time, when he calls his dog, the animal shrinks away from him with a piteous howl.

After this he leaves Cologne, still travelling on foot—of necessity now, for his money is getting low. He joins travelling hawkers, he walks side by side with labourers, he talks to every foot-passenger he falls in with, and tries from morning till night to get company on the road.

At night he sleeps by the fire in the kitchen of the inn at which he stops; but do what he will, he is often alone, and it is now a common thing for him to feel the cold arms around his neck.

Many months have passed since his cousin's death—autumn, winter, early spring. His money is nearly gone, his health is utterly broken, he is the shadow of his former self, and he is getting near to Paris. He will reach that city at the time of the Carnival. To this he looks forward. In Paris, in Carnival time, he need never, surely, be alone, never feel that deadly caress; he may even recover his lost gaiety, his lost health, once more resume his profession, once more earn fame and money by his art.

How hard he tries to get over the distance that divides him from Paris, while day by day he grows weaker, and his step slower and more heavy!

But there is an end at last; the long dreary roads are passed. This is Paris, which he enters for the first time—Paris, of which he has dreamed so much—Paris, whose million voices are to exorcise his phantom.

To him tonight Paris seems one vast chaos of lights, music, and confusion—lights which dance before his eyes and will not be still—music that rings in his ears and deafens him—confusion which makes his head whirl round and round.

But, in spite of all, he finds the opera-house, where there is a masked ball. He has enough money left to buy a ticket of admission, and to hire a domino to throw over his shabby dress. It seems only a moment after his entering the gates of Paris that he is in the very midst of all the wild gaiety of the opera-house ball.

No more darkness, no more loneliness, but a mad crowd, shouting and dancing, and a lovely Débardeuse hanging on his arm.

The boisterous gaiety he feels surely is his old light-heartedness come back. He hears the people round him talking of the outrageous conduct of some drunken student, and it is to him they point when they say this—to him, who has not moistened his lips since yesterday at noon, for even now he will not drink; though his lips are parched, and his throat burning, he cannot drink. His voice is thick and hoarse, and his utterance indistinct; but still this must be his old light-heartedness come back that makes him so wildly gay.

The little Débardeuse is wearied out—her arm rests on his shoulder heavier than lead—the other dancers one by one drop off.

The lights in the chandeliers one by one die out.

The decorations look pale and shadowy in that dim light which is neither night nor day.

A faint glimmer from the dying lamps, a pale streak of cold grey light from the new-born day, creeping in through half-opened shutters.

And by this light the bright-eyed Débardeuse fades sadly. He looks her in the face. How the brightness of her eyes dies out! Again he looks her in the face. How white that face has grown! Again—and now it is the shadow of a face alone that looks in his.

Again—and they are gone—the bright eyes, the face, the shadow of the face. He is alone; alone in that vast saloon.

Alone, and, in the terrible silence, he hears the echoes of his own footsteps in that dismal dance which has no music.

No music but the beating of his breast. The cold arms are round his neck—they whirl him round, they will not be flung off, or cast away; he can no more escape from their icy grasp than he can escape from death. He looks behind him—there is nothing but himself in the great empty salle; but he can feel—cold, deathlike, but O, how palpable!—the long slender fingers, and the ring which was his mother's.

He tries to shout, but he has no power in his burning throat. The silence of the place is only broken by the echoes of his own footsteps in the dance from which he cannot extricate himself. Who says he has no partner? The cold hands are clasped on his breast, and now he does not shun their caress. No! One more polka, if he drops down dead.

The lights are all out, and, half an hour after, the gendarmes come in with a lantern to see that the house is empty; they are followed by a great dog that they have found seated howling on the steps of the theatre. Near the principal entrance they stumble over—

The body of a student, who has died from want of food, exhaustion, and the breaking of a blood-vessel.

27

THE FACE

E.F. Benson

Hester Ward, sitting by the open window on this hot afternoon in June, began seriously to argue with herself about the cloud of foreboding and depression which had encompassed her all day, and, very sensibly, she enumerated to herself the manifold causes for happiness in the fortunate circumstances of her life. She was young, she was extremely good-looking, she was well-off, she enjoyed excellent health, and above all, she had an adorable husband and two small, adorable children. There was no break, indeed, anywhere in the circle of prosperity which surrounded her, and had the wishing-cap been handed to her that moment by some beneficent fairy, she would have hesitated to put it on her head, for there was positively nothing that she could think of which would have been worthy of such solemnity. Moreover, she could not accuse herself of a want of appreciation of her blessings; she appreciated enormously, she enjoyed enormously, and she thoroughly wanted all those who so munificently contributed to her happiness to share in it.

She made a very deliberate review of these things, for she was really anxious, more anxious, indeed, than she admitted to herself, to find anything tangible which could possibly warrant this ominous feeling of approaching disaster. Then there was the weather to consider; for the last week London had been stiflingly hot, but if that was the cause, why had she not felt it before? Perhaps the effect of these broiling, airless days had been cumulative. That was an idea, but, frankly, it did not seem a very good one, for, as a matter of fact, she loved the heat; Dick, who hated it, said that it was odd he should have fallen in love with a salamander.

She shifted her position, sitting up straight in this low window-seat, for she was intending to make a call on her courage. She had known from the moment she awoke this morning what it was that lay so heavy on her, and now, having done her best to shift the reason of her depression on to anything else, and having completely failed, she meant to look the thing in the face. She was ashamed of doing so, for the cause of this leaden mood of fear which held her in its grip, was so trivial, so fantastic, so excessively silly.

"Yes, there never was anything so silly," she said to herself. "I must look at it straight, and convince myself how silly it is." She paused a moment, clenching her hands.

"Now for it," she said.

She had had a dream the previous night, which, years ago, used to be familiar to her, for again and again when she was a child she had dreamed it. In itself the dream was nothing, but in those childish days, whenever she had this dream which had visited her last night, it was followed on the next night by another, which contained the source and the core of the horror, and she would awake screaming and struggling in the grip of overwhelming nightmare. For some ten years now she had not experienced it, and would have said that, though she remembered it, it had become dim and distant to her. But last night she had had that warning dream, which used to herald the visitation of the nightmare, and now that whole store-house of memory crammed as it was with bright things and beautiful contained nothing so vivid.

The warning dream, the curtain that was drawn up on the succeeding night, and disclosed the vision she dreaded, was simple and harmless enough in itself. She seemed to be walking on a high sandy cliff covered with short down-grass; twenty yards to the left came the edge of this cliff, which sloped steeply down to the sea that lay at its foot. The path she followed led through fields bounded by low hedges, and mounted gradually upwards. She went through some half-dozen of these, climbing over the wooden stiles that gave communication; sheep grazed there, but she never saw another human being, and always it was dusk, as if evening was falling, and she had to hurry on, because someone (she knew not whom) was waiting for her, and had been waiting not a few minutes only, but for many years. Presently, as she mounted this slope, she saw in front of her a copse of stunted trees, growing crookedly under the continual pressure of the wind that blew from the sea, and when she saw those she knew her journey was nearly done, and that the nameless one, who had been waiting for her so long was somewhere close at hand. The path she followed was cut through this wood, and the slanting boughs of the trees on the sea-ward side almost roofed it in; it was like walking through a tunnel. Soon the trees in front began to grow thin, and she saw through them the grey tower of a lonely church. It stood in a graveyard, apparently long disused, and the body of the church, which lay between the tower and the edge of the cliff, was in ruins, roofless, and with gaping windows, round which ivy grew thickly.

At that point this prefatory dream always stopped. It was a troubled, uneasy dream, for there was over it the sense of dusk and of the man who had been waiting for her so long, but it was not of the order of nightmare. Many times in childhood had she experienced it, and perhaps it was the subconscious knowledge of the night that so surely followed it, which gave it its disquiet. And now last night it had come again, identical in every particular but one. For last night it seemed to her that in the course of these ten years which had intervened since last it had visited her, the glimpse of the church and churchyard was changed. The edge of the cliff had come nearer to the tower, so that it now was within a yard or two of it, and the ruined body of the church, but for one broken arch that remained, had vanished. The sea had encroached, and for ten years had been busily eating at the cliff.

Hester knew well that it was this dream and this alone which had darkened the day for her, by reason of the nightmares that used to follow it, and, like a sensible woman, having looked it once in the face, she refused to admit into her mind any conscious calling-up of the sequel. If she let herself contemplate that, as likely or not the very thinking about it would be sufficient to ensure its return, and of one thing she was very certain, namely, that she didn't at all want it to do so. It was not like the confused jumble and jangle of ordinary nightmare, it was very simple, and she felt it concerned the nameless one who waited for her... But she must not think of it; her whole will and intention was set on not thinking of it, and to aid her resolution, there was the rattle of Dick's latch-key in the front-door, and his voice calling her.

She went out into the little square front hall; there he was, strong and large, and wonderfully undreamlike.

"This heat's a scandal, it's an outrage, it's an abomination of desolation," he cried, vigorously mopping. "What have we done that Providence should place us in this frying-pan? Let us thwart him, Hester! Let us drive out of this inferno and have our dinner at—I'll whisper it so that he shan't overhear—at Hampton Court!"

She laughed: this plan suited her excellently. They would return late, after the distraction of a fresh scene; and dining out at night was both delicious and stupefying.

"The very thing," she said, "and I'm sure Providence didn't hear. Let's start now!"

"Rather. Any letters for me?"

He walked to the table where there were a few rather uninteresting-looking envelopes with half penny stamps.

"Ah, receipted bill," he said. "Just a reminder of one's folly in paying it. Circular...unasked advice to invest in German marks... Circular begging letter, beginning 'Dear Sir or Madam.' Such impertinence to ask one to subscribe to something without ascertaining one's sex... Private view, portraits at the Walton Gallery... Can't go: business meetings all day. You might like to have a look in, Hester. Some one told me there were some fine Vandycks. That's all: let's be off."

Hester spent a thoroughly reassuring evening, and though she thought of telling Dick about the dream that had so deeply imprinted itself on her consciousness all day, in order to hear the great laugh he would have given her for being such a goose, she refrained from doing so, since nothing that he could say would be so tonic to these fantastic fears as his general robustness. Besides, she would have to account for its disturbing effect, tell him that it was once familiar to her, and recount the sequel of the nightmares that followed. She would neither think of them, nor mention them: it was wiser by far just to soak herself in his extraordinary sanity, and wrap herself in his affection... They dined out-of-doors at a river-side restaurant and strolled about afterwards, and it was very nearly midnight when, soothed with coolness and fresh air, and the vigour of his strong companionship, she let herself into the house, while he took the car back to the garage. And now she marvelled at the mood which had beset her all day, so distant and unreal had it become. She felt as if she had dreamed of shipwreck, and had awoke to find herself in some secure and sheltered garden where no tempest raged nor waves beat. But was there, ever so remotely, ever so dimly, the noise of far-off breakers somewhere?

He slept in the dressing-room which communicated with her bedroom, the door of which was left open for the sake of air and coolness, and she fell asleep almost as soon as her light was out, and while his was still burning. And immediately she began to dream.

She was standing on the sea-shore; the tide was out, for level sands strewn with stranded jetsam glimmered in a dusk that was deepening into night. Though she had never seen the place it was awfully familiar to her. At the head of the beach there was a steep cliff of sand, and perched on the edge of it was a grey church tower. The sea must have encroached and undermined the body of the church, for tumbled blocks of masonry lay close to her at the bottom of the cliff, and there were gravestones there, while others still in place were silhouetted whitely against the sky. To the right of the church tower there was a wood of stunted trees, combed sideways by the prevalent sea-wind, and she knew that along the top of the cliff a few yards inland there lay a path through fields, with wooden stiles to climb, which led through a tunnel of trees and so out into the churchyard. All this she saw in a glance, and waited, looking at the sand-cliff crowned by the church tower, for the terror that was going to reveal itself. Already she knew what it was, and, as so many times before, she tried to run away. But the catalepsy of nightmare was already on her; frantically she strove to move, but her utmost endeavour could not raise a foot from the sand. Frantically she tried to look away from the sand-cliffs close in front of her, where in a moment now the horror would be manifested...

It came. There formed a pale oval light, the size of a man's face, dimly luminous in front of her and a few inches above the level of her eyes. It outlined itself, short reddish hair grew low on the forehead, below were two grey eyes, set very close together, which steadily and fixedly regarded her. On each side the ears stood noticeably away from the head, and the lines of the jaw met in a short pointed chin. The nose was straight and rather long, below it came a hairless lip, and last of all the mouth took shape and colour, and there lay the crowning terror. One side of it, soft-curved and beautiful, trembled into a smile, the other side, thick and gathered together as by some physical deformity, sneered and lusted.

The whole face, dim at first, gradually focused itself into clear outline: it was pale and rather lean, the face of a young man. And then the lower lip dropped a little, showing the glint of teeth, and there was the sound of speech. "I shall soon come for you now," it said, and on the words it drew a little nearer to her, and the smile broadened. At that the full hot blast of nightmare poured in upon her. Again she tried to run, again she tried to scream, and now she could feel the breath of that terrible mouth upon her. Then with a crash and a rending like the tearing asunder of soul and body she broke the spell, and heard her own voice yelling, and felt with her fingers for the switch of her light. And then she saw that the room was not dark, for Dick's door was open, and the next moment, not yet undressed, he was with her.

"My darling, what is it?" he said. "What's the matter?"

She clung desperately to him, still distraught with terror.

"Ah, he has been here again," she cried. "He says he will soon come to me. Keep him away, Dick."

For one moment her fear infected him, and he found himself glancing round the room.

"But what do you mean?" he said. "No one has been here."

She raised her head from his shoulder.

"No, it was just a dream," she said. "But it was the old dream, and I was terrified. Why, you've not undressed yet. What time is it?"

"You haven't been in bed ten minutes, dear," he said. "You had hardly put out your light when I heard you screaming."

She shuddered.

"Ah, it's awful," she said. "And he will come again…"

He sat down by her.

"Now tell me all about it," he said.

She shook her head.

"No, it will never do to talk about it," she said, "it will only make it more real. I suppose the children are all right, are they?"

"Of course they are. I looked in on my way upstairs."

"That's good. But I'm better now, Dick. A dream hasn't anything real about it, has it? It doesn't mean anything?"

He was quite reassuring on this point, and soon she quieted down. Before he went to bed he looked in again on her, and she was asleep.

Hester had a stern interview with herself when Dick had gone down to his office next morning. She told herself that what she was afraid of was nothing more than her own fear. How many times had that ill-omened face come to her in dreams, and what significance had it ever proved to possess? Absolutely none at all, except to make her afraid. She was afraid where no fear was: she was guarded, sheltered, prosperous, and what if a nightmare of childhood returned? It had no more meaning now than it had then, and all those visitations of her childhood had passed away without trace... And then, despite herself, she began thinking over that vision again. It was grimly identical with all its previous occurrences, except... And then, with a sudden shrinking of the heart, she remembered that in earlier years those terrible lips had said: "I shall come for you when you are older," and last night they had said: "I shall soon come for you now." She remembered, too, that in the warning dream the sea had encroached, and it had now demolished the body of the church. There was an awful consistency about these two changes in the otherwise identical visions. The years had brought their change to them, for in the one the encroaching sea had brought down the body of the church, in the other the time was now near...

It was no use to scold or reprimand herself, for to bring her mind to the contemplation of the vision meant merely that the grip of terror closed on her again; it was far wiser to occupy herself, and starve her fear out by refusing to bring it the sustenance of thought. So she went about her household duties, she took the children out for their airing in the park, and then, determined to leave no moment unoccupied, set off with the card of invitation to see the pictures in the private view at the Walton Gallery. After that her day was full enough, she was lunching out, and going on to a matinée, and by the time she got home Dick would have returned, and they would drive down to his little house at Rye for the week-end. All Saturday and Sunday she would be playing golf, and she felt that fresh air and physical fatigue would exorcise the dread of these dreaming fantasies.

The gallery was crowded when she got there; there were friends among the sightseers, and the inspection of the pictures was diversified by cheerful conversation. There were two or three fine Raeburns, a couple of Sir Joshuas, but the gems, so she gathered, were three Vandycks that hung in a small room by themselves. Presently she strolled in there, looking at her catalogue. The first of them, she saw, was a portrait of Sir Roger Wyburn. Still chatting to her friend she raised her eye and saw it...

Her heart hammered in her throat, and then seemed to stand still altogether. A qualm, as of some mental sickness of the soul overcame her, for there in front of her was he who would soon come for her. There was the reddish hair, the projecting ears, the greedy eyes set close together, and the mouth smiling on one side, and on the other gathered up into the sneering menace that she knew so well. It might have been her own nightmare rather than a living model which had sat to the painter for that face.

"Ah, what a portrait, and what a brute!" said her companion. "Look, Hester, isn't that marvellous?"

She recovered herself with an effort. To give way to this ever-mastering dread would have been to allow nightmare to invade her waking life, and there, for sure, madness lay. She forced herself to look at it again, but there were the steady and eager eyes regarding her; she could almost fancy the mouth began to move. All round her the crowd bustled and chattered, but to her own sense she was alone there with Roger Wyburn.

And yet, so she reasoned with herself, this picture of him—for it was he and no other—should have reassured her. Roger Wyburn, to have been painted by Vandyck, must have been dead near on two hundred years; how could he be a menace to her? Had she seen that portrait by some chance as a child; had it made some dreadful impression on her, since overscored by other memories, but still alive in the mysterious subconsciousness, which flows eternally, like some dark underground river, beneath the surface of human life? Psychologists taught that these early impressions fester or poison the mind like some hidden abscess. That might account for this dread of one, nameless no longer, who waited for her.

That night down at Rye there came again to her the prefatory dream, followed by the nightmare, and clinging to her husband as the terror began to subside, she told him what she had resolved to keep to herself. Just to tell it brought a measure of comfort, for it was so outrageously fantastic, and his robust common sense upheld her. But when on their return to London there was a recurrence of these visions, he made short work of her demur and took her straight to her doctor.

"Tell him all, darling," he said. "Unless you promise to do that, I will. I can't have you worried like this. It's all nonsense, you know, and doctors are wonderful people for curing nonsense."

She turned to him.

"Dick, you're frightened," she said quietly.

He laughed.

"I'm nothing of the kind," he said, "but I don't like being awakened by your screaming. Not my idea of a peaceful night. Here we are."

The medical report was decisive and peremptory. There was nothing whatever to be alarmed about; in brain and body she was perfectly healthy, but she was run down. These disturbing dreams were, as likely as not, an effect, a symptom of her condition, rather than the cause of it, and Dr. Baring unhesitatingly recommended a complete change to some bracing place. The wise thing would be to send her out of this stuffy furnace to some quiet place to where she had never been. Complete change; quite so. For the same reason her husband had better not go with her; he must pack her off to, let us say, the East coast. Sea-air and coolness and complete idleness. No long walks; no long bathings; a dip, and a deck-chair on the sands. A lazy, soporific life. How about Rushton? He had no doubt that Rushton would set her up again. After a week or so, perhaps, her husband might go down and see her. Plenty of sleep—never mind the nightmares—plenty of fresh air.

Hester, rather to her husband's surprise, fell in with this suggestion at once, and the following evening saw her installed in solitude and tranquillity. The little hotel was still almost empty, for the rush of summer tourists had not yet begun, and all day she sat out on the beach with the sense of a struggle over. She need not fight the terror any more; dimly it seemed to her that its malignancy had been relaxed. Had she in some way yielded to it and done its secret bidding? At any rate no return of its nightly visitations had occurred, and she slept long and dreamlessly, and woke to another day of quiet. Every morning there was a line for her from Dick, with good news of himself and the children, but he and they alike seemed somehow remote, like memories of a very distant time. Something had driven in between her and them, and she saw them as if through glass. But equally did the memory of the face of Roger Wyburn, as seen on the master's canvas or hanging close in front of her against the crumbling sand-cliff, become blurred and indistinct, and no return of her nightly terrors visited her. This truce from all emotion reacted not on her mind alone, lulling her with a sense of soothed security, but on her body also, and she began to weary of this day-long inactivity.

The village lay on the lip of a stretch of land reclaimed from the sea. To the north the level marsh, now beginning to glow with the pale bloom of the sea-lavender, stretched away featureless till it lost itself in distance, but to the south a spur of hill came down to the shore ending in a wooded promontory. Gradually, as her physical health increased, she began to wonder what lay beyond this ridge which cut short the view, and one afternoon she walked across the intervening level and strolled up its wooded slopes. The day was close and windless, the invigorating sea-breeze which till now had spiced the heat with freshness had died, and she looked forward to finding a current of air stirring when she had topped the hill. To the south a mass of dark cloud lay along the horizon, but there was no imminent threat of storm. The slope was easily surmounted, and presently she stood at the top and found herself on the edge of a tableland of wooded pasture, and following the path, which ran not far from the edge of the cliff, she came out into more open country. Empty fields, where a few sheep were grazing, mounted gradually upwards. Wooden stiles made a communication in the hedges that bounded them. And there, not a mile in front of her, she saw a wood, with trees growing slantingly away from the push of the prevalent sea winds, crowning the upward slope, and over the top of it peered a grey church tower.

For the moment, as the awful and familiar scene identified itself, Hester's heart stood still: the next a wave of courage and resolution poured in upon her. Here, at last was the scene of that prefatory dream, and here was she presented with the opportunity of fathoming and dispelling it. Instantly her mind was made up, and under the strange twilight of the shrouded sky, she walked swiftly on through the fields she had so often traversed in sleep, and up to the wood, beyond which he was waiting for her. She closed her ears against the clanging bell of terror, which now she could silence for ever, and unfalteringly entered that dark tunnel of wood. Soon in front of her the trees began to thin, and through them, now close at hand, she saw the church tower. In a few yards farther she came out of the belt of trees, and round her were the monuments of a graveyard long disused. The cliff was broken off close to the church tower: between it and the edge there was no more of the body of the church than a broken arch, thick hung with ivy. Round this she passed and saw below the ruin of fallen masonry, and the level sands strewn with headstones and disjected rubble, and at the edge of the cliff were graves already cracked and toppling. But there was no one here, none waited for her, and the churchyard where she had so often pictured him was as empty as the fields she had just traversed.

A huge elation filled her; her courage had been rewarded, and all the terrors of the past became to her meaningless phantoms. But there was no time to linger, for now the storm threatened, and on the horizon a blink of lightning was followed by a crackling peal. Just as she turned to go her eye fell on a tombstone that was balanced on the very edge of the cliff, and she read on it that here lay the body of Roger Wyburn.

Fear, the catalepsy of nightmare, rooted her for the moment to the spot; she stared in stricken amazement at the moss-grown letters; almost she expected to see that fell terror of a face rise and hover over his resting-place. Then the fear which had frozen her lent her wings, and with hurrying feet she sped through the arched pathway in the wood and out into the fields. Not one backward glance did she give till she had come to the edge of the ridge above the village, and, turning, saw the pastures she had traversed empty of any living presence. None had followed; but the sheep, apprehensive of the coming storm, had ceased to feed, and were huddling under shelter of the stunted hedges.

Her first idea, in the panic of her mind, was to leave the place at once, but the last train for London had left an hour before, and besides, where was the use of flight if it was the spirit of a man long dead from which she fled? The distance from the place where his bones lay did not afford her safety; that must be sought for within. But she longed for Dick's sheltering and confident presence; he was arriving in any case to-morrow, but there were long dark hours before to-morrow, and who could say what the perils and dangers of the coming night might be? If he started this evening instead of to-morrow morning, he could motor down here in four hours, and would be with her by ten o'clock or eleven. She wrote an urgent telegram: "Come at once," she said. "Don't delay."

The storm which had flickered on the south now came quickly up, and soon after it burst in appalling violence. For preface there were but a few large drops that splashed and dried on the roadway as she came back from the post-office, and just as she reached the hotel again the roar of the approaching rain sounded, and the sluices of heaven were opened. Through the deluge flared the fire of the lightning, the thunder crashed and echoed overhead, and presently the street of the village was a torrent of sandy turbulent water, and sitting there in the dark one picture leapt floating before her eyes, that of the tombstone of Roger Wyburn, already tottering to its fall at the edge of the cliff of the church tower. In such rains as these, acres of the cliffs were loosened; she seemed to hear the whisper of the sliding sand that would precipitate those perished sepulchres and what lay within to the beach below.

By eight o'clock the storm was subsiding, and as she dined she was handed a telegram from Dick, saying that he had already started and sent this off *en route*. By half-past ten, therefore, if all was well, he would be here, and somehow he would stand between her and her fear. Strange how a few days ago both it and the thought of him had become distant and dim to her; now the one was as vivid as the other, and she counted the minutes to his arrival. Soon the rain ceased altogether, and looking out of the curtained window of her sitting-room where she sat watching the slow circle of the hands of the clock, she saw a tawny moon rising over the sea. Before it had climbed to the zenith, before her clock had twice told the hour again, Dick would be with her.

It had just struck ten when there came a knock at her door, and the page-boy entered with the message that a gentleman had come for her. Her heart leaped at the news; she had not expected Dick for half an hour yet, and now the lonely vigil was over. She ran downstairs, and there was the figure standing on the step outside. His face was turned away from her; no doubt he was giving some order to his chauffeur. He was outlined against the white moonlight, and in contrast with that, the gas-jet in the entrance just above his head gave his hair a warm, reddish tinge.

She ran across the hall to him.

"Ah, my darling, you've come," she said. "It was good of you. How quick you've been!" Just as she laid her hand on his shoulder he turned. His arm was thrown out round her, and she looked into a face with eyes close set, and a mouth smiling on one side, the other, thick and gathered together as by some physical deformity, sneered and lusted.

The nightmare was on her; she could neither run nor scream, and supporting her dragging steps, he went forth with her into the night.

Half an hour later Dick arrived. To his amazement he heard that a man had called for his wife not long before, and that she had gone out with him. He seemed to be a stranger here, for the boy who had taken his message to her had never seen him before, and presently surprise began to deepen into alarm; enquiries were made outside the hotel, and it appeared that a witness or two had seen the lady whom they knew to be staying there walking, hatless, along the top of the beach with a man whose arm was linked in hers. Neither of them knew him, but one had seen his face and could describe it.

The direction of the search thus became narrowed down, and though with a lantern to supplement the moonlight they came upon footprints which might have been hers, there were no marks of any who walked beside her. But they followed these until they came to an end, a mile away, in a great landslide of sand, which had fallen from the old churchyard on the cliff, and had brought down with it half the tower and a gravestone, with the body that had lain below.

The gravestone was that of Roger Wyburn, and his body lay by it, untouched by corruption or decay, though two hundred years had elapsed since it was interred there. For a week afterwards the work of searching the landslide went on, assisted by the high tides that gradually washed it away. But no further discovery was made.

28

THE MARK OF THE BEAST

Rudyard Kipling

Your Gods and my Gods—do you or I know which are the stronger?

—NATIVE PROVERB

East of Suez, some hold, the direct control of Providence ceases; Man being there handed over to the power of the Gods and Devils of Asia, and the Church of England Providence only exercising an occasional and modified supervision in the case of Englishmen. This theory accounts for some of the more unnecessary horrors of life in India: it may be stretched to explain my story.

My friend Strickland of the Police, who knows as much of natives of India as is good for any man, can bear witness to the facts of the case. Dumoise, our doctor, also saw what Strickland and I saw. The inference which he drew from the evidence was entirely incorrect. He is dead now; he died in a rather curious manner, which has been elsewhere described.

When Fleete came to India he owned a little money and some land in the Himalayas, near a place called Dharmsala. Both properties had been left him by an uncle, and he came out to finance them. He was a big, heavy, genial, and inoffensive man. His knowledge of natives was, of course, limited, and he complained of the difficulties of the language.

He rode in from his place in the hills to spend New Year in the station, and he stayed with Strickland. On New Year's Eve there was a big dinner at the club, and the night was excusably wet. When men foregather from the uttermost ends of the Empire they have a right to be riotous. The Frontier had sent down a contingent o' Catch-'em-Alive-O's who had not seen twenty white faces for a year, and were used to ride fifteen miles to dinner at the next Fort at the risk of a Khyberee bullet where their drinks should lie. They profited by their new security, for they tried to play pool with a curled-up hedgehog found in the garden, and one of them carried the marker round the room in his teeth. Half a dozen planters had come in from the south and were talking "horse" to the Biggest Liar in Asia, who was trying to cap all their stories at once. Everybody was there, and there was a general closing up of ranks and taking stock of our losses in dead or disabled that had fallen during the past year. It was a very wet night, and I remember that we sang "Auld Lang Syne" with our feet in the Polo Championship Cup, and our heads among the stars, and swore that we were all dear friends. Then some of us went away and annexed Burma, and some tried to open up the Soudan and were opened up by Fuzzies in that cruel scrub outside Suakim, and some found stars and medals, and some were married, which was bad, and some did other things which were worse, and the others of us stayed in our chains and strove to make money on insufficient experiences.

Fleete began the night with sherry and bitters, drank champagne steadily up to dessert, then raw, rasping Capri with all the strength of whisky, took Benedictine with his coffee, four or five whiskies and sodas to improve his pool strokes, beer and bones at half-past two, winding up with old brandy. Consequently, when he came out, at half-past three in the morning, into fourteen degrees of frost, he was very angry with his horse for coughing, and tried to leapfrog into the saddle. The horse broke away and went to his stables; so Strickland and I formed a Guard of Dishonour to take Fleete home.

Our road lay through the bazaar, close to a little temple of Hanuman, the Monkey-god, who is a leading divinity worthy of respect. All gods have good points, just as have all priests. Personally, I attach much importance to Hanuman, and am kind to his people—the great gray apes of the hills. One never knows when one may want a friend.

There was a light in the temple, and as we passed we could hear voices of men chanting hymns. In a native temple the priests rise at all hours of the night to do honour to their god. Before we could stop him, Fleete dashed up the steps, patted two priests on the back, and was gravely grinding the ashes of his cigar-butt in to the forehead of the red stone image of Hanuman. Strickland tried to drag him out, but he sat down and said solemnly:

"Shee that? 'Mark of the B——beasht! I made it. Ishn't it fine?"

In half a minute the temple was alive and noisy, and Strickland, who knew what came of polluting gods, said that things might occur. He, by virtue of his official position, long residence in the country, and weakness for going among the natives, was known to the priests and he felt unhappy. Fleete sat on the ground and refused to move. He said that "good old Hanuman" made a very soft pillow.

Then, without any warning, a Silver Man came out of a recess behind the image of the god. He was perfectly naked in that bitter, bitter cold, and his body shone like frosted silver, for he was what the Bible calls "a leper as white as snow." Also he had no face, because he was a leper of some years' standing, and his disease was heavy upon him. We two stooped to haul Fleete up, and the temple was filling and filling with folk who seemed to spring from the earth, when the Silver Man ran in under our arms, making a noise exactly like the mewing of an otter, caught Fleete round the body and dropped his head on Fleete's breast before we could wrench him away. Then he retired to a corner and sat mewing while the crowd blocked all the doors.

The priests were very angry until the Silver Man touched Fleete. That nuzzling seemed to sober them.

At the end of a few minutes' silence one of the priests came to Strickland and said, in perfect English, "Take your friend away. He has done with Hanuman but Hanuman has not done with him." The crowd gave room and we carried Fleete into the road.

Strickland was very angry. He said that we might all three have been knifed, and that Fleete should thank his stars that he had escaped without injury.

Fleete thanked no one. He said that he wanted to go to bed. He was gorgeously drunk.

We moved on, Strickland silent and wrathful, until Fleete was taken with violent shivering fits and sweating. He said that the smells of the bazaar were overpowering, and he wondered why slaughter-houses were permitted so near English residences. "Can't you smell the blood?" said Fleete.

We put him to bed at last, just as the dawn was breaking, and Strickland invited me to have another whisky and soda. While we were drinking he talked of the trouble in the temple, and admitted that it baffled him completely. Strickland hates being mystified by natives, because his business in life is to overmatch them with their own weapons. He has not yet succeeded in doing this, but in fifteen or twenty years he will have made some small progress.

"They should have mauled us," he said, "instead of mewing at us. I wonder what they meant. I don't like it one little bit."

I said that the Managing Committee of the temple would in all probability bring a criminal action against us for insulting their religion. There was a section of the Indian Penal Code which exactly met Fleete's offence. Strickland said he only hoped and prayed that they would do this. Before I left I looked into Fleete's room, and saw him lying on his right side, scratching his left breast. Then I went to bed cold, depressed, and unhappy, at seven o'clock in the morning.

At one o'clock I rode over to Strickland's house to inquire after Fleete's head. I imagined that it would be a sore one. Fleete was breakfasting and seemed unwell. His temper was gone, for he was abusing the cook for not supplying him with an underdone chop. A man who can eat raw meat after a wet night is a curiosity. I told Fleete this and he laughed.

"You breed queer mosquitoes in these parts," he said. "I've been bitten to pieces, but only in one place."

"Let's have a look at the bite," said Strickland. "It may have gone down since this morning."

While the chops were being cooked, Fleete opened his shirt and showed us, just over his left breast, a mark, the perfect double of the black rosettes—the five or six irregular blotches arranged in a circle—on a leopard's hide. Strickland looked and said, "It was only pink this morning. It's grown black now."

Fleete ran to a glass.

"By Jove!" he said, "this is nasty. What is it?"

We could not answer. Here the chops came in, all red and juicy, and Fleete bolted three in a most offensive manner. He ate on his right grinders only, and threw his head over his right shoulder as he snapped the meat. When he had finished, it struck him that he had been behaving strangely, for he said apologetically, "I don't think I ever felt so hungry in my life. I've bolted like an ostrich."

After breakfast Strickland said to me, "Don't go. Stay here, and stay for the night."

Seeing that my house was not three miles from Strickland's, this request was absurd. But Strickland insisted, and was going to say something, when Fleete interrupted by declaring in a shamefaced way that he felt hungry again. Strickland sent a man to my house to fetch over my bedding and a horse, and we three went down to Strickland's stables to pass the hours until it was time to go out for a ride. The man who has a weakness for horses never wearies of inspecting them; and when two men are killing time in this way they gather knowledge and lies the one from the other.

There were five horses in the stables, and I shall never forget the scene as we tried to look them over. They seemed to have gone mad. They reared and screamed and nearly tore up their pickets; they sweated and shivered and lathered and were distraught with fear. Strickland's horses used to know him as well as his dogs; which made the matter more curious. We left the stable for fear of the brutes throwing themselves in their panic. Then Strickland turned back and called me. The horses were still frightened, but they let us "gentle" and make much of them, and put their heads in our bosoms.

"They aren't afraid of *us*," said Strickland. "D' you know, I'd give three months' pay if *Outrage* here could talk."

But *Outrage* was dumb, and could only cuddle up to his master and blow out his nostrils, as is the custom of horses when they wish to explain things but can't. Fleete came up when we were in the stalls, and as soon as the horses saw him, their fright broke out afresh. It was all that we could do to escape from the place unkicked. Strickland said, "They don't seem to love you, Fleete."

"Nonsense," said Fleete; "my mare will follow me like a dog." He went to her; she was in a loose-box; but as he slipped the bars she plunged, knocked him down, and broke away into the garden. I laughed, but Strickland was not amused. He took his moustache in both fists and pulled at it till it nearly came out. Fleete, instead of going off to chase his property, yawned, saying that he felt sleepy. He went to the house to lie down, which was a foolish way of spending New Year's Day.

Strickland sat with me in the stables and asked if I had noticed anything peculiar in Fleete's manner. I said that he ate his food like a beast; but that this might have been the result of living alone in the hills out of the reach of society as refined and elevating as ours for instance. Strickland was not amused. I do not think that he listened to me, for his next sentence referred to the mark on Fleete's breast, and I said that it might have been caused by blister-flies, or that it was possibly a birth-mark newly born and now visible for the first time. We both agreed that it was unpleasant to look at, and Strickland found occasion to say that I was a fool.

"I can't tell you what I think now," said he, "because you would call me a madman; but you must stay with me for the next few days, if you can. I want you to watch Fleete, but don't tell me what you think till I have made up my mind."

"But I am dining out to-night," I said.

"So am I," said Strickland, "and so is Fleete. At least if he doesn't change his mind."

We walked about the garden smoking, but saying nothing— because we were friends, and talking spoils good tobacco—till our pipes were out. Then we went to wake up Fleete. He was wide awake and fidgeting about his room.

"I say, I want some more chops," he said. "Can I get them?"

We laughed and said, "Go and change. The ponies will be round in a minute."

"All right," said Fleete. "I'll go when I get the chops— underdone ones, mind."

He seemed to be quite in earnest. It was four o'clock, and we had had breakfast at one; still, for a long time, he demanded those underdone chops. Then he changed into riding clothes and went out into the verandah. His pony—the mare had not been caught—would not let him come near. All three horses were unmanageable—mad with fear—and finally Fleete said that he would stay at home and get something to eat. Strickland and I rode out wondering. As we passed the temple of Hanuman the Silver Man came out and mewed at us.

"He is not one of the regular priests of the temple," said

Strickland. "I think I should peculiarly like to lay my hands on him."

There was no spring in our gallop on the racecourse that evening. The horses were stale, and moved as though they had been ridden out.

"The fright after breakfast has been too much for them," said Strickland.

That was the only remark he made through the remainder of the ride. Once or twice, I think, he swore to himself; but that did not count.

We came back in the dark at seven o'clock, and saw that there were no lights in the bungalow. "Careless ruffians my servants are!" said Strickland.

My horse reared at something on the carriage drive, and Fleete stood up under its nose.

"What are you doing, grovelling about the garden?" said Strickland.

But both horses bolted and nearly threw us. We dismounted by the stables and returned to Fleete, who was on his hands and knees under the orange-bushes.

"What the devil's wrong with you?" said Strickland.

"Nothing, nothing in the world," said Fleete, speaking very quickly and thickly. "I've been gardening—botanising, you know. The smell of the earth is delightful. I think I'm going for a walk—a long walk—all night."

Then I saw that there was something excessively out of order somewhere, and I said to Strickland, "I am not dining out."

"Bless you!" said Strickland. "Here, Fleete, get up. You'll catch fever there. Come in to dinner and let's have the lamps lit. We'll all dine at home."

Fleete stood up unwillingly, and said, "No lamps—no lamps. It's much nicer here. Let's dine outside and have some more chops—lots of 'em and underdone—bloody ones with gristle."

Now a December evening in Northern India is bitterly cold, and Fleete's suggestion was that of a maniac.

"Come in," said Strickland sternly. "Come in at once."

Fleete came, and when the lamps were brought, we saw that he was literally plastered with dirt from head to foot. He must have been rolling in the garden. He shrank from the light and went to his room. His eyes were horrible to look at. There was a green light behind them, not in them, if you understand, and the man's lower lip hung down.

Strickland said, "There is going to be trouble—big trouble—to-night. Don't you change your riding-things."

We waited and waited for Fleete's reappearance, and ordered dinner in the meantime. We could hear him moving about his own room, but there was no light there. Presently from the room came the long-drawn howl of a wolf.

People write and talk lightly of blood running cold and hair standing up, and things of that kind. Both sensations are too horrible to be trifled with.

My heart stopped as though a knife had been driven through it, and Strickland turned as white as the tablecloth.

The howl was repeated, and was answered by another howl far across the fields.

That set the gilded roof on the horror. Strickland dashed into Fleete's room. I followed, and we saw Fleete getting out of the window. He made beast-noises in the back of his throat. He could not answer us when we shouted at him. He spat.

I don't quite remember what followed, but I think that Strickland must have stunned him with the long boot-jack, or else I should never have been able to sit on his chest. Fleete could not speak, he could only snarl, and his snarls were those of a wolf, not of a man. The human spirit must have been giving way all day and have died out with the twilight. We were dealing with a beast that had once been Fleete.

The affair was beyond any human and rational experience. I tried to say "Hydrophobia," but the word wouldn't come, because I knew that I was lying.

We bound this beast with leather thongs of the punkah-rope, and tied its thumbs and big toes together, and gagged it with a shoe-horn, which makes a very efficient gag if you know how to arrange it. Then we carried it into the dining-room, and sent a man to Dumoise, the doctor, telling him to come over at once. After we had despatched the messenger and were drawing breath, Strickland said, "It's no good. This isn't any doctor's work." I, also, knew that he spoke the truth.

The beast's head was free, and it threw it about from side to side. Any one entering the room would have believed that we were curing a wolf's pelt. That was the most loathsome accessory of all.

Strickland sat with his chin in the heel of his fist, watching the beast as it wriggled on the ground, but saying nothing. The shirt had been torn open in the scuffle and showed the black rosette mark on the left breast. It stood out like a blister.

In the silence of the watching we heard something without— mewing like a she-otter. We both rose to our feet, and, I answer for myself, not Strickland, felt sick—actually and physically sick. We told each other, as did the men in Pinafore, that it was the cat.

Dumoise arrived, and I never saw a little man so unprofessionally shocked. He said that it was a heart-rending case of hydrophobia, and that nothing could be done. At least any palliative measures would only prolong the agony. The beast was foaming at the mouth. Fleete, as we told Dumoise, had been bitten by dogs once or twice. Any man who keeps half a dozen terriers must expect a nip now and again. Dumoise could offer no help. He could only certify that Fleete was dying of hydrophobia. The beast was then howling, for it had managed to spit out the shoe-horn. Dumoise said that he would be ready to certify to the cause of death, and that the end was certain. He was a good little man, and he offered to remain with us; but Strickland refused the kindness. He did not wish to poison Dumoise's New Year. He would only ask him not to give the real cause of Fleete's death to the public.

So Dumoise left, deeply agitated; and as soon as the noise of the cart-wheels had died away, Strickland told me, in a whisper, his suspicions. They were so wildly improbable that he dared not say them out aloud; and I, who entertained all Strickland's beliefs, was so ashamed of owning to them that I pretended to disbelieve.

"Even if the Silver Man had bewitched Fleete for polluting the image of Hanuman, the punishment could not have fallen so quickly."

As I was whispering this the cry outside the house rose again, and the beast fell into a fresh paroxysm of struggling till we were afraid that the thongs that held it would give way.

"Watch!" said Strickland. "If this happens six times I shall take the law into my own hands. I order you to help me."

He went into his room and came out in a few minutes with the barrels of an old shot-gun, a piece of fishing-line, some thick cord, and his heavy wooden bedstead. I reported that the convulsions had followed the cry by two seconds in each case, and the beast seemed perceptibly weaker.

Strickland muttered, "But he can't take away the life! He can't take away the life!"

I said, though I knew that I was arguing against myself, "It may be a cat. It must be a cat. If the Silver Man is responsible, why does he dare to come here?"

Strickland arranged the wood on the hearth, put the gun-barrels into the glow of the fire, spread the twine on the table, and broke a walking stick in two. There was one yard of fishing line, gut lapped with wire, such as is used for mahseer-fishing, and he tied the two ends together in a loop.

Then he said, "How can we catch him? He must be taken alive and unhurt."

I said that we must trust in Providence, and go out softly with polo-sticks into the shrubbery at the front of the house. The man or animal that made the cry was evidently moving round the house as regularly as a night-watchman. We could wait in the bushes till he came by and knock him over.

Strickland accepted this suggestion, and we slipped out from a bath-room window into the front verandah and then across the carriage drive into the bushes.

In the moonlight we could see the leper coming round the corner of the house. He was perfectly naked, and from time to time he mewed and stopped to dance with his shadow. It was an unattractive sight, and thinking of poor Fleete, brought to such degradation by so foul a creature, I put away all my doubts and resolved to help Strickland from the heated gun-barrels to the loop of twine—from the loins to the head and back again—with all tortures that might be needful.

The leper halted in the front porch for a moment and we jumped out on him with the sticks. He was wonderfully strong, and we were afraid that he might escape or be fatally injured before we caught him. We had an idea that lepers were frail creatures, but this proved to be incorrect. Strickland knocked his legs from under him and I put my foot on his neck. He mewed hideously, and even through my riding-boots I could feel that his flesh was not the flesh of a clean man.

He struck at us with his hand and feet-stumps. We looped the lash of a dog-whip round him, under the arm-pits, and dragged him backwards into the hall and so into the dining-room where the beast lay. There we tied him with trunk-straps. He made no attempt to escape, but mewed.

When we confronted him with the beast the scene was beyond description. The beast doubled backwards into a bow as though he had been poisoned with strychnine, and moaned in the most pitiable fashion. Several other things happened also, but they cannot be put down here.

"I think I was right," said Strickland. "Now we will ask him to cure this case."

But the leper only mewed. Strickland wrapped a towel round his hand and took the gun-barrels out of the fire. I put the half of the broken walking stick through the loop of fishing-line and buckled the leper comfortably to Strickland's bedstead. I understood then how men and women and little children can endure to see a witch burnt alive; for the beast was moaning on the floor, and though the Silver Man had no face, you could see horrible feelings passing through the slab that took its place, exactly as waves of heat play across red-hot iron—gun-barrels for instance.

Strickland shaded his eyes with his hands for a moment and we got to work. This part is not to be printed.

The dawn was beginning to break when the leper spoke. His mewings had not been satisfactory up to that point. The beast had fainted from exhaustion and the house was very still. We unstrapped the leper and told him to take away the evil spirit. He crawled to the beast and laid his hand upon the left breast. That was all. Then he fell face down and whined, drawing in his breath as he did so.

We watched the face of the beast, and saw the soul of Fleete coming back into the eyes. Then a sweat broke out on the forehead and the eyes—they were human eyes—closed. We waited for an hour, but Fleete still slept. We carried him to his room and bade the leper go, giving him the bedstead, and the sheet on the bedstead to cover his nakedness, the gloves and the towels with which we had touched him, and the whip that had been hooked round his body. He put the sheet about him and went out into the early morning without speaking or mewing.

Strickland wiped his face and sat down. A night-gong, far away in the city, made seven o'clock.

"Exactly four-and-twenty hours!" said Strickland. "And I've done enough to ensure my dismissal from the service, besides permanent quarters in a lunatic asylum. Do you believe that we are awake?"

The red-hot gun-barrel had fallen on the floor and was singeing the carpet. The smell was entirely real.

That morning at eleven we two together went to wake up Fleete. We looked and saw that the black leopard-rosette on his chest had disappeared. He was very drowsy and tired, but as soon as he saw us, he said, "Oh! Confound you fellows. Happy New Year to you. Never mix your liquors. I'm nearly dead."

"Thanks for your kindness, but you're over time," said Strickland. "To-day is the morning of the second. You've slept the clock round with a vengeance."

The door opened, and little Dumoise put his head in. He had come on foot, and fancied that we were laying out Fleete.

"I've brought a nurse," said Dumoise. "I suppose that she can come in for…what is necessary."

"By all means," said Fleete cheerily, sitting up in bed. "Bring on your nurses."

Dumoise was dumb. Strickland led him out and explained that there must have been a mistake in the diagnosis. Dumoise remained dumb and left the house hastily. He considered that his professional reputation had been injured, and was inclined to make a personal matter of the recovery. Strickland went out too. When he came back, he said that he had been to call on the Temple of Hanuman to offer redress for the pollution of the god, and had been solemnly assured that no white man had ever touched the idol, and that he was an incarnation of all the virtues labouring under a delusion. "What do you think?" said Strickland.

I said, "There are more things..."

But Strickland hates that quotation. He says that I have worn it threadbare.

One other curious thing happened which frightened me as much as anything in all the night's work. When Fleete was dressed he came into the dining-room and sniffed. He had a quaint trick of moving his nose when he sniffed. "Horrid doggy smell, here," said he. "You should really keep those terriers of yours in better order. Try sulphur, Strick."

But Strickland did not answer. He caught hold of the back of a chair, and, without warning, went into an amazing fit of hysterics. It is terrible to see a strong man overtaken with hysteria. Then it struck me that we had fought for Fleete's soul with the Silver Man in that room, and had disgraced ourselves as Englishmen for ever, and I laughed and gasped and gurgled just as shamefully as Strickland, while Fleete thought that we had both gone mad. We never told him what we had done.

Some years later, when Strickland had married and was a church-going member of society for his wife's sake, we reviewed the incident dispassionately, and Strickland suggested that I should put it before the public.

I cannot myself see that this step is likely to clear up the mystery; because, in the first place, no one will believe a rather unpleasant story, and, in the second, it is well known to every right-minded man that the gods of the heathen are stone and brass, and any attempt to deal with them otherwise is justly condemned.

29

DICKON THE DEVIL

J.S. Le Fanu

About thirty years ago I was selected by two rich old maids to visit a property in that part of Lancashire which lies near the famous forest of Pendle, with which Mr. Ainsworth's "Lancashire Witches" has made us so pleasantly familiar. My business was to make partition of a small property, including a house and demesne, to which they had a long time before succeeded as co-heiresses.

The last forty miles of my journey I was obliged to post, chiefly by cross-roads, little known, and less frequented, and presenting scenery often extremely interesting and pretty. The picturesqueness of the landscape was enhanced by the season, the beginning of September, at which I was travelling.

I had never been in this part of the world before; I am told it is now a great deal less wild, and, consequently, less beautiful.

At the inn where I had stopped for a relay of horses and some dinner—for it was then past five o'clock—I found the host, a hale old fellow of five-and-sixty, as he told me, a man of easy and garrulous benevolence, willing to accommodate his guests with any amount of talk, which the slightest tap sufficed to set flowing, on any subject you pleased.

I was curious to learn something about Barwyke, which was the name of the demesne and house I was going to. As there was no inn within some miles of it, I had written to the steward to put me up there, the best way he could, for a night.

The host of the "Three Nuns," which was the sign under

which he entertained wayfarers, had not a great deal to tell. It was twenty years, or more, since old Squire Bowes died, and no one had lived in the Hall ever since, except the gardener and his wife.

"Tom Wyndsour will be as old a man as myself; but he's a bit taller, and not so much in flesh, quite," said the fat innkeeper.

"But there were stories about the house," I repeated, "that they said, prevented tenants from coming into it?"

"Old wives' tales; many years ago, that will be, sir; I forget 'em; I forget 'em all. Oh yes, there always will be, when a house is left so; foolish folk will always be talkin'; but I hadn't heard a word about it this twenty year."

It was vain trying to pump him; the old landlord of the "Three Nuns," for some reason, did not choose to tell tales of Barwyke Hall, if he really did, as I suspected, remember them.

I paid my reckoning, and resumed my journey, well pleased with the good cheer of that old-world inn, but a little disappointed.

We had been driving for more than an hour, when we began to cross a wild common; and I knew that, this passed, a quarter of an hour would bring me to the door of Barwyke Hall.

The peat and furze were pretty soon left behind; we were again in the wooded scenery that I enjoyed so much, so entirely natural and pretty, and so little disturbed by traffic of any kind. I was looking from the chaise-window, and soon detected the object of which, for some time, my eye had been in search. Barwyke Hall was a large, quaint house, of that cage-work fashion known as "black-and-white," in which the bars and angles of an oak framework contrast, black as ebony, with the white plaster that overspreads the masonry built into its interstices. This steep-roofed Elizabethan house stood in the midst of park-like grounds of no great extent, but rendered imposing by the noble stature of the old trees that now cast their lengthening shadows eastward over the sward, from the declining sun.

The park-wall was grey with age, and in many places laden with ivy. In deep grey shadow, that contrasted with the dim fires of evening reflected on the foliage above it, in a gentle hollow, stretched a lake that looked cold and black, and seemed, as it were, to skulk from observation with a guilty knowledge.

I had forgot that there was a lake at Barwyke; but the moment this caught my eye, like the cold polish of a snake in the shadow, my instinct seemed to recognise something dangerous, and I knew that the lake was connected, I could not remember how, with the story I had heard of this place in my boyhood.

I drove up a grass-grown avenue, under the boughs of these noble trees, whose foliage, dyed in autumnal red and yellow, returned the beams of the western sun gorgeously.

We drew up at the door. I got out, and had a good look at the front of the house; it was a large and melancholy mansion, with signs of long neglect upon it; great wooden shutters, in the old fashion, were barred, outside, across the windows; grass, and even nettles, were growing thick on the courtyard, and a thin moss streaked the timber beams; the plaster was discoloured by time and weather, and bore great russet and yellow stains. The gloom was increased by several grand old trees that crowded close about the house.

I mounted the steps, and looked round; the dark lake lay near me now, a little to the left. It was not large; it may have covered some ten or twelve acres; but it added to the melancholy of the scene. Near the centre of it was a small island, with two old ash trees, leaning toward each other, their pensive images reflected in the stirless water. The only cheery influence in this scene of antiquity, solitude, and neglect was that the house and landscape were warmed with the ruddy western beams. I knocked, and my summons resounded hollow and ungenial in my ear; and the bell, from far away, returned a deep-mouthed and surly ring, as if it resented being roused from a score years' slumber.

A light-limbed, jolly-looking old fellow, in a barracan jacket and gaiters, with a smile of welcome, and a very sharp, red nose, that seemed to promise good cheer, opened the door with a promptitude that indicated a hospitable expectation of my arrival.

There was but little light in the hall, and that little lost itself in darkness in the background. It was very spacious and lofty, with a gallery running round it, which, when the door was open, was visible at two or three points. Almost in the dark my new acquaintance led me across this wide hall into the room destined for my reception. It was spacious, and wainscoted up to the ceiling. The furniture of this capacious chamber was old-fashioned and clumsy. There were curtains still to the windows, and a piece of Turkey carpet lay upon the floor; those windows were two in number, looking out, through the trunks of the trees close to the house, upon the lake. It needed all the fire, and all the pleasant associations of my entertainer's red nose, to light up this melancholy chamber. A door at its farther end admitted to the room that was prepared for my sleeping apartment. It was wainscoted, like the other. It had a four-post bed, with heavy tapestry curtains, and in other respects was furnished in the same old-world and ponderous style as the other room. Its window, like those of that apartment, looked out upon the lake.

Sombre and sad as these rooms were, they were yet scrupulously clean. I had nothing to complain of; but the effect was rather dispiriting. Having given some directions about supper—a pleasant incident to look forward to—and made a rapid toilet, I called on my friend with the gaiters and red nose (Tom Wyndsour) whose occupation was that of a "bailiff," or under-steward, of the property, to accompany me, as we had still an hour or so of sun and twilight, in a walk over the grounds.

It was a sweet autumn evening, and my guide, a hardy old fellow, strode at a pace that tasked me to keep up with.

Among clumps of trees at the northern boundary of the

demesne we lighted upon the little antique parish church. I was looking down upon it, from an eminence, and the park-wall interposed; but a little way down was a stile affording access to the road, and by this we approached the iron gate of the churchyard. I saw the church door open; the sexton was replacing his pick, shovel and spade, with which he had just been digging a grave in the churchyard, in their little repository under the stone stair of the tower. He was a polite, shrewd little hunchback, who was very happy to show me over the church. Among the monuments was one that interested me; it was erected to commemorate the very Squire Bowes from whom my two old maids had inherited the house and estate of Barwyke. It spoke of him in terms of grandiloquent eulogy, and informed the Christian reader that he had died, in the bosom of the Church of England, at the age of seventy-one.

I read this inscription by the parting beams of the setting sun, which disappeared behind the horizon just as we passed out from under the porch.

"Twenty years since the Squire died," said I, reflecting as I loitered still in the churchyard.

"Ay, sir; 'twill be twenty year the ninth o' last month."

"And a very good old gentleman?"

"Good-natured enough, and an easy gentleman he was, sir; I don't think while he lived he ever hurt a fly," acquiesced Tom Wyndsour. "It ain't always easy sayin' what's in 'em though, and what they may take or turn to afterwards; and some o' them sort, I think, goes mad."

"You don't think he was out of his mind?" I asked.

"He? La! no; not he, sir; a bit lazy, mayhap, like other old fellows; but a knew devilish well what he was about."

Tom Wyndsour's account was a little enigmatical; but, like old Squire Bowes, I was "a bit lazy" that evening, and asked no more questions about him.

We got over the stile upon the narrow road that skirts the churchyard. It is overhung by elms more than a hundred years old, and in the twilight, which now prevailed, was growing very dark. As side-by-side we walked along this road, hemmed in by two loose stone-like walls, something running towards us in a zig-zag line passed us at a wild pace, with a sound like a frightened laugh or a shudder, and I saw, as it passed, that it was a human figure. I may confess now, that I was a little startled. The dress of this figure was, in part, white: I know I mistook it at first for a white horse coming down the road at a gallop. Tom Wyndsour turned about and looked after the retreating figure.

"He'll be on his travels to-night," he said, in a low tone. "Easy served with a bed, *that* lad be; six foot o' dry peat or heath, or a nook in a dry ditch. That lad hasn't slept once in a house this twenty year, and never will while grass grows."

"Is he mad?" I asked.

"Something that way, sir; he's an idiot, an awpy; we call him 'Dickon the devil,' because the devil's almost the only word that's ever in his mouth."

It struck me that this idiot was in some way connected with the story of old Squire Bowes.

"Queer things are told of him, I dare say?" I suggested.

"More or less, sir; more or less. Queer stories, some."

"Twenty years since he slept in a house? That's about the time the Squire died," I continued.

"So it will be, sir; and not very long after."

"You must tell me all about that, Tom, to-night, when I can hear it comfortably, after supper."

Tom did not seem to like my invitation; and looking straight before him as we trudged on, he said,

"You see, sir, the house has been quiet, and nout's been troubling folk inside the walls or out, all round the woods of Barwyke, this ten year, or more; and my old woman, down there, is clear against talking about such matters, and thinks it best—and so do I—to let sleepin' dogs be."

He dropped his voice towards the close of the sentence, and nodded significantly.

We soon reached a point where he unlocked a wicket in the park wall, by which we entered the grounds of Barwyke once more.

The twilight deepening over the landscape, the huge and solemn trees, and the distant outline of the haunted house, exercised a sombre influence on me, which, together with the fatigue of a day of travel, and the brisk walk we had had, disinclined me to interrupt the silence in which my companion now indulged.

A certain air of comparative comfort, on our arrival, in great measure dissipated the gloom that was stealing over me. Although it was by no means a cold night, I was very glad to see some wood blazing in the grate; and a pair of candles aiding the light of the fire, made the room look cheerful. A small table, with a very white cloth, and preparations for supper, was also a very agreeable object.

I should have liked very well, under these influences, to have listened to Tom Wyndsour's story; but after supper I grew too sleepy to attempt to lead him to the subject; and after yawning for a time, I found there was no use in contending against my drowsiness, so I betook myself to my bedroom, and by ten o'clock was fast asleep.

What interruption I experienced that night I shall tell you presently. It was not much, but it was very odd.

By next night I had completed my work at Barwyke. From early morning till then I was so incessantly occupied and hard-worked, that I had no time to think over the singular occurrence to which I have just referred. Behold me, however, at length once more seated at my little supper-table, having ended a comfortable meal. It had been a sultry day, and I had thrown one of the large windows up as high as it would go. I was sitting near it, with my brandy and water at my elbow, looking out into the dark. There was no moon, and the trees that are grouped about the house make the darkness round it supernaturally profound on such nights.

"Tom," said I, so soon as the jug of hot punch I had supplied him with began to exercise its genial and communicative influence; "you must tell me who beside your wife and you and myself slept in the house last night."

Tom, sitting near the door, set down his tumbler, and looked at me askance, while you might count seven, without speaking a word.

"Who else slept in the house?" he repeated, very deliberately. "Not a living soul, sir"; and he looked hard at me, still evidently expecting something more.

"That *is* very odd," I said returning his stare, and feeling really a little odd. "You are sure *you* were not in my room last night?"

"Not till I came to call you, sir, this morning; *I* can make oath of that."

"Well," said I, "there was some one there, *I* can make oath of that. I was so tired I could not make up my mind to get up; but I was waked by a sound that I thought was some one flinging down the two tin boxes in which my papers were locked up violently on the floor. I heard a slow step on the ground, and there was light in the room, although I remembered having put out my candle. I thought it must have been you, who had come in for my clothes, and upset the boxes by accident. Whoever it was, he went out and the light with him. I was about to settle again, when, the curtain being a little open at the foot of the bed, I saw a light on the wall opposite; such as a candle from outside would cast if the door were very cautiously opening. I started up in the bed, drew the side curtain, and saw that the door *was* opening, and admitting light from outside. It is close, you know, to the head of the bed. A hand was holding on the edge of the door and pushing it open; not a bit like yours; a very singular hand. Let me look at yours."

He extended it for my inspection.

"Oh no; there's nothing wrong with your hand. This was differently shaped; fatter; and the middle finger was stunted, and shorter than the rest, looking as if it had once been broken, and the nail was crooked like a claw. I called out 'Who's there?' and the light and the hand were withdrawn, and I saw and heard no more of my visitor."

"So sure as you're a living man, that was him!" exclaimed Tom Wyndsour, his very nose growing pale, and his eyes almost starting out of his head.

"Who?" I asked.

"Old Squire Bowes; 'twas *his* hand you saw; the Lord a' mercy on us!" answered Tom. "The broken finger, and the nail bent like a hoop. Well for you, sir, he didn't come back when you called, that time. You came here about them Miss Dymock's business, and he never meant they should have a foot o' ground in Barwyke; and he was making a will to give it away quite different, when death took him short. He never was uncivil to no one; but he couldn't abide them ladies. My mind misgave me when I heard 'twas about their business you were coming; and now you see how it is; he'll be at his old tricks again!"

With some pressure and a little more punch, I induced Tom Wyndsour to explain his mysterious allusions by recounting the occurrences which followed the old Squire's death.

"Squire Bowes of Barwyke died without making a will, as you know," said Tom. "And all the folk round were sorry; that is to say, sir, as sorry as folk will be for an old man that has seen a long tale of years, and has no right to grumble that death has knocked an hour too soon at his door. The Squire was well liked;

he was never in a passion, or said a hard word; and he would not hurt a fly; and that made what happened after his decease the more surprising.

"The first thing these ladies did, when they got the property was to buy stock for the park.

"It was not wise, in any case, to graze the land on their own account. But they little knew all they had to contend with.

"Before long something went wrong with the cattle; first one, and then another, took sick and died, and so on, till the loss began to grow heavy. Then, queer stories, little by little, began to be told. It was said, first by one, then by another, that Squire Bowes was seen, about evening time, walking, just as he used to do when he was alive, among the old trees, leaning on his stick; and, sometimes when he came up with the cattle, he would stop and lay his hand kindly like on the back of one of them; and that one was sure to fall sick next day, and die soon after.

"No one ever met him in the park, or in the woods, or ever saw him, except a good distance off. But they knew his gait and his figure well, and the clothes he used to wear; and they could tell the beast he laid his hand on by its colour—white, dun, or black; and that beast was sure to sicken and die. The neighbours grew shy of taking the path over the park; and no one liked to walk in the woods, or come inside the bounds of Barwyke; and the cattle went on sickening and dying as before.

"At that time there was one Thomas Pyke; he had been a groom to the old Squire; and he was in care of the place, and was the only one that used to sleep in the house.

"Tom was vexed, hearing these stories; which he did not believe the half on 'em; and more especial as he could not get man or boy to herd the cattle; all being afeared. So he wrote to Matlock in Derbyshire, for his brother, Richard Pyke, a clever lad, and one that knew nout o' the story of the old Squire walking.

"Dick came; and the cattle was better; folk said they could

still see the old Squire, sometimes, walking, as before, in openings of the wood, with his stick in his hand; but he was shy of coming nigh the cattle, whatever his reason might be, since Dickon Pyke came; and he used to stand a long bit off, looking at them, with no more stir in him than a trunk o' one of the old trees, for an hour at a time, till the shape melted away, little by little, like the smoke of a fire that burns out.

"Tom Pyke and his brother Dickon, being the only living souls in the house, lay in the big bed in the servants' room, the house being fast barred and locked, one night in November.

"Tom was lying next the wall, and he told me, as wide awake as ever he was at noonday. His brother Dickon lay outside, and was sound asleep.

"Well, as Tom lay thinking, with his eyes turned toward the door, it opens slowly, and who should come in but old Squire Bowes, his face lookin' as dead as he was in his coffin.

"Tom's very breath left his body; he could not take his eyes off him; and he felt the hair rising up on his head.

"The Squire came to the side of the bed, and put his arms under Dickon, and lifted the boy—in a dead sleep all the time—and carried him out so, at the door.

"Such was the appearance, to Tom Pyke's eyes, and he was ready to swear to it, anywhere.

"When this happened, the light, wherever it came from, all on a sudden went out, and Tom could not see his own hand before him.

"More dead than alive, he lay till daylight.

"Sure enough his brother Dickon was gone. No sign of him could he discover about the house; and with some trouble he got a couple of the neighbours to help him to search the woods and grounds. Not a sign of him anywhere.

"At last one of them thought of the island in the lake; the little boat was moored to the old post at the water's edge. In they got, though with small hope of finding him there. Find him, nevertheless, they did, sitting under the big ash tree, quite out of his wits; and to all their questions he answered nothing but one cry—'Bowes, the devil! See him; see him; Bowes, the devil!' An idiot they found him; and so he will be till God sets all things right. No one could ever get him to sleep under roof-tree more. He wanders from house to house while daylight lasts; and no one cares to lock the harmless creature in the workhouse. And folk would rather not meet him after nightfall, for they think where he is there may be worse things near."

A silence followed Tom's story. He and I were alone in that large room; I was sitting near the open window, looking into the dark night air. I fancied I saw something white move across it; and I heard a sound like low talking that swelled into a discordant shriek—"Hoo-oo-oo! Bowes, the devil! Over your shoulder. Hoo-oo-oo! ha! ha! ha!" I started up, and saw, by the light of the candle with which Tom strode to the window, the wild eyes and blighted face of the idiot, as, with a sudden change of mood, he drew off, whispering and tittering to himself, and holding up his long fingers, and looking at the tips like a "hand of glory."

Tom pulled down the window. The story and its epilogue were over. I confess I was rather glad when I heard the sound of the horses' hoofs on the courtyard, a few minutes later; and still gladder when, having bidden Tom a kind farewell, I had left the neglected house of Barwyke a mile behind me.

30

CELEPHAÏS

H.P. Lovecraft

In a dream Kuranes saw the city in the valley, and the sea-coast beyond, and the snowy peak overlooking the sea, and the gaily painted galleys that sail out of the harbour toward the distant regions where the sea meets the sky. In a dream it was also that he came by his name of Kuranes, for when awake he was called by another name. Perhaps it was natural for him to dream a new name; for he was the last of his family, and alone among the indifferent millions of London, so there were not many to speak to him and remind him who he had been. His money and lands were gone, and he did not care for the ways of people about him, but preferred to dream and write of his dreams. What he wrote was laughed at by those to whom he showed it, so that after a time he kept his writings to himself, and finally ceased to write. The more he withdrew from the world about him, the more wonderful became his dreams; and it would have been quite futile to try to describe them on paper. Kuranes was not modern, and did not think like others who wrote. Whilst they strove to strip from life its embroidered robes of myth, and to show in naked ugliness the foul thing that is reality, Kuranes sought for beauty alone. When truth and experience failed to reveal it, he sought it in fancy and illusion, and found it on his very doorstep, amid the nebulous memories of childhood tales and dreams.

There are not many persons who know what wonders are opened to them in the stories and visions of their youth; for when as children we listen and dream, we think but half-formed thoughts, and when as men we try to remember, we are dulled and prosaic with the poison of life. But some of us awake in the night with strange phantasms of enchanted hills and gardens, of fountains that sing in the sun, of golden cliffs overhanging murmuring seas, of plains that stretch down to sleeping cities of bronze and stone, and of shadowy companies of heroes that ride caparisoned white horses along the edges of thick forests; and then we know that we have looked back through the ivory gates into that world of wonder which was ours before we were wise and unhappy.

Kuranes came very suddenly upon his old world of childhood. He had been dreaming of the house where he was born; the great stone house covered with ivy, where thirteen generations of his ancestors had lived, and where he had hoped to die. It was moonlight, and he had stolen out into the fragrant summer night, through the gardens, down the terraces, past the great oaks of the park, and along the long white road to the village. The village seemed very old, eaten away at the edge like the moon which had commenced to wane, and Kuranes wondered whether the peaked roofs of the small houses hid sleep or death. In the streets were spears of long grass, and the window-panes on either side were either broken or filmily staring. Kuranes had not lingered, but had plodded on as though summoned toward some goal. He dared not disobey the summons for fear it might prove an illusion like the urges and aspirations of waking life, which do not lead to any goal. Then he had been drawn down a lane that led off from the village street toward the channel cliffs, and had come to the end of things—to the precipice and the abyss where all the village and all the world fell abruptly into the unechoing emptiness of infinity, and where even the sky ahead was empty and unlit by the crumbling moon and the peering stars. Faith had urged him on, over the precipice and into the gulf, where he had floated down, down, down; past dark, shapeless, undreamed dreams, faintly glowing spheres that may have been partly dreamed dreams, and laughing winged things that seemed to mock the dreamers of all the worlds. Then a rift seemed to open in the darkness before him, and he saw the city of the valley, glistening radiantly far, far below, with a background of sea and sky, and a snow-capped mountain near the shore.

Kuranes had awaked the very moment he beheld the city, yet he knew from his brief glance that it was none other than Celephaïs, in the Valley of Ooth-Nargai beyond the Tanarian Hills, where his spirit had dwelt all the eternity of an hour one summer afternoon very long ago, when he had slipt away from his nurse and let the warm sea-breeze lull him to sleep as he watched the clouds from the cliff near the village. He had protested then, when they had found him, waked him, and carried him home, for just as he was aroused he had been about to sail in a golden galley for those alluring regions where the sea meets the sky. And now he was equally resentful of awaking, for he had found his fabulous city after forty weary years.

But three nights afterward Kuranes came again to Celephaïs. As before, he dreamed first of the village that was asleep or dead, and of the abyss down which one must float silently; then the rift appeared again, and he beheld the glittering minarets of the city, and saw the graceful galleys riding at anchor in the blue harbour, and watched the gingko trees of Mount Aran swaying in the sea-breeze. But this time he was not snatched away, and like a winged being settled gradually over a grassy hillside till finally his feet rested gently on the turf. He had indeed come back to the Valley of Ooth-Nargai and the splendid city of Celephaïs.

Down the hill amid scented grasses and brilliant flowers walked Kuranes, over the bubbling Naraxa on the small wooden bridge where he had carved his name so many years ago, and through the whispering grove to the great stone bridge by the city gate. All was as of old, nor were the marble walls discoloured, nor the polished bronze statues upon them tarnished. And Kuranes saw that he need not tremble lest the things he knew be vanished; for even the sentries on the ramparts were the same, and still as young as he remembered them. When he entered the city, past the bronze gates and over the onyx pavements, the merchants and camel-drivers greeted him as if he had never been away; and it was the same at the turquoise temple of Nath-Horthath, where the orchid-wreathed priests told him that there is no time in Ooth-Nargai, but only perpetual youth. Then Kuranes walked through the Street of Pillars to the seaward wall, where gathered the traders and sailors, and strange men from the regions where the sea meets the sky. There he stayed long, gazing out over the bright harbour where the ripples sparkled beneath an unknown sun, and where rode lightly the galleys from far places over the water. And he gazed also upon Mount Aran rising regally from the shore, its lower slopes green with swaying trees and its white summit touching the sky.

More than ever Kuranes wished to sail in a galley to the far places of which he had heard so many strange tales, and he sought again the captain who had agreed to carry him so long ago. He found the man, Athib, sitting on the same chest of spices he had sat upon before, and Athib seemed not to realise that any time had passed. Then the two rowed to a galley in the harbour, and giving orders to the oarsmen, commenced to sail out into the billowy Cerenerian Sea that leads to the sky. For several days they glided undulatingly over the water, till finally they came to the horizon, where the sea meets the sky. Here the galley paused not at all, but floated easily in the blue of the sky among fleecy clouds tinted with rose. And far beneath the keel Kuranes could see strange lands and rivers and cities of surpassing beauty, spread indolently in the sunshine which seemed never to lessen or disappear. At length Athib told him that their journey was near its end, and that they would soon enter the harbour of Serannian, the pink marble city of the clouds, which is built on that ethereal coast where the west wind flows into the sky; but as the highest of the city's carven towers came into sight there was a sound somewhere in space, and Kuranes awaked in his London garret.

For many months after that Kuranes sought the marvellous city of Celephaïs and its sky-bound galleys in vain; and though his dreams carried him to many gorgeous and unheard-of places, no one whom he met could tell him how to find Ooth-Nargai, beyond the Tanarian Hills. One night he went flying over dark mountains where there were faint, lone campfires at great distances apart, and strange, shaggy herds with tinkling bells on the leaders; and in the wildest part of this hilly country, so remote that few men could ever have seen it, he found a hideously ancient wall or causeway of stone zigzagging along the ridges and valleys; too gigantic ever to have risen by human hands, and of such a length that neither end of it could be seen. Beyond that wall in the grey dawn he came to a land of quaint gardens and cherry trees, and when the sun rose he beheld such beauty of red and white flowers, green foliage and lawns, white paths, diamond brooks, blue lakelets, carven bridges, and red-roofed pagodas, that he for a moment forgot Celephaïs in sheer delight. But he remembered it again when he walked down a white path toward a red-roofed pagoda, and would have questioned the people of that land about it, had he not found that there were no people there, but only birds and bees and butterflies. On another night Kuranes walked up a damp stone spiral stairway endlessly, and came to a tower window overlooking a mighty plain and river lit by the full moon; and in the silent city that spread away from the river-bank he thought he beheld some feature or arrangement which he had known before. He would have descended and asked the way to Ooth-Nargai had not a fearsome aurora sputtered up from some remote place beyond the horizon, showing the ruin and antiquity of the city, and the stagnation of the reedy river, and the death lying upon that land, as it had lain since King Kynaratholis came home from his conquests to find the vengeance of the gods.

So Kuranes sought fruitlessly for the marvellous city of Celephaïs and its galleys that sail to Serannian in the sky, meanwhile seeing many wonders and once barely escaping from the high-priest not to be described, which wears a yellow silken mask over its face and dwells all alone in a prehistoric stone monastery on the cold desert plateau of Leng. In time he grew so impatient of the bleak intervals of day that he began buying drugs in order to increase his periods of sleep. Hasheesh helped a great deal, and once sent him to a part of space where form does not exist, but where glowing gases study the secrets of existence. And a violet-coloured gas told him that this part of space was outside what he had called infinity. The gas had not heard of planets and organisms before, but identified Kuranes merely as one from the infinity where matter, energy, and gravitation exist. Kuranes was now very anxious to return to minaret-studded Celephaïs, and increased his doses of drugs; but eventually he had no more money left, and could buy no drugs. Then one summer day he was turned out of his garret, and wandered aimlessly through the streets, drifting over a bridge to a place where the houses grew thinner and thinner. And it was there that fulfilment came, and he met the cortege of knights come from Celephaïs to bear him thither forever.

Handsome knights they were, astride roan horses and clad in shining armour with tabards of cloth-of-gold curiously emblazoned. So numerous were they, that Kuranes almost mistook them for an army, but their leader told him they were sent in his honour; since it was he who had created Ooth-Nargai in his dreams, on which account he was now to be appointed its chief god for evermore. Then they gave Kuranes a horse and placed him at the head of the cavalcade, and all rode majestically through the downs of Surrey and onward toward the region where Kuranes and his ancestors were born. It was very strange, but as the riders went on they seemed to gallop back through Time; for whenever they passed through a village in the twilight they saw only such houses and villages as Chaucer or men before him might have seen, and sometimes they saw knights on horseback with small companies of retainers. When it grew dark they travelled more swiftly, till soon they were flying uncannily as if in the air. In the dim dawn they came upon the village which Kuranes had seen alive in his childhood, and asleep or dead in his dreams. It was alive now, and early villagers curtesied as the horsemen clattered down the street and turned off into the lane that ends in the abyss of dream. Kuranes had previously entered that abyss only at night, and wondered what it would look like by day; so he watched anxiously as the column approached its brink. Just as they galloped up the rising ground to the precipice a golden glare came somewhere out of the east and hid all the landscape in its effulgent draperies. The abyss was now a seething chaos of roseate and cerulean splendour, and invisible voices sang exultantly as the knightly entourage plunged over the edge and floated gracefully down past glittering clouds and silvery coruscations. Endlessly down the horsemen floated, their chargers pawing the aether as if galloping over golden sands; and then the luminous vapours spread apart to reveal a greater brightness, the brightness of the city Celephaïs, and the sea-coast beyond, and the snowy peak overlooking the sea, and the gaily painted galleys that sail out of the harbour toward distant regions where the sea meets the sky.

And Kuranes reigned thereafter over Ooth-Nargai and all the neighbouring regions of dream, and held his court alternately in Celephaïs and in the cloud-fashioned Serannian. He reigns there still, and will reign happily forever, though below the cliffs at Innsmouth the channel tides played mockingly with the body of a tramp who had stumbled through the half-deserted village at dawn; played mockingly, and cast it upon the rocks by ivy-covered Trevor Towers, where a notably fat and especially offensive millionaire brewer enjoys the purchased atmosphere of extinct nobility.

31

THE DEVIL IN A NUNNERY

Francis Oscar Mann

Buckingham is as pleasant a shire as a man shall see on a seven days' journey. Neither was it any less pleasant in the days of our Lord King Edward, the third of that name, he who fought and put the French to shameful discomfiture at Crecy and Poitiers and at many another hard-fought field. May God rest his soul, for he now sleeps in the great Church at Westminster.

Buckinghamshire is full of smooth round hills and woodlands of hawthorn and beech, and it is a famous country for its brooks and shaded waterways running through the low hay meadows. Upon its hills feed a thousand sheep, scattered like the remnants of the spring snow, and it was from these that the merchants made themselves fat purses, sending the wool into Flanders in exchange for silver crowns. There were many strong castles there too, and rich abbeys, and the King's Highway ran through it from North to South, upon which the pilgrims went in crowds to worship at the Shrine of the Blessed Saint Alban. Thereon also rode noble knights and stout men-at-arms, and these you could follow with the eye by their glistening armour, as they wound over hill and dale, mile after mile, with shining spears and shields and fluttering pennons, and anon a trumpet or two sounding the same keen note as that which rang out dreadfully on those bloody fields of France. The girls used to come to the cottage doors or run to hide themselves in the wayside woods to see them go trampling by; for Buckinghamshire girls love a soldier above all men. Nor, I warrant you, were jolly friars lacking in the highways and the by-ways and under the hedges, good men of religion, comfortable of penance and easy of life, who could tip a wink to a housewife, and drink and crack a joke with the good man, going on their several ways with tight paunches, skins full of ale and a merry salutation for every one. A fat pleasant land was this Buckinghamshire; always plenty to eat and drink therein, and pretty girls and lusty fellows; and God knows what more a man can expect in a world where all is vanity, as the Preacher truly says.

There was a nunnery at Maids Moreton, two miles out from Buckingham Borough, on the road to Stony Stratford, and the place was called Maids Moreton because of the nunnery. Very devout creatures were the nuns, being holy ladies out of families of gentle blood. They punctually fulfilled to the letter all the commands of the pious founder, just as they were blazoned on the great parchment Regula, which the Lady Mother kept on her reading-desk in her little cell. If ever any of the nuns, by any chance or subtle machination of the Evil One, was guilty of the smallest backsliding from the conduct that beseemed them, they made full and devout confession thereof to the Holy Father who visited them for this purpose. This good man loved swan's meat and galingale, and the charitable nuns never failed to provide of their best for him on his visiting days; and whatsoever penance he laid upon them they performed to the utmost, and with due contrition of heart.

From Matins to Compline they regularly and decently carried out the services of Holy Mother Church. After dinner, one read aloud to them from the Rule, and again after supper there was reading from the life of some notable Saint or Virgin, that thereby they might find ensample for themselves on their own earthly pilgrimage. For the rest, they tended their herb garden, reared their chickens, which were famous for miles around, and kept strict watch over their haywards and swineherds. If time was when they had nothing more important on hand, they set to and made the prettiest blood bandages imaginable for the Bishop, the Bishop's Chaplain, the Archdeacon, the neighbouring Abbot and other godly men of religion round about, who were forced often to bleed themselves for their health's sake and their eternal salvation, so that these venerable men in process of time came to have by them great chests full of these useful articles. If little tongues wagged now and then as the sisters sat at their sewing in the great hall, who shall blame them, *Eva peccatrice?* Not I; besides, some of them were something stricken in years, and old women are garrulous and hard to be constrained from chattering and gossiping. But being devout women they could have spoken no evil.

One evening after Vespers all these good nuns sat at supper, the Abbess on her high dais and the nuns ranged up and down the hall at the long trestled tables. The Abbess had just said "*Gratias*" and the sisters had sung "*Qui vivit et regnat per omnia saecula saeculorum, Amen,*" when in came the Manciple mysteriously, and, with many deprecating bows and outstretchings of the hands, sidled himself up upon the dais, and, permission having been given him, spoke to the Lady Mother thus:

"Madam, there is a certain pilgrim at the gate who asks refreshment and a night's lodging." It is true he spoke softly, but little pink ears are sharp of hearing, and nuns, from their secluded way of life, love to hear news of the great world.

"Send him away," said the Abbess. "It is not fit that a man should lie within this house."

"Madam, he asks food and a bed of straw lest he should starve of hunger and exhaustion on his way to do penance and worship at the Holy Shrine of the Blessed Saint Alban."

"What kind of pilgrim is he?"

"Madam, to speak truly, I know not; but he appears of a reverend and gracious aspect, a young man well spoken and well disposed. Madam knows it waxeth late, and the ways are dark and foul."

"I would not have a young man, who is given to pilgrimages and good works, to faint and starve by the wayside. Let him sleep with the haywards."

"But, Madam, he is a young man of goodly appearance and conversation; saving your reverence, I would not wish to ask him to eat and sleep with churls."

"He must sleep without. Let him, however, enter and eat of our poor table."

"Madam, I will strictly enjoin him what you command. He hath with him, however, an instrument of music and would fain cheer you with spiritual songs."

A little shiver of anticipation ran down the benches of the great hall, and the nuns fell to whispering.

"Take care, Sir Manciple, that he be not some light juggler, a singer of vain songs, a mocker. I would not have these quiet halls disturbed by wanton music and unholy words. God forbid." And she crossed herself.

"Madam, I will answer for it."

The Manciple bowed himself from the dais and went down the middle of the hall, his keys rattling at his belt. A little buzz of conversation rose from the sisters and went up to the oak roof-trees, like the singing of bees. The Abbess told her beads.

The hall door opened and in came the pilgrim. God knows what manner of man he was; I cannot tell you. He certainly was lean and lithe like a cat, his eyes danced in his head like the very devil, but his cheeks and jaws were as bare of flesh as any hermit's that lives on roots and ditchwater. His yellow-hosed legs went like the tune of a May game, and he screwed and twisted his scarlet-jerkined body in time with them. In his left hand he held a cithern, on which he twanged with his right, making a cunning noise that titillated the backbones of those who heard it, and teased every delicate nerve in the body. Such a tune would have tickled the ribs of Death himself. A queer fellow to go pilgrimaging certainly, but why, when they saw him, all the young nuns tittered and the old nuns grinned, until they showed their red gums, it is hard to tell. Even the Lady Mother on the dais smiled, though she tried to frown a moment later.

The pilgrim stepped lightly up to the dais, the infernal devil in his legs making the nuns think of the games the village folk play all night in the churchyard on Saint John's Eve.

"Gracious Mother," he cried, bowing deeply and in comely wise, "allow a poor pilgrim on his way to confess and do penance at the shrine of Saint Alban to take food in your hall, and to rest with the haywards this night, and let me thereof make some small recompense with a few sacred numbers, such as your pious founder would not have disdained to hear."

"Young man," returned the Abbess, "right glad am I to hear that God has moved thy heart to godly works and to go on pilgrimages, and verily I wish it may be to thy soul's health and to the respite of thy pains hereafter. I am right willing that thou shouldst refresh thyself with meat and rest at this holy place."

"Madam, I thank thee from my heart, but as some slight token of gratitude for so large a favour, let me, I pray thee, sing one or two of my divine songs, to the uplifting of these holy Sisters' hearts."

Another burst of chatter, louder than before, from the benches in the hall. One or two of the younger Sisters clapped their plump white hands and cried, "Oh!" The Lady Abbess held up her hand for silence.

"Verily, I should be glad to hear some sweet songs of religion, and I think it would be to the uplifting of these Sisters' hearts. But, young man, take warning against singing any wanton lines of vain imagination, such as the ribalds use on the highways, and the idlers and haunters of taverns. I have heard them in my youth, although my ears tingle to think of them now, and I should think it shame that any such light words should echo among these sacred rafters or disturb the slumber of our pious founder, who now sleeps in Christ. Let me remind you of what saith Saint Jeremie, *Onager solitarius, in desiderio animae suae, attraxit ventum amoris;* the wild ass of the wilderness, in the desire of his heart, snuffeth up the wind of love; whereby that holy man signifies that vain earthly love, which is but wind and air, and shall avail nothing at all, when this weak, impure flesh is sloughed away."

"Madam, such songs as I shall sing, I learnt at the mouth of our holy parish priest, Sir Thomas, a man of all good learning and purity of heart."

"In that case," said the Abbess, "sing in God's name, but stand at the end of the hall, for it suits not the dignity of my office a man should stand so near this dais."

Whereon the pilgrim, making obeisance, went to the end of the hall, and the eyes of all the nuns danced after his dancing legs, and their ears hung on the clear, sweet notes he struck out of his cithern as he walked. He took his place with his back against the great hall door, in such attitude as men use when they play the cithern. A little trembling ran through the nuns, and some rose from their seats and knelt on the benches, leaning over the table, the better to see and hear him. Their eyes sparkled like dew on meadowsweet on a fair morning.

Certainly his fingers were bewitched or else the devil was in his cithern, for such sweet sounds had never been heard in the hall since the day when it was built and consecrated to the service of the servants of God. The shrill notes fell like a tinkling rain from the high roof in mad, fantastic trills and dying falls that brought all one's soul to one's lips to suck them in. What he sang about, God only knows; not one of the nuns or even the holy Abbess herself could have told you, although you had offered her a piece of the True Cross or a hair of the Blessed Virgin for a single word. But a divine yearning filled all their hearts; they seemed to hear ten thousand thousand angels singing in choruses, Alleluia, Alleluia, Alleluia; they floated up on impalpable clouds of azure and silver, up through the blissful paradises of the uppermost heaven; their nostrils were filled with the odours of exquisite spices and herbs and smoke of incense; their eyes dazzled at splendours and lights and glories; their ears were full of gorgeous harmonies and all created concords of sweet sounds; the very fibres of being were loosened within them, as though their souls would leap forth from their bodies in exquisite dissolution. The eyes of the younger nuns grew round and large and tender, and their breath almost died upon their velvet lips. As for the old nuns, the great, salt tears coursed down their withered cheeks and fell like rain on their gnarled hands. The Abbess sat on her dais with her lips apart, looking into space, ten thousand thousand miles away. But no one saw her and she saw no one; every one had forgotten every one else in that delicious intoxication.

Then with a shrill cry, full of human yearnings and desire, the minstrel came to a sudden stop—

"Western wind, when wilt thou blow,
"And the small rain will down rain?
Christ, if my love were in my arms,
"And I in my bed again."

Silence!—not one of the holy Sisters spoke, but some sighed; some put their hands over their hearts, and one put her hand in her hood, but when she felt her hair shorn close to her scalp, drew it out again sharply, as though she had touched red-hot iron, and cried, "O Jesu."

Sister Peronelle, a toothless old woman, began to speak in a cracked, high voice, quickly and monotonously, as though she spoke in a dream. Her eyes were wet and red, and her thin lips trembled. "God knows," she said, "I loved him; God knows it.

But I bid all those who be maids here, to be mindful of the woods. For they are green, but they are deep and dark, and it is merry in the springtime with the thick turf below and the good boughs above, all alone with your heart's darling—all alone in the green wood. But God help me, he would not stay any more than snow at Easter. I thought just now that I was back with him in the woods. God keep all those that be maids from the green woods."

The pretty Sister Ursula, who had only just finished her novitiate, was as white as a sheet. Her breath came thickly and quick as though she bore a great burden up hill. A great sigh made her comely shoulders rise and fall. "Blessed Virgin," she cried. "Ah, ye ask too much; I did not know; God help me, I did not know," and her grey eyes filled with sudden tears, and she dropped her head on her arms on the table, and sobbed aloud.

Then cried out Sister Katherine, who looked as old and dead as a twig dropped from a tree of last autumn, and at whom the younger Sisters privily mocked, "It is the wars, the wars, the cursed wars. I have held his head in this lap, I tell you; I have kissed his soul into mine. But now he lies dead, and his pretty limbs all dropped away into earth. Holy Mother, have pity on me. I shall never kiss his sweet lips again or look into his jolly eyes. My heart is broken long since. Holy Mother! Holy Mother!"

"He must come oftener," said a plump Sister of thirty, with a little nose turned up at the end, eyes black as sloes and lips round as a plum. "I go to the orchard day after day, and gather my lap full of apples. He is my darling. Why does he not come? I look for him every time that I gather the ripe apples. He used to come; but that was in the spring, and Our Lady knows that is long ago. Will it not be spring again soon? I have gathered many ripe apples."

Sister Margarita rocked herself to and fro in her seat and crossed her arms on her breast. She was singing quietly to herself.

"Lulla, lullay, thou tiny little child,
"Lulla, lullay, lullay;
Suck at my breast that am thereat beguiled.,
"Lulla, lullay, lullay."

She moaned to herself, "I have seen the village women go to the well, carrying their babies with them, and they laugh as they go by on the way. Their babies hold them tight round the neck, and their mothers comfort them, saying, 'Hey, hey, my little son; hey, hey, my sweeting.' Christ and the blessed Saints know that I have never felt a baby's little hand in my bosom—and now I shall die without it, for I am old and past the age of bearing children.

"Lulla, lullay, thou tiny little boy,
"Lulla, lullay, lullay;
To feel thee suck doth soothe my great annoy,
"Lulla, lullay, lullay."

"I have heard them on a May morning, with their pipes and tabors and jolly, jolly music," cried Sister Helen; "I have seen them too, and my heart has gone with them to bring back the white hawthorn from the woods. 'A man and a maid to a hawthorn bough,' as it says in the song. They sing outside my window all Saint John's Eve so that I cannot say my prayers for the wild thoughts they put into my brain, as they go dancing up and down in the churchyard; I cannot forget the pretty words they say to each other, 'Sweet love, a kiss'; 'kiss me, my love, nor let me go'; 'As I went through the garden gate'; 'A bonny black knight, a bonny black knight, and what will you give to me? A kiss, and a kiss, and no more than a kiss, under the wild rose tree.' Oh, Mary Mother, have pity on a poor girl's heart, I shall die, if no one love me, I shall die."

"In faith, I am truly sorry, William," said Sister Agnes, who was gaunt and hollow-eyed with long vigils and overfasting, for which the good father had rebuked her time after time, saying that she overtasked the poor weak flesh. "I am truly sorry that I could not wait. But the neighbours made such a clamour, and my father and mother buffeted me too sorely. It is under the oak tree, no more than a foot deep, and covered with the red and brown leaves. It was a pretty sight to see the red blood on its neck, as white as whalebone, and it neither cried nor wept, so I put it down among the leaves, the pretty poppet; and it was like thee, William, it was like thee. I am sorry I did not wait, and now I'm worn and wan for thy sake, this many a long year, and all in vain, for thou never comst. I am an old woman now, and I shall soon be quiet and not complain any more."

Some of the Sisters were sobbing as if their hearts would break; some sat quiet and still, and let the tears fall from their eyes unchecked; some smiled and cried together; some sighed a little and trembled like aspen leaves in a southern wind. The great candles in the hall were burning down to their sockets. One by one they spluttered out. A ghostly, flickering light fell upon the legend over the broad dais, "*Connubium mundum sed virginitas paradisum complet*"—"Marriage replenisheth the World, but virginity Paradise."

"Dong, dong, dong." Suddenly the great bell of the Nunnery began to toll. With a cry the Abbess sprang to her feet; there were tear stains on her white cheeks, and her hand shook as she pointed fiercely to the door.

"Away, false pilgrim," she cried. "Silence, foul blasphemer! *Retro me, Satanas*," She crossed herself again and again, saying *Pater Noster*.

The nuns screamed and trembled with terror. A little cloud of blue smoke arose from where the minstrel had stood. There was a little tongue of flame, and he had disappeared. It was almost dark in the hall. A few sobs broke the silence. The dying light of a single candle fell on the form of the Lady Mother.

"Tomorrow," she said, "we shall fast and sing *Placebo* and *Dirige* and the *Seven Penitential Psalms*. May the Holy God have mercy upon us for all we have done and said and thought amiss this night. Amen."

32

THE FLAYED HAND

Guy De Maupassant

One evening about eight months ago I met with some college comrades at the lodgings of our friend Louis R. We drank punch and smoked, talked of literature and art, and made jokes like any other company of young men. Suddenly the door flew open, and one who had been my friend since boyhood burst in like a hurricane.

"Guess where I come from?" he cried.

"I bet on the Mabille," responded one. "No," said another, "you are too gay; you come from borrowing money, from burying a rich uncle, or from pawning your watch." "You are getting sober," cried a third, "and, as you scented the punch in Louis' room, you came up here to get drunk again."

"You are all wrong," he replied. "I come from P., in Normandy, where I have spent eight days, and whence I have brought one of my friends, a great criminal, whom I ask permission to present to you."

With these words he drew from his pocket a long, black hand, from which the skin had been stripped. It had been severed at the wrist. Its dry and shriveled shape, and the narrow, yellowed nails still clinging to the fingers, made it frightful to look upon. The muscles, which showed that Its first owner had been possessed of great strength, were bound in place by a strip of parchment-like skin.

"Just fancy," said my friend, "the other day they sold the effects of an old sorcerer, recently deceased, well known in all the country. Every Saturday night he used to go to witch gatherings on a broomstick; he practised the white magic and the black, gave blue milk to the cows, and made them wear tails like that of the companion of Saint Anthony. The old scoundrel always had a deep affection for this hand, which, he said, was that of a celebrated criminal, executed in 1736 for having thrown his lawful wife head first into a well—for which I do not blame him—and then hanging in the belfry the priest who had married him. After this double exploit he went away, and, during his subsequent career, which was brief but exciting, he robbed twelve travelers, smoked a score of monks in their monastery, and made a seraglio of a convent."

"But what are you going to do with this horror?" we cried.

"Eh! parbleu! I will make it the handle to my door-bell and frighten my creditors."

"My friend," said Henry Smith, a big, phlegmatic Englishman, "I believe that this hand is only a kind of Indian meat, preserved by a new process; I advise you to make bouillon of it."

"Rail not, messieurs," said, with the utmost sang froid, a medical student who was three-quarters drunk, "but if you follow my advice, Pierre, you will give this piece of human debris Christian burial, for fear lest its owner should come to demand it. Then, too, this hand has acquired some bad habits, for you know the proverb, 'Who has killed will kill.'"

"And who has drank will drink," replied the host as he poured out a big glass of punch for the student, who emptied it at a draught and slid dead drunk under the table. His sudden dropping out of the company was greeted with a burst of laughter, and Pierre, raising his glass and saluting the hand, cried:

"I drink to the next visit of thy master."

Then the conversation turned upon other subjects, and shortly afterward each returned to his lodgings.

About two o'clock the next day, as I was passing Pierre's door,

I entered and found him reading and smoking.

"Well, how goes it?" said I. "Very well," he responded. "And your hand?" "My hand? Did you not see it on the bell-pull? I put it there when I returned home last night. But, apropos of this, what do you think? Some idiot, doubtless to play a stupid joke on me, came ringing at my door towards midnight. I demanded who was there, but as no one replied, I went back to bed again, and to sleep."

At this moment the door opened and the landlord, a fat and extremely impertinent person, entered without saluting us.

"Sir," said he, "I pray you to take away immediately that carrion which you have hung to your bell-pull. Unless you do this I shall be compelled to ask you to leave."

"Sir," responded Pierre, with much gravity, "you insult a hand which does not merit it. Know you that it belonged to a man of high breeding?"

The landlord turned on his heel and made his exit, without speaking. Pierre followed him, detached the hand and affixed it to the bell-cord hanging in his alcove.

"That is better," he said. "This hand, like the 'Brother, all must die,' of the Trappists, will give my thoughts a serious turn every night before I sleep."

At the end of an hour I left him and returned to my own apartment.

I slept badly the following night, was nervous and agitated, and several times awoke with a start. Once I imagined, even, that a man had broken into my room, and I sprang up and searched the closets and under the bed. Towards six o'clock in the morning I was commencing to doze at last, when a loud knocking at my door made me jump from my couch. It was my friend Pierre's servant, half dressed, pale and trembling.

"Ah, sir!" cried he, sobbing, "my poor master. Someone has murdered him."

I dressed myself hastily and ran to Pierre's lodgings. The house was full of people disputing together, and everything was in a commotion. Everyone was talking at the same time, recounting and commenting on the occurrence in all sorts of ways. With great difficulty I reached the bed-room, made myself known to those guarding the door and was permitted to enter. Four agents of police were standing in the middle of the apartment, pencils in hand, examining every detail, conferring in low voices and writing from time to time in their note-books. Two doctors were in consultation by the bed on which lay the unconscious form of Pierre. He was not dead, but his face was fixed in an expression of the most awful terror. His eyes were open their widest, and the dilated pupils seemed to regard fixedly, with unspeakable horror, something unknown and frightful. His hands were clinched. I raised the quilt, which covered his body from the chin downward, and saw on his neck, deeply sunk in the flesh, the marks of fingers. Some drops of blood spotted his shirt. At that moment one thing struck me. I chanced to notice that the shriveled hand was no longer attached to the bell-cord. The doctors had doubtless removed it to avoid the comments of those entering the chamber where the wounded man lay, because the appearance of this hand was indeed frightful. I did not inquire what had become of it.

I now clip from a newspaper of the next day the story of the crime with all the details that the police were able to procure:

"A frightful attempt was made yesterday on the life of young M. Pierre B., student, who belongs to one of the best families in Normandy. He returned home about ten o'clock in the evening, and excused his valet, Bouvin, from further attendance upon him, saying that he felt fatigued and was going to bed. Towards midnight Bouvin was suddenly awakened by the furious ringing of his master's bell. He was afraid, and lighted a lamp and waited. The bell was silent about a minute, then rang again with such vehemence that the domestic, mad with fright, flew from his room to awaken the concierge, who ran to summon the police, and, at the end of about fifteen minutes, two policemen forced open the door. A horrible sight met their eyes. The furniture was overturned, giving evidence of a fearful struggle between the victim and his assailant. In the middle of the room, upon his back, his body rigid, with livid face and frightfully dilated eyes, lay, motionless, young Pierre B., bearing upon his neck the deep imprints of five fingers. Dr. Bourdean was called immediately, and his report says that the aggressor must have been possessed of prodigious strength and have had an extraordinarily thin and sinewy hand, because the fingers left in the flesh of the victim five holes like those from a pistol ball, and had penetrated until they almost met. There is no clue to the motive of the crime or to its perpetrator. The police are making a thorough investigation."

The following appeared in the same newspaper next day:

"M. Pierre B., the victim of the frightful assault of which we published an account yesterday, has regained consciousness after two hours of the most assiduous care by Dr. Bourdean. His life is not in danger, but it is strongly feared that he has lost his reason. No trace has been found of his assailant."

My poor friend was indeed insane. For seven months I visited him daily at the hospital where we had placed him, but he did not recover the light of reason. In his delirium strange words escaped him, and, like all madmen, he had one fixed idea: he believed himself continually pursued by a specter. One day they came for me in haste, saying he was worse, and when I arrived I found him dying. For two hours he remained very calm, then, suddenly, rising from his bed in spite of our efforts, he cried, waving his arms as if a prey to the most awful terror: "Take it away! Take it away! It strangles me! Help! Help!" Twice he made the circuit of the room, uttering horrible screams, then fell face downward, dead.

As he was an orphan I was charged to take his body to the

little village of P., in Normandy, where his parents were buried. It was the place from which he had arrived the evening he found us drinking punch in Louis R.'s room, when he had presented to us the flayed hand. His body was inclosed in a leaden coffin, and four days afterwards I walked sadly beside the old curé, who had given him his first lessons, to the little cemetery where they dug his grave. It was a beautiful day, and sunshine from a cloudless sky flooded the earth. Birds sang from the blackberry bushes where many a time when we were children we had stolen to eat the fruit. Again I saw Pierre and myself creeping along behind the hedge and slipping through the gap that we knew so well, down at the end of the little plot where they bury the poor. Again we would return to the house with cheeks and lips black with the juice of the berries we had eaten. I looked at the bushes; they were covered with fruit; mechanically I picked some and bore it to my mouth. The curé had opened his breviary, and was muttering his prayers in a low voice. I heard at the end of the walk the spades of the grave-diggers who were opening the tomb. Suddenly they called out, the curé closed his book, and we went to see what they wished of us. They had found a coffin; in digging a stroke of the pickaxe had started the cover, and we perceived within a skeleton of unusual stature, lying on its back, its hollow eyes seeming yet to menace and defy us. I was troubled, I know not why, and almost afraid.

"Hold!" cried one of the men, "look there! One of the rascal's hands has been severed at the wrist. Ah, here it is!" and he picked up from beside the body a huge withered hand, and held it out to us.

"See," cried the other, laughing, "see how he glares at you, as if he would spring at your throat to make you give him back his hand."

"Go," said the curé, "leave the dead in peace, and close the coffin. We will make poor Pierre's grave elsewhere."

The next day all was finished, and I returned to Paris, after having left fifty francs with the old curé for masses to be said for the repose of the soul of him whose sepulchre we had troubled.

33

THE CONJURER

Richard Middleton

Certainly the audience was restive. In the first place it felt that it had been defrauded, seeing that Cissie Bradford, whose smiling face adorned the bills outside, had, failed to appear, and secondly, it considered that the deputy for that famous lady was more than inadequate. To the little man who sweated in the glare of the limelight and juggled desperately with glass balls in a vain effort to steady his nerve it was apparent that his turn was a failure. And as he worked he could have cried with disappointment, for his was a trial performance, and a year's engagement in the Hennings' group of music-halls would have rewarded success. Yet his tricks, things that he had done with the utmost ease a thousand times, had been a succession of blunders, rather mirth-provoking than mystifying to the audience. Presently one of the glass balls fell crashing on the stage, and amidst the jeers of the gallery he turned to his wife, who served as his assistant.

"I've lost my chance," he said, with a sob; "I can't do it!"

"Never mind, dear," she whispered. "There's a nice steak and onions at home for supper."

"It's no use," he said despairingly. "I'll try the disappearing trick and then get off. I'm done here." He turned back to the audience.

"Ladies and gentlemen," he said to the mockers in a wavering voice, "I will now present to you the concluding item of my entertainment. I will cause this lady to disappear under your very eyes, without the aid of any mechanical contrivance or artificial device." This was the merest showman's patter, for, as a matter of fact, it was not a very wonderful illusion. But as he led his wife forward to present her to the audience the conjurer was wondering whether the mishaps that had ruined his chance would meet him even here. If something should go wrong—he felt his wife's hand tremble in his, and he pressed it tightly to reassure her. He must make an effort, an effort of will, and then no mistakes would happen. For a second the lights danced before his eyes, then he pulled himself together. If an earthquake should disturb the curtains and show Molly creeping ignominiously away behind he would still meet his fate like a man. He turned round to conduct his wife to the little alcove from which she should vanish. She was not on the stage!

For a minute he did not guess the greatness of the disaster. Then he realised that the theatre was intensely quiet, and that he would have to explain that the last item of his programme was even more of a fiasco than the rest. Owing to a sudden indisposition—his skin tingled at the thought of the hooting. His tongue rasped upon cracking lips as he braced himself and bowed to the audience.

Then came the applause. Again and again it broke out from all over the house, while the curtain rose and fell, and the conjurer stood on the stage, mute, uncomprehending. What had happened? At first he had thought they were mocking him, but it was impossible to misjudge the nature of the applause. Besides, the stage-manager was allowing him call after call, as if he were a star. When at length the curtain remained down, and the orchestra struck up the opening bars of the next song, he staggered off into the wings as if he were drunk. There he met Mr. James Hennings himself.

"You'll do," said the great man; "that last trick was neat. You ought to polish up the others though. I suppose you don't want to tell me how you did it? Well, well, come in the morning and we'll fix up a contract."

And so, without having said a word, the conjurer found himself hustled off by the Vaudeville Napoleon. Mr. Hennings had something more to say to his manager.

"Bit rum," he said. "Did you see it?"

"Queerest thing we've struck."

"How was it done do you think?"

"Can't imagine. There one minute on his arm, gone the next, no trap, or curtain, or anything."

"Money in it, eh?"

"Biggest hit of the century, I should think."

"I'll go and fix up a contract and get him to sign it tonight. Get on with it." And Mr. James Hennings fled to his office.

Meanwhile the conjurer was wandering in the wings with the drooping heart of a lost child. What had happened? Why was he a success, and why did people stare so oddly, and what had become of his wife? When he asked them the stage hands laughed, and said they had not seen her. Why should they laugh? He wanted her to explain things, and hear their good luck. But she was not in her dressing-room, she was not anywhere. For a moment he felt like crying.

Then, for the second time that night, he pulled himself together. After all, there was no reason to be upset. He ought to feel very pleased about the contract, however it had happened. It seemed that his wife had left the stage in some queer way without being seen. Probably to increase the mystery she had gone straight home in her stage dress, and had succeeded in dodging the stage-door keeper. It was all very strange; but, of course, there must be some simple explanation like that. He would take a cab home and find her there already. There was a steak and onions for supper.

As he drove along in the cab he became convinced that this

theory was right. Molly had always been clever, and this time she had certainly succeeded in surprising everybody. At the door of his house he gave the cabman a shilling for himself with a light heart. He could afford it now. He ran up the steps cheerfully and opened the door. The passage was quite dark, and he wondered why his wife hadn't lit the gas.

"Molly!" he cried, "Molly!"

The small, weary-eyed servant came out of the kitchen on a savoury wind of onions.

"Hasn't missus come home with you, sir?" she said.

The conjurer thrust his hand against the wall to steady himself, and the pattern of the wall-paper seemed to burn his finger-tips.

"Not here!" he gasped at the frightened girl. "Then where is she? Where is she?"

"I don't know, sir," she began stuttering; but the conjurer turned quickly and ran out of the house. Of course, his wife must be at the theatre. It was absurd ever to have supposed that she could leave the theatre in her stage dress unnoticed; and now she was probably worrying because he had not waited for her. How foolish he had been.

It was a quarter of an hour before he found a cab, and the theatre was dark and empty when he got back to it. He knocked at the stage door, and the night watchman opened it.

"My wife?" he cried. "There's no one here now, sir," the man answered respectfully, for he knew that a new star had risen that night.

The conjurer leant against the doorpost faintly.

"Take me up to the dressing-rooms," he said. "I want to see whether she has been there while I was away."

The watchman led the way along the dark passages. "I shouldn't worry if I were you, sir," he said. "She can't have gone far." He did not know anything about it, but he wanted to be sympathetic.

"God knows," the conjurer muttered, "I can't understand this at all."

In the dressing-room Molly's clothes still lay neatly folded as she had left them when they went on the stage that night, and when he saw them his last hope left the conjurer, and a strange thought came into his mind.

"I should like to go down on the stage," he said, "and see if there is anything to tell me of her."

The night watchman looked at the conjurer as if he thought he was mad, but he followed him down to the stage in silence. When he was there the conjurer leaned forward suddenly, and his face was filled with a wistful eagerness.

"Molly!" he called, "Molly!"

But the empty theatre gave him nothing but echoes in reply.

34

THE VAMPIRE

Jan Neruda

The excursion steamer brought us from Constantinople to the shore of the island of Prinkipo and we disembarked. The number of passengers was not large. There was one Polish family, a father, a mother, a daughter and her bridegroom, and then we two. Oh, yes, I must not forget that when we were already on the wooden bridge which crosses the Golden Horn to Constantinople, a Greek, a rather youthful man, joined us. He was probably an artist, judging by the portfolio he carried under his arm. Long black locks floated to his shoulders, his face was pale, and his black eyes were deeply set in their sockets. From the first moment he interested me, especially for his obligingness and for his knowledge of local conditions. But he talked too much, and I then turned away from him.

All the more agreeable was the Polish family. The father and mother were good-natured, fine people, the lover a handsome young fellow, of direct and refined manners. They had come to Prinkipo to spend the summer months for the sake of the daughter, who was slightly ailing. The beautiful pale girl was either just recovering from a severe illness or else a serious disease was just fastening its hold upon her. She leaned upon her lover when she walked and very often sat down to rest, while a frequent dry little cough interrupted her whispers. Whenever she coughed, her escort would considerately pause in their walk. He always cast upon her a glance of sympathetic suffering and she would look back at him as if she would say: "It is nothing. I am happy!"

They believed in health and happiness.

On the recommendation of the Greek, who departed from us immediately at the pier, the family secured quarters in the hotel on the hill. The hotel-keeper was a Frenchman and his entire building was equipped comfortably and artistically, according to the French style.

We breakfasted together and when the noon heat had abated somewhat we all betook ourselves to the heights, where in the grove of Siberian stone-pines we could refresh ourselves with the view. Hardly had we found a suitable spot and settled ourselves when the Greek appeared again. He greeted us lightly, looked about and seated himself only a few steps from us. He opened his portfolio and began to sketch.

"I think he purposely sits with his back to the rocks so that we can't look at his sketch," I said.

"We don't have to," said the young Pole. "We have enough before us to look at." After a while he added, "It seems to me he's sketching us in as a sort of background. Well—let him!"

We truly did have enough to gaze at. There is not a more beautiful or more happy corner in the world than that very Prinkipo! The political martyr, Irene, contemporary of Charles the Great, lived there for a month as an exile. If I could live a month of my life there I would be happy for the memory of it for the rest of my days! I shall never forget even that one day spent at Prinkipo.

The air was as clear as a diamond, so soft, so caressing, that one's whole soul swung out upon it into the distance. At the right beyond the sea projected the brown Asiatic summits; to the left in the distance purpled the steep coasts of Europe. The neighboring Chalki, one of the nine islands of the "Prince's Archipelago," rose with its cypress forests into the peaceful heights like a sorrowful dream, crowned by a great structure—an asylum for those whose minds are sick.

The Sea of Marmora was but slightly ruffled and played in all colors like a sparkling opal. In the distance the sea was as white as milk, then rosy, between the two islands a glowing orange and below us it was beautifully greenish blue, like a transparent sapphire. It was resplendent in its own beauty. Nowhere were there any large ships—only two small craft flying the English flag sped along the shore. One was a steamboat as big as a watchman's booth, the second had about twelve oarsmen, and when their oars rose simultaneously molten silver dripped from them. Trustful dolphins darted in and out among them and dove with long, arching flights above the surface of the water. Through the blue heavens now and then calm eagles winged their way, measuring the space between two continents.

The entire slope below us was covered with blossoming roses whose fragrance filled the air. From the coffee-house near the sea music was carried up to us through the clear air, hushed somewhat by the distance.

The effect was enchanting. We all sat silent and steeped our souls completely in the picture of paradise. The young Polish girl lay on the grass with her head supported on the bosom of her lover. The pale oval of her delicate face was slightly tinged with soft color, and from her blue eyes tears suddenly gushed forth. The lover understood, bent down and kissed tear after tear. Her mother also was moved to tears, and I—even I—felt a strange twinge.

"Here mind and body both must get well," whispered the girl. "How happy a land this is!"

"God knows I haven't any enemies, but if I had I would forgive them here!" said the father in a trembling voice.

And again we became silent. We were all in such a wonderful mood—so unspeakably sweet it all was! Each felt for himself a whole world of happiness and each one would have shared his happiness with the whole world. All felt the same—and so no one disturbed another. We had scarcely even noticed the Greek, after an hour or so, had arisen, folded his portfolio and with a slight nod had taken his departure. We remained.

Finally after several hours, when the distance was becoming overspread with a darker violet, so magically beautiful in the south, the mother reminded us it was time to depart. We arose and walked down towards the hotel with the easy, elastic steps that characterize carefree children. We sat down in the hotel under the handsome veranda.

Hardly had we been seated when we heard below the sounds of quarreling and oaths. Our Greek was wrangling the hotel-keeper, and for the entertainment of it we listened.

The amusement did not last long. "If I didn't have other guests," growled the hotel-keeper, and ascended the steps towards us.

"I beg you to tell me, sir," asked the young Pole of the approaching hotel-keeper, "who is that gentleman? What's his name?"

"Eh—who knows what the fellow's name is?" grumbled the hotel-keeper, and he gazed venomously downwards. "We call him the Vampire."

"An artist?"

"Fine trade! He sketches only corpses. Just as soon as someone in Constantinople or here in the neighborhood dies, that very day he has a picture of the dead one completed. That fellow paints them beforehand—and he never makes a mistake—just like a vulture!"

The old Polish woman shrieked affrightedly. In her arms lay her daughter pale as chalk. She had fainted.

In one bound the lover had leaped down the steps. With one hand he seized the Greek and with the other reached for the portfolio.

We ran down after him. Both men were rolling in the sand.

The contents of the portfolio were scattered all about. On one sheet, sketched with a crayon, was the head of the young Polish girl, her eyes closed and a wreath of myrtle on her brow.

35

THE MASS FOR THE DEAD

Edith Nesbit

I was awake—widely, cruelly awake. I had been awake all night; what sleep could there be for me when the woman I loved was to be married next morning—married, and not to me?

I went to my room early; the family party in the drawing-room maddened me. Grouped about the round table with the stamped plush cover, each was busy with work, or book, or newspaper, but not too busy to stab my heart through and through with their talk of the wedding.

Her people were near neighbours of mine, so why should her marriage not be canvassed in my home circle?

They did not mean to be cruel; they did not know that I loved her; but she knew it. I told her, but she knew it before that. She knew it from the moment when I came back from three years of musical study in Germany—came back and met her in the wood where we used to go nutting when we were children.

I looked into her eyes, and my whole soul trembled with thankfulness that I was living in a world that held her also. I turned and walked by her side, through the tangled green wood, and we talked of the long-ago days, and it was, "Have you forgotten?" and "Do you remember?" till we reached her garden gate. Then I said—

"Good-bye; no, *auf wiedersehn*, and in a very little time, I hope."

And she answered—

"Good-bye. By the way, you haven't congratulated me yet."

"Congratulated you?"

"Yes, did I not tell you I am to marry Mr. Benoliel next month?"

And she turned away, and went up the garden slowly.

I asked my people, and they said it was true. Kate, my dear playfellow, was to marry this Spaniard, rich, wilful, accustomed to win, polished in manners and base in life. Why was she to marry him?

"No one knows," said my father, "but her father is talked about in the city, and Benoliel, the Spaniard, is rich. Perhaps that's it."

That was it. She told me so when, after two weeks spent with her and near her, I implored her to break so vile a chain and to come to me, who loved her—whom she loved.

"You are quite right," she said calmly. We were sitting in the window-seat of the oak parlour in her father's desolate old house. "I do love you, and I shall marry Mr. Benoliel."

"Why?"

"Look around you and ask me why, if you can."

I looked around—on the shabby, bare room, with its faded hangings of sage-green moreen, its threadbare carpet, its patched, washed-out chintz chair-covers. I looked out through the square, latticed window at the ragged, unkempt lawn, at her own gown—of poor material, though she wore it as queens might desire to wear ermine—and I understood.

Kate is obstinate; it is her one fault; I knew how vain would be my entreaties, yet I offered them; how unavailing my arguments, yet they were set forth; how useless my love and my sorrow, yet I showed them to her.

"No," she answered, but she flung her arms round my neck as she spoke, and held me as one may hold one's best treasure. "No, no; you are poor, and he is rich. You wouldn't have me break my father's heart: he's so proud, and if he doesn't get some money next month, he will be ruined. I'm not deceiving any one.

Mr. Benoliel knows I don't care for him; and if I marry him, he is going to advance my father a large sum of money. Oh, I assure you that everything has been talked over and settled. There is no going from it."

"Child! child!" I cried, "how calmly you speak of it! Don't you see that you are selling your soul and throwing mine away?"

"Father Fabian says I am doing right," she answered, unclasping her hands, but holding mine in them, and looking at me with those clear, grey eyes of hers. "Are we to be unselfish in everything else, and in love to think only of our own happiness? I love you, and I shall marry him. Would you rather the positions were reversed?"

"Yes," I said, "for then I would make you love me."

"Perhaps *he* will," she said bitterly. Even in that moment her mouth trembled with the ghost of a smile. She always loved to tease. She goes through more moods in a day than most other women in a year. Drowning the smile came tears, but she controlled them, and she said—

"Good-bye; you see I am right, don't you? Oh, Jasper, I wish I hadn't told you I loved you. It will only make you more unhappy."

"It makes my one happiness," I answered; "nothing can take that from me. And that happiness *he* will never have. Say again that you love me!"

"I love you! I love you! I love you!"

With further folly of tears and mad loving words we parted, and I bore my heartache away, leaving her to bear hers into her new life.

And now she was to be married to-morrow, and I could not sleep.

When the darkness became unbearable I lighted a candle, and then lay staring vacantly at the roses on the wall-paper, or following with my eyes the lines and curves of the heavy mahogany furniture.

The solidity of my surroundings oppressed me. In the dull light the wardrobe loomed like a hearse, and my violin case looked like a child's coffin.

I reached a book and read till my eyes ached and the letters danced a *pas fantastique* up and down the page.

I got up and had ten minutes with the dumbbells. I sponged my face and hands with cold water and tried again to sleep—vainly. I lay there, miserably wide awake.

I tried to say poetry, the half-forgotten tasks of my school days even, but through everything ran the refrain—

"Kate is to be married to-morrow, and not to me, not to me!"

I tried counting up to a thousand. I tried to imagine sheep in a lane, and to count them as they jumped through a gap in an imaginary hedge—all the time-honoured spells with which sleep is wooed—vainly.

Then the Waits came, and a torture to the nerves was superadded to the torture of the heart. After fifteen minutes of carols every fibre of me seemed vibrating in an agony of physical misery.

To banish the echo of "The Mistletoe Bough," I hummed softly to myself a melody of Palestrina's, and felt more awake than ever.

Then the thing happened which nothing will ever explain. As I lay there I heard, breaking through and gradually overpowering the air I was suggesting, a harmony which I had never heard before, beautiful beyond description, and as distinct and definite as any song man's ears have ever listened to.

My first half-formed thought was, "more Waits," but the music was choral music, true and sweet; with it mingled an organ's notes, and with every note the music grew in volume. It is absurd to suggest that I dreamed it, for, still hearing the music, I leaped out of bed and opened the window. The music grew fainter. There was no one to be seen in the snowy garden below.

Shivering, I shut the window. The music grew more distinct, and I became aware that I was listening to a mass—a funeral mass, and one which I had never heard before. I lay in my bed and followed the whole course of the office.

The music ceased.

I was sitting up in bed, my candle alight, and myself as wide awake as ever, and more than ever possessed by the thought of *her*.

But with a difference. Before, I had only mourned the loss of her: now, my thoughts of her were mingled with an indescribable dread. The sense of death and decay that had come to me with that strange, beautiful music, coloured all my thoughts. I was filled with fancies of hushed houses, black garments, rooms where white flowers and white linen lay in a deathly stillness. I heard echoes of tears, and of dim-voiced bells tolling monotonously. I shivered, as it were on the brink of irreparable woe, and in its contemplation I watched the dull dawn slowly overcome the pale flame of my candle, now burnt down into its socket.

I felt that I must see Kate once again before she gave herself away. Before ten o'clock I was in the oak parlour. She came to me. As she entered the room, her pallor, her swollen eyelids and the misery in her eyes wrung my heart as even that night of agony had not done. I literally could not speak. I held out my hands.

Would she reproach me for coming to her again, for forcing upon her a second time the anguish of parting?

She did not. She laid her hands in mine, and said—

"I am thankful you have come; do you know, I think I am going mad? Don't let me go mad, Jasper."

The look in her eyes underlined her words.

I stammered something and kissed her hands. I was with her again, and joy fought again with grief.

"I must tell some one. If I am mad, don't lock me up. Take care of me, won't you?"

Would I not?

"Understand," she went on, "it was not a dream. I was wide awake, thinking of you. The Waits had not long gone, and I—I was looking at your likeness. I was not asleep."

I shivered as I held her fast.

"As Heaven sees us, I did not dream it. I heard a mass sung, and, Jasper, it was a mass for the dead. I followed the office. You are not a Catholic, but I thought—I feared—oh, I don't know what I thought. I am thankful there is nothing wrong with you."

I felt a sudden certainty, and complete sense of power possess me. Now, in this her moment of weakness, while she was so completely under the influence of a strong emotion, I could and would save her from Benoliel, and myself from life-long pain.

"Kate," I said, "I believe it is a warning. You shall not marry this man. You shall marry me, and none other."

She leaned her head against my shoulder; she seemed to have forgotten her father and all the reasons for her marriage with Benoliel.

"You don't think I'm mad? No? Then take care of me; take me away; I feel safe with you."

Thus all obstacles vanished in less time than the length of a lover's kiss. I dared not stop to consider the coincidence of supernatural warning—nor what it might mean. Face to face with crowned hope, I am proud to remember that common sense held her own. The room in which we were had a French window. I fetched her garden hat and a shawl from the hall, and we went out through the still, white garden. We did not meet a soul. When we reached my father's garden I took her in by the back way, to the summer-house, and left her, though I was half afraid to leave her, while I went into the house. I snatched my violin and cheque book, took all my spare money, scrawled a line to my father and rejoined her.

Still no one had seen us.

We walked to a station five miles away; and by the time Benoliel would reach the church, I was leaving Doctors' Commons with a special licence in my pocket. Two hours later Kate was my wife, and we were quietly and prosaically eating our wedding-breakfast in the dining-room of the Grand Hotel.

"And where shall we go?" I said.

"I don't know," she answered, smiling; "you have not much money, have you?"

"Oh dear me, yes. I'm not rich, but I'm not absolutely a church mouse."

"Could we go to Devonshire?" she asked, twisting her new ring round and round.

"Devonshire! Why, that is where——"

"Yes, I know: Benoliel arranged to go there. Jasper, I am afraid of Benoliel."

"Then why——"

"Foolish person," she answered. "Do you think that Benoliel will be likely to go to Devonshire *now*?"

We went to Devonshire—I had had a small legacy a few months earlier, and I did not permit money cares to trouble my new and beautiful happiness. My only fear was that she would be saddened by thoughts of her father; but I am thankful to remember that in those first days she, too, was happy—so happy that there seemed to be hardly room in her mind for any thought but of me. And every hour of every day I said to my soul—

"But for that portent, whatever it boded, she might have been not my wife but his."

The first four or five days of our marriage are flowers that memory keeps always fresh. Kate's face had recovered its wild-rose bloom, and she laughed and sang and jested and enjoyed all our little daily adventures with the fullest, freest-hearted gaiety. Then I committed the supreme imbecility of my life—one of those acts of folly on which one looks back all one's life with a half stamp of the foot, and the unanswerable question, "How on earth could I have been such a fool?"

We were sitting in a little sitting-room, hideous in intention, but redeemed by blazing fire and the fact that two were there, sitting hand-in-hand, gazing into the fire and talking of their future and of their love. There was nothing to trouble us; no one had discovered our whereabouts, and my wife's fear of Benoliel's revenge seemed to have dissolved before the flame of our happiness.

And as we sat there, peaceful and untroubled, the Imp of the Perverse jogged my elbow, as, alas! he does so often, and I was moved to tell my wife that I, too, had heard that unearthly midnight music—that her hearing of it was not, as she had grown to think, a mere nightmare—a strange dream—but something more strange, more significant. I told her how I had heard the mass for the dead, and all the tale of that night. She listened silently, and I thought her strangely indifferent. When I had finished, she took her hand from mine and covered her face.

"I believe it was a warning to us to flee temptation. We ought never to have married. Oh, my poor father!"

Her tone was one that I had never heard before. Its hopeless misery appalled me. And justly. For no arguments, no entreaties, no caresses, could win my wife back to the mood of an hour before.

She tried to be cheerful, but her gaiety was forced, and her laughter stung my heart.

She spoke no more about the music, and when I tried to reason with her about it she smiled a gloomy little smile, and said—

"I cannot be happy. I will not be happy. It is wrong. I have been very selfish and wicked. You think me very idiotic, I know, but I believe there is a curse on us. We shall never be happy again."

"Don't you love me any more?" I asked like a fool.

"Love you?" She only repeated my words, but I was satisfied on that score. But those were miserable days. We loved each other passionately, yet our hours were spent like those of lovers on the eve of parting. Long, long silences took the place of foolish little jokes and childish talk which happy lovers know. And more than once, waking in the night, I heard my wife sobbing, and feigned sleep, with the bitter knowledge that I had no power to comfort her. I knew that the thought of her father was with her always, and that her anxiety about him grew, day by day. I wore myself out in trying to think of some way to divert her thoughts from him. I could not, indeed, pay his debts, but I could have him to live with us, a much greater sacrifice; and having a good connection, both as a musician and composer, I did not doubt that I could support her and him in comfort.

But Kate had made up her mind that the disgrace of bankruptcy would break her father's heart; and my Kate is not easy to convince or persuade.

At Torquay it occurred to me that perhaps it would be well for her to see a priest. True, Father Fabian had counselled her to marry Benoliel, but I could hardly believe that most priests would advise a girl to marry a bad man, whom she did not love, for the sake of any worldly gain whatsoever.

She received the suggestion with favour, but without enthusiasm, and we sought out a Catholic church to make inquiries. As we opened the outer door of the church we heard music, and as we stood in the entrance and I laid my hand on the heavy inner door, my other hand was caught by Kate.

"Jasper," she whispered, "it is the same!"

Some person opening the door behind us compelled us to move forward. In another moment we stood in the dusky church—stood hand-in-hand in dim daylight, listening to the same music that each had heard in the lonely night on the eve of our wedding.

I put my arm round my wife and drew her back.

"Come away, my darling," I whispered; "it is a funeral service."

She turned her eyes on me. "I *must* understand, I must see who it is. I shall go mad if you take me away now. I cannot bear any more."

We walked up the aisle, and placed ourselves as near as possible to the spot where the coffin lay, covered with flowers and with tapers burning about it. And we heard that music again, every note of it the same that each had heard before. And when the service was over I whispered to the sacristan—

"Whose music was that?"

"Our organist's," he answered; "it is the first time they've had it. Fine, wasn't it?"

"Who is the—who was—who is being buried?"

"A foreign gentleman, sir; they do say as his lady as was to be gave him the slip on his wedding day, and he'd given her father thousands they say, if the truth was known."

"But what was he doing here?"

"Well, that's the curious part, sir. To show his independence what does he do but go the same tour he'd planned for wedding trip. And there was a railway accident, and him every one in his carriage killed in a twinkling, so to speak for the young lady she was off with somebody else."

The sacristan laughed softly to himself.

Kate's fingers gripped my arm.

"What was his name?" she asked.

I would not have asked: I did not wish to

"Benoliel," said the sacristan. "Curious na'

Every one's talking of it."

Every one had something else to tal¹

that Benoliel's pride, which had permitr

shrunk from reclaiming the purchasᶠ

was lost to him. And to the man who had been willing to sell his daughter, the retention of her price seemed perfectly natural.

From the moment when she heard Benoliel's name on the sacristan's lips, all Kate's gaiety and happiness returned. She loved me, and she hated Benoliel. She was married to me, and he was dead; and his death was far more of a shock to me than to her. Women are curiously kind and curiously cruel. And she never could see why her father should not have kept the money. It is noteworthy that women, even the cleverest and the best of them, have no perception of what men mean by honour.

How do I account for the music? My good critic, my business is to tell my story—not to account for it.

And do I not pity Benoliel? Yes. I can afford, now, to pity most men, alive or dead.

36

WHEN I WAS DEAD

Vincent O'Sullivan

That was the worst of Ravenel Hall. The passages were long and gloomy, the rooms were musty and dull, even the pictures were sombre and their subjects dire. On an autumn evening, when the wind soughed and ailed through the trees in the park, and the dead leaves whistled and chattered, while the rain clamoured at the windows, small wonder that folks with gentle nerves went a-straying in their wits! An acute nervous system is a grievous burthen on the deck of a yacht under sunlit skies: at Ravenel the chain of nerves was prone to clash and jangle a funeral march. Nerves must be pampered in a tea-drinking community; and the ghost that your grandfather, with a skinful of port, could face and never tremble, sets you, in your sobriety, sweating and shivering; or, becoming scared (poor ghost!) of your bulged eyes and dropping jaw, he quenches expectation by not appearing at all. So I am left to conclude that it was tea which made my acquaintance afraid to stay at Ravenel. Even Wilvern gave over; and as he is in the Guards, and a polo player his nerves ought to be strong enough. On the night before he went I was explaining to him my theory, that if you place some drops of human blood near you, and then concentrate your thoughts, you will after a while see before you a man or a woman who will stay with you during long hours of the night, and even meet you at unexpected places during the day. I was explaining this theory, I repeat, when he interrupted me with words, senseless enough, which sent me fencing and parrying strangers,—on my guard.

"I say, Alistair, my dear chap!" he began, "you ought to get out of this place and go up to Town and knock about a bit—you really ought, you know."

"Yes," I replied, "and get poisoned at the hotels by bad food and at the clubs by bad talk, I suppose. No, thank you: and let me say that your care for my health enervates me."

"Well, you can do as you like," says he, rapping with his feet on the floor. "I'm hanged if I stay here after to-morrow I'll be staring mad if I do!"

He was my last visitor. Some weeks after his departure I was sitting in the library with my drops of blood by me. I had got my theory nearly perfect by this time; but there was one difficulty. The figure which I had ever before me was the figure of an old woman with her hair divided in the middle, and her hair fell to her shoulders, white on one side and black on the other. She as a very complete old woman; but, alas! she was eyeless, and when I tried to construct the eyes she would shrivel and rot in my sight. But to-night I was thinking, thinking, as I had never thought before, and the eyes were just creeping into the head when I heard terrible crash outside as if some heavy substance had fallen. Of a sudden the door was flung open and two maid-servants entered they glanced at the rug under my chair, and at that they turned a sick white, cried on God, and huddled out.

"How dare you enter the library in this manner?" I demanded sternly. No answer came back from them, so I started in pursuit. I found all the servants in the house gathered in a knot at the end of the passage.

"Mrs. Pebble," I said smartly, to the housekeeper, "I want those two women discharged to-morrow. It's an outrage! You ought to be more careful." But she was not attending to me. Her face was distorted with terror.

"Ah dear, ah dear!" she went. "We had better all go to the library together," says she to the others.

"Am I master of my own house, Mrs. Pebble?" I inquired, bringing my knuckles down with a bang on the table.

None of them seemed to see me or hear me: I might as well have been shrieking in a desert. I followed them down the passage, and forbade them to enter the library.

But they trooped past me, and stood with a clutter round the hearth-rug. Then three or four of them began dragging and lifting, as if they were lifting a helpless body, and stumbled with their imaginary burthen over to a sofa. Old Soames, the butler, stood near.

"Poor young gentleman!" he said with a sob. "I've knowed him since he was a baby. And to think of him being dead like this and so young, too!"

I crossed the room. "What's all this, Soames!" I cried, shaking him roughly by the shoulders. "I'm not dead. I'm here—here!" As he did not stir I got a little scared. "Soames, old friend!" I called, "don't you know me! Don't you know the little boy you used to play with? Say I'm not dead, Soames, please, Soames!"

He stooped down and kissed the sofa. "I think one of the men ought to ride over to the village for the doctor, Mr. Soames," says Mrs. Pebble; and he shuffled out to give the order.

Now, this doctor was an ignorant dog, whom I had been forced to exclude from the house because he went about proclaiming his belief in a saving God, at the same time that he proclaimed himself a man of science. He, I was resolved, should never cross my threshold, and I followed Mrs. Pebble through the house, screaming out prohibition. But I did not catch even a groan from her, not a nod of the head, nor a cast of the eye, to show that she had heard.

I met the doctor at the door of the library. "Well," I sneered, throwing my hand in his face, "have you come to teach me some new prayers?"

He brushed by me as if he had not felt the blow, and knelt down by the sofa.

"Rupture of a vessel on the brain, I think," he says to Soames and Mrs. Pebble after a short moment. "He has been dead some hours. Poor fellow! You had better telegraph for his sister, and I will send up the undertaker to arrange the body."

"You liar!" I yelled. "You whining liar! How have you the insolence to tell my servants that I am dead, when you see me here face to face?"

He was far in the passage, with Soames and Mrs. Pebble at his heels, ere I had ended, and not one of the three turned round.

All that night I sat in the library. Strangely enough, I had no wish to sleep nor during the time that followed, had I any craving to eat. In the morning the men came, and although I ordered them out, they proceeded to minister about something I could not see. So all day I stayed in the library or wandered about the house, and at night the men came again bringing with them a coffin. Then, in my humour, thinking it shame that so fine a coffin should be empty I lay the night in it and slept a soft dreamless sleep—the softest sleep I have ever slept. And when the men came the next day I rested still, and the undertaker shaved me. A strange valet!

On the evening after that, I was coming downstairs, when I noted some luggage in the hall, and so learned that my sister had arrived. I had not seen this woman since her marriage, and I loathed her more than I loathed any creature in this ill-organised world. She was very beautiful, I think—tall, and dark, and straight as a ram-rod—and she had an unruly passion for scandal and dress. I suppose the reason I disliked her so intensely was, that she had a habit of making one aware of her presence when she was several yards off. At half-past nine o'clock my sister came down to the library in a very charming wrap, and I soon found that she was as insensible to my presence as the others. I trembled with rage to see her kneel down by the coffin—my coffin; but when she bent over to kiss the pillow I threw away control.

A knife which had been used to cut string was lying upon a table: I seized it and drove it into her neck. She fled from the room screaming.

"Come! come!" she cried, her voice quivering with anguish. "The corpse is bleeding from the nose."

Then I cursed her.

On the evening of the third day there was a heavy fall of snow. About eleven o'clock I observed that the house was filled with blacks and mutes and folk of the county, who came for the obsequies. I went into the library and sat still, and waited. Soon came the men, and they closed the lid of the coffin and bore it out on their shoulders. And yet I sat, feeling rather sadly that something of mine had been taken away: I could not quite think what. For half-an-hour perhaps—dreaming, dreaming: and then I glided to the hall door. There was no trace left of the funeral; but after a while I sighted a black thread winding slowly across the white plain.

"I'm not dead!" I moaned, and rubbed my face in the pure snow, and tossed it on my neck and hair. "Sweet God, I am not dead."

37

A DREAM OF RED HANDS

Bram Stoker

The first opinion given to me regarding Jacob Settle was a simple descriptive statement. "He's a down-in-the-mouth chap": but I found that it embodied the thoughts and ideas of all his fellow-workmen. There was in the phrase a certain easy tolerance, an absence of positive feeling of any kind, rather than any complete opinion, which marked pretty accurately the man's place in public esteem. Still, there was some dissimilarity between this and his appearance which unconsciously set me thinking, and by degrees, as I saw more of the place and the workmen, I came to have a special interest in him. He was, I found, for ever doing kindnesses, not involving money expenses beyond his humble means, but in the manifold ways of forethought and forbearance and self-repression which are of the truer charities of life. Women and children trusted him implicitly, though, strangely enough, he rather shunned them, except when anyone was sick, and then he made his appearance to help if he could, timidly and awkwardly. He led a very solitary life, keeping house by himself in a tiny cottage, or rather hut, of one room, far on the edge of the moorland. His existence seemed so sad and solitary that I wished to cheer it up, and for the purpose took the occasion when we had both been sitting up with a child, injured by me through accident, to offer to lend him books. He gladly accepted, and as we parted in the grey of the dawn I felt that something of mutual confidence had been established between us.

The books were always most carefully and punctually

returned, and in time Jacob Settle and I became quite friends. Once or twice as I crossed the moorland on Sundays I looked in on him; but on such occasions he was shy and ill at ease so that I felt diffident about calling to see him. He would never under any circumstances come into my own lodgings.

One Sunday afternoon, I was coming back from a long walk beyond the moor, and as I passed Settle's cottage stopped at the door to say "how do you do?" to him. As the door was shut, I thought that he was out, and merely knocked for form's sake, or through habit, not expecting to get any answer. To my surprise, I heard a feeble voice from within, though what was said I could not hear. I entered at once, and found Jacob lying half-dressed upon his bed. He was as pale as death, and the sweat was simply rolling off his face. His hands were unconsciously gripping the bed-clothes as a drowning man holds on to whatever he may grasp. As I came in he half arose, with a wild, hunted look in his eyes, which were wide open and staring, as though something of horror had come before him; but when he recognised me he sank back on the couch with a smothered sob of relief and closed his eyes. I stood by him for a while, quiet a minute or two, while he gasped. Then he opened his eyes and looked at me, but with such a despairing, woeful expression that, as I am a living man, I would have rather seen that frozen look of horror. I sat down beside him and asked after his health. For a while he would not answer me except to say that he was not ill; but then, after scrutinising me closely, he half arose on his elbow and said—

"I thank you kindly, sir, but I'm simply telling you the truth. I am not ill, as men call it, though God knows whether there be not worse sicknesses than doctors know of. I'll tell you, as you are so kind, but I trust that you won't even mention such a think to a living soul, for it might work me more and greater woe. I am suffering from a bad dream."

"A bad dream!" I said, hoping to cheer him; "but dreams

pass away with the light-even with waking." There I stopped, for before he spoke I saw the answer in his desolate look round the little place.

"No! no! that's all well for people that live in comfort and with those they love around them. It is a thousand times worse for those who live alone and have to do so. What cheer is there for me, waking here in the silence of the night, with the wide moor around me full of voices and full of faces that make my waking a worse dream than my sleep? Ah, young sir, you have no past that can send its legions to people the darkness and the empty space, and I pray the good God that you may never have! As he spoke, there was such an almost irresistible gravity of conviction in his manner that I abandoned my remonstrance about his solitary life. I felt that I was in the presence of some secret influence which I could not fathom. To my relief, for I knew not what to say, he went on—

"Two nights past have I dreamed it. It was hard enough the first night, but I came through it. Last night the expectation was in itself almost worse than the dream-until the dream came, and then it swept away every remembrance of lesser pain. I stayed awake till just before the dawn, and then it came again, and ever since I have been in such an agony as I am sure the dying feel, and with it all the dread of to-night." Before he had got to the end of the sentence my mind was made up, and I felt that I could speak to him more cheerfully.

"Try and get to sleep early to-night in fact, before the evening has passed away. The sleep will refresh you, and I promise you there will not be any bad dreams after to-night." He shook his head hopelessly, so I sat a little longer and then left him.

When I got home I made my arrangements for the night, for I had made up my mind to share Jacob Settle's lonely vigil in his cottage on the moor. I judged that if he got to sleep before sunset he would wake well before midnight, and so, just as the bells of the city were striking eleven, I stood opposite his door armed with a bag, in which were my supper, and extra large flask, a couple of candles, and a book. The moonlight was bright, and flooded the whole moor, till it was almost as light as day; but ever and anon black clouds drove across the sky, and made a darkness which by comparison seemed almost tangible. I opened the door softly, and entered without waking Jacob, who lay asleep with his white face upward. He was still, and again bathed in sweat. I tried to imagine what visions were passing before those closed eyes which could bring with them the misery and woe which were stamped on the face, but fancy failed me, and I waited for the awakening. It came suddenly, and in a fashion which touched me to the quick, for the hollow groan that broke from the man's white lips as he half arose and sank back was manifestly the realisation or completion of some train of thought which had gone before.

"If this be dreaming," said I to myself, "then it must be based on some very terrible reality. What can have been that unhappy fact that he spoke of?"

While I thus spoke, he realised that I was with him. It struck me as strange that he had no period of that doubt as to whether dream or reality surrounded him which commonly marks an expected environment of waking men. With a positive cry of joy, he seized my hand and held it in his two wet, trembling hands, as a frightened child clings on to someone whom it loves. I tried to soothe him—

"There, there! it is all right. I have come to stay with you to-night, and together we will try to fight this evil dream." He let go my hand suddenly, and sank back on his bed and covered his eyes with his hands.

"Fight it?—the evil dream! Ah! no sir no! No mortal power can fight that dream, for it comes form God-and is burned in here;" and he beat upon his forehead. Then he went on—

It is the same dream, ever the same, and yet it grows in its power to torture me every time it comes."

"What is the dream?" I asked, thinking that the speaking of it might give him some relief, but he shrank away from me, and after a long pause said—

"No, I had better not tell it. It may not come again."

There was manifestly something to conceal from me—something that lay behind the dream, so I answered—

"All right. I hope you have seen the last of it. But if it should come again, you will tell me, will you not? I ask, not out of curiosity, but because I think it may relieve you to speak." He answered with what I thought was almost an undue amount of solemnity—

"If it comes again, I shall tell you all."

Then I tried to get his mind away from the subject to more mundane things, so I produced supper, and made him share it with me, including the contents of the flask. After a little he braced up, and when I lit my cigar, having given him another, we smoked a full hour, and talked of many things. Little by little the comfort of his body stole over his mind, and I could see sleep laying her gentle hands on his eyelids. He felt it, too, and told me that now he felt all right, and I might safely leave him; but I told him that, right or wrong, I was going to see in the daylight. So I lit my other candle, and began to read as he fell asleep.

By degrees I got interested in my book, so interested that presently I was startled by its dropping out of my hands. I looked and saw that Jacob was still asleep, and I was rejoiced to see that there was on his face a look of unwonted happiness, while his lips seemed to move with unspoken words. Then I turned to my work again, and again woke, but this time to feel chilled to my very marrow by hearing the voice from the bed beside me—

"Not with those red hands! Never! never!" On looking at

him, I found that he was still asleep. He woke, however, in an instant, and did not seem surprised to see me; there was again that strange apathy as to his surroundings. Then I said:

"Settle, tell me your dream. You may speak freely, for I shall hold your confidence sacred. While we both live I shall never mention what you may choose to tell me."

"I said I would; but I had better tell you first what goes before the dream, that you may understand. I was a schoolmaster when I was a very young man; it was only a parish school in a little village in the West Country. No need to mention any names. Better not. I was engaged to be married to a young girl whom I loved and almost reverenced. It was the old story. While we were waiting for the time when we could afford to set up house together, another man came along. He was nearly as young as I was, and handsome, and a gentleman, with all a gentleman's attractive ways for a woman of our class. He would go fishing, and she would meet him while I was at my work in school. I reasoned with her and implored her to give him up. I offered to get married at once and go away and begin the world in a strange country; but she would not listen to anything I could say, and I could see that she was infatuated with him. Then I took it on myself to meet the man and ask him to deal well with the girl, for I thought he might mean honestly by her, so that there might be no talk or chance of talk on the part of others. I went where I should meet him with none by, and we met!" Here Jacob Settle had to pause, for something seemed to rise in his throat, and he almost gasped for breath. Then went on—

"Sir, as God is above us, there was no selfish thought in my heart that day, I loved my pretty Mabel too well to be content with a part of her love, and I had thought of my own unhappiness too often not to have come to realise that, whatever might come to her, my hope was gone. He was insolent to me—you, sir, who are a gentleman, cannot know, perhaps, how galling can be the insolence of one who is above you in station—but I bore with that. I implored him to deal well with the girl, for what might be only a pastime of an idle hour with him might be the breaking of her heart. For I never had a thought of her truth, or that the worst of harm could come to her—it was only the unhappiness to her heart I feared. But when I asked him when he intended to marry her his laughter galled me so that I lost my temper and told him that I would not stand by and see her life made unhappy. Then he grew angry too, and in his anger said such cruel things of her that then and there I swore he should not live to do her harm. God knows how it came about, for in such moments of passion it is hard to remember the steps from a word to a blow, but I found myself standing over his dead body, with my hands crimson with the blood that welled from his torn throat. We were alone and he was a stranger, with none of his kin to seek for him and murder does not always out—not all at once. His bones may be whitening still, for all I know, in the pool of the river where I left him. No one suspected his absence, or why it was, except my poor Mabel, and she dared not speak. But it was all in vain, for when I came back again after an absence of months—for I could not live in the place—I learned that her shame had come and that she had died in it. Hitherto I had been borne up by the thought that my ill deed had saved her future, but now, when I learned that I had been too late, and that my poor love was smirched with that man's sin, I fled away with the sense of my useless guilt upon me more heavily than I could bear. Ah! Sir, you that have not done such a sin don't know what it is to carry it with you. You may think that custom makes it easy to you, but it is not so. It grows and grows with every hour, till it becomes intolerable, and with it growing, too, the feeling that you must for ever stand outside Heaven. You don't know what that means, and I pray God that you never may. Ordinary men, to whom all things are possible, don't often, if ever, think of Heaven. It is a name, and nothing more, and they are content to wait and let things be, but to those who are doomed to be shut out for ever you cannot think what it means, you cannot guess or measure the terrible endless longing to see the gates opened, and to be able to join the white figures within.

"And this brings me to my dream. It seemed that the portal was before me, with great gates of massive steel with bars of the thickness of a mast, rising to the very clouds, and so close that between them was just a glimpse of a crystal grotto, on whose shinning walls were figured many white-clad forms with faces radiant with joy. When I stood before the gate my heart and my soul were so full of rapture and longing that I forgot. And there stood at the gate two mighty angels with sweeping wings, and, oh! so stern of countenance. They held each in one hand a flaming sword, and in the other the latchet, which moved to and fro at their lightest touch. Nearer were figures all draped in black, with heads covered so that only the eyes were seen, and they handed to each who came white garments such as the angels wear. A low murmur came that told that all should put on their own robes, and without soil, or the angels would not pass them in, but would smite them down with the flaming swords. I was eager to don my own garment, and hurriedly threw it over me and stepped swiftly to the gate; but it moved not, and the angels, loosing the latchet, pointed to my dress, I looked down, and was aghast, for the whole robe was smeared with blood. My hands were red; they glittered with the blood that dripped form them as on that day by the river bank. And then the angels raised their flaming swords to smite me down, and the horror was complete—I awoke. Again, and again, and again, that awful dream comes to me. I never learn form the experience, I never remember, but at the beginning the hope if ever there to make the end more appalling; and I know that the dream does not come out of the common darkness where the dreams abide, but that it is sent from God as a punishment! Never, never shall I be able to pass the gate, for the soil on the angel garments must ever come from these bloody hands!"

I listened as in a spell as Jacob Settle spoke. There was something so far away in the tone of his voice—something so dreamy and mystic in the eyes that looked as if through me at some spirit beyond—something so lofty in his very diction and in such marked contrast to his workworn clothes and his poor surroundings that I wondered if the whole thing were not a dream.

We were both silent for a long time. I kept looking at the man before me in growing wonderment. Now that his confession had been made, his soul, which had been crushed to the very earth, seemed to leap back again to uprightness with some resilient force. I suppose I ought to have been horrified with his story, but, strange to say, I was not. It certainly is not pleasant to be made the recipient of the confidence of a murderer, but this poor fellow seemed to have had, not only so much provocation, but so much self-denying purpose in his deed of blood that I did not feel called upon to pass judgment upon him. My purpose was to comfort, so I spoke out with what calmness I could, for my heart was beating fast and heavily—

"You need not despair, Jacob Settle. God is very good, and his mercy is great. Live on and work on in the hope that some day you may feel that you have atoned for the past." Here I paused, for I could see that sleep, natural sleep this time, was creeping upon him. "Go to sleep," I said; "I shall watch with you here, and we shall have no more evil dreams to-night."

He made an effort to pull himself together, and answered—

"I don't know how to thank you for your goodness to me this night, but I think you had best leave me now. I'll try and sleep this out; I feel a weight off my mind since I have told you all. If there's anything of the man left in me, I must try and fight out life alone."

"I'll go to-night, as you wish it," I said; "but take my advice, and do not live in such a solitary way. Go among men and women; live among them. Share their joys and sorrows, and it will help you to forget. This solitude will make you melancholy mad."

"I will!" he answered, half unconsciously, for sleep was overmastering him.

I turned to go, and he looked after me. When I had touched the latch I dropped it, and, coming back to the bed, held out my hand. He grasped it with both his as he rose to a sitting posture, and I said my good-night, trying to cheer him—

"Heart, man, heart! There is work in the world for you to do, Jacob Settle. You can wear those white robes yet and pass through that gate of steel!"

Then I left him.

A week after I found his cottage deserted, and on asking at the works was told that he had "gone north," no one exactly knew whither.

Two years afterwards, I was staying for a few days with my friend Dr. Munro in Glasgow. He was a busy man, and could not spare much time for going about with me, so I spent my days in excursions to the Trossachs and Loch Katrine and down the Clyde. On the second last evening of my stay I came back somewhat later than I had arranged, but found that my host was late too. The maid told me that he had been sent for to the hospital—a case of accident at the gas-works, and the dinner was postponed an hour; so telling her I would stroll down to find her master and walk back with him, I went out. At the hospital I found him washing his hands preparatory to starting for home. Casually, I asked him what his case was.

"Oh, the usual thing! A rotten rope and men's lives of no account. Two men were working in a gasometer, when the rope that held their scaffolding broke. It must have occurred just before the dinner hour, for no one noticed their absence till the men had returned. There was about seven feet of water in the gasometer, so they had a hard fight for it, poor fellows. However, one of them was alive, just alive, but we have had a hard job to pull him through. It seems that he owes his life to his mate, for I have never heard of greater heroism. They swam together while their strength lasted, but at the end they were so done up that even the lights above, and the men slung with ropes, coming down to help them, could not keep them up. But one of them stood on the bottom and held up his comrade over his head, and those few breaths made all the difference between life and death. They were a shocking sight when they were taken out, for that water is like a purple dye with the gas and the tar. The man upstairs looked as if he had been washed in blood. Ugh!"

"And the other?"

"Oh, he's worse still. But he must have been a very noble fellow. That struggle under the water must have been fearful; one can see that by the way the blood has been drawn from the extremities. It makes the idea of the Stigmata possible to look at him. Resolution like this could, you would think, do anything in the world. Ay! it might almost unbar the gates of Heaven. Look here, old man, it is not a very pleasant sight, especially just before dinner, but you are a writer, and this is an odd case. Here is something you would not like to miss, for in all human probability you will never see anything like it again." While he was speaking he had brought me into the mortuary of the hospital.

On the bier lay a body covered with a white sheet, which was wrapped close round it.

"Looks like a chrysalis, don't it? I say, Jack, if there be anything in the old myth that a soul is typified by a butterfly, well, then the one that this chrysalis sent forth was a very noble specimen and took all the sunlight on its wings. See here!" He uncovered the face. Horrible, indeed, it looked, as though stained with blood. But I knew him at once, Jacob Settle! My friend pulled the winding sheet further down.

The hands were crossed on the purple breast as they had been reverently placed by some tenderhearted person. As I saw them my heart throbbed with a great exultation, for the memory of his harrowing dream rushed across my mind. There was no stain now on those poor, brave hands, for they were blanched white as snow.

And somehow as I looked I felt that the evil dream was all over. That noble soul had won a way through the gate at last. The white robe had now no stain from the hands that had put it on.

38

THE CASK OF AMONTILLADO

Edgar Allen Poe

The thousand injuries of Fortunato I had borne as I best could, but when he ventured upon insult I vowed revenge. You, who so well know the nature of my soul, will not suppose, however, that I gave utterance to a threat. *At length* I would be avenged; this was a point definitively settled—but the very definitiveness with which it was resolved precluded the idea of risk. I must not only punish but punish with impunity. A wrong is unredressed when retribution overtakes its redresser. It is equally unredressed when the avenger fails to make himself felt as such to him who has done the wrong.

It must be understood that neither by word nor deed had I given Fortunato cause to doubt my good will. I continued, as was my wont, to smile in his face, and he did not perceive that my smile *now* was at the thought of his immolation.

He had a weak point—this Fortunato—although in other regards he was a man to be respected and even feared. He prided himself on his connoisseurship in wine. Few Italians have the true virtuoso spirit. For the most part their enthusiasm is adopted to suit the time and opportunity, to practice imposture upon the British and Austrian millionaires. In painting and gemmary, Fortunato, like his countrymen, was a quack, but in the matter of old wines he was sincere. In this respect I did not differ from him materially;—I was skilful in the Italian vintages myself, and bought largely whenever I could.

It was about dusk, one evening during the supreme madness

of the carnival season, that I encountered my friend. He accosted me with excessive warmth, for he had been drinking much. The man wore motley. He had on a tight-fitting parti-striped dress, and his head was surmounted by the conical cap and bells. I was so pleased to see him that I thought I should never have done wringing his hand.

I said to him—"My dear Fortunato, you are luckily met. How remarkably well you are looking to-day! But I have received a pipe of what passes for Amontillado, and I have my doubts."

"How?" said he. "Amontillado? A pipe? Impossible! And in the middle of the carnival!"

"I have my doubts," I replied; "and I was silly enough to pay the full Amontillado price without consulting you in the matter. You were not to be found, and I was fearful of losing a bargain."

"Amontillado!"

"I have my doubts."

"Amontillado!"

"And I must satisfy them."

"Amontillado!"

"As you are engaged, I am on my way to Luchesi. If any one has a critical turn it is he. He will tell me—"

"Luchesi cannot tell Amontillado from Sherry."

"And yet some fools will have it that his taste is a match for your own."

"Come, let us go."

"Whither?"

"To your vaults."

"My friend, no; I will not impose upon your good nature. I perceive you have an engagement. Luchesi—"

"I have no engagement;— come."

"My friend, no. It is not the engagement, but the severe cold with which I perceive you are afflicted. The vaults are insufferably damp. They are encrusted with nitre."

"Let us go, nevertheless. The cold is merely nothing. Amontillado! You have been imposed upon. And as for Luchesi, he cannot distinguish Sherry from Amontillado."

Thus speaking, Fortunato possessed himself of my arm. Putting on a mask of black silk and drawing a roquelaire closely about my person, I suffered him to hurry me to my palazzo.

There were no attendants at home; they had absconded to make merry in honour of the time. I had told them that I should not return until the morning, and had given them explicit orders not to stir from the house. These orders were sufficient, I well knew, to insure their immediate disappearance, one and all, as soon as my back was turned.

I took from their sconces two flambeaux, and giving one to Fortunato, bowed him through several suites of rooms to the archway that led into the vaults. I passed down a long and winding staircase, requesting him to be cautious as he followed. We came at length to the foot of the descent, and stood together on the damp ground of the catacombs of the Montresors.

The gait of my friend was unsteady, and the bells upon his cap jingled as he strode.

"The pipe," said he.

"It is farther on," said I; "but observe the white web-work which gleams from these cavern walls."

He turned towards me, and looked into my eyes with two filmy orbs that distilled the rheum of intoxication .

"Nitre?" he asked, at length.

"Nitre," I replied. "How long have you had that cough?"

"Ugh! ugh! ugh!—ugh!ugh!ugh!—ugh!ugh!ugh!—ugh!ugh! ugh!—ugh!ugh!ugh!"

My poor friend found it impossible to reply for many minutes.

"It is nothing," he said, at last.

"Come," I said, with decision, "we will go back; your health is precious. You are rich, respected, admired, beloved; you are happy, as once I was. You are a man to be missed. For me it is no matter. We will go back; you will be ill, and I cannot be responsible. Besides, there is Luchesi—"

"Enough," he said; "the cough is a mere nothing; it will not kill me. I shall not die of a cough."

"True—true," I replied; "and, indeed, I had no intention of alarming you unnecessarily—but you should use all proper caution. A draught of this Medoc will defend us from the damps."

Here I knocked off the neck of a bottle which I drew from a long row of its fellows that lay upon the mould.

"Drink," I said, presenting him the wine.

He raised it to his lips with a leer. He paused and nodded to me familiarly, while his bells jingled.

"I drink," he said, "to the buried that repose around us."

"And I to your long life."

He again took my arm, and we proceeded.

"These vaults," he said, "are extensive."

"The Montresors," I replied, "were a great and numerous family."

"I forget your arms."

"A huge human foot d'or, in a field azure; the foot crushes a serpent rampant whose fangs are imbedded in the heel."

"And the motto?"

"*Nemo me impune lacessit.*"

"Good!" he said.

The wine sparkled in his eyes and the bells jingled. My own fancy grew warm with the Medoc. We had passed through walls of piled bones, with casks and puncheons intermingling, into the inmost recesses of the catacombs. I paused again, and this time I made bold to seize Fortunato by an arm above the elbow.

"The nitre!" I said: "see, it increases. It hangs like moss upon the vaults. We are below the river's bed. The drops of moisture trickle among the bones. Come, we will go back ere it is too late. Your cough—"

"It is nothing," he said; "let us go on. But first, another draught of the Medoc."

I broke and reached him a flaçon of De Grâve. He emptied it at a breath. His eyes flashed with a fierce light. He laughed and threw the bottle upwards with a gesticulation I did not understand.

I looked at him in surprise. He repeated the movement—a grotesque one.

"You do not comprehend?" he said.

"Not I," I replied.

"Then you are not of the brotherhood."

"How?"

"You are not of the masons."

"Yes, yes," I said; "yes, yes."

"You? Impossible! A mason?"

"A mason," I replied.

"A sign," he said.

"It is this," I answered, producing a trowel from beneath the folds of my *roquelaire*.

"You jest," he exclaimed, recoiling a few paces. "But let us proceed to the Amontillado."

"Be it so," I said, replacing the tool beneath the cloak and again offering him my arm. He leaned upon it heavily. We continued our route in search of the Amontillado. We passed through a range of low arches, descended, passed on, and descending again, arrived at a deep crypt, in which the foulness of the air caused our flambeaux rather to glow than flame.

At the most remote end of the crypt there appeared another less spacious. Its walls had been lined with human remains, piled to the vault overhead, in the fashion of the great catacombs of Paris. Three sides of this interior crypt were still ornamented in this manner. From the fourth the bones had been thrown down, and lay promiscuously upon the earth, forming at one point a mound of some size. Within the wall thus exposed by the displacing of the bones, we perceived a still interior recess, in depth about four feet, in width three, in height six or seven. It seemed to have been constructed for no especial use within itself, but formed merely the interval between two of the colossal supports of the roof of the catacombs, and was backed by one of their circumscribing walls of solid granite.

It was in vain that Fortunato, uplifting his dull torch, endeavoured to pry into the depths of the recess. Its termination the feeble light did not enable us to see.

"Proceed," I said; "herein is the Amontillado. As for Luchesi—"

"He is an ignoramus," interrupted my friend, as he stepped unsteadily forward, while I followed immediately at his heels. In an instant he had reached the extremity of the niche, and finding his progress arrested by the rock, stood stupidly bewildered. A moment more and I had fettered him to the granite. In its surface were two iron staples, distant from each other about two feet, horizontally. From one of these depended a short chain, from the other a padlock. Throwing the links about his waist, it was but the work of a few seconds to secure it. He was too much astounded to resist. Withdrawing the key I stepped back from the recess.

"Pass your hand," I said, "over the wall; you cannot help feeling the nitre. Indeed, it is very damp. Once more let me *implore* you to return. No? Then I will positively leave you. But I must first render you all the little attentions in my power."

"The Amontillado!" ejaculated my friend, not yet recovered from his astonishment.

"True," I replied; "the Amontillado."

As I said these words I busied myself among the pile of bones of which I have before spoken. Throwing them aside, I soon uncovered a quantity of building stone and mortar. With these materials and with the aid of my trowel, I began vigorously to wall up the entrance of the niche.

I had scarcely laid the first tier of my masonry when I discovered that the intoxication of Fortunato had in a great measure worn off. The earliest indication I had of this was a low moaning cry from the depth of the recess. It was *not* the cry of a drunken man. There was then a long and obstinate silence. I laid the second tier, and the third, and the fourth; and then I heard the furious vibrations of the chain. The noise lasted for several minutes, during which, that I might hearken to it with the more satisfaction, I ceased my labours and sat down upon the bones. When at last the clanking subsided, I resumed the trowel, and finished without interruption the fifth, the sixth, and the seventh tier. The wall was now nearly upon a level with my breast. I again paused, and holding the flambeaux over the mason-work, threw a few feeble rays upon the figure within.

A succession of loud and shrill screams, bursting suddenly from the throat of the chained form, seemed to thrust me violently back. For a brief moment I hesitated, I trembled. Unsheathing my rapier, I began to grope with it about the recess; but the thought of an instant reassured me. I placed my hand upon the solid fabric of the catacombs, and felt satisfied. I reapproached the wall. I replied to the yells of him who clamoured. I re-echoed—I aided—I surpassed them in volume and in strength. I did this, and the clamourer grew still.

It was now midnight, and my task was drawing to a close. I had completed the eighth, the ninth, and the tenth tier. I had finished a portion of the last and the eleventh; there remained but a single stone to be fitted and plastered in. I struggled with its weight; I placed it partially in its destined position. But now there came from out the niche a low laugh that erected the hairs upon my head. It was succeeded by a sad voice, which I had difficulty in recognising as that of the noble Fortunato. The voice said—

"Ha! ha! ha!— he! he! he!—a very good joke, indeed—an excellent jest. We will have many a rich laugh about it at the palazzo—he! he! he!—over our wine—he! he! he!"

"The Amontillado!" I said.

"He! he! he!—he! he! he!—yes, the Amontillado. But is it not getting late? Will not they be awaiting us at the palazzo—the Lady Fortunato and the rest? Let us be gone."

"Yes," I said, "let us be gone."

"For the love of God, Montresor!"

"Yes," I said, "for the love of God!"

But to these words I hearkened in vain for a reply. I grew impatient. I called aloud—

"Fortunato!"

No answer. I called again—

"Fortunato!" No answer still. I thrust a torch through the remaining aperture and let it fall within. There came forth in return only a jingling of the bells. My heart grew sick—on account of the dampness of the catacombs. I hastened to make an end of my labour. I forced the last stone into its position; I plastered it up. Against the new masonry I re-erected the old rampart of bones. For the half of a century no mortal has disturbed them. *In pace requiescat!*

39

THE RED ROOM

H.G. Wells

"I can assure you," said I, "that it will take a very tangible ghost to frighten me." And I stood up before the fire with my glass in my hand.

"It is your own choosing," said the man with the withered arm, and glanced at me askance.

"Eight-and-twenty years," said I, "I have lived, and never a ghost have I seen as yet."

The old woman sat staring hard into the fire, her pale eyes wide open. "Ay," she broke in; "and eight-and-twenty years you have lived and never seen the likes of this house, I reckon. There's a many things to see, when one's still but eight-and-twenty." She swayed her head slowly from side to side. "A many things to see and sorrow for."

I half suspected the old people were trying to enhance the spiritual terrors of their house by their droning insistence. I put down my empty glass on the table and looked about the room, and caught a glimpse of myself, abbreviated and broadened to an impossible sturdiness, in the queer old mirror at the end of the room. "Well," I said, "if I see anything to-night, I shall be so much the wiser. For I come to the business with an open mind."

"It's your own choosing," said the man with the withered arm once more.

I heard the faint sound of a stick and a shambling step on the flags in the passage outside. The door creaked on its hinges as a second old man entered, more bent, more wrinkled, more aged even than the first. He supported himself by the help of a crutch, his eyes were covered by a shade, and his lower lip, half averted, hung pale and pink from his decaying yellow teeth. He made straight for an armchair on the opposite side of the table, sat down clumsily, and began to cough. The man with the withered hand gave the newcomer a short glance of positive dislike; the old woman took no notice of his arrival, but remained with her eyes fixed steadily on the fire.

"I said—it's your own choosing," said the man with the withered hand, when the coughing had ceased for a while.

"It's my own choosing," I answered.

The man with the shade became aware of my presence for the first time, and threw his head back for a moment, and sidewise, to see me. I caught a momentary glimpse of his eyes, small and bright and inflamed. Then he began to cough and splutter again.

"Why don't you drink?" said the man with the withered arm, pushing the beer toward him. The man with the shade poured out a glassful with a shaking hand, that splashed half as much again on the deal table. A monstrous shadow of him crouched upon the wall, and mocked his action as he poured and drank. I must confess I had scarcely expected these grotesque custodians. There is, to my mind, something inhuman in senility, something crouching and atavistic; the human qualities seem to drop from old people insensibly day by day. The three of them made me feel uncomfortable with their gaunt silences, their bent carriage, their evident unfriendliness to me and to one another. And that night, perhaps, I was in the mood for uncomfortable impressions. I resolved to get away from their vague fore-shadowings of the evil things upstairs.

"If," said I, "you will show me to this haunted room of yours, I will make myself comfortable there."

The old man with the cough jerked his head back so suddenly that it startled me, and shot another glance of his red eyes at me from out of the darkness under the shade, but no one answered me. I waited a minute, glancing from one to the other. The old woman stared like a dead body, glaring into the fire with lack-lustre eyes.

"If," I said, a little louder, "if you will show me to this haunted room of yours, I will relieve you from the task of entertaining me."

"There's a candle on the slab outside the door," said the man with the withered hand, looking at my feet as he addressed me. "But if you go to the Red Room to-night—"

"This night of all nights!" said the old woman, softly.

"—You go alone."

"Very well," I answered, shortly, "and which way do I go?"

"You go along the passage for a bit," said he, nodding his head on his shoulder at the door, "until you come to a spiral staircase; and on the second landing is a door covered with green baize. Go through that, and down the long corridor to the end, and the Red Room is on your left up the steps."

"Have I got that right?" I said, and repeated his directions.

He corrected me in one particular.

"And you are really going?" said the man with the shade, looking at me again for the third time with that queer, unnatural tilting of the face.

"This night of all nights!" whispered the old woman.

"It is what I came for," I said, and moved toward the door. As I did so, the old man with the shade rose and staggered round the table, so as to be closer to the others and to the fire. At the door I turned and looked at them, and saw they were all close together, dark against the firelight, staring at me over their shoulders, with an intent expression on their ancient faces.

"Good-night," I said, setting the door open. "It's your own choosing," said the man with the withered arm.

I left the door wide open until the candle was well alight, and then I shut them in, and walked down the chilly, echoing passage.

I must confess that the oddness of these three old pensioners in whose charge her ladyship had left the castle, and the deep-toned, old-fashioned furniture of the housekeeper's room, in which they foregathered, had affected me curiously in spite of my effort to keep myself at a matter-of-fact phase. They seemed to belong to another age, an older age, an age when things spiritual were indeed to be feared, when common sense was uncommon, an age when omens and witches were credible, and ghosts beyond denying. Their very existence, thought I, is spectral; the cut of their clothing, fashions born in dead brains; the ornaments and conveniences in the room about them even are ghostly—the thoughts of vanished men, which still haunt rather than participate in the world of to-day. And the passage I was in, long and shadowy, with a film of moisture glistening on the wall, was as gaunt and cold as a thing that is dead and rigid. But with an effort I sent such thoughts to the right-about. The long, drafty subterranean passage was chilly and dusty, and my candle flared and made the shadows cower and quiver. The echoes rang up and down the spiral staircase, and a shadow came sweeping up after me, and another fled before me into the darkness overhead. I came to the wide landing and stopped there for a moment listening to a rustling that I fancied I heard creeping behind me, and then, satisfied of the absolute silence, pushed open the unwilling baize-covered door and stood in the silent corridor.

The effect was scarcely what I expected, for the moonlight, coming in by the great window on the grand staircase, picked out everything in vivid black shadow or reticulated silvery illumination. Everything seemed in its proper position; the house might have been deserted on the yesterday instead of twelve months ago. There were candles in the sockets of the sconces, and whatever dust had gathered on the carpets or upon the polished flooring was distributed so evenly as to be invisible in my candlelight.

A waiting stillness was over everything. I was about to advance, and stopped abruptly. A bronze group stood upon the landing hidden from me by a corner of the wall; but its shadow fell with marvelous distinctness upon the white paneling, and gave me the impression of some one crouching to waylay me. The thing jumped upon my attention suddenly. I stood rigid for half a moment, perhaps. Then, with my hand in the pocket that held the revolver, I advanced, only to discover a Ganymede and Eagle, glistening in the moonlight. That incident for a time restored my nerve, and a dim porcelain Chinaman on a buhl table, whose head rocked as I passed, scarcely startled me.

The door of the Red Room and the steps up to it were in a shadowy corner. I moved my candle from side to side in order to see clearly the nature of the recess in which I stood, before opening the door. Here it was, thought I, that my predecessor was found, and the memory of that story gave me a sudden twinge of apprehension. I glanced over my shoulder at the black Ganymede in the moonlight, and opened the door of the Red Room rather hastily, with my face half turned to the pallid silence of the corridor.

I entered, closed the door behind me at once, turned the key I found in the lock within, and stood with the candle held aloft surveying the scene of my vigil, the great Red Room of Lorraine Castle, in which the young Duke had died; or rather in which he had begun his dying, for he had opened the door and fallen headlong down the steps I had just ascended. That had been the end of his vigil, of his gallant attempt to conquer the ghostly tradition of the place, and never, I thought, had apoplexy better served the ends of superstition. There were other and older stories that clung to the room, back to the half-incredible beginning of it all, the tale of a timid wife and the tragic end that came to her husband's jest of frightening her. And looking round that huge shadowy room with its black window bays, its recesses and alcoves, its dusty brown-red hangings and dark gigantic furniture, one could well understand the legends that had sprouted in its black corners, its germinating darknesses. My candle was a little tongue of light in the vastness of the chamber; its rays failed to pierce to the opposite end of the room, and left an ocean of dull red mystery and suggestion, sentinel shadows and watching darknesses beyond its island of light. And the stillness of desolation brooded over it all.

I must confess some impalpable quality of that ancient room disturbed me. I tried to fight the feeling down. I resolved to make a systematic examination of the place, and so, by leaving nothing to the imagination, dispel the fanciful suggestions of the obscurity before they obtained a hold upon me. After satisfying myself of the fastening of the door, I began to walk round the room, peering round each article of furniture, tucking up the valances of the bed and opening its curtains wide. In one place there was a distinct echo to my footsteps, the noises I made seemed so little that they enhanced rather than broke the silence of the place. I pulled up the blinds and examined the fastenings of the several windows. Attracted by the fall of a particle of dust, I leaned forward and looked up the blackness of the wide chimney. Then, trying to preserve my scientific attitude of mind, I walked round and began tapping the oak paneling for any secret opening, but I desisted before reaching the alcove. I saw my face in a mirror—white.

There were two big mirrors in the room, each with a pair of sconces bearing candles, and on the mantelshelf, too, were candles in china candle-sticks. All these I lit one after the other. The fire was laid—an unexpected consideration from the old housekeeper—and I lit it, to keep down any disposition to shiver, and when it was burning well I stood round with my back to it and regarded the room again. I had pulled up a chintz-covered armchair and a table to form a kind of barricade before me. On this lay my revolver, ready to hand. My precise examination had done me a little good, but I still found the remoter darkness of the place and its perfect stillness too stimulating for the imagination. The echoing of the stir and crackling of the fire was no sort of comfort to me. The shadow in the alcove at the end of the room began to display that undefinable quality of a presence, that odd suggestion of a lurking living thing that comes so easily in silence and solitude. And to reassure myself, I walked with a candle into it and satisfied myself that there was nothing tangible there. I stood that candle upon the floor of the alcove and left it in that position.

By this time I was in a state of considerable nervous tension, although to my reason there was no adequate cause for my condition. My mind, however, was perfectly clear. I postulated quite unreservedly that nothing supernatural could happen, and to pass the time I began stringing some rhymes together, Ingoldsby fashion, concerning the original legend of the place. A few I spoke aloud, but the echoes were not pleasant. For the same reason I also abandoned, after a time, a conversation with myself upon the impossibility of ghosts and haunting. My mind reverted to the three old and distorted people downstairs, and I tried to keep it upon that topic.

The sombre reds and grays of the room troubled me; even with its seven candles the place was merely dim. The light in the alcove flaring in a draft, and the fire flickering, kept the shadows and penumbra perpetually shifting and stirring in a noiseless flighty dance. Casting about for a remedy, I recalled the wax candles I had seen in the corridor, and, with a slight effort, carrying a candle and leaving the door open, I walked out into the moonlight, and presently returned with as many as ten. These I put in the various knick-knacks of china with which the room was sparsely adorned, and lit and placed them where the shadows had lain deepest, some on the floor, some in the window recesses, arranging and rearranging them until at last my seventeen candles were so placed that not an inch of the room but had the direct light of at least one of them. It occurred to me that when the ghost came I could warn him not to trip over them. The room was now quite brightly illuminated. There was something very cheering and reassuring in these little silent streaming flames, and to notice their steady diminution of length offered me an occupation and gave me a reassuring sense of the passage of time.

Even with that, however, the brooding expectation of the vigil weighed heavily enough upon me. I stood watching the minute hand of my watch creep towards midnight.

Then something happened in the alcove. I did not see the candle go out, I simply turned and saw that the darkness was there, as one might start and see the unexpected presence of a stranger. The black shadow had sprung back to its place. "By Jove," said I aloud, recovering from my surprise, "that draft's a strong one;" and taking the matchbox from the table, I walked across the room in a leisurely manner to relight the corner again. My first match would not strike, and as I succeeded with the second, something seemed to blink on the wall before me. I turned my head involuntarily and saw that the two candles on the little table by the fireplace were extinguished. I rose at once to my feet.

"Odd," I said. "Did I do that myself in a flash of absent-mindedness?"

I walked back, relit one, and as I did so I saw the candle in the right sconce of one of the mirrors wink and go right out, and almost immediately its companion followed it. The flames vanished as if the wick had been suddenly nipped between a finger and thumb, leaving the wick neither glowing nor smoking, but black. While I stood gaping the candle at the foot of the bed went out, and the shadows seemed to take another step toward me.

"This won't do!" said I, and first one and then another candle on the mantelshelf followed.

"What's up?" I cried, with a queer high note getting into my voice somehow. At that the candle on the corner of the wardrobe went out, and the one I had relit in the alcove followed.

"Steady on!" I said, "those candles are wanted," speaking with a half-hysterical facetiousness, and scratching away at a match the while, "for the mantel candlesticks." My hands trembled so much that twice I missed the rough paper of the matchbox. As the mantel emerged from darkness again, two candles in the remoter end of the room were eclipsed. But with the same match I also relit the larger mirror candles, and those on the floor near the doorway, so that for the moment I seemed to gain on the extinctions. But then in a noiseless volley there vanished four lights at once in different corners of the room, and I struck another match in quivering haste, and stood hesitating whither to take it.

As I stood undecided, an invisible hand seemed to sweep out the two candles on the table. With a cry of terror I dashed at the alcove, then into the corner and then into the window, relighting three as two more vanished by the fireplace, and then, perceiving a better way, I dropped matches on the iron-bound deedbox in the corner, and caught up the bedroom candlestick. With this I avoided the delay of striking matches, but for all that the steady process of extinction went on, and the shadows I feared and fought against returned, and crept in upon me, first a step gained on this side of me, then on that. I was now almost frantic with the horror of the coming darkness, and my self-possession deserted me. I leaped panting from candle to candle in a vain struggle against that remorseless advance.

I bruised myself in the thigh against the table, I sent a chair headlong, I stumbled and fell and whisked the cloth from the table in my fall. My candle rolled away from me and I snatched another as I rose. Abruptly this was blown out as I swung it off the table by the wind of my sudden movement, and immediately the two remaining candles followed. But there was light still in the room, a red light, that streamed across the ceiling and staved off the shadows from me. The fire! Of course I could still thrust my candle between the bars and relight it.

I turned to where the flames were still dancing between the glowing coals and splashing red reflections upon the furniture; made two steps toward the grate, and incontinently the flames dwindled and vanished, the glow vanished, the reflections rushed together and disappeared, and as I thrust the candle between the bars darkness closed upon me like the shutting of an eye, wrapped about me in a stifling embrace, sealed my vision, and crushed the last vestiges of self-possession from my brain. And it was not only palpable darkness, but intolerable terror. The candle fell from my hands. I flung out my arms in a vain effort to thrust that ponderous blackness away from me, and lifting up my voice, screamed with all my might, once, twice, thrice. Then I think I must have staggered to my feet. I know I thought suddenly of the moonlit corridor, and with my head bowed and my arms over my face, made a stumbling run for the door.

But I had forgotten the exact position of the door, and I struck myself heavily against the corner of the bed. I staggered back, turned, and was either struck or struck myself against some other bulky furnishing. I have a vague memory of battering myself thus to and fro in the darkness, of a heavy blow at last upon my forehead, of a horrible sensation of falling that lasted an age, of my last frantic effort to keep my footing, and then I remember no more.

I opened my eyes in daylight. My head was roughly bandaged, and the man with the withered hand was watching my face. I looked about me trying to remember what had happened, and for a space I could not recollect. I rolled my eyes into the corner and saw the old woman, no longer abstracted, no longer terrible, pouring out some drops of medicine from a little blue phial into a glass. "Where am I?" I said. "I seem to remember you, and yet I can not remember who you are."

They told me then, and I heard of the haunted Red Room as one who hears a tale. "We found you at dawn," said he, "and there was blood on your forehead and lips."

I wondered that I had ever disliked him. The three of them in the daylight seemed commonplace old folk enough. The man with the green shade had his head bent as one who sleeps.

It was very slowly I recovered the memory of my experience. "You believe now," said the old man with the withered hand, "that the room is haunted?" He spoke no longer as one who greets an intruder, but as one who condoles with a friend.

"Yes," said I, "the room is haunted."

"And you have seen it. And we who have been here all our lives have never set eyes upon it. Because we have never dared. Tell us, is it truly the old earl who—"

"No," said I, "it is not."

"I told you so," said the old lady, with the glass in her hand. "It is his poor young countess who was frightened—"

"It is not," I said. "There is neither ghost of earl nor ghost of countess in that room; there is no ghost there at all, but worse, far worse, something impalpable—"

"Well?" they said.

"The worst of all the things that haunt poor mortal men," said I; "and that is, in all its nakedness—'Fear!' Fear that will not have light nor sound, that will not bear with reason, that deafens and darkens and overwhelms. It followed me through the corridor, it fought against me in the room—"

I stopped abruptly. There was an interval of silence. My hand went up to my bandages. "The candles went out one after another, and I fled—"

Then the man with the shade lifted his face sideways to see me and spoke.

"That is it," said he. "I knew that was it. A Power of Darkness. To put such a curse upon a home! It lurks there always. You can feel it even in the daytime, even of a bright summer's day, in the hangings, in the curtains, keeping behind you however you face about. In the dusk it creeps in the corridor and follows you, so that you dare not turn. It is even as you say. Fear itself is in that room. Black Fear... And there it will be...so long as this house of sin endures."

40

THE SQUAW

Bram Stoker

Nurnberg at the time was not so much exploited as it has been since then. Irving had not been playing *Faust*, and the very name of the old town was hardly known to the great bulk of the travelling public. My wife and I being in the second week of our honeymoon, naturally wanted someone else to join our party, so that when the cheery stranger, Elias P. Hutcheson, hailing from Isthmian City, Bleeding Gulch, Maple Tree County, Neb. turned up at the station at Frankfort, and casually remarked that he was going on to see the most all-fired old Methuselah of a town in Yurrup, and that he guessed that so much travelling alone was enough to send an intelligent, active citizen into the melancholy ward of a daft house, we took the pretty broad hint and suggested that we should join forces. We found, on comparing notes afterwards, that we had each intended to speak with some diffidence or hesitation so as not to appear too eager, such not being a good compliment to the success of our married life; but the effect was entirely marred by our both beginning to speak at the same instant—stopping simultaneously and then going on together again. Anyhow, no matter how, it was done; and Elias P. Hutcheson became one of our party. Straightway Amelia and I found the pleasant benefit; instead of quarrelling, as we had been doing, we found that the restraining influence of a third party was such that we now took every opportunity of spooning in odd corners. Amelia declares that ever since she has, as the result of that experience, advised all her friends to take a friend on the honeymoon. Well, we 'did' Nurnberg together, and much enjoyed the racy remarks of our Transatlantic friend, who, from his quaint speech and his wonderful stock of adventures, might have stepped out of a novel. We kept for the last object of interest in the city to be visited the Burg, and on the day appointed for the visit strolled round the outer wall of the city by the eastern side. The Burg is seated on a rock dominating the town and an immensely deep fosse guards it on the northern side. Nurnberg has been happy in that it was never sacked; had it been it would certainly not be so spick and span perfect as it is at present. The ditch has not been used for centuries, and now its base is spread with tea-gardens and orchards, of which some of the trees are of quite respectable growth. As we wandered round the wall, dawdling in the hot July sunshine, we often paused to admire the views spread before us, and in especial the great plain covered with towns and villages and bounded with a blue line of hills, like a landscape of Claude Lorraine. From this we always turned with new delight to the city itself, with its myriad of quaint old gables and acre-wide red roofs dotted with dormer windows, tier upon tier. A little to our right rose the towers of the Burg, and nearer still, standing grim, the Torture Tower, which was, and is, perhaps, the most interesting place in the city. For centuries the tradition of the Iron Virgin of Nurnberg has been handed down as an instance of the horrors of cruelty of which man is capable; we had long looked forward to seeing it; and here at last was its home.

In one of our pauses we leaned over the wall of the moat and looked down. The garden seemed quite fifty or sixty feet below us, and the sun pouring into it with an intense, moveless heat like that of an oven. Beyond rose the grey, grim wall seemingly of endless height, and losing itself right and left in the angles of bastion and counterscarp. Trees and bushes crowned the wall, and above again towered the lofty houses on whose massive beauty

Time has only set the hand of approval. The sun was hot and we were lazy; time was our own, and we lingered, leaning on the wall. Just below us was a pretty sight—a great black cat lying stretched in the sun, whilst round her gambolled prettily a tiny black kitten. The mother would wave her tail for the kitten to play with, or would raise her feet and push away the little one as an encouragement to further play. They were just at the foot of the wall, and Elias P. Hutcheson, in order to help the play, stooped and took from the walk a moderate sized pebble.

"See!" he said, "I will drop it near the kitten, and they will both wonder where it came from."

"Oh, be careful," said my wife; "you might hit the dear little thing!"

"Not me, ma'am," said Elias P. "Why, I'm as tender as a Maine cherry-tree. Lor, bless ye. I wouldn't hurt the poor pooty little critter more'n I'd scalp a baby. An' you may bet your variegated socks on that! See, I'll drop it fur away on the outside so's not to go near her!" Thus saying, he leaned over and held his arm out at full length and dropped the stone. It may be that there is some attractive force which draws lesser matters to greater; or more probably that the wall was not plumb but sloped to its base—we not noticing the inclination from above; but the stone fell with a sickening thud that came up to us through the hot air, right on the kitten's head, and shattered out its little brains then and there. The black cat cast a swift upward glance, and we saw her eyes like green fire fixed an instant on Elias P. Hutcheson; and then her attention was given to the kitten, which lay still with just a quiver of her tiny limbs, whilst a thin red stream trickled from a gaping wound. With a muffled cry, such as a human being might give, she bent over the kitten licking its wounds and moaning. Suddenly she seemed to realise that it was dead, and again threw her eyes up at us. I shall never forget the sight, for she looked the perfect incarnation of hate. Her green eyes blazed with lurid fire, and the white, sharp teeth seemed to almost shine through the blood which dabbled her mouth and whiskers. She gnashed her teeth, and her claws stood out stark and at full length on every paw. Then she made a wild rush up the wall as if to reach us, but when the momentum ended fell back, and further added to her horrible appearance for she fell on the kitten, and rose with her black fur smeared with its brains and blood. Amelia turned quite faint, and I had to lift her back from the wall. There was a seat close by in shade of a spreading plane-tree, and here I placed her whilst she composed herself. Then I went back to Hutcheson, who stood without moving, looking down on the angry cat below.

As I joined him, he said:

"Wall, I guess that air the savagest beast I ever see—'cept once when an Apache squaw had an edge on a half-breed what they nicknamed 'Splinters' 'cos of the way he fixed up her papoose which he stole on a raid just to show that he appreciated the way they had given his mother the fire torture. She got that kinder look so set on her face that it jest seemed to grow there. She followed Splinters mor'n three year till at last the braves got him and handed him over to her. They did say that no man, white or Injun, had ever been so long a-dying under the tortures of the Apaches. The only time I ever see her smile was when I wiped her out. I kem on the camp just in time to see Splinters pass in his checks, and he wasn't sorry to go either. He was a hard citizen, and though I never could shake with him after that papoose business—for it was bitter bad, and he should have been a white man, for he looked like one—I see he had got paid out in full. Durn me, but I took a piece of his hide from one of his skinnin' posts an' had it made into a pocket-book. It's here now!" and he slapped the breast pocket of his coat.

Whilst he was speaking the cat was continuing her frantic efforts to get up the wall. She would take a run back and then charge up, sometimes reaching an incredible height. She did not seem to mind the heavy fall which she got each time but started with renewed vigour; and at every tumble her appearance became more horrible. Hutcheson was a kind-hearted man—my wife and I had both noticed little acts of kindness to animals as well as to persons—and he seemed concerned at the state of fury to which the cat had wrought herself.

"Wall, now!" he said, "I du declare that that poor critter seems quite desperate. There! there! poor thing, it was all an accident—though that won't bring back your little one to you. Say! I wouldn't have had such a thing happen for a thousand! Just shows what a clumsy fool of a man can do when he tries to play! Seems I'm too darned slipperhanded to even play with a cat. Say Colonel!" it was a pleasant way he had to bestow titles freely—"I hope your wife don't hold no grudge against me on account of this unpleasantness? Why, I wouldn't have had it occur on no account."

He came over to Amelia and apologised profusely, and she with her usual kindness of heart hastened to assure him that she quite understood that it was an accident. Then we all went again to the wall and looked over.

The cat missing Hutcheson's face had drawn back across the moat, and was sitting on her haunches as though ready to spring. Indeed, the very instant she saw him she did spring, and with a blind unreasoning fury, which would have been grotesque, only that it was so frightfully real. She did not try to run up the wall, but simply launched herself at him as though hate and fury could lend her wings to pass straight through the great distance between them. Amelia, womanlike, got quite concerned, and said to Elias P. in a warning voice:

"Oh! you must be very careful. That animal would try to kill you if she were here; her eyes look like positive murder."

He laughed out jovially. "Excuse me, ma'am," he said, "but

I can't help laughin'. Fancy a man that has fought grizzlies an' Injuns bein' careful of bein' murdered by a cat!"

When the cat heard him laugh, her whole demeanour seemed to change. She no longer tried to jump or run up the wall, but went quietly over, and sitting again beside the dead kitten began to lick and fondle it as though it were alive.

"See!" said I, "the effect of a really strong man. Even that animal in the midst of her fury recognises the voice of a master, and bows to him!"

"Like a squaw!" was the only comment of Elias P. Hutcheson, as we moved on our way round the city fosse. Every now and then we looked over the wall and each time saw the cat following us. At first she had kept going back to the dead kitten, and then as the distance grew greater took it in her mouth and so followed. After a while, however, she abandoned this, for we saw her following all alone; she had evidently hidden the body somewhere. Amelia's alarm grew at the cat's persistence, and more than once she repeated her warning; but the American always laughed with amusement, till finally, seeing that she was beginning to be worried, he said:

"I say, ma'am, you needn't be skeered over that cat. I go heeled, I du!" Here he slapped his pistol pocket at the back of his lumbar region. "Why sooner'n have you worried, I'll shoot the critter, right here, an' risk the police interferin' with a citizen of the United States for carryin' arms contrairy to reg'lations!" As he spoke he looked over the wall, but the cat on seeing him, retreated, with a growl, into a bed of tall flowers, and was hidden. He went on: "Blest if that ar critter ain't got more sense of what's good for her than most Christians. I guess we've seen the last of her! You bet, she'll go back now to that busted kitten and have a private funeral of it, all to herself!"

Amelia did not like to say more, lest he might, in mistaken kindness to her, fulfil his threat of shooting the cat: and so we went on and crossed the little wooden bridge leading to the gateway whence ran the steep paved roadway between the Burg and the pentagonal Torture Tower. As we crossed the bridge we saw the cat again down below us. When she saw us her fury seemed to return, and she made frantic efforts to get up the steep wall. Hutcheson laughed as he looked down at her, and said:

"Goodbye, old girl. Sorry I injured your feelin's, but you'll get over it in time! So long!" And then we passed through the long, dim archway and came to the gate of the Burg.

When we came out again after our survey of this most beautiful old place which not even the well-intentioned efforts of the Gothic restorers of forty years ago have been able to spoil— though their restoration was then glaring white—we seemed to have quite forgotten the unpleasant episode of the morning. The old lime tree with its great trunk gnarled with the passing of nearly nine centuries, the deep well cut through the heart of the rock by those captives of old, and the lovely view from the city wall whence we heard, spread over almost a full quarter of an hour, the multitudinous chimes of the city, had all helped to wipe out from our minds the incident of the slain kitten.

We were the only visitors who had entered the Torture Tower that morning—so at least said the old custodian—and as we had the place all to ourselves were able to make a minute and more satisfactory survey than would have otherwise been possible. The custodian, looking to us as the sole source of his gains for the day, was willing to meet our wishes in any way. The Torture Tower is truly a grim place, even now when many thousands of visitors have sent a stream of life, and the joy that follows life, into the place; but at the time I mention it wore its grimmest and most gruesome aspect. The dust of ages seemed to have settled on it, and the darkness and the horror of its memories seem to have become sentient in a way that would have satisfied the Pantheistic souls of Philo or Spinoza. The lower chamber where we entered was seemingly, in its normal state, filled with incarnate darkness; even the hot sunlight streaming in through the door seemed to be lost in the vast thickness of the walls, and only showed the masonry rough as when the builder's scaffolding had come down, but coated with dust and marked here and there with patches of dark stain which, if walls could speak, could have given their own dread memories of fear and pain. We were glad to pass up the dusty wooden staircase, the custodian leaving the outer door open to light us somewhat on our way; for to our eyes the one long-wick'd, evil-smelling candle stuck in a sconce on the wall gave an inadequate light. When we came up through the open trap in the corner of the chamber overhead, Amelia held on to me so tightly that I could actually feel her heart beat. I must say for my own part that I was not surprised at her fear, for this room was even more gruesome than that below. Here there was certainly more light, but only just sufficient to realise the horrible surroundings of the place. The builders of the tower had evidently intended that only they who should gain the top should have any of the joys of light and prospect. There, as we had noticed from below, were ranges of windows, albeit of mediaeval smallness, but elsewhere in the tower were only a very few narrow slits such as were habitual in places of mediaeval defence. A few of these only lit the chamber, and these so high up in the wall that from no part could the sky be seen through the thickness of the walls. In racks, and leaning in disorder against the walls, were a number of headsmen's swords, great double-handed weapons with broad blade and keen edge. Hard by were several blocks whereon the necks of the victims had lain, with here and there deep notches where the steel had bitten through the guard of flesh and shored into the wood. Round the chamber, placed in all sorts of irregular ways, were many implements of torture which made one's heart ache to see—chairs full of spikes which gave instant and excruciating pain; chairs and couches with dull knobs whose torture was seemingly less, but which, though slower, were equally efficacious; racks, belts, boots, gloves, collars, all made for compressing at will; steel baskets in which the head could be slowly crushed into a pulp if necessary; watchmen's hooks with long handle and knife that cut at resistance—this a speciality of the old Nurnberg police system; and many, many other devices for man's injury to man. Amelia grew quite pale with the horror of the things, but fortunately did not faint, for being a little overcome she sat down on a torture chair, but jumped up again with a shriek, all tendency to faint gone. We both pretended that it was the injury done to her dress by the dust of the chair, and the rusty spikes which had upset her, and Mr. Hutcheson acquiesced in accepting the explanation with a kind-hearted laugh.

But the central object in the whole of this chamber of horrors was the engine known as the Iron Virgin, which stood near the centre of the room. It was a rudely-shaped figure of a woman, something of the bell order, or, to make a closer comparison, of the figure of Mrs. Noah in the children's Ark, but without that slimness of waist and perfect *rondeur* of hip which marks the aesthetic type of the Noah family. One would hardly have recognised it as intended for a human figure at all had not the founder shaped on the forehead a rude semblance of a woman's face. This machine was coated with rust without, and covered with dust; a rope was fastened to a ring in the front of the figure, about where the waist should have been, and was drawn through a pulley, fastened on the wooden pillar which sustained the flooring above. The custodian pulling this rope showed that a section of the front was hinged like a door at one side; we then saw that the engine was of considerable thickness, leaving just room enough inside for a man to be placed. The door was of equal thickness and of great weight, for it took the custodian all his strength, aided though he was by the contrivance of the pulley, to open it. This weight was partly due to the fact that the door was of manifest purpose hung so as to throw its weight downwards, so that it might shut of its own accord when the strain was released. The inside was honeycombed with rust—nay more, the rust alone that comes through time would hardly have eaten so deep into the iron walls; the rust of the cruel stains was deep indeed! It was only, however, when we came to look at the inside of the door that the diabolical intention was manifest to the full. Here were several long spikes, square and massive, broad at the base and sharp at the points, placed in such a position that when the door should close the upper ones would pierce the eyes of the victim, and the lower ones his heart and vitals. The sight was too much for poor Amelia, and this time she fainted dead off, and I had to carry her down the stairs, and place her on a bench outside till she recovered. That she felt it to the quick was afterwards shown by the fact that my eldest son bears to this day a rude birthmark on his breast, which has, by family consent, been accepted as representing the Nurnberg Virgin.

When we got back to the chamber we found Hutcheson still opposite the Iron Virgin; he had been evidently philosophising, and now gave us the benefit of his thought in the shape of a sort of exordium.

"Wall, I guess I've been learnin' somethin' here while madam has been gettin' over her faint. 'Pears to me that we're a long way behind the times on our side of the big drink. We uster think out on the plains that the Injun could give us points in tryin' to make a man uncomfortable; but I guess your old mediaeval law-and-order party could raise him every time. Splinters was pretty good in his bluff on the squaw, but this here young miss held a straight flush all high on him. The points of them spikes air sharp enough still, though even the edges air eaten out by what uster be on them. It'd be a good thing for our Indian section to get some specimens of this here play-toy to send round to the

Reservations jest to knock the stuffin' out of the bucks, and the squaws too, by showing them as how old civilisation lays over them at their best. Guess but I'll get in that box a minute jest to see how it feels!"

"Oh no! no!" said Amelia. "It is too terrible!"

"Guess, ma'am, nothin's too terrible to the explorin' mind. I've been in some queer places in my time. Spent a night inside a dead horse while a prairie fire swept over me in Montana Territory—an' another time slept inside a dead buffler when the Comanches was on the war path an' I didn't keer to leave my kyard on them. I've been two days in a caved-in tunnel in the Billy Broncho gold mine in New Mexico, an' was one of the four shut up for three parts of a day in the caisson what slid over on her side when we was settin' the foundations of the Buffalo Bridge. I've not funked an odd experience yet, an' I don't propose to begin now!"

We saw that he was set on the experiment, so I said: "Well, hurry up, old man, and get through it quick!"

"All right, General," said he, "but I calculate we ain't quite ready yet. The gentlemen, my predecessors, what stood in that thar canister, didn't volunteer for the office—not much! And I guess there was some ornamental tyin' up before the big stroke was made. I want to go into this thing fair and square, so I must get fixed up proper first. I dare say this old galoot can rise some string and tie me up accordin' to sample?"

This was said interrogatively to the old custodian, but the latter, who understood the drift of his speech, though perhaps not appreciating to the full the niceties of dialect and imagery, shook his head. His protest was, however, only formal and made to be overcome. The American thrust a gold piece into his hand, saying: "Take it, pard! it's your pot; and don't be skeer'd. This ain't no necktie party that you're asked to assist in!" He produced some thin frayed rope and proceeded to bind our companion with sufficient strictness for the purpose. When the upper part of his body was bound, Hutcheson said:

"Hold on a moment, Judge. Guess I'm too heavy for you to tote into the canister. You jest let me walk in, and then you can wash up regardin' my legs!"

Whilst speaking he had backed himself into the opening which was just enough to hold him. It was a close fit and no mistake. Amelia looked on with fear in her eyes, but she evidently did not like to say anything. Then the custodian completed his task by tying the American's feet together so that he was now absolutely helpless and fixed in his voluntary prison. He seemed to really enjoy it, and the incipient smile which was habitual to his face blossomed into actuality as he said:

"Guess this here Eve was made out of the rib of a dwarf! There ain't much room for a full-grown citizen of the United States to hustle. We uster make our coffins more roomier in Idaho territory. Now, Judge, you jest begin to let this door down, slow, on to me. I want to feel the same pleasure as the other jays had when those spikes began to move toward their eyes!"

"Oh no! no! no!" broke in Amelia hysterically. "It is too terrible! I can't bear to see it!—I can't! I can't!" But the American was obdurate. "Say, Colonel," said he, "why not take Madame for a little promenade? I wouldn't hurt her feelin's for the world; but now that I am here, havin' kem eight thousand miles, wouldn't it be too hard to give up the very experience I've been pinin' an' pantin' fur? A man can't get to feel like canned goods every time! Me and the Judge here'll fix up this thing in no time, an' then you'll come back, an' we'll all laugh together!"

Once more the resolution that is born of curiosity triumphed, and Amelia stayed holding tight to my arm and shivering whilst the custodian began to slacken slowly inch by inch the rope that held back the iron door. Hutcheson's face was positively radiant as his eyes followed the first movement of the spikes.

"Wall!" he said, "I guess I've not had enjoyment like this since I left Noo York. Bar a scrap with a French sailor at Wapping—an' that warn't much of a picnic neither—I've not had a show fur real pleasure in this dod-rotted Continent, where there ain't no b'ars nor no Injuns, an' wheer nary man goes heeled. Slow there, Judge! Don't you rush this business! I want a show for my money this game—I du!"

The custodian must have had in him some of the blood of his predecessors in that ghastly tower, for he worked the engine with a deliberate and excruciating slowness which after five minutes, in which the outer edge of the door had not moved half as many inches, began to overcome Amelia. I saw her lips whiten, and felt her hold upon my arm relax. I looked around an instant for a place whereon to lay her, and when I looked at her again found that her eye had become fixed on the side of the Virgin. Following its direction I saw the black cat crouching out of sight. Her green eyes shone like danger lamps in the gloom of the place, and their colour was heightened by the blood which still smeared her coat and reddened her mouth. I cried out:

"The cat! look out for the cat!" for even then she sprang out before the engine. At this moment she looked like a triumphant demon. Her eyes blazed with ferocity, her hair bristled out till she seemed twice her normal size, and her tail lashed about as does a tiger's when the quarry is before it. Elias P. Hutcheson when he saw her was amused, and his eyes positively sparkled with fun as he said:

"Darned if the squaw hain't got on all her war paint! Jest give her a shove off if she comes any of her tricks on me, for I'm so fixed everlastingly by the boss, that durn my skin if I can keep my eyes from her if she wants them! Easy there, Judge! don't you slack that ar rope or I'm euchered!"

At this moment Amelia completed her faint, and I had to clutch hold of her round the waist or she would have fallen to the floor. Whilst attending to her I saw the black cat crouching for a spring, and jumped up to turn the creature out.

But at that instant, with a sort of hellish scream, she hurled herself, not as we expected at Hutcheson, but straight at the face of the custodian. Her claws seemed to be tearing wildly as one sees in the Chinese drawings of the dragon rampant, and as I looked I saw one of them light on the poor man's eye, and actually tear through it and down his cheek, leaving a wide band of red where the blood seemed to spurt from every vein.

With a yell of sheer terror which came quicker than even his sense of pain, the man leaped back, dropping as he did so the rope which held back the iron door. I jumped for it, but was too late, for the cord ran like lightning through the pulley-block, and the heavy mass fell forward from its own weight.

As the door closed I caught a glimpse of our poor companion's face. He seemed frozen with terror. His eyes stared with a horrible anguish as if dazed, and no sound came from his lips.

And then the spikes did their work. Happily the end was quick, for when I wrenched open the door they had pierced so deep that they had locked in the bones of the skull through which they had crushed, and actually tore him—it—out of his iron prison till, bound as he was, he fell at full length with a sickly thud upon the floor, the face turning upward as he fell.

I rushed to my wife, lifted her up and carried her out, for I feared for her very reason if she should wake from her faint to such a scene. I laid her on the bench outside and ran back. Leaning against the wooden column was the custodian moaning in pain whilst he held his reddening handkerchief to his eyes. And sitting on the head of the poor American was the cat, purring loudly as she licked the blood which trickled through the gashed socket of his eyes.

I think no one will call me cruel because I seized one of the old executioner's swords and shore her in two as she sat.

41

A GHOST STORY

Mark Twain

I took a large room, far up Broadway, in a huge old building whose upper stories had been wholly unoccupied for years until I came. The place had long been given up to dust and cobwebs, to solitude and silence. I seemed groping among the tombs and invading the privacy of the dead, that first night I climbed up to my quarters. For the first time in my life a superstitious dread came over me; and as I turned a dark angle of the stairway and an invisible cobweb swung its slazy woof in my face and clung there, I shuddered as one who had encountered a phantom. I was glad enough when I reached my room and locked out the mold and the darkness. A cheery fire was burning in the grate, and I sat down before it with a comforting sense of relief. For two hours I sat there, thinking of bygone times; recalling old scenes, and summoning half- forgotten faces out of the mists of the past; listening, in fancy, to voices that long ago grew silent for all time, and to once familiar songs that nobody sings now. And as my reverie softened down to a sadder and sadder pathos, the shrieking of the winds outside softened to a wail, the angry beating of the rain against the panes diminished to a tranquil patter, and one by one the noises in the street subsided, until the hurrying footsteps of the last belated straggler died away in the distance and left no sound behind.

The fire had burned low. A sense of loneliness crept over me. I arose and undressed, moving on tiptoe about the room, doing stealthily what I had to do, as if I were environed by sleeping enemies whose slumbers it would be fatal to break. I covered up in bed, and lay listening to the rain and wind and the faint creaking of distant shutters, till they lulled me to sleep.

I slept profoundly, but how long I do not know. All at once I found myself awake, and filled with a shuddering expectancy. All was still. All but my own heart—I could hear it beat. Presently the bedclothes began to slip away slowly toward the foot of the bed, as if some one were pulling them! I could not stir; I could not speak. Still the blankets slipped deliberately away, till my breast was uncovered. Then with a great effort I seized them and drew them over my head. I waited, listened, waited. Once more that steady pull began, and once more I lay torpid a century of dragging seconds till my breast was naked again. At last I roused my energies and snatched the covers back to their place and held them with a strong grip. I waited. By and by I felt a faint tug, and took a fresh grip. The tug strengthened to a steady strain—it grew stronger and stronger. My hold parted, and for the third time the blankets slid away. I groaned. An answering groan came from the foot of the bed! Beaded drops of sweat stood upon my forehead. I was more dead than alive. Presently I heard a heavy footstep in my room—the step of an elephant, it seemed to me—it was not like anything human. But it was moving *from* me—there was relief in that. I heard it approach the door—pass out without moving bolt or lock—and wander away among the dismal corridors, straining the floors and joists till they creaked again as it passed—and then silence reigned once more.

When my excitement had calmed, I said to myself, "This is a dream—simply a hideous dream." And so I lay thinking it over until I convinced myself that it *was* a dream, and then a comforting laugh relaxed my lips and I was happy again. I got up and struck a light; and when I found that the locks and bolts were just as I had left them, another soothing laugh welled in my heart and rippled from my lips. I took my pipe and lit it, and was just sitting down before the fire, when—down went the pipe out of my nerveless fingers, the blood forsook my cheeks, and my placid breathing was cut short with a gasp! In the ashes on the hearth, side by side with my own bare footprint, was another, so vast that in comparison mine was but an infant's! Then I had *had* a visitor, and the elephantine tread was explained.

I put out the light and returned to bed, palsied with fear. I lay a long time, peering into the darkness, and listening. Then I heard a grating noise overhead, like the dragging of a heavy body across the floor; then the throwing down of the body, and the shaking of my windows in response to the concussion. In distant parts of the building I heard the muffled slamming of doors. I heard, at intervals, stealthy footsteps creeping in and out among the corridors, and up and down the stairs. Sometimes these noises approached my door, hesitated, and went away again. I heard the clanking of chains faintly, in remote passages, and listened while the clanking grew nearer—while it wearily climbed the stairways, marking each move by the loose surplus of chain that fell with an accented rattle upon each succeeding step as the goblin that bore it advanced. I heard muttered sentences; half-uttered screams that seemed smothered violently; and the swish of invisible garments, the rush of invisible wings. Then I became conscious that my chamber was invaded—that I was not alone. I heard sighs and breathings about my bed, and mysterious whisperings. Three little spheres of soft phosphorescent light appeared on the ceiling directly over my head, clung and glowed there a moment, and then dropped—two of them upon my face and one upon the pillow. They, spattered, liquidly, and felt warm. Intuition told me they had—turned to gouts of blood as they fell—I needed no light to satisfy myself of that. Then I saw pallid faces, dimly luminous, and white uplifted hands, floating bodiless in the air—floating a moment and then disappearing. The whispering ceased, and the voices and the sounds, and a solemn stillness followed.

I waited and listened. I felt that I must have light or die. I was weak with fear. I slowly raised myself toward a sitting posture, and my face came in contact with a clammy hand! All strength went from me apparently, and I fell back like a stricken invalid. Then I heard the rustle of a garment it seemed to pass to the door and go out.

When everything was still once more, I crept out of bed, sick and feeble, and lit the gas with a hand that trembled as if it were aged with a hundred years. The light brought some little cheer to my spirits. I sat down and fell into a dreamy contemplation of that great footprint in the ashes. By and by its outlines began to waver and grow dim. I glanced up and the broad gas-flame was slowly wilting away. In the same moment I heard that elephantine tread again. I noted its approach, nearer and nearer, along the musty halls, and dimmer and dimmer the light waned. The tread reached my very door and paused—the light had dwindled to a sickly blue, and all things about me lay in a spectral twilight. The door did not open, and yet I felt a faint gust of air fan my cheek, and presently was conscious of a huge, cloudy presence before me. I watched it with fascinated eyes. A pale glow stole over the Thing; gradually its cloudy folds took shape—an arm appeared, then legs, then a body, and last a great sad face looked out of the vapor. Stripped of its filmy housings, naked, muscular and comely, the majestic Cardiff Giant loomed above me!

All my misery vanished—for a child might know that no harm could come with that benignant countenance. My cheerful spirits returned at once, and in sympathy with them the gas flamed up brightly again. Never a lonely outcast was so glad to welcome company as I was to greet the friendly giant. I said:

"Why, is it nobody but you? Do you know, I have been scared to death for the last two or three hours? I am most honestly glad to see you. I wish I had a chair——Here, here, don't try to sit down in that thing—"

But it was too late. He was in it before I could stop him and down he went—I never saw a chair shivered so in my life.

"Stop, stop, you'll ruin ev——"

Too late again. There was another crash, and another chair was resolved into its original elements.

"Confound it, haven't you got any judgment at' all? Do you want to ruin all the furniture on the place? Here, here, you petrified fool——"

But it was no use. Before I could arrest him he had sat down on the bed, and it was a melancholy ruin.

"Now what sort of a way is that to do? First you come lumbering about the place bringing a legion of vagabond goblins along with you to worry me to death, and then when I overlook an indelicacy of costume which would not be tolerated anywhere by cultivated people except in a respectable theater, and not even there if the nudity were of *your* sex, you repay me by wrecking all the furniture you can find to sit down on. And why will you? You damage yourself as much as you do me. You have broken off the end of your spinal column, and littered up the floor with chips of your hams till the place looks like a marble yard. You ought to be ashamed of yourself—you are big enough to know better."

"Well, I will not break any more furniture. But what am I to do? I have not had a chance to sit down for a century." And the tears came into his eyes.

"Poor devil," I said, "I should not have been so harsh with you. And you are an orphan, too, no doubt. But sit down on the floor here—nothing else can stand your weight—and besides, we cannot be sociable with you away up there above me; I want you down where I can perch on this high counting-house stool and gossip with you face to face." So he sat down on the floor, and lit a pipe which I gave him, threw one of my red blankets over his shoulders, inverted my sitz-bath on his head, helmet fashion, and made himself picturesque and comfortable. Then he crossed his ankles, while I renewed the fire, and exposed the flat, honeycombed bottoms of his prodigious feet to the grateful warmth.

"What is the matter with the bottom of your feet and the back of your legs, that they are gouged up so?"

"Infernal chilblains—I caught them clear up to the back of my head, roosting out there under Newell's farm. But I love the place; I love it as one loves his old home. There is no peace for me like the peace I feel when I am there."

We talked along for half an hour, and then I noticed that he looked tired, and spoke of it.

"Tired?" he said. "Well, I should think so. And now I will tell you all about it, since you have treated me so well. I am the spirit of the Petrified Man that lies across the street there in the museum. I am the ghost of the Cardiff Giant. I can have no rest, no peace, till they have given that poor body burial again. Now what was the most natural thing for me to do, to make men satisfy this wish? Terrify them into it! haunt the place where the body lay! So I haunted the museum night after night. I even got other spirits to help me. But it did no good, for nobody ever came to the museum at midnight. Then it occurred to me to come over the way and haunt this place a little. I felt that if I ever got a hearing I must succeed, for I had the most efficient company that perdition could furnish. Night after night we have shivered around through these mildewed halls, dragging chains, groaning, whispering, tramping up and down stairs, till, to tell you the truth, I am almost worn out. But when I saw a light in your room to-night I roused my energies again and went at it with a deal of the old freshness. But I am tired out—entirely fagged out. Give me, I beseech you, give me some hope!" I lit off my perch in a burst of excitement, and exclaimed:

"This transcends everything! everything that ever did occur! Why you poor blundering old fossil, you have had all your trouble for nothing—you have been haunting a *plaster cast* of yourself—the real Cardiff Giant is in Albany! Confound it, don't you know your own remains?"

I never saw such an eloquent look of shame, of pitiable humiliation, overspread a countenance before.

The Petrified Man rose slowly to his feet, and said:

"Honestly, *is* that true?"

"As true as I am sitting here."

He took the pipe from his mouth and laid it on the mantel, then stood irresolute a moment (unconsciously, from old habit, thrusting his hands where his pantaloons pockets should have been, and meditatively dropping his chin on his breast); and finally said:

"Well—I *never* felt so absurd before. The Petrified Man has sold everybody else, and now the mean fraud has ended by selling its own ghost! My son, if there is any charity left in your heart for a poor friendless phantom like me, don't let this get out. Think how *you* would feel if you had made such an ass of yourself."

I heard his stately tramp die away, step by step down the stairs and out into the deserted street, and felt sorry that he was gone, poor fellow—and sorrier still that he had carried off my red blanket and my bath-tub.

42

THE SHADOWS ON THE WALL

Mary Eleanor Wilkins Freeman

"Henry had words with Edward in the study the night before Edward died," said Caroline Glynn.

She was elderly, tall, and harshly thin, with a hard colourlessness of face. She spoke not with acrimony, but with grave severity. Rebecca Ann Glynn, younger, stouter and rosy of face between her crinkling puffs of gray hair, gasped, by way of assent. She sat in a wide flounce of black silk in the corner of the sofa, and rolled terrified eyes from her sister Caroline to her sister Mrs. Stephen Brigham, who had been Emma Glynn, the one beauty of the family. She was beautiful still, with a large, splendid, full-blown beauty; she filled a great rocking-chair with her superb bulk of femininity, and swayed gently back and forth, her black silks whispering and her black frills fluttering. Even the shock of death (for her brother Edward lay dead in the house,) could not disturb her outward serenity of demeanour. She was grieved over the loss of her brother: he had been the youngest, and she had been fond of him, but never had Emma Brigham lost sight of her own importance amidst the waters of tribulation. She was always awake to the consciousness of her own stability in the midst of vicissitudes and the splendour of her permanent bearing.

But even her expression of masterly placidity changed before her sister Caroline's announcement and her sister Rebecca Ann's gasp of terror and distress in response.

"I think Henry might have controlled his temper, when poor Edward was so near his end," said she with an asperity which disturbed slightly the roseate curves of her beautiful mouth.

"Of course he did not *know*," murmured Rebecca Ann in a faint tone strangely out of keeping with her appearance.

One involuntarily looked again to be sure that such a feeble pipe came from that full-swelling chest.

"Of course he did not know it," said Caroline quickly. She turned on her sister with a strange sharp look of suspicion. "How could he have known it?" said she. Then she shrank as if from the other's possible answer. "Of course you and I both know he could not," said she conclusively, but her pale face was paler than it had been before.

Rebecca gasped again. The married sister, Mrs. Emma Brigham, was now sitting up straight in her chair; she had ceased rocking, and was eyeing them both intently with a sudden accentuation of family likeness in her face. Given one common intensity of emotion and similar lines showed forth, and the three sisters of one race were evident.

"What do you mean?" said she impartially to them both. Then she, too, seemed to shrink before a possible answer. She even laughed an evasive sort of laugh. "I guess you don't mean anything," said she, but her face wore still the expression of shrinking horror.

"Nobody means anything," said Caroline firmly. She rose and crossed the room toward the door with grim decisiveness.

"Where are you going?" asked Mrs. Brigham.

"I have something to see to," replied Caroline, and the others at once knew by her tone that she had some solemn and sad duty to perform in the chamber of death.

"Oh," said Mrs. Brigham.

After the door had closed behind Caroline, she turned to Rebecca.

"Did Henry have many words with him?" she asked.

"They were talking very loud," replied Rebecca evasively, yet with an answering gleam of ready response to the other's curiosity in the quick lift of her soft blue eyes.

Mrs. Brigham looked at her. She had not resumed rocking. She still sat up straight with a slight knitting of intensity on her fair forehead, between the pretty rippling curves of her auburn hair.

"Did you—hear anything?" she asked in a low voice with a glance toward the door.

"I was just across the hall in the south parlour, and that door was open and this door ajar," replied Rebecca with a slight flush.

"Then you must have—"

"I couldn't help it."

"Everything?"

"Most of it."

"What was it?"

"The old story."

"I suppose Henry was mad, as he always was, because Edward was living on here for nothing, when he had wasted all the money father left him."

Rebecca nodded with a fearful glance at the door.

When Emma spoke again her voice was still more hushed. "I know how he felt," said she. "He had always been so prudent himself, and worked hard at his profession, and there Edward had never done anything but spend, and it must have looked to him as if Edward was living at his expense, but he wasn't."

"No, he wasn't."

"It was the way father left the property—that all the children should have a home here—and he left money enough to buy the food and all if we had all come home."

"Yes."

"And Edward had a right here according to the terms of father's will, and Henry ought to have remembered it."

"Yes, he ought."

"Did he say hard things?"

"Pretty hard from what I heard."

"What?"

"I heard him tell Edward that he had no business here at all, and he thought he had better go away."

"What did Edward say?"

"That he would stay here as long as he lived and afterward, too, if he was a mind to, and he would like to see Henry get him out; and then—"

"What?"

"Then he laughed."

"What did Henry say."

"I didn't hear him say anything, but—"

"But what?"

"I saw him when he came out of this room."

"He looked mad?"

"You've seen him when he looked so."

Emma nodded; the expression of horror on her face had deepened.

"Do you remember that time he killed the cat because she had scratched him?"

"Yes. Don't!"

Then Caroline reentered the room. She went up to the stove in which a wood fire was burning—it was a cold, gloomy day of fall—and she warmed her hands, which were reddened from recent washing in cold water.

Mrs. Brigham looked at her and hesitated. She glanced at the door, which was still ajar, as it did not easily shut, being still swollen with the damp weather of the summer. She rose and pushed it together with a sharp thud which jarred the house. Rebecca started painfully with a half exclamation. Caroline looked at her disapprovingly.

"It is time you controlled your nerves, Rebecca," said she.

"I can't help it," replied Rebecca with almost a wail. "I am nervous. There's enough to make me so, the Lord knows."

"What do you mean by that?" asked Caroline with her old air of sharp suspicion, and something between challenge and dread of its being met.

Rebecca shrank.

"Nothing," said she.

"Then I wouldn't keep speaking in such a fashion."

Emma, returning from the closed door, said imperiously that it ought to be fixed, it shut so hard.

"It will shrink enough after we have had the fire a few days," replied Caroline. "If anything is done to it it will be too small; there will be a crack at the sill."

"I think Henry ought to be ashamed of himself for talking as he did to Edward," said Mrs. Brigham abruptly, but in an almost inaudible voice.

"Hush!" said Caroline, with a glance of actual fear at the closed door.

"Nobody can hear with the door shut."

"He must have heard it shut, and—"

"Well, I can say what I want to before he comes down, and I am not afraid of him."

"I don't know who is afraid of him! What reason is there for anybody to be afraid of Henry?" demanded Caroline.

Mrs. Brigham trembled before her sister's look. Rebecca gasped again. "There isn't any reason, of course. Why should there be?"

"I wouldn't speak so, then. Somebody might overhear you and think it was queer. Miranda Joy is in the south parlour sewing, you know."

"I thought she went upstairs to stitch on the machine."

"She did, but she has come down again."

"Well, she can't hear."

"I say again I think Henry ought to be ashamed of himself.

I shouldn't think he'd ever get over it, having words with poor Edward the very night before he died. Edward was enough sight better disposition than Henry, with all his faults. I always thought a great deal of poor Edward, myself."

Mrs. Brigham passed a large fluff of handkerchief across her eyes; Rebecca sobbed outright.

"Rebecca," said Caroline admonishingly, keeping her mouth stiff and swallowing determinately.

"I never heard him speak a cross word, unless he spoke cross to Henry that last night. I don't know, but he did from what Rebecca overheard," said Emma.

"Not so much cross as sort of soft, and sweet, and aggravating," sniffled Rebecca.

"He never raised his voice," said Caroline; "but he had his way."

"He had a right to in this case."

"Yes, he did."

"He had as much of a right here as Henry," sobbed Rebecca, "and now he's gone, and he will never be in this home that poor father left him and the rest of us again."

"What do you really think ailed Edward?" asked Emma in hardly more than a whisper. She did not look at her sister.

Caroline sat down in a nearby armchair, and clutched the arms convulsively until her thin knuckles whitened.

"I told you," said she.

Rebecca held her handkerchief over her mouth, and looked at them above it with terrified, streaming eyes.

"I know you said that he had terrible pains in his stomach, and had spasms, but what do you think made him have them?"

"Henry called it gastric trouble. You know Edward has always had dyspepsia."

Mrs. Brigham hesitated a moment. "Was there any talk of an—examination?" said she.

Then Caroline turned on her fiercely.

"No," said she in a terrible voice. "No."

The three sisters' souls seemed to meet on one common ground of terrified understanding through their eyes. The old-fashioned latch of the door was heard to rattle, and a push from without made the door shake ineffectually. "It's Henry," Rebecca sighed rather than whispered. Mrs. Brigham settled herself after a noiseless rush across the floor into her rocking-chair again, and was swaying back and forth with her head comfortably leaning back, when the door at last yielded and Henry Glynn entered. He cast a covertly sharp, comprehensive glance at Mrs. Brigham with her elaborate calm; at Rebecca quietly huddled in the corner of the sofa with her handkerchief to her face and only one small reddened ear as attentive as a dog's uncovered and revealing her alertness for his presence; at Caroline sitting with a strained composure in her armchair by the stove. She met his eyes quite firmly with a look of inscrutable fear, and defiance of the fear and of him.

Henry Glynn looked more like this sister than the others. Both had the same hard delicacy of form and feature, both were tall and almost emaciated, both had a sparse growth of gray blond hair far back from high intellectual foreheads, both had an almost noble aquilinity of feature. They confronted each other with the pitiless immovability of two statues in whose marble lineaments emotions were fixed for all eternity.

Then Henry Glynn smiled and the smile transformed his face. He looked suddenly years younger, and an almost boyish recklessness and irresolution appeared in his face. He flung himself into a chair with a gesture which was bewildering from its incongruity with his general appearance. He leaned his head back, flung one leg over the other, and looked laughingly at Mrs. Brigham.

"I declare, Emma, you grow younger every year," he said.

She flushed a little, and her placid mouth widened at the corners. She was susceptible to praise.

"Our thoughts to-day ought to belong to the one of us who will NEVER grow older," said Caroline in a hard voice.

Henry looked at her, still smiling. "Of course, we none of us forget that," said he, in a deep, gentle voice, "but we have to speak to the living, Caroline, and I have not seen Emma for a long time, and the living are as dear as the dead."

"Not to me," said Caroline.

She rose, and went abruptly out of the room again. Rebecca also rose and hurried after her, sobbing loudly.

Henry looked slowly after them.

"Caroline is completely unstrung," said he. Mrs. Brigham rocked. A confidence in him inspired by his manner was stealing over her. Out of that confidence she spoke quite easily and naturally.

"His death was very sudden," said she.

Henry's eyelids quivered slightly but his gaze was unswerving.

"Yes," said he; "it was very sudden. He was sick only a few hours."

"What did you call it?"

"Gastric."

"You did not think of an examination?"

"There was no need. I am perfectly certain as to the cause of his death."

Suddenly Mrs. Brigham felt a creep as of some live horror over her very soul. Her flesh prickled with cold, before an inflection of his voice. She rose, tottering on weak knees.

"Where are you going?" asked Henry in a strange, breathless voice.

Mrs. Brigham said something incoherent about some sewing which she had to do, some black for the funeral, and was out of the room. She went up to the front chamber which she occupied.

Caroline was there. She went close to her and took her hands, and the two sisters looked at each other.

"Don't speak, don't, I won't have it!" said Caroline finally in an awful whisper.

"I won't," replied Emma.

That afternoon the three sisters were in the study, the large front room on the ground floor across the hall from the south parlour, when the dusk deepened.

Mrs. Brigham was hemming some black material. She sat close to the west window for the waning light. At last she laid her work on her lap.

"It's no use, I cannot see to sew another stitch until we have a light," said she.

Caroline, who was writing some letters at the table, turned to Rebecca, in her usual place on the sofa.

"Rebecca, you had better get a lamp," she said.

Rebecca started up; even in the dusk her face showed her agitation.

"It doesn't seem to me that we need a lamp quite yet," she said in a piteous, pleading voice like a child's.

"Yes, we do," returned Mrs. Brigham peremptorily. "We must have a light. I must finish this to-night or I can't go to the funeral, and I can't see to sew another stitch."

"Caroline can see to write letters, and she is farther from the window than you are," said Rebecca.

"Are you trying to save kerosene or are you lazy, Rebecca Glynn?" cried Mrs. Brigham. "I can go and get the light myself, but I have this work all in my lap."

Caroline's pen stopped scratching.

"Rebecca, we must have the light," said she.

"Had we better have it in here?" asked Rebecca weakly.

"Of course! Why not?" cried Caroline sternly.

"I am sure I don't want to take my sewing into the other

room, when it is all cleaned up for to-morrow," said Mrs. Brigham.

"Why, I never heard such a to-do about lighting a lamp."

Rebecca rose and left the room. Presently she entered with a lamp—a large one with a white porcelain shade. She set it on a table, an old-fashioned card-table which was placed against the opposite wall from the window. That wall was clear of bookcases and books, which were only on three sides of the room. That opposite wall was taken up with three doors, the one small space being occupied by the table. Above the table on the old-fashioned paper, of a white satin gloss, traversed by an indeterminate green scroll, hung quite high a small gilt and black-framed ivory miniature taken in her girlhood of the mother of the family. When the lamp was set on the table beneath it, the tiny pretty face painted on the ivory seemed to gleam out with a look of intelligence.

"What have you put that lamp over there for?" asked Mrs. Brigham, with more of impatience than her voice usually revealed. "Why didn't you set it in the hall and have done with it. Neither Caroline nor I can see if it is on that table."

"I thought perhaps you would move," replied Rebecca hoarsely.

"If I do move, we can't both sit at that table. Caroline has her paper all spread around. Why don't you set the lamp on the study table in the middle of the room, then we can both see?"

Rebecca hesitated. Her face was very pale. She looked with an appeal that was fairly agonizing at her sister Caroline.

"Why don't you put the lamp on this table, as she says?" asked Caroline, almost fiercely. "Why do you act so, Rebecca?"

"I should think you *would* ask her that," said Mrs. Brigham. "She doesn't act like herself at all."

Rebecca took the lamp and set it on the table in the middle of the room without another word. Then she turned her back upon it quickly and seated herself on the sofa, and placed a hand over her eyes as if to shade them, and remained so.

"Does the light hurt your eyes, and is that the reason why you didn't want the lamp?" asked Mrs. Brigham kindly.

"I always like to sit in the dark," replied Rebecca chokingly. Then she snatched her handkerchief hastily from her pocket and began to weep. Caroline continued to write, Mrs. Brigham to sew.

Suddenly Mrs. Brigham as she sewed glanced at the opposite wall. The glance became a steady stare. She looked intently, her work suspended in her hands. Then she looked away again and took a few more stitches, then she looked again, and again turned to her task. At last she laid her work in her lap and stared concentratedly. She looked from the wall around the room, taking note of the various objects; she looked at the wall long and intently. Then she turned to her sisters.

"What *is* that?" said she.

"What?" asked Caroline harshly; her pen scratched loudly across the paper.

Rebecca gave one of her convulsive gasps.

"That strange shadow on the wall," replied Mrs. Brigham.

Rebecca sat with her face hidden: Caroline dipped her pen in the inkstand.

"Why don't you turn around and look?" asked Mrs. Brigham in a wondering and somewhat aggrieved way.

"I am in a hurry to finish this letter, if Mrs. Wilson Ebbit is going to get word in time to come to the funeral," replied Caroline shortly.

Mrs. Brigham rose, her work slipping to the floor, and she began walking around the room, moving various articles of furniture, with her eyes on the shadow.

Then suddenly she shrieked out:

"Look at this awful shadow! What is it? Caroline, look, look! Rebecca, look! *What is it?*"

All Mrs. Brigham's triumphant placidity was gone. Her handsome face was livid with horror. She stood stiffly pointing at the shadow.

"Look!" said she, pointing her finger at it. "Look! What is it?"

Then Rebecca burst out in a wild wail after a shuddering glance at the wall:

"Oh, Caroline, there it is again! There it is again!"

"Caroline Glynn, you look!" said Mrs. Brigham. "Look! What is that dreadful shadow?"

Caroline rose, turned, and stood confronting the wall.

"How should I know?" she said.

"It has been there every night since he died," cried Rebecca.

"Every night?"

"Yes. He died Thursday and this is Saturday; that makes three nights," said Caroline rigidly. She stood as if holding herself calm with a vise of concentrated will.

"It—it looks like—like—" stammered Mrs. Brigham in a tone of intense horror.

"I know what it looks like well enough," said Caroline. "I've got eyes in my head."

"It looks like Edward," burst out Rebecca in a sort of frenzy of fear. "Only—"

"Yes, it does," assented Mrs. Brigham, whose horror-stricken tone matched her sister's, "only— Oh, it is awful! What is it, Caroline?"

"I ask you again, how should I know?" replied Caroline. "I see it there like you. How should I know any more than you?"

"It *must* be something in the room," said Mrs. Brigham, staring wildly around.

"We moved everything in the room the first night it came," said Rebecca; "it is not anything in the room."

Caroline turned upon her with a sort of fury. "Of course it is something in the room," said she. "How you act! What do you mean by talking so? Of course it is something in the room."

"Of course, it is," agreed Mrs. Brigham, looking at Caroline suspiciously. "Of course it must be. It is only a coincidence. It just happens so. Perhaps it is that fold of the window curtain that makes it. It must be something in the room."

"It is not anything in the room," repeated Rebecca with obstinate horror.

The door opened suddenly and Henry Glynn entered. He began to speak, then his eyes followed the direction of the others'. He stood stock still staring at the shadow on the wall. It was life size and stretched across the white parallelogram of a door, half across the wall space on which the picture hung.

"What is that?" he demanded in a strange voice.

"It must be due to something in the room," Mrs. Brigham said faintly.

"It is not due to anything in the room," said Rebecca again with the shrill insistency of terror.

"How you act, Rebecca Glynn," said Caroline.

Henry Glynn stood and stared a moment longer. His face showed a gamut of emotions—horror, conviction, then furious incredulity. Suddenly he began hastening hither and thither about the room. He moved the furniture with fierce jerks, turning ever to see the effect upon the shadow on the wall. Not a line of its terrible outlines wavered.

"It must be something in the room!" he declared in a voice which seemed to snap like a lash.

His face changed. The inmost secrecy of his nature seemed evident until one almost lost sight of his lineaments. Rebecca stood close to her sofa, regarding him with woeful, fascinated eyes. Mrs. Brigham clutched Caroline's hand. They both stood in a corner out of his way. For a few moments he raged about the room like a caged wild animal. He moved every piece of furniture; when the moving of a piece did not affect the shadow, he flung it to the floor, the sisters watching.

Then suddenly he desisted. He laughed and began straightening the furniture which he had flung down.

"What an absurdity," he said easily. "Such a to-do about a shadow."

"That's so," assented Mrs. Brigham, in a scared voice which she tried to make natural. As she spoke she lifted a chair near her.

"I think you have broken the chair that Edward was so fond of," said Caroline.

Terror and wrath were struggling for expression on her face. Her mouth was set, her eyes shrinking. Henry lifted the chair with a show of anxiety.

"Just as good as ever," he said pleasantly. He laughed again, looking at his sisters. "Did I scare you?" he said. "I should think you might be used to me by this time. You know my way of wanting to leap to the bottom of a mystery, and that shadow does look—queer, like—and I thought if there was any way of accounting for it I would like to without any delay."

"You don't seem to have succeeded," remarked Caroline dryly, with a slight glance at the wall.

Henry's eyes followed hers and he quivered perceptibly.

"Oh, there is no accounting for shadows," he said, and he laughed again. "A man is a fool to try to account for shadows."

Then the supper bell rang, and they all left the room, but Henry kept his back to the wall, as did, indeed, the others.

Mrs. Brigham pressed close to Caroline as she crossed the hall. "He looked like a demon!" she breathed in her ear.

Henry led the way with an alert motion like a boy; Rebecca brought up the rear; she could scarcely walk, her knees trembled so.

"I can't sit in that room again this evening," she whispered to Caroline after supper.

"Very well, we will sit in the south room," replied Caroline.

"I think we will sit in the south parlour," she said aloud; "it isn't as damp as the study, and I have a cold."

So they all sat in the south room with their sewing. Henry read the newspaper, his chair drawn close to the lamp on the table. About nine o'clock he rose abruptly and crossed the hall to the study. The three sisters looked at one another. Mrs. Brigham rose, folded her rustling skirts compactly around her, and began tiptoeing toward the door.

"What are you going to do?" inquired Rebecca agitatedly.

"I am going to see what he is about," replied Mrs. Brigham cautiously.

She pointed as she spoke to the study door across the hall; it was ajar. Henry had striven to pull it together behind him, but it had somehow swollen beyond the limit with curious speed. It was still ajar and a streak of light showed from top to bottom. The hall lamp was not lit.

"You had better stay where you are," said Caroline with guarded sharpness.

"I am going to see," repeated Mrs. Brigham firmly.

Then she folded her skirts so tightly that her bulk with its swelling curves was revealed in a black silk sheath, and she went with a slow toddle across the hall to the study door. She stood there, her eye at the crack.

In the south room Rebecca stopped sewing and sat watching with dilated eyes. Caroline sewed steadily. What Mrs. Brigham, standing at the crack in the study door, saw was this:

Henry Glynn, evidently reasoning that the source of the strange shadow must be between the table on which the lamp stood and the wall, was making systematic passes and thrusts all over and through the intervening space with an old sword which had belonged to his father. Not an inch was left unpierced. He seemed to have divided the space into mathematical sections. He brandished the sword with a sort of cold fury and calculation; the blade gave out flashes of light, the shadow remained unmoved. Mrs. Brigham, watching, felt herself cold with horror.

Finally Henry ceased and stood with the sword in hand and raised as if to strike, surveying the shadow on the wall threateningly. Mrs. Brigham toddled back across the hall and shut the south room door behind her before she related what she had seen.

"He looked like a demon!" she said again. "Have you got any of that old wine in the house, Caroline? I don't feel as if I could stand much more."

Indeed, she looked overcome. Her handsome placid face was worn and strained and pale.

"Yes, there's plenty," said Caroline; "you can have some when you go to bed."

"I think we had all better take some," said Mrs. Brigham. "Oh, my God, Caroline, what—"

"Don't ask and don't speak," said Caroline.

"No, I am not going to," replied Mrs. Brigham; "but—"

Rebecca moaned aloud.

"What are you doing that for?" asked Caroline harshly.

"Poor Edward," returned Rebecca.

"That is all you have to groan for," said Caroline. "There is nothing else."

"I am going to bed," said Mrs. Brigham. "I sha'n't be able to be at the funeral if I don't."

Soon the three sisters went to their chambers and the south parlour was deserted. Caroline called to Henry in the study to put out the light before he came upstairs. They had been gone about an hour when he came into the room bringing the lamp which had stood in the study. He set it on the table and waited a few minutes, pacing up and down. His face was terrible, his fair complexion showed livid; his blue eyes seemed dark blanks of awful reflections.

Then he took the lamp up and returned to the library. He set the lamp on the centre table, and the shadow sprang out on the wall. Again he studied the furniture and moved it about, but deliberately, with none of his former frenzy. Nothing affected the shadow. Then he returned to the south room with the lamp and again waited. Again he returned to the study and placed the lamp on the table, and the shadow sprang out upon the wall. It was midnight before he went upstairs. Mrs. Brigham and the other sisters, who could not sleep, heard him.

The next day was the funeral. That evening the family sat in the south room. Some relatives were with them. Nobody entered the study until Henry carried a lamp in there after the others had retired for the night. He saw again the shadow on the wall leap to an awful life before the light.

The next morning at breakfast Henry Glynn announced that he had to go to the city for three days. The sisters looked at him with surprise. He very seldom left home, and just now his practice had been neglected on account of Edward's death. He was a physician.

"How can you leave your patients now?" asked Mrs. Brigham wonderingly.

"I don't know how to, but there is no other way," replied Henry easily. "I have had a telegram from Doctor Mitford."

"Consultation?" inquired Mrs. Brigham.

"I have business," replied Henry.

Doctor Mitford was an old classmate of his who lived in a neighbouring city and who occasionally called upon him in the case of a consultation.

After he had gone Mrs. Brigham said to Caroline that after all Henry had not said that he was going to consult with Doctor Mitford, and she thought it very strange.

"Everything is very strange," said Rebecca with a shudder.

"What do you mean?" inquired Caroline sharply.

"Nothing," replied Rebecca.

Nobody entered the library that day, nor the next, nor the next. The third day Henry was expected home, but he did not arrive and the last train from the city had come.

"I call it pretty queer work," said Mrs. Brigham. "The idea of a doctor leaving his patients for three days anyhow, at such a time as this, and I know he has some very sick ones; he said so. And the idea of a consultation lasting three days! There is no sense in it, and *now* he has not come. I don't understand it, for my part."

"I don't either," said Rebecca.

They were all in the south parlour. There was no light in the study opposite, and the door was ajar.

Presently Mrs. Brigham rose—she could not have told why; something seemed to impel her, some will outside her own. She went out of the room, again wrapping her rustling skirts around that she might pass noiselessly, and began pushing at the swollen door of the study.

"She has not got any lamp," said Rebecca in a shaking voice.

Caroline, who was writing letters, rose again, took a lamp (there were two in the room) and followed her sister. Rebecca had risen, but she stood trembling, not venturing to follow.

The doorbell rang, but the others did not hear it; it was on the south door on the other side of the house from the study. Rebecca, after hesitating until the bell rang the second time, went to the door; she remembered that the servant was out.

Caroline and her sister Emma entered the study. Caroline set the lamp on the table. They looked at the wall. "Oh, my God," gasped Mrs. Brigham, "there are—there are *two*—shadows." The sisters stood clutching each other, staring at the awful things on the wall. Then Rebecca came in, staggering, with a telegram in her hand. "Here is—a telegram," she gasped. "Henry is—dead."

43

THE TERROR BY NIGHT

E.F. Benson

The transference of emotion is a phenomenon so common, so constantly witnessed, that mankind in general have long ceased to be conscious of its existence, as a thing worth our wonder or consideration, regarding it as being as natural and commonplace as the transference of things that act by the ascertained laws of matter. Nobody, for instance, is surprised, if when the room is too hot, the opening of a window causes the cold fresh air of outside to be transferred into the room, and in the same way no one is surprised when into the same room, perhaps, which we will imagine as being peopled with dull and gloomy persons, there enters some one of fresh and sunny mind, who instantly brings into the stuffy mental atmosphere a change analogous to that of the opened windows. Exactly how this infection is conveyed we do not know; considering the wireless wonders (that act by material laws) which are already beginning to lose their wonder now that we have our newspaper brought as a matter of course every morning in mid-Atlantic, it would not perhaps be rash to conjecture that in some subtle and occult way the transference of emotion is in reality material too. Certainly (to take another instance) the sight of definitely material things, like writing on a page, conveys emotion apparently direct to our minds, as when our pleasure or pity is stirred by a book, and it is therefore possible that mind may act on mind by means as material as that.

Occasionally, however, we come across phenomena which,

though they may easily be as material as any of these things, are rarer, and therefore more astounding. Some people call them ghosts, some conjuring tricks, and some nonsense. It seems simpler to group them under the head of transferred emotions, and they may appeal to any of the senses. Some ghosts are seen, some heard, some felt, and though I know of no instance of a ghost being tasted, yet it will seem in the following pages that these occult phenomena may appeal at any rate to the senses that perceive heat, cold, or smell. For, to take the analogy of wireless telegraphy, we are all of us probably "receivers" to some extent, and catch now and then a message or part of a message that the eternal waves of emotion are ceaselessly shouting aloud to those who have ears to hear, and materialising themselves for those who have eyes to see. Not being, as a rule, perfectly tuned, we grasp but pieces and fragments of such messages, a few coherent words it may be, or a few words which seem to have no sense. The following story, however, to my mind, is interesting, because it shows how different pieces of what no doubt was one message were received and recorded by several different people simultaneously. Ten years have elapsed since the events recorded took place, but they were written down at the time.

Jack Lorimer and I were very old friends before he married, and his marriage to a first cousin of mine did not make, as so often happens, a slackening in our intimacy. Within a few months after, it was found out that his wife had consumption, and, without any loss of time, she was sent off to Davos, with her sister to look after her. The disease had evidently been detected at a very early stage, and there was excellent ground for hoping that with proper care and strict regime she would be cured by the life-giving frosts of that wonderful valley.

The two had gone out in the November of which I am speaking, and Jack and I joined them for a month at Christmas, and found that week after week she was steadily and quickly gaining ground. We had to be back in town by the end of January, but it was settled that Ida should remain out with her sister for a week or two more. They both, I remember, came down to the station to see us off, and I am not likely to forget the last words that passed:

"Oh, don't look so woebegone, Jack," his wife had said; "you'll see me again before long."

Then the fussy little mountain engine squeaked, as a puppy squeaks when its toe is trodden on, and we puffed our way up the pass.

London was in its usual desperate February plight when we got back, full of fogs and still-born frosts that seemed to produce a cold far more bitter than the piercing temperature of those sunny altitudes from which we had come. We both, I think, felt rather lonely, and even before we had got to our journey's end we had settled that for the present it was ridiculous that we should keep open two houses when one would suffice, and would also be far more cheerful for us both.

So, as we both lived in almost identical houses in the same street in Chelsea, we decided to "toss," live in the house which the coin indicated (heads mine, tails his), share expenses, attempt to let the other house, and, if successful, share the proceeds. A French five-franc piece of the Second Empire told us it was "heads."

We had been back some ten days, receiving every day the most excellent accounts from Davos, when, first on him, then on me, there descended, like some tropical storm, a feeling of indefinable fear. Very possibly this sense of apprehension (for there is nothing in the world so virulently infectious) reached me through him: on the other hand both these attacks of vague foreboding may have come from the same source. But it is true that it did not attack me till he spoke of it, so the possibility perhaps inclines to my having caught it from him. He spoke of it first, I remember, one evening when we had met for a good-night talk, after having come back from separate houses where we had dined.

"I have felt most awfully down all day," he said; "and just after receiving this splendid account from Daisy, I can't think what is the matter."

He poured himself out some whisky and soda as he spoke.

"Oh, touch of liver," I said. "I shouldn't drink that if I were you. Give it me instead."

"I was never better in my life," he said.

I was opening letters, as we talked, and came across one from the house agent, which, with trembling eagerness, I read.

"Hurrah," I cried, "offer of five gu"—why can't he write it in proper English—"five guineas a week till Easter for number 31. We shall roll in guineas!"

"Oh, but I can't stop here till Easter," he said.

"I don't see why not. Nor by the way does Daisy. I heard from her this morning, and she told me to persuade you to stop. That's to say, if you like. It really is more cheerful for you here. I forgot, you were telling me something."

The glorious news about the weekly guineas did not cheer him up in the least.

"Thanks awfully. Of course I'll stop."

He moved up and down the room once or twice.

"No, it's not me that is wrong," he said, "it's It, whatever It is. The terror by night."

"Which you are commanded not to be afraid of," I remarked.

"I know; it's easy commanding. I'm frightened: something's coming."

"Five guineas a week are coming," I said. "I shan't sit up and be infected by your fears. All that matters, Davos, is going as well as it can. What was the last report? Incredibly better. Take that to bed with you."

The infection—if infection it was—did not take hold of me then, for I remember going to sleep feeling quite cheerful, but I awoke in some dark still house and It, the terror by night, had come while I slept. Fear and misgiving, blind, unreasonable, and paralysing, had taken and gripped me. What was it? Just as by an aneroid we can foretell the approach of storm, so by this sinking of the spirit, unlike anything I had ever felt before, I felt sure that disaster of some sort was presaged.

Jack saw it at once when we met at breakfast next morning, in the brown haggard light of a foggy day, not dark enough for candles, but dismal beyond all telling.

"So it has come to you too," he said.

And I had not even the fighting-power left to tell him that I was merely slightly unwell.

Besides, never in my life had I felt better.

All next day, all the day after that fear lay like a black cloak over my mind; I did not know what I dreaded, but it was something very acute, something that was very near. It was coming nearer every moment, spreading like a pall of clouds over the sky; but on the third day, after miserably cowering under it, I suppose some sort of courage came back to me: either this was pure imagination, some trick of disordered nerves or what not, in which case we were both "disquieting ourselves in vain," or from the immeasurable waves of emotion that beat upon the minds of men, something within both of us had caught a current, a pressure. In either case it was infinitely better to try, however ineffectively, to stand up against it. For these two days I had neither worked nor played; I had only shrunk and shuddered; I planned for myself a busy day, with diversion for us both in the evening.

"We will dine early," I said, "and go to the 'Man from Blankley's.' I have already asked Philip to come, and he is coming, and I have telephoned for tickets. Dinner at seven."

Philip, I may remark, is an old friend of ours, neighbour in this street, and by profession a much-respected doctor.

Jack laid down his paper.

"Yes, I expect you're right," he said. "It's no use doing nothing, it doesn't help things. Did you sleep well?"

"Yes, beautifully," I said rather snappishly, for I was all on edge with the added burden of an almost sleepless night.

"I wish I had," said he.

This would not do at all.

"We have got to play up!" I said. "Here are we two strong and stalwart persons, with as much cause for satisfaction with life as any you can mention, letting ourselves behave like worms. Our fear may be over things imaginary or over things that are real, but it is the fact of being afraid that is so despicable. There is nothing in the world to fear except fear. You know that as well as I do. Now let's read our papers with interest. Which do you back, Mr. Druce, or the Duke of Portland, or the Times Book Club?"

That day, therefore, passed very busily for me; and there were enough events moving in front of that black background, which I was conscious was there all the time, to enable me to keep my eyes away from it, and I was detained rather late at the office, and had to drive back to Chelsea, in order to be in time to dress for dinner instead of walking back as I had intended.

Then the message, which for these three days had been twittering in our minds, the receivers, just making them quiver and rattle, came through.

I found Jack already dressed, since it was within a minute or two of seven when I got in, and sitting in the drawing-room. The day had been warm and muggy, but when I looked in on the way up to my room, it seemed to me to have grown suddenly and bitterly cold, not with the dampness of English frost, but with the clear and stinging exhilaration of such days as we had recently spent in Switzerland. Fire was laid in the grate but not lit, and I went down on my knees on the hearth-rug to light it.

"Why, it's freezing in here," I said. "What donkeys servants are! It never occurs to them that you want fires in cold weather, and no fires in hot weather."

"Oh, for heaven's sake don't light the fire," said he, "it's the warmest muggiest evening I ever remember."

I stared at him in astonishment. My hands were shaking with the cold. He saw this.

"Why, you are shivering!" he said. "Have you caught a chill? But as to the room being cold let us look at the thermometer."

There was one on the writing-table.

"Sixty-five," he said.

There was no disputing that, nor did I want to, for at that moment it suddenly struck us, dimly and distantly, that It was "coming through." I felt it like some curious internal vibration.

"Hot or cold, I must go and dress," I said.

Still shivering, but feeling as if I was breathing some rarefied exhilarating air, I went up to my room. My clothes were already laid out, but, by an oversight, no hot water had been brought up, and I rang for my man. He came up almost at once, but he looked scared, or, to my already-startled senses, he appeared so.

"What's the matter?" I said.

"Nothing, sir," he said, and he could hardly articulate the words. "I thought you rang."

"Yes. Hot water. But what's the matter?"

He shifted from one foot to the other.

"I thought I saw a lady on the stairs," he said, "coming up close behind me. And the front-door bell hadn't rung that I heard."

"Where did you think you saw her?" I asked.

"On the stairs. Then on the landing outside the drawing-room door, sir," he said. "She stood there as if she didn't know whether to go in or not."

"One—one of the servants," I said. But again I felt that It was coming through.

"No, sir. It was none of the servants," he said.

"Who was it then?"

"Couldn't see distinctly, sir, it was dim-like. But I thought it was Mrs. Lorimer."

"Oh, go and get me some hot water," I said.

But he lingered; he was quite clearly frightened.

At this moment the front door bell rang. It was just seven, and already Philip had come with brutal punctuality while I was not yet half dressed.

"That's Dr. Enderly," I said. "Perhaps if he is on the stairs you may be able to pass the place where you saw the lady."

Then quite suddenly there rang through the house a scream, so terrible, so appalling in its agony and supreme terror, that I simply stood still and shuddered, unable to move. Then by an effort so violent that I felt as if something must break, I recalled the power of motion, and ran downstairs, my man at my heels, to meet Philip who was running up from the ground floor. He had heard it too.

"What's the matter?" he said. "What was that?"

Together we went into the drawing-room. Jack was lying in front of the fireplace, with the chair in which he had been sitting a few minutes before overturned. Philip went straight to him and bent over him, tearing open his white shirt.

"Open all the windows," he said, "the place reeks."

We flung open the windows, and there poured in so it seemed to me, a stream of hot air into the bitter cold. Eventually Philip got up.

"He is dead," he said. "Keep the windows open. The place is still thick with chloroform."

Gradually to my sense the room got warmer, to Philip's the drug-laden atmosphere dispersed.

But neither my servant nor I had smelt anything at all.

A couple of hours later there came a telegram from Davos for me. It was to tell me to break the news of Daisy's death to Jack, and was sent by her sister. She supposed he would come out immediately. But he had been gone two hours now.

I left for Davos next day, and learned what had happened. Daisy had been suffering for three days from a little abscess which had to be opened, and, though the operation was of the slightest, she had been so nervous about it that the doctor gave her chloroform. She made a good recovery from the anesthetic, but an hour later had a sudden attack of syncope, and had died that night at a few minutes before eight, by Central European time, corresponding to seven in English time. She had insisted that Jack should be told nothing about this little operation till it was over, since the matter was quite unconnected with her general health, and she did not wish to cause him needless anxiety.

And there the story ends. To my servant there came the sight of a woman outside the drawing-room door, where Jack was, hesitating about her entrance, at the moment when Daisy's soul hovered between the two worlds; to me there came—I do not think it is fanciful to suppose this—the keen exhilarating cold of Davos; to Philip there came the fumes of chloroform. And to Jack, I must suppose, came his wife. So he joined her.

44

THE NIGHT-DOINGS AT "DEADMAN'S"

Ambrose Bierce

It was a singularly sharp night, and clear as the heart of a diamond. Clear nights have a trick of being keen. In darkness you may be cold and not know it; when you see, you suffer. This night was bright enough to bite like a serpent. The moon was moving mysteriously along behind the giant pines crowning the South Mountain, striking a cold sparkle from the crusted snow, and bringing out against the black west and ghostly outlines of the Coast Range, beyond which lay the invisible Pacific. The snow had piled itself, in the open spaces along the bottom of the gulch, into long ridges that seemed to heave, and into hills that appeared to toss and scatter spray. The spray was sunlight, twice reflected: dashed once from the moon, once from the snow.

In this snow many of the shanties of the abandoned mining camp were obliterated (a sailor might have said they had gone down), and at irregular intervals it had overtopped the tall trestles which had once supported a river called a flume; for, of course, "flume" is flumen. Among the advantages of which the mountains cannot deprive the gold-hunter is the privilege of speaking Latin. He says of his dead neighbour, "He has gone up the flume." This is not a bad way to say, "His life has returned to the Fountain of Life."

While putting on its armour against the assaults of the wind, this snow had neglected no coign of vantage. Snow pursued by the wind is not wholly unlike a retreating army. In the open field it ranges itself in ranks and battalions; where it can get a foothold it makes a stand; where it can take cover it does so. You may see whole platoons of snow cowering behind a bit of broken wall. The devious old road, hewn out of the mountainside, was full of it. Squadron upon squadron had struggled to escape by this line, when suddenly pursuit had ceased. A more desolate and dreary spot than Deadman's Gulch in a winter midnight it is impossible to imagine. Yet Mr. Hiram Beeson elected to live there, the sole inhabitant.

Away up the side of the North Mountain his little pine-log shanty projected from its single pane of glass a long, thin beam of light, and looked not altogether unlike a black beetle fastened to the hillside with a bright new pin. Within it sat Mr. Beeson himself, before a roaring fire, staring into its hot heart as if he had never before seen such a thing in all his life. He was not a comely man. He was grey; he was ragged and slovenly in his attire; his face was wan and haggard; his eyes were too bright. As to his age, if one had attempted to guess it, one might have said forty-seven, then corrected himself and said seventy-four. He was really twenty-eight. Emaciated he was; as much, perhaps, as he dared be, with a needy undertaker at Bentley's Flat and a new and enterprising coroner at Sonora. Poverty and zeal are an upper and a nether millstone. It is dangerous to make a third in that kind of sandwich.

As Mr. Beeson sat there, with his ragged elbows on his ragged knees, his lean jaws buried in his lean hands, and with no apparent intention of going to bed, he looked as if the slightest movement would tumble him to pieces. Yet during the last hour he had winked no fewer than three times.

There was a sharp rapping at the door. A rap at that time of night and in that weather might have surprised an ordinary mortal who had dwelt two years in the gulch without seeing a human face, and could not fail to know that the country was impassable; but Mr. Beeson did not so much as pull his eyes out of the coals. And even when the door was pushed open he only shrugged a little more closely into himself, as one does who is expecting something that he would rather not see. You may observe this movement in women when, in a mortuary chapel, the coffin is borne up the aisle behind them.

But when a long old man in a blanket overcoat, his head tied up in a handkerchief and nearly his entire face in a muffler, wearing green goggles and with a complexion of glittering whiteness where it could be seen, strode silently into the room, laying a hard, gloved hand on Mr. Beeson's shoulder, the latter so far forgot himself as to look up with an appearance of no small astonishment; whomever he may have been expecting, he had evidently not counted on meeting anyone like this. Nevertheless, the sight of this unexpected guest produced in Mr. Beeson the following sequence: a feeling of astonishment; a sense of gratification; a sentiment of profound good will. Rising from his seat, he took the knotty hand from his shoulder, and shook it up and down with a fervour quite unaccountable; for in the old man's aspect was nothing to attract, much to repel. However, attraction is too general a property for repulsion to be without it. The most attractive object in the world is the face we instinctively cover with a cloth. When it becomes still more attractive—fascinating—we put seven feet of earth above it.

"Sir," said Mr. Beeson, releasing the old man's hand, which fell passively against his thigh with a quiet clack, "it is an extremely disagreeable night. Pray be seated; I am very glad to see you."

Mr. Beeson spoke with an easy good breeding that one would hardly have expected, considering all things. Indeed, the contrast between his appearance and his manner was sufficiently surprising to be one of the commonest of social phenomena in the mines. The old man advanced a step toward the fire, glowing cavernously in the green goggles. Mr. Beeson resumed.

"You bet your life I am!"

Mr. Beeson's elegance was not too refined; it had made reasonable concessions to local taste. He paused a moment, letting his eyes drop from the muffled head of his guest, down along the row of mouldy buttons confining the blanket overcoat, to the greenish cowhide boots powdered with snow, which had begun to melt and run along the floor in little rills. He took an inventory of his guest, and appeared satisfied. Who would not have been? Then he continued:

"The cheer I can offer you is, unfortunately, in keeping with my surroundings; but I shall esteem myself highly favoured if it is your pleasure to partake of it, rather than seek better at Bentley's Flat."

With a singular refinement of hospitable humility Mr. Beeson spoke as if a sojourn in his warm cabin on such a night, as compared with walking fourteen miles up to the throat in snow with a cutting crust, would be an intolerable hardship. By way of reply, his guest unbuttoned the blanket overcoat. The host laid fresh fuel on the fire, swept the hearth with the tail of a wolf, and added:

"But I think you'd better skedaddle."

The old man took a seat by the fire, spreading his broad soles to the heat without removing his hat. In the mines the hat is seldom removed except when the boots are. Without further remark Mr. Beeson also seated himself in a chair which had been a barrel, and which, retaining much of its original character, seemed to have been designed with a view to preserving his dust if it should please him to crumble. For a moment there was silence; then, from somewhere among the pines, came the snarling yelp of a coyote; and simultaneously the door rattled in its frame. There was no other connection between the two incidents than that the coyote has an aversion to storms, and the wind was rising; yet there seemed somehow a kind of supernatural conspiracy between the two, and Mr. Beeson shuddered with a vague sense of terror.

He recovered himself in a moment and again addressed his guest.

"There are strange doings here. I will tell you everything, and then if you decide to go I shall hope to accompany you over the worst of the way; as far as where Baldy Peterson shot Ben Hike—I dare say you know the place."

The old man nodded emphatically, as intimating not merely that he did, but that he did indeed.

"Two years ago," began Mr. Beeson, "I, with two companions, occupied this house; but when the rush to the Flat occurred we left, along with the rest. In ten hours the gulch was deserted. That evening, however, I discovered I had left behind me a valuable pistol (that is it) and returned for it, passing the night here alone, as I have passed every night since. I must explain that a few days before we left, our Chinese domestic had the misfortune to die while the ground was frozen so hard that it was impossible to dig a grave in the usual way. So, on the day of our hasty departure, we cut through the floor there, and gave him such burial as we could. But before putting him down I had the extremely bad taste to cut off his pigtail and spike it to that beam above his grave, where you may see it at this moment, or, preferably, when warmth has given you leisure for observation.

"I stated, did I not, that the Chinaman came to his death from natural causes? I had, of course, nothing to do with that, and returned through no irresistible attraction, or morbid fascination, but only because I had forgotten a pistol. That is clear to you, is it not, sir?"

The visitor nodded gravely. He appeared to be a man of few words, if any. Mr. Beeson continued:

"According to the Chinese faith, a man is like a kite: he cannot go to heaven without a tail. Well, to shorten this tedious story—which, however, I thought it my duty to relate—on that night, while I was here alone and thinking of anything but him, that Chinaman came back for his pigtail.

"He did not get it."

At this point Mr. Beeson relapsed into blank silence. Perhaps he was fatigued by the unwonted exercise of speaking; perhaps he had conjured up a memory that demanded his undivided attention. The wind was now fairly abroad, and the pines along the mountainside sang with singular distinctness. The narrator continued:

"You say you do not see much in that, and I must confess I do not myself.

"But he keeps coming!"

There was another long silence, during which both stared into the fire without the movement of a limb. Then Mr. Beeson broke out, almost fiercely, fixing his eyes on what he could see of the impassive face of his auditor:

"Give it him? Sir, in this matter I have no intention of troubling anyone for advice. You will pardon me, I am sure"— here he became singularly persuasive—"but I have ventured to nail that pigtail fast, and have assumed that somewhat onerous obligation of guarding it. So it is quite impossible to act on your considerate suggestion.

"Do you play me for a Modoc?"

Nothing could exceed the sudden ferocity with which he thrust this indignant remonstrance into the ear of his guest. It was as if he had struck him on the side of the head with a steel gauntlet. It was a protest, but it was a challenge. To be mistaken for a coward—to be played for a Modoc: these two expressions are one. Sometimes it is a Chinaman. Do you play me for a Chinaman? is a question frequently addressed to the ear of the suddenly dead.

Mr. Beeson's buffet produced no effect, and after a moment's pause, during which the wind thundered in the chimney like the sound of clods upon a coffin, he resumed:

"But, as you say, it is wearing me out. I feel that the life of the last two years has been a mistake—a mistake that corrects itself; you see how. The grave! No; there is no one to dig it. The ground is frozen, too. But you are very welcome. You may say at Bentley's—but that is not important. It was very tough to cut; they braid silk into their pigtails. Kwaagh."

Mr. Beeson was speaking with his eyes shut, and he wandered. His last word was a snore. A moment later he drew a long breath, opened his eyes with an effort, made a single remark, and fell into a deep sleep. What he said was this:

"They are swiping my dust!"

Then the aged stranger, who had not uttered one word since his arrival, arose from his seat and deliberately laid off his outer clothing, looking as angular in his flannels as the late Signorina Festorazzi, an Irish woman, six feet in height, and weighing fifty-six pounds, who used to exhibit herself in her chemise to the people of San Francisco. He then crept into one of the "bunks," having first placed a revolver in easy reach, according to the custom of the country. This revolver he took from a shelf, and it was the one which Mr. Beeson had mentioned as that for which he had returned to the gulch two years before.

In a few moments Mr. Beeson awoke, and seeing that his guest had retired he did likewise. But before doing so he approached the long, plaited wisp of pagan hair and gave it a powerful tug, to assure himself that it was fast and firm. The two beds-mere shelves covered with blankets not overclean-faced each other from opposite sides of the room, the little square trap-door that had given access to the Chinaman's grave being midway between. This, by the way, was crossed by a double row of spikeheads. In his resistance to the supernatural, Mr. Beeson had not disdained the use of material precautions.

The fire was now low, the flames burning bluely and petulantly, with occasional flashes, projecting spectral shadows on the walls—shadows that moved mysteriously about, now dividing, now uniting. The shadow of the pendent queue, however, kept moodily apart, near the roof at the farther end of the room, looking like a note of admiration. The song of the pines outside had now risen to the dignity of a triumphal hymn. In the pauses the silence was dreadful.

It was during one of these intervals that the trap in the floor began to lift. Slowly and steadily it rose, and slowly and steadily rose the swaddled head of the old man in the bunk to observe it. Then, with a clap that shook the house to its foundation, it was thrown clean back, where it lay with its unsightly spikes pointing threateningly upward. Mr. Beeson awoke, and without rising, pressed his fingers into his eyes. He shuddered; his teeth chattered. His guest was now reclining on one elbow, watching the proceedings with the goggles that glowed like lamps.

Suddenly a howling gust of wind swooped down the chimney, scattering ashes and smoke in all directions, for a moment obscuring everything. When the fire-light again illuminated the room there was seen, sitting gingerly on the edge of a stool by the hearth-side, a swarthy little man of prepossessing appearance and dressed with faultless taste, nodding to the old man with a friendly and engaging smile.

"From San Francisco, evidently," thought Mr. Beeson, who having somewhat recovered from his fright was groping his way to a solution of the evening's events.

But now another actor appeared upon the scene. Out of the square black hole in the middle of the floor protruded the head of the departed Chinaman, his glassy eyes turned upward in their angular slits and fastened on the dangling queue above with a look of yearning unspeakable. Mr. Beeson groaned, and again spread his hands upon his face. A mild odour of opium pervaded the place. The phantom, clad only in a short blue tunic quilted and silken but covered with grave-mould, rose slowly, as if pushed by a weak spiral spring. Its knees were at the level of the floor, when with a quick upward impulse like the silent leaping of a flame it grasped the queue with both hands, drew up its body and took the tip in its horrible yellow teeth. To this it clung in a seeming frenzy, grimacing ghastly, surging and plunging from side to side in its efforts to disengage its property from the beam, but uttering no sound. It was like a corpse artificially convulsed by means of a galvanic battery. The contrast between its superhuman activity and its silence was no less than hideous!

Mr. Beeson cowered in his bed. The swarthy little gentleman uncrossed his legs, beat an impatient tattoo with the toe of his boot and consulted a heavy gold watch. The old man sat erect and quietly laid hold of the revolver.

Bang!

Like a body cut from the gallows the Chinaman plumped into the black hole below, carrying his tail in his teeth. The trapdoor turned over, shutting down with a snap. The swarthy little gentleman from San Francisco sprang nimbly from his perch, caught something in the air with his hat, as a boy catches a butterfly, and vanished into the chimney as if drawn up by suction.

From away somewhere in the outer darkness floated in through the open door a faint, far cry—a long, sobbing wail, as of a child death-strangled in the desert, or a lost soul borne away by the Adversary. It may have been the coyote.

In the early days of the following spring a party of miners on their way to new diggings passed along the gulch, and straying through the deserted shanties found in one of them the body of Hiram Beeson, stretched upon a bunk, with a bullet hole through the heart. The ball had evidently been fired from the opposite side of the room, for in one of the oaken beams overhead was a shallow blue dint, where it had struck a knot and been deflected downward to the breast of its victim. Strongly attached to the same beam was what appeared to be an end of a rope of braided horsehair, which had been cut by the bullet in its passage to the knot. Nothing else of interest was noted, excepting a suit of mouldy and incongruous clothing, several articles of which were afterward identified by respectable witnesses as those in which certain deceased citizen's of Deadman's had been buried years before. But it is not easy to understand how that could be, unless, indeed, the garments had been worn as a disguise by Death himself—which is hardly credible.

45

THE PHANTOM COACH

Amelia B. Edwards

The circumstances I am about to relate to you have truth to recommend them. They happened to myself, and my recollection of them is as vivid as if they had taken place only yesterday. Twenty years, however, have gone by since that night. During those twenty years I have told the story to but one other person. I tell it now with a reluctance which I find it difficult to overcome. All I entreat, meanwhile, is that you will abstain from forcing your own conclusions upon me. I want nothing explained away. I desire no arguments. My mind on this subject is quite made up, and, having the testimony of my own senses to rely upon, I prefer to abide by it.

Well! It was just twenty years ago, and within a day or two of the end of the grouse season. I had been out all day with my gun, and had had no sport to speak of. The wind was due east; the month, December; the place, a bleak wide moor in the far north of England. And I had lost my way. It was not a pleasant place in which to lose one's way, with the first feathery flakes of a coming snowstorm just fluttering down upon the heather, and the leaden evening closing in all around. I shaded my eyes with my hand, and staled anxiously into the gathering darkness, where the purple moorland melted into a range of low hills, some ten or twelve miles distant. Not the faintest smoke-wreath, not the tiniest cultivated patch, or fence, or sheep-track, met my eyes in any direction. There was nothing for it but to walk on, and take my chance of finding what shelter I could, by the way. So

I shouldered my gun again, and pushed wearily forward; for I had been on foot since an hour after daybreak, and had eaten nothing since breakfast.

Meanwhile, the snow began to come down with ominous steadiness, and the wind fell. After this, the cold became more intense, and the night came rapidly up. As for me, my prospects darkened with the darkening sky, and my heart grew heavy as I thought how my young wife was already watching for me through the window of our little inn parlour, and thought of all the suffering in store for her throughout this weary night. We had been married four months, and, having spent our autumn in the Highlands, were now lodging in a remote little village situated just on the verge of the great English moorlands. We were very much in love, and, of course, very happy. This morning, when we parted, she had implored me to return before dusk, and I had promised her that I would. What would I not have given to have kept my word!

Even now, weary as I was, I felt that with a supper, an hour's rest, and a guide, I might still get back to her before midnight, if only guide and shelter could be found.

And all this time, the snow fell and the night thickened. I stopped and shouted every now and then, but my shouts seemed only to make the silence deeper. Then a vague sense of uneasiness came upon me, and I began to remember stories of travellers who had walked on and on in the falling snow until, wearied out, they were fain to lie down and sleep their lives away. Would it be possible, I asked myself, to keep on thus through all the long dark night? Would there not come a time when my limbs must fail, and my resolution give way? When I, too, must sleep the sleep of death. Death! I shuddered. How hard to die just now, when life lay all so bright before me! How hard for my darling, whose whole loving heart but that thought was not to be borne! To banish it, I shouted again, louder and longer, and then listened eagerly. Was my shout answered, or did I only fancy that I heard a far-off cry? I hallooed again, and again the echo followed. Then a wavering speck of light came suddenly out of the dark, shifting, disappearing, growing momentarily nearer and brighter. Running towards it at full speed, I found myself, to my great joy, face to face with an old man and a lantern.

"Thank God!" was the exclamation that burst involuntarily from my lips.

Blinking and frowning, he lifted his lantern and peered into my face.

"What for?" growled he, sulkily.

"Well—for you. I began to fear I should be lost in the snow."

"Eh, then, folks do get cast away hereabouts fra' time to time, an' what's to hinder you from bein' cast away likewise, if the Lord's so minded?"

"If the Lord is so minded that you and I shall be lost together, friend, we must submit," I replied; "but I don't mean to be lost without you. How far am I now from Dwolding?"

"A gude twenty mile, more or less."

"And the nearest village?"

"The nearest village is Wyke, an' that's twelve mile t'other side."

"Where do you live, then?"

"Out yonder," said he, with a vague jerk of the lantern.

"You're going home, I presume?"

"Maybe I am."

"Then I'm going with you."

The old man shook his head, and rubbed his nose reflectively with the handle of the lantern.

"It ain't o' no use," growled he. "He 'ont let you in—not he."

"We'll see about that," I replied, briskly. "Who is He?"

"The master."

"Who is the master?"

"That's nowt to you," was the unceremonious reply.

"Well, well; you lead the way, and I'll engage that the master shall give me shelter and a supper to-night."

"Eh, you can try him!" muttered my reluctant guide; and, still shaking his head, he hobbled, gnome-like, away through the falling snow. A large mass loomed up presently out of the darkness, and a huge dog rushed out, barking furiously.

"Is this the house?" I asked.

"Ay, it's the house. Down, Bey!" And he fumbled in his pocket for the key.

I drew up close behind him, prepared to lose no chance of entrance, and saw in the little circle of light shed by the lantern that the door was heavily studded with iron nails, like the door of a prison. In another minute he had turned the key and I had pushed past him into the house.

Once inside, I looked round with curiosity, and found myself in a great raftered hall, which served, apparently, a variety of uses. One end was piled to the roof with corn, like a barn. The other was stored with flour-sacks, agricultural implements, casks, and all kinds of miscellaneous lumber; while from the beams overhead hung rows of hams, flitches, and bunches of dried herbs for winter use. In the centre of the floor stood some huge object gauntly dressed in a dingy wrapping-cloth, and reaching half way to the rafters. Lifting a corner of this cloth, I saw, to my surprise, a telescope of very considerable size, mounted on a rude movable platform, with four small wheels. The tube was made of painted wood, bound round with bands of metal rudely fashioned; the speculum, so far as I could estimate its size in the dim light, measured at least fifteen inches in diameter. While I was yet examining the instrument, and asking myself whether it was not the work of some self-taught optician, a bell rang sharply.

"That's for you," said my guide, with a malicious grin. "Yonder's his room."

He pointed to a low black door at the opposite side of the hall. I crossed over, rapped somewhat loudly, and went in, without waiting for an invitation. A huge, white-haired old man rose from a table covered with books and papers, and confronted me sternly.

"Who are you?" said he. "How came you here? What do you want?"

"James Murray, barrister-at-law. On foot across the moor. Meat, drink, and sleep."

He bent his bushy brows into a portentous frown.

"Mine is not a house of entertainment," he said, haughtily. "Jacob, how dared you admit this stranger?"

"I didn't admit him," grumbled the old man. "He followed me over the muir, and shouldered his way in before me. I'm no match for six foot two."

"And pray, sir, by what right have you forced an entrance into my house?"

"The same by which I should have clung to your boat, if I were drowning. The right of self-preservation."

"Self-preservation?"

"There's an inch of snow on the ground already," I replied, briefly; "and it would be deep enough to cover my body before daybreak."

He strode to the window, pulled aside a heavy black curtain, and looked out.

"It is true," he said. "You can stay, if you choose, till morning. Jacob, serve the supper."

With this he waved me to a seat, resumed his own, and became at once absorbed in the studies from which I had disturbed him.

I placed my gun in a corner, drew a chair to the hearth, and examined my quarters at leisure. Smaller and less incongruous in its arrangements than the hall, this room contained, nevertheless, much to awaken my curiosity. The floor was carpetless. The whitewashed walls were in parts scrawled over with strange diagrams, and in others covered with shelves crowded with philosophical instruments, the uses of many of which were unknown to me. On one side of the fireplace, stood a bookcase filled with dingy folios; on the other, a small organ, fantastically decorated with painted carvings of mediæval saints and devils. Through the half-opened door of a cupboard at the further end of the room, I saw a long array of geological specimens, surgical preparations, crucibles, retorts, and jars of chemicals; while on the mantelshelf beside me, amid a number of small objects, stood a model of the solar system, a small galvanic battery, and a microscope. Every chair had its burden. Every corner was heaped high with books. The very floor was littered over with maps, casts, papers, tracings, and learned lumber of all conceivable kinds.

I stared about me with an amazement increased by every fresh object upon which my eyes chanced to rest. So strange a room I had never seen; yet seemed it stranger still, to find such a room in a lone farmhouse amid those wild and solitary moors! Over and over again, I looked from my host to his surroundings, and from his surroundings back to my host, asking myself who and what he could be? His head was singularly fine; but it was more the head of a poet than of a philosopher. Broad in the temples, prominent over the eyes, and clothed with a rough profusion of perfectly white hair, it had all the ideality and much of the ruggedness that characterises the head of Louis von Beethoven. There were the same deep lines about the mouth, and the same stern furrows in the brow. There was the same concentration of expression. While I was yet observing him, the door opened, and Jacob brought in the supper. His master then closed his book, rose, and with more courtesy of manner than he had yet shown, invited me to the table.

A dish of ham and eggs, a loaf of brown bread, and a bottle

of admirable sherry, were placed before me.

"I have but the homeliest farmhouse fare to offer you, sir," said my entertainer. "Your appetite, I trust, will make up for the deficiencies of our larder."

I had already fallen upon the viands, and now protested, with the enthusiasm of a starving sportsman, that I had never eaten anything so delicious.

He bowed stiffly, and sat down to his own supper, which consisted, primitively, of a jug of milk and a basin of porridge. We ate in silence, and, when we had done, Jacob removed the tray. I then drew my chair back to the fireside. My host, somewhat to my surprise, did the same, and turning abruptly towards me, said:

"Sir, I have lived here in strict retirement for three-and-twenty years. During that time, I have not seen as many strange faces, and I have not read a single newspaper. You are the first stranger who has crossed my threshold for more than four years. Will you favour me with a few words of information respecting that outer world from which I have parted company so long?"

"Pray interrogate me," I replied. "I am heartily at your service."

He bent his head in acknowledgment; leaned forward, with his elbows resting on his knees and his chin supported in the palms of his hands; stared fixedly into the fire; and proceeded to question me.

His inquiries related chiefly to scientific matters, with the later progress of which, as applied to the practical purposes of life, he was almost wholly unacquainted. No student of science myself, I replied as well as my slight information permitted; but the task was far from easy, and I was much relieved when, passing from interrogation to discussion, he began pouring forth his own conclusions upon the facts which I had been attempting to place before him. He talked, and I listened spellbound. He talked till I believe he almost forgot my presence, and only thought aloud. I had never heard anything like it then; I have never heard anything like it since. Familiar with all systems of all philosophies, subtle in analysis, bold in generalisation, he poured forth his thoughts in an uninterrupted stream, and, still leaning forward in the same moody attitude with his eyes fixed upon the fire, wandered from topic to topic, from speculation to speculation, like an inspired dreamer. From practical science to mental philosophy; from electricity in the wire to electricity in the nerve; from Watts to Mesmer, from Mesmer to Reichenbach, from Reichenbach to Swedenborg, Spinoza, Condillac, Descartes, Berkeley, Aristotle, Plato, and the Magi and mystics of the East, were transitions which, however bewildering in their variety and scope, seemed easy and harmonious upon his lips as sequences in music. By-and-by—I forget now by what link of conjecture or illustration—he passed on to that field which lies beyond the boundary line of even conjectural philosophy, and reaches no man knows whither. He spoke of the soul and its aspirations; of the spirit and its powers; of second sight; of prophecy; of those phenomena which, under the names of ghosts, spectres, and supernatural appearances, have been denied by the sceptics and attested by the credulous, of all ages.

"The world," he said, "grows hourly more and more sceptical of all that lies beyond its own narrow radius; and our men of science foster the fatal tendency. They condemn as fable all that resists experiment. They reject as false all that cannot be brought to the test of the laboratory or the dissecting-room. Against what superstition have they waged so long and obstinate a war, as against the belief in apparitions? And yet what superstition has maintained its hold upon the minds of men so long and so firmly? Show me any fact in physics, in history, in archæology, which is supported by testimony so wide and so various. Attested by all races of men, in all ages, and in all climates, by the soberest sages of antiquity, by the rudest savage of to-day, by the Christian, the Pagan, the Pantheist, the Materialist, this phenomenon is treated as a nursery tale by the philosophers of our century. Circumstantial evidence weighs with them as a feather in the balance. The comparison of causes with effects, however valuable in physical science, is put aside as worthless and unreliable. The evidence of competent witnesses, however conclusive in a court of justice, counts for nothing. He who pauses before he pronounces, is condemned as a trifler. He who believes, is a dreamer or a fool."

He spoke with bitterness, and, having said thus, relapsed for some minutes into silence. Presently he raised his head from his hands, and added, with an altered voice and manner, "I, sir, paused, investigated, believed, and was not ashamed to state my convictions to the world. I, too, was branded as a visionary, held up to ridicule by my contemporaries, and hooted from that field of science in which I had laboured with honour during all the best years of my life. These things happened just three-and-twenty years ago. Since then, I have lived as you see me living now, and the world has forgotten me, as I have forgot—ten the world. You have my history."

"It is a very sad one," I murmured, scarcely knowing what to answer.

"It is a very common one," he replied. "I have only suffered for the truth, as many a better and wiser man has suffered before me."

He rose, as if desirous of ending the conversation, and went over to the window.

"It has ceased snowing," he observed, as he dropped the curtain, and came back to the fireside.

"Ceased!" I exclaimed, starting eagerly to my feet. "Oh, if it were only possible—but no! it is hopeless. Even if I could find my way across the moor, I could not walk twenty miles to-night."

"Walk twenty miles to-night!" repeated my host. "What are you thinking of?"

"Of my wife," I replied, impatiently. "Of my young wife, who does not know that I have lost my way, and who is at this moment breaking her heart with suspense and terror."

"Where is she?"

"At Dwolding, twenty miles away."

"At Dwolding," he echoed, thoughtfully. "Yes, the distance, it is true, is twenty miles; but—are you so very anxious to save the next six or eight hours?"

"So very, very anxious, that I would give ten guineas at this moment for a guide and a horse."

"Your wish can be gratified at a less costly rate," said he, smiling. "The night mail from the north, which changes horses at Dwolding, passes within five miles of this spot, and will be due at a certain cross-road in about an hour and a quarter. If Jacob were to go with you across the moor, and put you into the old coach-road, you could find your way, I suppose, to where it joins the new one?"

"Easily—gladly."

He smiled again, rang the bell, gave the old servant his directions, and, taking a bottle of whisky and a wineglass from the cupboard in which he kept his chemicals, said:

"The snow lies deep, and it will be difficult walking to-night on the moor. A glass of usquebaugh before you start?"

I would have declined the spirit, but he pressed it on me, and I drank it. It went down my throat like liquid flame, and almost took my breath away.

"It is strong," he said; "but it will help to keep out the cold. And now you have no moments to spare. Good night!"

I thanked him for his hospitality, and would have shaken hands, but that he had turned away before I could finish my sentence. In another minute I had traversed the hall, Jacob had locked the outer door behind me, and we were out on the wide white moor.

Although the wind had fallen, it was still bitterly cold. Not a star glimmered in the black vault overhead. Not a sound, save the rapid crunching of the snow beneath our feet, disturbed the heavy stillness of the night. Jacob, not too well pleased with his mission, shambled on before in sullen silence, his lantern in his hand, and his shadow at his feet. I followed, with my gun over my shoulder, as little inclined for conversation as himself. My thoughts were full of my late host. His voice yet rang in my ears. His eloquence yet held my imagination captive. I remember to this day, with surprise, how my over-excited brain retained whole sentences and parts of sentences, troops of brilliant images, and fragments of splendid reasoning, in the very words in which he had uttered them. Musing thus over what I had heard, and striving to recall a lost link here and there, I strode on at the heels of my guide, absorbed and unobservant. Presently—at the end, as it seemed to me, of only a few minutes—he came to a sudden halt, and said:

"Yon's your road. Keep the stone fence to your right hand, and you can't fail of the way."

"This, then, is the old coach-road?"

"Ay, 'tis the old coach-road."

"And how far do I go, before I reach the cross-roads?"

"Nigh upon three mile."

I pulled out my purse, and he became more communicative.

"The road's a fair road enough," said he, "for foot passengers; but 'twas over steep and narrow for the northern traffic. You'll mind where the parapet's broken away, close again the sign-post. It's never been mended since the accident."

"What accident?"

"Eh, the night mail pitched right over into the valley below—a gude fifty feet an' more—just at the worst bit o' road in the whole county."

"Horrible! Were many lives lost?"

"All. Four were found dead, and t'other two died next morning."

"How long is it since this happened?"

"Just nine year."

"Near the sign-post, you say? I will bear it in mind. Good night."

"Gude night, sir, and thankee." Jacob pocketed his half-crown, made a faint pretence of touching his hat, and trudged back by the way he had come.

I watched the light of his lantern till it quite disappeared, and then turned to pursue my way alone. This was no longer matter of the slightest difficulty, for, despite the dead darkness overhead, the line of stone fence showed distinctly enough against the pale gleam of the snow. How silent it seemed now, with only my footsteps to listen to; how silent and how solitary! A strange disagreeable sense of loneliness stole over me. I walked faster. I hummed a fragment of a tune. I cast up enormous sums in my head, and accumulated them at compound interest. I did my best, in short, to forget the startling speculations to which I had but just been listening, and, to some extent, I succeeded.

Meanwhile the night air seemed to become colder and colder, and though I walked fast I found it impossible to keep myself warm. My feet were like ice. I lost sensation in my hands, and grasped my gun mechanically. I even breathed with difficulty, as though, instead of traversing a quiet north country highway, I were scaling the uppermost heights of some gigantic Alp. This last symptom became presently so distressing, that I was forced to stop for a few minutes, and lean against the stone fence. As I did so, I chanced to look back up the road, and there, to my infinite relief, I saw a distant point of light, like the gleam of an approaching lantern. I at first concluded that Jacob had retraced his steps and followed me; but even as the conjecture presented itself, a second light flashed into sight—a light evidently parallel with the first, and approaching at the same rate of motion. It needed no second thought to show me that these must be the carriage-lamps of some private vehicle, though it seemed strange that any private vehicle should take a road professedly disused and dangerous.

There could be no doubt, however, of the fact, for the lamps grew larger and brighter every moment, and I even fancied I could already see the dark outline of the carriage between them. It was coming up very fast, and quite noiselessly, the snow being nearly a foot deep under the wheels.

And now the body of the vehicle became distinctly visible behind the lamps. It looked strangely lofty. A sudden suspicion flashed upon me. Was it possible that I had passed the cross-roads in the dark without observing the sign-post, and could this be the very coach which I had come to meet?

No need to ask myself that question a second time, for here it came round the bend of the road, guard and driver, one outside passenger, and four steaming greys, all wrapped in a soft haze of light, through which the lamps blazed out, like a pair of fiery meteors.

I jumped forward, waved my hat, and shouted. The mail came down at full speed, and passed me. For a moment I feared that I had not been seen or heard, but it was only for a moment. The coachman pulled up; the guard, muffled to the eyes in capes and comforters, and apparently sound asleep in the rumble, neither answered my hail nor made the slightest effort to dismount; the outside passenger did not even turn his head. I opened the door for myself, and looked in. There were but three travellers inside, so I stepped in, shut the door, slipped into the vacant corner, and congratulated myself on my good fortune.

The atmosphere of the coach seemed, if possible, colder than that of the outer air, and was pervaded by a singularly damp and disagreeable smell. I looked round at my fellow-passengers. They were all three, men, and all silent. They did not seem to be asleep, but each leaned back in his corner of the vehicle, as if absorbed in his own reflections. I attempted to open a conversation.

"How intensely cold it is to-night," I said, addressing my opposite neighbour.

He lifted his head, looked at me, but made no reply.

"The winter," I added, "seems to have begun in earnest."

Although the corner in which he sat was so dim that I could distinguish none of his features very clearly, I saw that his eyes were still turned full upon me. And yet he answered never a word.

At any other time I should have felt, and perhaps expressed, some annoyance, but at the moment I felt too ill to do either. The icy coldness of the night air had struck a chill to my very marrow, and the strange smell inside the coach was affecting me with an intolerable nausea. I shivered from head to foot, and, turning to my left-hand neighbour, asked if he had any objection to an open window?

He neither spoke nor stirred.

I repeated the question somewhat more loudly, but with the same result. Then I lost patience, and let the sash down. As I did so, the leather strap broke in my hand, and I observed that the glass was covered with a thick coat of mildew, the accumulation, apparently, of years. My attention being thus drawn to the condition of the coach, I examined it more narrowly, and saw by the uncertain light of the outer lamps that it was in the last stage of dilapidation. Every part of it was not only out of repair, but in a condition of decay. The sashes splintered at a touch. The leather fittings were crusted over with mould, and literally rotting from the woodwork. The floor was almost breaking away beneath my feet. The whole machine, in short, was foul with damp, and had evidently been dragged from some outhouse in which it had been mouldering away for years, to do another day or two of duty on the road.

I turned to the third passenger, whom I had not yet addressed, and hazarded one more remark.

"This coach," I said, "is in a deplorable condition. The regular mail, I suppose, is under repair?"

He moved his head slowly, and looked me in the face, without speaking a word. I shall never forget that look while I live. I turned cold at heart under it. I turn cold at heart even now when I recall it. His eyes glowed with a fiery unnatural lustre. His face was livid as the face of a corpse. His bloodless lips were drawn back as if in the agony of death, and showed the gleaming teeth between.

The words that I was about to utter died upon my lips, and a strange horror—a dreadful horror—came upon me. My sight had by this time become used to the gloom of the coach, and I could see with tolerable distinctness. I turned to my opposite neighbour. He, too, was looking at me, with the same startling pallor in his face, and the same stony glitter in his eyes. I passed my hand across my brow. I turned to the passenger on the seat beside my own, and saw—oh Heaven! how shall I describe what I saw? I saw that he was no living man—that none of them were living men, like myself! A pale phosphorescent light—the light of putrefaction—played upon their awful faces; upon their hair, dank with the dews of the grave; upon their clothes, earth-stained and dropping to pieces; upon their hands, which were as the hands of corpses long buried. Only their eyes, their terrible eyes, were living; and those eyes were all turned menacingly upon me!

A shriek of terror, a wild unintelligible cry for help and mercy; burst from my lips as I flung myself against the door, and strove in vain to open it.

In that single instant, brief and vivid as a landscape beheld in the flash of summer lightning, I saw the moon shining down through a rift of stormy cloud—the ghastly sign-post rearing its warning finger by the wayside—the broken parapet—the plunging horses—the black gulf below. Then, the coach reeled like a ship at sea. Then, came a mighty crash—a sense of crushing pain—and then, darkness.

It seemed as if years had gone by when I awoke one morning from a deep sleep, and found my wife watching by my bedside I will pass over the scene that ensued, and give you, in half a dozen words, the tale she told me with tears of thanksgiving. I had fallen over a precipice, close against the junction of the old coach-road and the new, and had only been saved from certain death by lighting upon a deep snowdrift that had accumulated at the foot of the rock beneath. In this snowdrift I was discovered at daybreak, by a couple of shepherds, who carried me to the nearest shelter, and brought a surgeon to my aid. The surgeon found me in a state of raving delirium, with a broken arm and a compound fracture of the skull. The letters in my pocket-book showed my name and address; my wife was summoned to nurse me; and, thanks to youth and a fine constitution, I came out of danger at last. The place of my fall, I need scarcely say, was precisely that at which a frightful accident had happened to the north mail nine years before.

I never told my wife the fearful events which I have just related to you. I told the surgeon who attended me; but he treated the whole adventure as a mere dream born of the fever in my brain. We discussed the question over and over again, until we found that we could discuss it with temper no longer, and then we dropped it. Others may form what conclusions they please—I know that twenty years ago I was the fourth inside passenger in that Phantom Coach.

46

THE SECRET OF THE TWO PLASTER CASTS

J.S. Le Fanu

Years before the accession of her Majesty Queen Victoria, and yet at not so remote a date as to be utterly beyond the period to which the reminiscences of our middle-aged readers extend, it happened that two English gentlemen sat at table on a summer's evening, after dinner, quietly sipping their wine and engaged in desultory conversation. They were both men known to fame. One of them was a sculptor whose statues adorned the palaces of princes, and whose chiselled busts were the pride of half the nobility of his nation; the other was no less renowned as an anatomist and surgeon. The age of the anatomist might have been guessed at fifty, but the guess would have erred on the side of youth by at least ten years. That of the sculptor could scarcely be more than five-and-thirty. A bust of the anatomist, so admirably executed as to present, although in stone, the perfect similitude of life and flesh, stood upon a pedestal opposite to the table at which sat the pair, and at once explained at least one connecting-link of companionship between them. The anatomist was exhibiting for the criticism of his friend a rare gem which he had just drawn from his cabinet: it was a crucifix magnificently carved in ivory, and incased in a setting of pure gold.

"The carving, my dear sir," observed Mr. Fiddyes, the sculptor, "is indeed, as you say, exquisite. The muscles are admirably made out, the flesh well modelled, wonderfully so for the size and material; and yet—by the bye, on this point you must know more than I—the more I think upon the matter, the more I regard the artistic conception as utterly false and wrong."

"You speak in a riddle," replied Dr. Carnell; "but pray go on, and explain."

"It is a fancy I first had in my student-days," replied Fiddyes. "Conventionality, not to say a most proper and becoming reverence, prevents people by no means ignorant from considering the point. But once think upon it, and you at least, of all men, must at once perceive how utterly impossible it would be for a victim nailed upon a cross by hands and feet to preserve the position invariably displayed in figures of the Crucifixion. Those who so portray it fail in what should be their most awful and agonizing effect. Think for one moment, and imagine, if you can, what would be the attitude of a man, living or dead, under this frightful torture."

"You startle me," returned the great surgeon, "not only by the truth of your remarks, but by their obviousness. It is strange indeed that such a matter should have so long been overlooked. The more I think upon it the more the bare idea of actual crucifixion seems to horrify me, though heaven knows I am accustomed enough to scenes of suffering. How would you represent such a terrible agony?"

"Indeed I cannot tell," replied the sculptor; "to guess would be almost vain. The fearful strain upon the muscles, their utter helplessness and inactivity, the frightful swellings, the effect of weight upon the racked and tortured sinews, appal me too much even for speculation."

"But this," replied the surgeon, "one might think a matter of importance, not only to art, but, higher still, to religion itself."

"Maybe so," returned the sculptor. "But perhaps the appeal to the senses through a true representation might be too horrible for either the one or the other."

"Still," persisted the surgeon, "I should like—say for curiosity—though I am weak enough to believe even in my own motive as a higher one—to ascertain the effect from actual observation."

"So should I, could it be done, and of course without pain to the object, which, as a condition, seems to present at the outset an impossibility."

"Perhaps not," mused the anatomist; "I think I have a notion. Stay—we may contrive this matter. I will tell you my plan, and it will be strange indeed if we two cannot manage to carry it out."

The discourse here, owing to the rapt attention of both speakers, assumed a low and earnest tone, but had perhaps better be narrated by a relation of the events to which it gave rise. Suffice it to say that the Sovereign was more than once mentioned during its progress, and in a manner which plainly told that the two speakers each possessed sufficient influence to obtain the assistance of royalty, and that such assistance would be required in their scheme.

The shades of evening deepened while the two were still conversing. And leaving this scene, let us cast one hurried glimpse at another taking place contemporaneously.

Between Pimlico and Chelsea, and across a canal of which the bed has since been used for the railway terminating at Victoria Station, there was at the time of which we speak a rude timber footway, long since replaced by a more substantial and convenient erection, but then known as the Wooden Bridge. It was named shortly afterward Cutthroat Bridge, and for this reason.

While Mr. Fiddyes and Dr. Carnell were discoursing over their wine, as we have already seen, one Peter Starke, a drunken Chelsea pensioner, was murdering his wife upon the spot we have last indicated. The coincidence was curious.

In those days the punishment of criminals followed closely upon their conviction. The Chelsea pensioner whom we have mentioned was found guilty one Friday and sentenced to die on the following Monday. He was a sad scoundrel, impenitent to the last, glorying in the deeds of slaughter which he had witnessed and acted during the series of campaigns which had ended just previously at Waterloo. He was a tall, well-built fellow enough, of middle age, for his class was not then, as now, composed chiefly of veterans, but comprised many young men, just sufficiently disabled to be unfit for service. Peter Starke, although but slightly wounded, had nearly completed his term of service, and had obtained his pension and presentment to Chelsea Hospital. With his life we have but little to do, save as regards its close, which we shall shortly endeavor to describe far more veraciously, and at some greater length than set forth in the brief account which satisfied the public of his own day, and which, as embodied in the columns of the few journals then appearing, ran thus:

"On Monday last Peter Starke was executed at Newgate for the murder at the Wooden Bridge, Chelsea, with four others for various offences. After he had been hanging only for a few minutes a respite arrived, but although he was promptly cut down, life was pronounced to be extinct. His body was buried within the prison walls."

Thus far history. But the conciseness of history far more frequently embodies falsehood than truth. Perhaps the following narration may approach more nearly to the facts.

A room within the prison had been, upon that special occasion and by high authority, allotted to the use of Dr. Carnell and Mr. Fiddyes, the famous sculptor, for the purpose of certain investigations connected with art and science. In that room Mr. Fiddyes, while wretched Peter Starke was yet swinging between heaven and earth, was busily engaged in arranging a variety of implements and materials, consisting of a large quantity of plaster-of-Paris, two large pails of water, some tubs, and other necessaries of the moulder's art. The room contained a large deal table, and a wooden cross, not neatly planed and squared at the angles, but of thick, narrow, rudely-sawn oaken plank, fixed by strong, heavy nails. And while Mr. Fiddyes was thus occupied, the executioner entered, bearing upon his shoulders the body of the wretched Peter, which he flung heavily upon the table.

"You are sure he is dead?" asked Mr. Fiddyes.

"Dead as a herring," replied the other. "And yet just as warm and limp as if he had only fainted."

"Then go to work at once," replied the sculptor, as turning his back upon the hangman, he resumed his occupation.

The "work" was soon done. Peter was stripped and nailed upon the timber, which was instantly propped against the wall.

"As fine a one as ever I see," exclaimed the executioner, as he regarded the defunct murderer with an expression of admiration, as if at his own handiwork, in having abruptly demolished such a magnificent animal. "Drops a good bit for'ard, though. Shall I tie him up round the waist, sir?"

"Certainly not," returned the sculptor. "Just rub him well over with this oil, especially his head, and then you can go. Dr. Carnell will settle with you."

"All right, sir."

The fellow did as ordered, and retired without another word; leaving this strange couple, the living and the dead, in that dismal chamber.

Mr. Fiddyes was a man of strong nerve in such matters. He had been too much accustomed to taking posthumous casts to trouble himself with any sentiment of repugnance at his approaching task of taking what is called a "piece-mould" from a body. He emptied a number of bags of the white powdery plaster-of-Paris into one of the larger vessels, poured into it a pail of water, and was carefully stirring up the mass, when a sound of dropping arrested his ear.

Drip, drip.

"There's something leaking," he muttered, as he took a second pail, and emptying it, again stirred the composition.

Drip, drip, drip.

"It's strange," he soliloquized, half aloud. "There is no more water, and yet——"

The sound was heard again.

He gazed at the ceiling; there was no sign of damp. He turned his eyes to the body, and something suddenly caused him a violent start. The murderer was bleeding.

The sculptor, spite of his command over himself, turned pale. At that moment the head of Starke moved—clearly moved. It raised itself convulsively for a single moment; its eyes rolled, and it gave vent to a subdued moan of intense agony. Mr. Fiddyes fell fainting on the floor as Dr. Carnell entered. It needed but a glance to tell the doctor what had happened, even had not Peter just then given vent to another low cry. The surgeon's measures were soon taken. Locking the door, he bore a chair to the wall which supported the body of the malefactor. He drew from his pocket a case of glittering instruments, and with one of these, so small and delicate that it scarcely seemed larger than a needle, he rapidly, but dexterously and firmly, touched Peter just at the back of the neck. There was no wound larger than the head of a small pin, and yet the head fell instantly as though the heart had been pierced. The doctor had divided the spinal cord, and Peter Starke was dead indeed.

A few minutes sufficed to recall the sculptor to his senses. He at first gazed wildly upon the still suspended body, so painfully recalled to life by the rough venesection of the hangman and the subsequent friction of anointing his body to prevent the adhesion of the plaster.

"You need not fear now," said Dr. Carnell; "I assure you he is dead."

"But he *was* alive, surely!"

"Only for a moment, and even that scarcely to be called life—mere muscular contraction, my dear sir, mere muscular contraction."

The sculptor resumed his labor. The body was girt at various circumferences with fine twine, to be afterward withdrawn through a thick coating of plaster, so as to separate the various pieces of the mould, which was at last completed; and after this Dr. Carnell skilfully flayed the body, to enable a second mould to be taken of the entire figure, showing every muscle of the outer layer.

The two moulds were thus taken. It is difficult to conceive more ghastly appearances than they presented. For sculptor's work they were utterly useless; for no artist except the most daring of realists would have ventured to indicate the horrors which they presented. Fiddyes refused to receive them. Dr. Carnell, hard and cruel as he was, for kindness' sake, in his profession, was a gentle, genial father of a family of daughters. He received the casts, and at once consigned them to a garret, to which he forbade access. His youngest daughter, one unfortunate day, during her father's absence, was impelled by feminine curiosity—perhaps a little increased by the prohibition—to enter the mysterious chamber.

Whether she imagined in the pallid figure upon the cross a celestial rebuke for her disobedience, or whether she was overcome by the mere mortal horror of one or both of those dreadful casts, can now never be known. But this is true: she became a maniac.

The writer of this has more than once seen (as, no doubt, have many others) the plaster effigies of Peter Starke, after their removal from Dr. Carnell's to a famous studio near the Regent's Park. It was there that he heard whispered the strange story of their origin. Sculptor and surgeon are now both long since dead, and it is no longer necessary to keep *the secret of the two plaster casts*.

MADEMOISELLE COCOTTE

Guy de Maupassant

We were just leaving the asylum when I saw a tall, thin man in a corner of the court who kept on calling an imaginary dog. He was crying in a soft, tender voice: "Cocotte! Come here, Cocotte, my beauty!" and slapping his thigh as one does when calling an animal. I asked the physician, "Who is that man?" He answered: "Oh! he is not at all interesting. He is a coachman named Francois, who became insane after drowning his dog."

I insisted: "Tell me his story. The most simple and humble things are sometimes those which touch our hearts most deeply."

Here is this man's adventure, which was obtained from a friend of his, a groom:

There was a family of rich bourgeois who lived in a suburb of Paris. They had a villa in the middle of a park, at the edge of the Seine. Their coachman was this Francois, a country fellow, somewhat dull, kind-hearted, simple and easy to deceive.

One evening, as he was returning home, a dog began to follow him. At first he paid no attention to it, but the creature's obstinacy at last made him turn round. He looked to see if he knew this dog. No, he had never seen it. It was a female dog and frightfully thin. She was trotting behind him with a mournful and famished look, her tail between her legs, her ears flattened against her head and stopping and starting whenever he did.

He tried to chase this skeleton away and cried:

"Run along! Get out! Kss! kss!" She retreated a few steps, then sat down and waited. And when the coachman started to walk again she followed along behind him.

He pretended to pick up some stones. The animal ran a little farther away, but came back again as soon as the man's back was turned.

Then the coachman Francois took pity on the beast and called her. The dog approached timidly. The man patted her protruding ribs, moved by the beast's misery, and he cried: "Come! come here!" Immediately she began to wag her tail, and, feeling herself taken in, adopted, she began to run along ahead of her new master.

He made her a bed on the straw in the stable, then he ran to the kitchen for some bread. When she had eaten all she could she curled up and went to sleep.

When his employers heard of this the next day they allowed the coachman to keep the animal. It was a good beast, caressing and faithful, intelligent and gentle.

Nevertheless Francois adored Cocotte, and he kept repeating: "That beast is human. She only lacks speech."

He had a magnificent red leather collar made for her which bore these words engraved on a copper plate: "Mademoiselle Cocotte, belonging to the coachman Francois."

She was remarkably prolific and four times a year would give birth to a batch of little animals belonging to every variety of the canine race. Francois would pick out one which he would leave her and then he would unmercifully throw the others into the river. But soon the cook joined her complaints to those of the gardener. She would find dogs under the stove, in the ice box, in the coal bin, and they would steal everything they came across.

Finally the master, tired of complaints, impatiently ordered Francois to get rid of Cocotte. In despair the man tried to give her away. Nobody wanted her. Then he decided to lose her, and he gave her to a teamster, who was to drop her on the other side of Paris, near Joinville-le-Pont.

Cocotte returned the same day. Some decision had to be taken. Five francs was given to a train conductor to take her to Havre. He was to drop her there.

Three days later she returned to the stable, thin, footsore and tired out.

The master took pity on her and let her stay. But other dogs were attracted as before, and one evening, when a big dinner party was on, a stuffed turkey was carried away by one of them right under the cook's nose, and she did not dare to stop him.

This time the master completely lost his temper and said angrily to Francois: "If you don't throw this beast into the water before—to-morrow morning, I'll put you out, do you hear?"

The man was dumbfounded, and he returned to his room to pack his trunk, preferring to leave the place. Then he bethought himself that he could find no other situation as long as he dragged this animal about with him. He thought of his good position, where he was well paid and well fed, and he decided that a dog was really not worth all that. At last he decided to rid himself of Cocotte at daybreak.

He slept badly. He rose at dawn, and taking a strong rope, went to get the dog. She stood up slowly, shook herself, stretched and came to welcome her master.

Then his courage forsook him, and he began to pet her affectionately, stroking her long ears, kissing her muzzle and calling her tender names.

But a neighboring clock struck six. He could no longer hesitate. He opened the door, calling: "Come!" The beast wagged her tail, understanding that she was to be taken out.

They reached the beach, and he chose a place where the water seemed deep. Then he knotted the rope round the leather collar and tied a heavy stone to the other end. He seized Cocotte in his arms and kissed her madly, as though he were taking leave of some human being. He held her to his breast, rocked her and called her "my dear little Cocotte, my sweet little Cocotte," and she grunted with pleasure.

Ten times he tried to throw her into the water and each time he lost courage.

But suddenly he made up his mind and threw her as far from him as he could. At first she tried to swim, as she did when he gave her a bath, but her head, dragged down by the stone, kept going under, and she looked at her master with wild, human glances as she struggled like a drowning person. Then the front part of her body sank, while her hind legs waved wildly out of the water. Finally those also disappeared.

Then, for five minutes, bubbles rose to the surface as though the river were boiling, and Francois, haggard, his heart beating, thought that he saw Cocotte struggling in the mud, and, with the simplicity of a peasant, he kept saying to himself: "What does the poor beast think of me now?"

He almost lost his mind. He was ill for a month and every night he dreamed of his dog. He could feel her licking his hands and hear her barking. It was necessary to call in a physician. At last he recovered, and toward the 2nd of June his employers took him to their estate at Biesard, near Rouen.

There again he was near the Seine. He began to take baths. Each morning he would go down with the groom and they would swim across the river.

One day, as they were disporting themselves in the water, Francois suddenly cried to his companion: "Look what's coming! I'm going to give you a chop!"

It was an enormous, swollen corpse that was floating down with its feet sticking straight up in the air.

Francois swam up to it, still joking: "Whew! it's not fresh. What a catch, old man! It isn't thin, either!" He kept swimming about at a distance from the animal that was in a state of decomposition. Then, suddenly, he was silent and looked at it: attentively. This time he came near enough to touch it. He looked fixedly at the collar, then he stretched out his arm, seized the neck, swung the corpse round and drew it up close to him and read on the copper which had turned green and which still stuck to the discolored leather: "Mademoiselle Cocotte, belonging to the coachman Francois."

The dead dog had come more than a hundred miles to find its master.

He let out a frightful shriek and began to swim for the beach with all his might, still howling; and as soon as he touched land he ran away wildly, stark naked, through the country. He was insane!

48

BRICKETT BOTTOM

Amyas Northcote

The Reverend Arthur Maydew was the hard-working incumbent of a large parish in one of our manufacturing towns. He was also a student and a man of no strong physique, so that when an opportunity was presented to him to take an annual holiday by exchanging parsonages with an elderly clergyman, Mr. Roberts, the Squarson of the Parish of Overbury, and an acquaintance of his own, he was glad to avail himself of it.

Overbury is a small and very remote village in one of our most lovely and rural counties, and Mr. Roberts had long held the living of it.

Without further delay we can transport Mr. Maydew and his family, which consisted only of two daughters, to their temporary home. The two young ladies, Alice and Maggie, the heroines of this narrative, were at that time aged twenty-six and twenty-four years respectively. Both of them were attractive girls, fond of such society as they could find in their own parish and, the former especially, always pleased to extend the circle of their acquaintance. Although the elder in years, Alice in many ways yielded place to her sister, who was the more energetic and practical and upon whose shoulders the bulk of the family cares and responsibilities rested. Alice was inclined to be absent-minded and emotional and to devote more of her thoughts and time to speculations of an abstract nature than her sister.

Both of the girls, however, rejoiced at the prospect of a period of quiet and rest in a pleasant country neighbourhood, and both were gratified at knowing that their father would find in Mr. Roberts' library much that would entertain his mind, and in Mr. Roberts' garden an opportunity to indulge freely in his favourite game of croquet. They would have, no doubt, preferred some cheerful neighbours, but Mr. Roberts was positive in his assurances that there was no one in the neighbourhood whose acquaintance would be of interest to them.

The first few weeks of their new life passed pleasantly for the Maydew family. Mr. Maydew quickly gained renewed vigour in his quiet and congenial surroundings, and in the delightful air, while his daughters spent much of their time in long walks about the country and in exploring its beauties.

One evening late in August the two girls were returning from a long walk along one of their favourite paths, which led along the side of the Downs. On their right, as they walked, the ground fell away sharply to a narrow glen, named Brickett Bottom, about three-quarters of a mile in length, along the bottom of which ran a little-used country road leading to a farm, known as Blaise's Farm, and then onward and upward to lose itself as a sheep track on the higher Downs.

On their side of the slope some scattered trees and bushes grew, but beyond the lane and running up over the farther slope of the glen was a thick wood, which extended away to Carew Court, the seat of a neighbouring magnate, Lord Carew. On their left the open Down rose above them and beyond its crest lay Overbury.

The girls were walking hastily, as they were later than they had intended to be and were anxious to reach home. At a certain point at which they had now arrived the path forked, the right hand branch leading down into Brickett Bottom and the left hand turning up over the Down to Overbury.

Just as they were about to turn into the left hand path Alice suddenly stopped and pointing downwards exclaimed: "How very curious, Maggie! Look, there is a house down there in the Bottom, which we have, or at least I have, never noticed before, often as we have walked up the Bottom."

Maggie followed with her eyes her sister's pointing finger.

"I don't see any house," she said.

"Why, Maggie," said her sister, "can't you see it! A quaint-looking, old-fashioned red brick house, there just where the road bends to the right. It seems to be standing in a nice, well-kept garden too."

Maggie looked again, but the light was beginning to fade in the glen and she was short-sighted to boot.

"I certainly don't see anything," she said, "but then I am so blind and the light is getting bad; yes, perhaps I do see a house," she added, straining her eyes.

"Well, it is there," replied her sister, "and to-morrow we will come and explore it."

Maggie agreed readily enough, and the sisters went home, still speculating on how they had happened not to notice the house before and resolving firmly on an expedition thither the next day. However, the expedition did not come off as planned, for that evening Maggie slipped on the stairs and fell, spraining her ankle in such a fashion as to preclude walking for some time.

Notwithstanding the accident to her sister, Alice remained possessed by the idea of making further investigations into the house she had looked down upon from the hill the evening before; and the next day, having seen Maggie carefully settled for the afternoon, she started off for Brickett Bottom. She returned in triumph and much intrigued over her discoveries, which she eagerly narrated to her sister.

Yes. There was a nice, old-fashioned red brick house, not very large and set in a charming, old-world garden in the Bottom. It stood on a tongue of land jutting out from the woods, just at the point where the lane, after a fairly straight course from its junction with the main road half a mile away, turned sharply to the right in the direction of Blaise's Farm. More than that, Alice had seen the people of the house, whom she described as an old gentleman and a lady, presumably his wife. She had not clearly made out the gentleman, who was sitting in the porch, but the old lady, who had been in the garden busy with her flowers, had looked up and smiled pleasantly at her as she passed. She was sure, she said, that they were nice people and that it would be pleasant to make their acquaintance.

Maggie was not quite satisfied with Alice's story. She was of a more prudent and retiring nature than her sister; she had an uneasy feeling that, if the old couple had been desirable or attractive neighbours, Mr. Roberts would have mentioned them, and knowing Alice's nature she said what she could to discourage her vague idea of endeavouring to make acquaintance with the owners of the red brick house.

On the following morning, when Alice came to her sister's room to inquire how she did, Maggie noticed that she looked pale and rather absent-minded, and, after a few commonplace remarks had passed, she asked:

"What is the matter, Alice? You don't look yourself this morning."

Her sister gave a slightly embarrassed laugh.

"Oh, I am all right," she replied, "only I did not sleep very well. I kept on dreaming about the house. It was such an odd dream too the house seemed to be home, and yet to be different."

"What, that house in Brickett Bottom?" said Maggie. "Why, what is the matter with you, you seem to be quite crazy about the place?"

"Well, it is curious, isn't it, Maggie, that we should have only just discovered it, and that it looks to be lived in by nice people? I wish we could get to know them."

Maggie did not care to resume the argument of the night

before and the subject dropped, nor did Alice again refer to the house or its inhabitants for some little time. In fact, for some days the weather was wet and Alice was forced to abandon her walks, but when the weather once more became fine she resumed them, and Maggie suspected that Brickett Bottom formed one of her sister's favourite expeditions. Maggie became anxious over her sister, who seemed to grow daily more absent-minded and silent, but she refused to be drawn into any confidential talk, and Maggie was nonplussed.

One day, however, Alice returned from her afternoon walk in an unusually excited state of mind, of which Maggie sought an explanation. It came with a rush. Alice said that, that afternoon, as she approached the house in Brickett Bottom, the old lady, who as usual was busy in her garden, had walked down to the gate as she passed and had wished her good day.

Alice had replied and, pausing, a short conversation had followed. Alice could not remember the exact tenor of it, but, after she had paid a compliment to the old lady's flowers, the latter had rather diffidently asked her to enter the garden for a closer view. Alice had hesitated, and the old lady had said "Don't be afraid of me, my dear, I like to see young ladies about me and my husband finds their society quite necessary to him." After a pause she went on: "Of course nobody has told you about us. My husband is Colonel Paxton, late of the Indian Army, and we have been here for many, many years. It's rather lonely, for so few people ever see us. Do come in and meet the Colonel."

"I hope you didn't go in," said Maggie rather sharply.

"Why not?" replied Alice.

"Well, I don't like Mrs. Paxton asking you in that way," answered Maggie.

"I don't see what harm there was in the invitation," said Alice.

"I didn't go in because it was getting late and I was anxious to get home; but—"

"But what?" asked Maggie.

Alice shrugged her shoulders.

"Well," she said, "I have accepted Mrs. Paxton's invitation to pay her a little visit to-morrow."

And she gazed defiantly at Maggie.

Maggie became distinctly uneasy on hearing of this resolution. She did not like the idea of her impulsive sister visiting people on such slight acquaintance, especially as they had never heard them mentioned before. She endeavoured by all means, short of appealing to Mr. Maydew, to dissuade her sister from going, at any rate until there had been time to make some inquiries as to the Paxtons. Alice, however, was obdurate.

What harm could happen to her? she asked. Mrs. Paxton was a charming old lady. She was going early in the afternoon for a short visit. She would be back for tea and croquet with her father and, anyway, now that Maggie was laid up, long solitary walks were unendurable and she was not going to let slip the chance of following up what promised to be a pleasant acquaintance.

Maggie could do nothing more. Her ankle was better and she was able to get down to the garden and sit in a long chair near her father, but walking was still quite out of the question, and it was with some misgivings that on the following day she watched Alice depart gaily for her visit, promising to be back by half-past four at the very latest.

The afternoon passed quietly till nearly five, when Mr. Maydew, looking up from his book, noticed Maggie's uneasy expression and asked:

"Where is Alice?"

"Out for a walk," replied Maggie; and then after a short pause she went on: "And she has also gone to pay a call on some neighbours whom she has recently discovered."

"Neighbours," ejaculated Mr. Maydew, "what neighbours? Mr. Roberts never spoke of any neighbours to me."

"Well, I don't know much about them," answered Maggie. "Only Alice and I were out walking the day of my accident and saw or at least she saw, for I am so blind I could not quite make it out, a house in Brickett Bottom. The next day she went to look at it closer, and yesterday she told me that she had made the acquaintance of the people living in it. She says that they are a retired Indian officer and his wife, a Colonel and Mrs. Paxton, and Alice describes Mrs. Paxton as a charming old lady, who pressed her to come and see them. So she has gone this afternoon, but she promised me she would be back long before this."

Mr. Maydew was silent for a moment and then said:

"I am not well pleased about this. Alice should not be so impulsive and scrape acquaintance with absolutely unknown people. Had there been nice neighbours in Brickett Bottom, I am certain Mr. Roberts would have told us."

The conversation dropped; but both father and daughter were disturbed and uneasy and, tea having been finished and the clock striking half-past five, Mr. Maydew asked Maggie:

"When did you say Alice would be back?"

"Before half-past four at the latest, father."

"Well, what can she be doing? What can have delayed her? You say you did not see the house," he went on.

"No," said Maggie, "I cannot say I did. It was getting dark and you know how short-sighted I am."

"But surely you must have seen it at some other time," said her father.

"That is the strangest part of the whole affair," answered Maggie. "We have often walked up the Bottom, but I never noticed the house, nor had Alice till that evening. I wonder," she went on after a short pause, "if it would not be well to ask Smith to harness the pony and drive over to bring her back. I am not happy about her—I am afraid—"

"Afraid of what?" said her father in the irritated voice of a man who is growing frightened.

"What can have gone wrong in this quiet place? Still, I'll send Smith over for her."

So saying he rose from his chair and sought out Smith, the rather dull-witted gardener-groom attached to Mr. Roberts' service.

"Smith," he said, "I want you to harness the pony at once and go over to Colonel Paxton's in Brickett Bottom and bring Miss Maydew home."

The man stared at him.

"Go where, sir?" he said.

Mr. Maydew repeated the order and the man, still staring stupidly, answered:

"I never heard of Colonel Paxton, sir. I don't know what house you mean."

Mr. Maydew was now growing really anxious.

"Well, harness the pony at once," he said; and going back to Maggie he told her of what he called Smith's stupidity, and asked her if she felt that her ankle would be strong enough to permit her to go with him and Smith to the Bottom to point out the house.

Maggie agreed readily and in a few minutes the party started off. Brickett Bottom, although not more than three-quarters of a mile away over the Downs, was at least three miles by road; and as it was nearly six o'clock before Mr. Maydew left time Vicarage, and the pony was old and slow, it was getting late before the entrance to Brickett Bottom was reached. Turning into the lane the cart proceeded slowly up the Bottom, Mr. Maydew and Maggie looking anxiously from side to side, whilst Smith drove stolidly on looking neither to time right nor left.

"Where is the house?" said Mr. Maydew presently.

"At the bend of the road," answered Maggie, her heart sickening as she looked out through the failing light to see the trees stretching their ranks in unbroken formation along it. The cart reached the bend. "It should be here," whispered Maggie.

They pulled up. Just in front of them the road bent to the right round a tongue of land, which, unlike the rest of the right hand side of the road, was free from trees and was covered only by rough grass and stray bushes. A closer inspection disclosed evident signs of terraces having once been formed on it, but of a house there was no trace.

"Is this the place?" said Mr. Maydew in a low voice.

Maggie nodded.

"But there is no house here," said her father. "What does it all mean? Are you sure of yourself, Maggie? Where is Alice?"

Before Maggie could answer a voice was heard calling "Father! Maggie!" The sound of the voice was thin and high and, paradoxically, it sounded both very near and yet as if it came from some infinite distance. The cry was thrice repeated and then silence fell. Mr. Maydew and Maggie stared at each other.

"That was Alice's voice," said Mr. Maydew huskily, "she is near and in trouble, and is calling us. Which way did you think it came from, Smith?" he added, turning to the gardener.

"I didn't hear anybody calling," said the man.

"Nonsense!" answered Mr. Maydew.

And then he and Maggie both began to call "Alice. Alice. Where are you?" There was no reply and Mr. Maydew sprang from the cart, at the same time bidding Smith to hand the reins to Maggie and come and search for the missing girl. Smith obeyed him and both men, scrambling up the turfy bit of ground, began to search and call through the neighbouring wood. They heard and saw nothing, however, and after an agonised search Mr. Maydew ran down to the cart and begged Maggie to drive on to Blaise's Farm for help leaving himself and Smith to continue the search. Maggie followed her father's instructions and was fortunate enough to find Mr. Rumbold, the farmer, his two sons and a couple of labourers just returning from the harvest field.

She explained what had happened, and the farmer and his men promptly volunteered to form a search party, though Maggie, in spite of her anxiety, noticed a queer expression on Mr. Rumbold's face as she told him her tale.

The party, provided with lanterns, now went down the Bottom, joined Mr. Maydew and Smith and made an exhaustive but absolutely fruitless search of the woods near the bend of the road.

No trace of the missing girl was to be found, and after a long and anxious time the search was abandoned, one of the young Rumbolds volunteering to ride into the nearest town and notify the police.

Maggie, though with little hope in her own heart, endeavoured to cheer her father on their homeward way with the idea that Alice might have returned to Overbury over the Downs whilst they were going by road to the Bottom, and that she had seen them and called to them in jest when they were opposite the tongue of land.

However, when they reached home there was no Alice and, though the next day the search was resumed and full inquiries were instituted by the police, all was to no purpose. No trace of Alice was ever found, the last human being that saw her having been an old woman, who had met her going down the path into the Bottom on the afternoon of her disappearance, and who described her as smiling but looking "queerlike."

This is the end of the story, but the following may throw some light upon it.

The history of Alice's mysterious disappearance became widely known through the medium of the Press and Mr. Roberts, distressed beyond measure at what had taken place, returned in all haste to Overbury to offer what comfort and help he could give to his afflicted friend and tenant.

He called upon the Maydews and, having heard their tale, sat for a short time in silence. Then he said:

"Have you ever heard any local gossip concerning this Colonel and Mrs. Paxton?"

"No," replied Mr. Maydew, "I never heard their names until the day of my poor daughter's fatal visit."

"Well," said Mr. Roberts, "I will tell you all I can about them, which is not very much, I fear."

He paused and then went on: "I am now nearly seventy-five years old, and for nearly seventy years no house has stood in Brickett Bottom. But when I was a child of about five there was an old-fashioned, red brick house standing in a garden at the bend of the road, such as you have described. It was owned and lived in by a retired Indian soldier and his wife, a Colonel and Mrs. Paxton. At the time I speak of, certain events having taken place at the house and the old couple having died, it was sold by their heirs to Lord Carew, who shortly after pulled it down on the ground that it interfered with his shooting. Colonel and Mrs. Paxton were well known to my father, who was the clergyman here before me, and to the neighbourhood in general. They lived quietly and were not unpopular, but the Colonel was supposed to possess a violent and vindictive temper. Their family consisted only of themselves, their daughter and a couple of servants, the Colonel's old Army servant and his Eurasian wife. Well, I cannot tell you details of what happened, I was only a child; my father never liked gossip and in later years, when he talked to me on the subject, he always avoided any appearance of exaggeration or sensationalism."

"However, it is known that Miss Paxton fell in love with and became engaged to a young man to whom her parents took a strong dislike. They used every possible means to break off the match, and many rumours were set on foot as to their conduct—undue influence, even cruelty were charged against them. I do not know the truth, all I can say is that Miss Paxton died and a very bitter feeling against her parents sprang up. My father, however, continued to call, but was rarely admitted. In fact, he never saw Colonel Paxton after his daughter's death and only saw Mrs. Paxton once or twice. He described her as an utterly broken woman, and was not surprised at her following her daughter to the grave in about three months' time. Colonel Paxton became, if possible, more of a recluse than ever after his wife's death and himself died not more than a month after her under circumstances which pointed to suicide. Again a crop of rumours sprang up, but there was no one in particular to take action, the doctor certified Death from Natural Causes, and Colonel Paxton, like his wife and daughter, was buried in this churchyard. The property passed to a distant relative, who came down to it for one night shortly afterwards; he never came again, having apparently conceived a violent dislike to the place, but arranged to pension off the servants and then sold the house to Lord Carew, who was glad to purchase this little island in the middle of his property. He pulled it down soon after he had bought it, and the garden was left to relapse into a wilderness."

Mr. Roberts paused.

"Those are all the facts," he added.

"But there is something more," said Maggie.

Mr. Roberts hesitated for a while.

"You have a right to know all," he said almost to himself; then louder he continued: "What I am now going to tell you is really rumour, vague and uncertain; I cannot fathom its truth or its meaning. About five years after the house had been pulled down a young maidservant at Carew Court was out walking one afternoon. She was a stranger to the village and a new-coiner to the Court. On returning home to tea she told her fellow-servants that as she walked down Brickett Bottom, which place she described clearly, she passed a red brick house at the bend of the road and that a kind-faced old lady had asked her to step in for a while. She did not go in, not because she had any suspicions of there being anything uncanny, but simply because she feared to be late for tea.

"I do not think she ever visited the Bottom again and she had no other similar experience, so far as I am aware.

"Two or three years later, shortly after my father's death, a travelling tinker with his wife and daughter camped for the night at the foot of the Bottom. The girl strolled away up the glen to gather blackberries and was never seen or heard of again. She was searched for in vain—of course, one does not know the truth—and she may have run away voluntarily from her parents, although there was no known cause for her doing so.

"That," concluded Mr. Roberts, "is all I can tell you of either facts or rumours; all that I can now do is to pray for you and for her."

THE TELL-TALE HEART

Edgar Allen Poe

True!—nervous—very, very dreadfully nervous I had been and am; but why *will* you say that I am mad? The disease had sharpened my senses—not destroyed—not dulled them. Above all was the sense of hearing acute. I heard all things in the heaven and in the earth. I heard many things in hell. How, then, am I mad? Hearken! and observe how healthily—how calmly I can tell you the whole story.

It is impossible to say how first the idea entered my brain; but once conceived, it haunted me day and night. Object there was none. Passion there was none. I loved the old man. He had never wronged me. He had never given me insult. For his gold I had no desire. I think it was his eye! yes, it was this! One of his eyes resembled that of a vulture—a pale blue eye, with a film over it. Whenever it fell upon me, my blood ran cold; and so by degrees—very gradually—I made up my mind to take the life of the old man, and thus rid myself of the eye forever.

Now this is the point. You fancy me mad. Madmen know nothing. But you should have seen *me*. You should have seen how wisely I proceeded—with what caution—with what foresight—with what dissimulation I went to work! I was never kinder to the old man than during the whole week before I killed him. And every night, about midnight, I turned the latch of his door and opened it—oh, so gently! And then, when I had made an opening sufficient for my head, I put in a dark lantern, all closed, closed, so that no light shone out, and then I thrust in my head.

Oh, you would have laughed to see how cunningly I thrust it in! I moved it slowly—very, very slowly, so that I might not disturb the old man's sleep. It took me an hour to place my whole head within the opening so far that I could see him as he lay upon his bed. Ha!—would a madman have been so wise as this? And then, when my head was well in the room, I undid the lantern cautiously—oh, so cautiously—cautiously (for the hinges creaked)—I undid it just so much that a single thin ray fell upon the vulture eye. And this I did for seven long nights—every night just at midnight—but I found the eye always closed; and so it was impossible to do the work; for it was not the old man who vexed me, but his Evil Eye. And every morning, when the day broke, I went boldly into the chamber, and spoke courageously to him, calling him by name in a hearty tone, and inquiring how he had passed the night. So you see he would have been a very profound old man, indeed, to suspect that every night, just at twelve, I looked in upon him while he slept.

Upon the eighth night I was more than usually cautious in opening the door. A watch's minute hand moves more quickly than did mine. Never before that night had I *felt* the extent of my own powers—of my sagacity. I could scarcely contain my feelings of triumph. To think that there I was, opening the door, little by little, and he not even to dream of my secret deeds or thoughts. I fairly chuckled at the idea; and perhaps he heard me; for he moved on the bed suddenly, as if startled. Now you may think that I drew back—but no. His room was as black as pitch with the thick darkness, (for the shutters were close fastened, through fear of robbers,) and so I knew that he could not see the opening of the door, and I kept pushing it on steadily, steadily.

I had my head in, and was about to open the lantern, when my thumb slipped upon the tin fastening, and the old man sprang up in the bed, crying out—"Who's there?"

I kept quite still and said nothing. For a whole hour I did

not move a muscle, and in the meantime I did not hear him lie down. He was still sitting up in the bed listening;—just as I have done, night after night, hearkening to the death watches in the wall.

Presently I heard a slight groan, and I knew it was the groan of mortal terror. It was not a groan of pain or of grief—oh, no!—it was the low stifled sound that arises from the bottom of the soul when overcharged with awe. I knew the sound well. Many a night, just at midnight, when all the world slept, it has welled up from my own bosom, deepening, with its dreadful echo, the terrors that distracted me. I say I knew it well. I knew what the old man felt, and pitied him, although I chuckled at heart. I knew that he had been lying awake ever since the first slight noise, when he had turned in the bed. His fears had been ever since growing upon him. He had been trying to fancy them causeless, but could not. He had been saying to himself—"It is nothing but the wind in the chimney—it is only a mouse crossing the floor," or "it is merely a cricket which has made a single chirp." Yes, he has been trying to comfort himself with these suppositions: but he had found all in vain. *All in vain*; because Death, in approaching him had stalked with his black shadow before him, and enveloped the victim. And it was the mournful influence of the unperceived shadow that caused him to feel—although he neither saw nor heard—to *feel* the presence of my head within the room.

When I had waited a long time, very patiently, without hearing him lie down, I resolved to open a little—a very, very little crevice in the lantern. So I opened it—you cannot imagine how stealthily, stealthily—until, at length a single dim ray, like the thread of the spider, shot from out the crevice and fell upon the vulture eye.

It was open—wide, wide open—and I grew furious as I gazed upon it. I saw it with perfect distinctness—all a dull blue, with a hideous veil over it that chilled the very marrow in my bones; but I could see nothing else of the old man's face or person: for I had directed the ray as if by instinct, precisely upon the damned spot.

And now have I not told you that what you mistake for madness is but over acuteness of the senses?—now, I say, there came to my ears a low, dull, quick sound, such as a watch makes when enveloped in cotton. I knew *that* sound well, too. It was the beating of the old man's heart. It increased my fury, as the beating of a drum stimulates the soldier into courage.

But even yet I refrained and kept still. I scarcely breathed. I held the lantern motionless. I tried how steadily I could maintain the ray upon the eye. Meantime the hellish tattoo of the heart increased. It grew quicker and quicker, and louder and louder every instant. The old man's terror *must* have been extreme! It grew louder, I say, louder every moment!—do you mark me well? I have told you that I am nervous: so I am. And now at the dead hour of the night, amid the dreadful silence of that old house, so strange a noise as this excited me to uncontrollable terror. Yet, for some minutes longer I refrained and stood still. But the beating grew louder, louder! I thought the heart must burst. And now a new anxiety seized me—the sound would be heard by a neighbor! The old man's hour had come! With a loud yell, I threw open the lantern and leaped into the room. He shrieked once—once only. In an instant I dragged him to the floor, and pulled the heavy bed over him. I then smiled gaily, to find the deed so far done. But, for many minutes, the heart beat on with a muffled sound. This, however, did not vex me; it would not be heard through the wall. At length it ceased. The old man was dead. I removed the bed and examined the corpse. Yes, he was stone, stone dead. I placed my hand upon the heart and held it there many minutes. There was no pulsation. He was stone dead. His eye would trouble me no more.

If still you think me mad, you will think so no longer when I describe the wise precautions I took for the concealment of the body. The night waned, and I worked hastily, but in silence. First of all I dismembered the corpse. I cut off the head and the arms and the legs.

I then took up three planks from the flooring of the chamber, and deposited all between the scantlings. I then replaced the boards so cleverly, so cunningly, that no human eye—not even *his*—could have detected any thing wrong. There was nothing to wash out—no stain of any kind—no blood-spot whatever. I had been too wary for that. A tub had caught all—ha! ha!

When I had made an end of these labors, it was four o'clock—still dark as midnight. As the bell sounded the hour, there came a knocking at the street door. I went down to open it with a light heart—for what had I *now* to fear? There entered three men, who introduced themselves, with perfect suavity, as officers of the police. A shriek had been heard by a neighbor during the night; suspicion of foul play had been aroused; information had been lodged at the police office, and they (the officers) had been deputed to search the premises.

I smiled—for *what* had I to fear? I bade the gentlemen welcome. The shriek, I said, was my own in a dream. The old man, I mentioned, was absent in the country. I took my visitors all over the house. I bade them search—search *well*. I led them, at length, to *his* chamber. I showed them his treasures, secure, undisturbed. In the enthusiasm of my confidence, I brought chairs into the room, and desired them *here* to rest from their fatigues, while I myself, in the wild audacity of my perfect triumph, placed my own seat upon the very spot beneath which reposed the corpse of the victim.

The officers were satisfied. My *manner* had convinced them. I was singularly at ease. They sat, and while I answered cheerily, they chatted of familiar things. But, ere long, I felt myself getting pale and wished them gone. My head ached, and I fancied a ringing in my ears: but still they sat and still chatted. The ringing became more distinct:—it continued and became more distinct: I talked more freely to get rid of the feeling: but it continued and gained definitiveness—until, at length, I found that the noise was *not* within my ears.

No doubt I now grew *very* pale;—but I talked more fluently, and with a heightened voice. Yet the sound increased—and what could I do? It was *a low, dull, quick sound—much such a sound as a watch makes when enveloped in cotton*. I gasped for breath—and yet the officers heard it not. I talked more quickly—more vehemently; but the noise steadily increased. I arose and argued about trifles, in a high key and with violent gesticulations; but the noise steadily increased. Why *would* they not be gone? I paced the floor to and fro with heavy strides, as if excited to fury by the observations of the men—but the noise steadily increased. Oh God! what *could* I do? I foamed—I raved—I swore! I swung the chair upon which I had been sitting, and grated it upon the boards, but the noise arose over all and continually increased. It grew louder—louder—*louder*! And still the men chatted pleasantly, and smiled. Was it possible they heard not? Almighty God!—no, no! They heard!—they suspected!—they *knew*!—they were making a mockery of my horror!—this I thought, and this I think. But anything was better than this agony! Anything was more tolerable than this derision! I could bear those hypocritical smiles no longer! I felt that I must scream or die!—and now—again!—hark! louder! louder! louder! *louder*!—

"Villains!" I shrieked, "dissemble no more! I admit the deed!—tear up the planks!—here, here!—it is the beating of his hideous heart!"

50

A PHANTOM TOE

W. Bob Holland

I am not a superstitious man, far from it, but despite all my efforts to the contrary I could not help thinking, directly I had taken a survey of my chamber, that I should never quit it without going through a strange adventure. There was something in its immense size, heaviness and gloom that seemed to annihilate at one blow all my resolute skepticism as regards supernatural visitations. It appeared to me totally impossible to go into that room and disbelieve in ghosts.

The fact is, I had incautiously partaken at supper of that favorite Dutch dish, sauerkraut, and I suppose it had disagreed with me and put strange fancies into my head. Be this as it may I only know that after parting with my friend for the night I gradually worked myself up into such a state of fidgetiness that at last I wasn't sure whether I hadn't become a ghost myself.

"Supposing," ruminated I, "supposing the landlord himself should be a practical robber and should have taken the lock and bolt from off this door for the purpose of entering here in the dead of the night, abstracting all my property, and perhaps murdering me! I thought the dog had a very cutthroat air about him." Now, I had never had any such idea until that moment, for my host was a fat (all Dutchmen are fat), stupid-looking fellow, who I don't believe had sense enough to understand what a robbery or murder meant, but somehow or other, whenever we have anything really to annoy us (and it certainly was not pleasant to go to bed in a strange place without being able to fasten one's door), we are sure to aggravate it by myriads of chimeras of our own brain.

So, on the present occasion, in the midst of a thousand disagreeable reveries, some of the most wild absurdity, I jumped very gloomily into bed, having first put out my candle (for total darkness was far preferable to its flickering, ghostly light, which transformed rather than revealed objects), and soon fell asleep, perfectly tired out with my day's riding.

How long I lay asleep I don't know, but I suddenly awoke from a disagreeable dream of cutthroats, ghosts and long, winding passages in a haunted inn. An indescribable feeling, such as I never before experienced, hung upon me. It seemed as if every nerve in my body had a hundred spirits tickling it, and this was accompanied by so great a heat that, inwardly cursing mine host's sauerkraut and wondering how the Dutchmen could endure such poison, I was forced to sit up in bed to cool myself. The whole of the room was profoundly dark, excepting at one place, where the moonlight, falling through a crevice in the shutters, threw a straight line of about an inch or so thick upon the floor—clear, sharp and intensely brilliant against the darkness. I leave you to conceive my horror when, upon looking at this said line of light, I saw there a naked human toe—nothing more.

For the first instant I thought the vision must be some effect of moonlight, then that I was only half awake and could not see distinctly. So I rubbed my eyes two or three times and looked again. Still there was the accursed thing—plain, distinct, immovable—marblelike in its fixedness and rigidity, but in everything else horribly human.

I am not an easily frightened man. No one who has traveled so much and seen so much and been exposed to so many dangers as I, can be, but there was something so mysterious and unusual in the appearance of this single toe that for a short time I could not think what to be at, so I did nothing but stare at it in a state of utter bewilderment.

At length, however, as the toe did not vanish under my steady gaze, I thought I might as well change my tactics, and remembering that all midnight invaders, be they thieves, ghosts or devils, dislike nothing so much as a good noise I shouted out in a loud voice:

"Who's there?"

The toe immediately disappeared in the darkness.

Almost simultaneously with my words I leaped out of bed and rushed toward the place where I had beheld the strange appearance. The next instant I ran against something and felt an iron grip round my body. After this I have no distinct recollection of what occurred, excepting that a fearful struggle ensued between me and my unseen opponent; that every now and then we were violently hurled to the floor, from which we always rose again in an instant, locked in a deadly embrace; that we tugged and strained and pulled and pushed, I in the convulsive and frantic energy of a fight for life, he (for by this time I had discovered that the intruder was a human being) actuated by some passion of which I was ignorant; that we whirled round and round, cheek to cheek and arm to arm, in fierce contest, until the room appeared to whiz round with us, and that at least a dozen people (my fellow traveler among them), roused, I suppose, by our repeated falls, came pouring into the room with lights and showed me struggling with a man having nothing on but a shirt, whose long, tangled hair and wild, unsettled eyes told me he was insane. And then, for the first time, I became aware that I had received in the conflict several gashes from a knife, which my opponent still held in his hand.

To conclude my story in a few words (for I daresay all of you by this time are getting very tired), it turned out that my midnight visitor was a madman who was being conveyed to a lunatic asylum at The Hague, and that he and his keeper had been obliged to stop at Delft on their way. The poor fellow had contrived during the night to escape from his keeper, who had carelessly forgotten to lock the door of his chamber, and with that irresistible desire to shed blood peculiar to many insane people had possessed himself of a pocketknife belonging to the man who had charge of him, entered my room, which was most likely the only one in the house unfastened, and was probably meditating the fatal stroke when I saw his toe in the moonlight, the rest of his body being hidden in the shade.

After this terrible freak of his he was watched with much greater strictness, but I ought to observe, as some excuse for the keeper's negligence, that this was the first act of violence he had ever attempted.